"Where are we going?" ...

"Across these, the waters of the sea whose existence you refuse to acknowledge, Princess," said Auda ibn Jad with a smile and a gesture of his hand. "We go to the island fortress of Galos, where dwells the last remnant of those who worship Zhakrin, God of Darkness."

"I have never heard of this god," Zohra stated.

"This is because he has been deposed from his heavenly throne. Some think him dead—a costly mistake. Zhakrin lives and we gather now in his palace to prepare for his return."

"We?"

Auda ibn Jad's voice became cool, reverent. "The Black Paladins, the Holy Knights of Evil."

ROSE OF THE PROPHET
Volume Two

# THE PALADIN OF THE NIGHT

## MARGARET WEIS AND TRACY HICKMAN

BANTAM BOOKS
NEW YORK · TORONTO · LONDON · SYDNEY · AUCKLAND

THE PALADIN OF THE NIGHT

*A Bantam Spectra Book / May 1989*

ISBN 0-553-27902-5

*Published simultaneously in the United States and Canada*

PRINTED IN THE UNITED STATES OF AMERICA

O  0  9  8  7  6  5  4  3

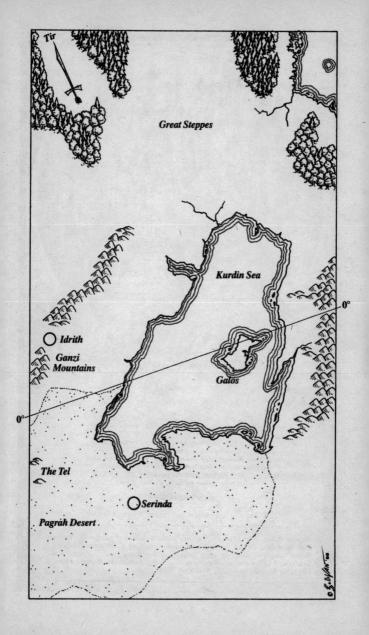

# Book One

# THE BOOK OF THE IMMORTALS 1

# Chapter 1

The theories about the creation of the world of Sularin numbered the same as the Gods who kept it in motion. The followers of Benario, God of Thieves, were firm in their belief that their God stole the world from Sul, who had been going to set it as another jewel in the firmament. Uevin's worshipers portrayed Sul as a craftsman, holding calipers and a T square in his hand and spending his spare time considering the nature of the dodecahedron. Quar taught that Sul molded the world from a lump of clay, used the sun to bake it, then bathed it with his tears when he was finished. Akhran told his followers nothing at all. The Wandering God hadn't the least interest in the creation of the world. That it was here and now was enough for him. Consequently each Sheykh had his own view, handed down from great-great-grandfather to great-grandfather to grandfather to father to son. Each Sheykh's view was the right one, all others were wrong, and it was a matter over which blood had been spilled on countless occasions.

In the Emperor's court in Khandar, renowned for advanced thought, learned men and women spent long hours debating the differing theories and even longer hours proving, eventually, that Quar's teachings were undoubtedly the most scientific. Certainly it was the only theory to explain adequately the phenomenon of the Kurdin Sea—an ocean of salt water populated with seagoing fish and completely surrounded on all sides by desert.

The landlocked Kurdin Sea was populated by other things,

3

too; dark and shadowy things that the learned men and women, living in the safety and comfort of the court of Khandar, saw only in their sleep or in fevered delirium. One of these dark things (and not the darkest by any means) was Quar's minion, Kaug.

Three figures, standing on the shore of the sea, were discussing this very subject intently. The figures were not human; no human had ever crossed the Sun's Anvil whose empty dunes surrounded the sea. The three were immortals— not gods, but those who served both gods and humans.

"You're telling me that his dwelling is down there, in *that*?" said a djinn, staring at both the water and his fellow djinn with deep disgust.

The water of the Kurdin Sea was a deep cobalt blue, its color made more vivid and intense by the stark, glaring whiteness of the desert. In the distance, what appeared to be a cloud of smoke was a white smudge against a pale blue sky.

"Yes," replied the younger djinn. "And don't look so amazed, Sond. I told you before we left—"

"You said *on* the Kurdin Sea, Pukah! You never said anything about *in* the Kurdin Sea!"

"Unless Kaug's taken up boating, how could he live *on* the Kurdin Sea?"

"There's an island in the center, you know."

"Galos!" Pukah's eyes opened wide. "From what I've heard of Galos, not even Kaug would dare live on that accursed rock."

"Bah!" Sond sneered. "You've been listening to the *meddah's* stories with ears soaked in *qumiz*."

"I haven't either! I'm extensively traveled. My former master—"

"—was a thief and a liar!"

"Don't pay any attention to him, Asrial, my beautiful enchanter," said Pukah, turning his back upon Sond and facing a silver-haired woman clad in white robes, who was looking from one to the other with increasing wonder. "My former master *was* a follower of Benario, but only because that was the religion in which he was raised. What could he do? He didn't want to offend his parents—"

"—by earning an honest living," interposed Sond.

"He was an entertainer at heart, with such a wonderful way with animals—"

"Snake charmer. That was his ploy to get into other people's houses."

"He was not a devout believer! Certainly Benario never blessed him!"

"That's true. He got caught with his hand in the money jar—"

"He was misunderstood!" Pukah shouted.

"When they were through with him, he was missing more than understanding," Sond said dryly, folding his gold-braceleted arms across his bare chest.

Drawing his saber from the green sash at his waist, Pukah rounded on the older djinn. "You and I have been friends for centuries, Sond, but I will not allow you to insult me before the angel I love!"

"We've never been friends, that I knew of," Sond growled, drawing his saber in turn. Steel flashing in the bright sunlight, the two began to circle each other. "And if hearing the truth insults you—"

"What are you two doing?" the angel demanded. "Have you forgotten why we are here? What about your Nedjma?" She glared at Sond. "Last night you shed tears over her cruel fate—being held captive by this evil afright—"

"—'efreet," corrected Sond.

"Whatever it is called in your crude language," Asrial said loftily. "You said you would give your life for her—which, considering you are immortal, doesn't seem to me to be much of a sacrifice. We have spent weary weeks searching the heavens for her and now you quibble about going into the sea!"

"I am of the desert," Sond protested sullenly. "I don't like water. It's cold and wet and slimy."

"You can't really feel anything, you know! We are immortal." Asrial glanced at Pukah coolly from the corner of her blue eyes. "We are above such things as love and physical sensations and other human frailties!"

"Above love?" cried Pukah jealously. "Where did the tears I saw you shedding over your mad master come from, if you have no eyes? If you have no hand, why do you caress his forehead and, for all I know, other parts of his body as well!"

"As for my tears," retorted Asrial angrily, "all know the adage, The drops of rain are the tears the Gods shed over the follies of man—"

"*Hazrat* Akhran goes about with dry eyes, then," Pukah interrupted, laughing.

Asrial pointedly ignored him. "And as for your insinuation that I have had carnal knowledge of my 'protégé'—Mathew is *not* my master and he's *not* mad—your statement is absurd and what I would expect of one who has been living around humans so long he has tricked himself into believing he can feel what they feel—"

"Hush!" said Sond suddenly, cocking his turbaned head to one side.

"What?"

"Shhh!" the djinn hissed urgently. He stared far off into nothing, his gaze abstracted. "My master," he murmured. "He's calling for me."

"Is that all?" Pukah raised his eyes to heaven. "He's called for you before. Let Majiid tie his headcloth himself this morning."

"No, it is more urgent than that! I think I should attend him!"

"Come now, Sond. Majiid gave you permission to leave. I know you don't want to go swimming, but this is ridiculous—"

"It isn't that! Something's wrong! Something's been wrong ever since we left."

"Bah! If something was wrong, Khardan would be calling for me. He can't get along without me for even the smallest thing, you know." The young djinn heaved the sigh of the vastly overworked. "I rarely have a moment's peace. He begged me to stay, in fact, but I told him that the wishes of *Hazrat* Akhran held preference over those of a human, even my master—"

"And is your master calling for you?" Sond interrupted impatiently.

"No! So you see—"

"I see nothing except a braggart and a buffoon—" Sond fell silent. "That's odd," he said after a moment's pause. "Majiid's calls just ceased."

"There, what did I tell you. The old man pulled his trousers on all by himself—"

"I don't like this," muttered Sond, putting his hand over his breast. "I feel strange—empty and hollow."

"What does he mean?" Asrial drew near Pukah. Slipping her hand into the hand of the djinn, she held onto him tightly. "He looks terrible, Pukah!"

"I know, my dear. I never could understand what women see in him!" said Pukah. Looking down at the small white hand he was holding, the djinn squeezed it teasingly. "A pity you can't feel this—"

Angrily, Asrial snatched her hand away. Spreading her white wings, she smoothed her robes about her and waded into the water of the cobalt blue sea. Pukah followed instantly, plunging headlong into the sea water with a splash that drenched the angel and sent a school of small fish into a panicked frenzy. "Coming?" he yelled.

"I'll be along," Sond answered softly.

Facing the west, the djinn's eyes scanned the horizon. He saw nothing but blowing sand, heard nothing but the eerie song the dunes sing as they shift and move in their eternal dance with the wind.

Shaking his head, the djinn turned away and slowly entered the Kurdin Sea.

# Chapter 2

Sinking deeper and deeper into the Kurdin Sea, Asrial tried to appear as nonplussed and casual as if she were drifting through a clear blue sky in the heavens of Promenthas. Inwardly, however, she was a prey to growing terror. The guardian angel had never encountered a place as fearsome as this.

It wasn't the cold or the wetness that sent shudders through her ethereal body—Asrial had not been around humans nearly as long as either Pukah or Sond and so did not feel these sensations. It was the darkness.

Night steals over the surface of the world like the shadow of an angel's wing and it is just that—a shadow. Night hides objects from our vision and this is what frightens mortals— not the darkness itself, but the unknown lurking beneath it. Night on the world's surface merely affects the sight, however, and mortals have learned to fight back. Light a candle and drive the darkness away. Night above does not affect hearing—the growls of animals, the rustling of trees, the sleepy murmur of the birds are easily detected, perhaps more easily than in daylight, for night seems to sharpen the other senses in return for dimming one.

But the night of the water is different. The darkness of the sea isn't a shadow cast over mortal vision. The sea's night is an entity. It has weight and form and substance. It smothers the breath from the lungs. The sea's night is eternal. The sun's rays cannot pierce it. No candle will light it. The sea's

8

night is alive. Creatures populate the darkness and mortals are the trespassers in their domain.

The sea's night is silent.

The silence, the weight, the aliveness of the darkness pressed in on Asrial. Though she had no need to breathe, she felt herself gasping for breath. Though her immortal vision could see, she wished desperately for light. More than once she caught herself in what appeared to be the act of swimming, as were Sond and Pukah. Asrial did not cleave the water with clean, strong strokes like Sond or flounder through it fishlike, as did Pukah. It was, with her, more as if she sought to push the water aside with her hands, as if she were trying to clear a path for herself.

"You're growing more human all the time," commented Pukah teasingly, bobbing up near her.

"If you mean that I am frightened of this terrible place and want very much to leave, then you are right," Asrial said miserably. Brushing aside the silver hair that floated into her face, she glanced around in dismay. "Surely this must be the dwelling place of Astafas!"

"Asta-who?"

"Astafas, the God who sits opposite Promenthas in the Great Jewel. He is cruel and evil, delighting in suffering and misery. He rules over a world that is dark and terrible. Demons serve him, bringing him human souls on which he feeds."

"That sounds a lot like Kaug, only he eats things more substantial than souls. Why, you're trembling all over! Pukah, you are a swine, a goat," he muttered beneath his breath. "You should never have brought her in the first place." He started to slip his arm comfortingly around the angel, only to discover that her wings were in the way. If he put his arm above where the wings sprouted from her back, it looked as if he were attempting to choke her. Sliding his arm under the wings, he became entangled in the feathers. Finally, in exasperation, he gave up and contented himself with patting her hand soothingly. "I'll take you back up to the surface," he offered. "Sond can deal with Kaug."

"No!" cried Asrial, looking alarmed. "I'm all right. Truly. It was wrong of me to complain." She smoothed her silver hair and her white robes and was endeavoring to appear composed and calm when a tentacle snaked out of the darkness and wrapped around her wrist. Asrial jerked her hand away with a smothered shriek. Pukah surged forward.

"A squid. Go on, get out of here! Do we look edible? Stupid fish. There, there, my dearest! It's all right. The creature's gone. . . ."

Completely unnerved, Asrial was sobbing, her wings folded tightly about her in a protective, feathered cocoon.

"Sond!" shouted Pukah into the thick darkness. "I'm taking Asrial to the surface— Sond! Sond? Drat! Where in Sul has he got to? Asrial, my angel, come with me—"

"No!" Asrial's wings parted suddenly. Resolutely, she began floating through the water. "I must stay! I must do this for Mathew! Fish, you said. The fish told me— Mathew would die a horrible death . . . unless I came—"

"Fish? What fish?"

"Oh, Pukah!" Asrial halted, staring at the djinn in horror. "I wasn't supposed to tell!"

"Well, you did. 'The sheep is dead', as they say. Might as well eat it as cry over it. You spoke with a fish? How? Where?"

"My protégé carries with him two fish—"

"In the middle of the desert? And you say he isn't mad!"

"No! No! It isn't like that at all! There's something . . . strange"—Asrial shivered—"about these fish. Something magical. They were given to Mathew by a man—a terrible man. The slave trader who took my protégé captive. The one who ordered the slaughter of the helpless priests and magi of Promenthas.

"When we came to the city of Kich, the slave trader was stopped outside the city walls by guards, who told him he must give up all his magical objects and sacrifice them to Quar. The slave trader gave up every magic item he had—except for one."

"I've heard of fish that swallowed magic rings, but magic fish?" Pukah appeared highly skeptical. "What do they do? Charm the bait?"

"This is serious, Pukah!" Asrial said softly. "One life has been lost over them already. And my poor Mathew . . ." She covered her face with her hands.

"Pukah, you are a low form of life. A worm, a snake is higher than you." The djinn gazed at the angel remorsefully. "I'm sorry. Go on, Asrial."

"He . . . the slave trader . . . called Mathew over to the white palanquin in which the trader always traveled. He handed my protégé a crystal globe decorated on the top and bottom with costly gold work. The globe was filled with water and inside swam two fish—one gold and one black. The trader ordered Mathew to keep them hidden from the guards. There was a poor girl standing there, watching—a slave girl. The trader told Mathew to witness what would happen if he betrayed him and he . . . he murdered the girl, right before Mathew's eyes!"

"Why did he choose Mathew to carry these fish?"

Asrial blushed faintly. "The trader mistook my protégé for a female—"

"Ah, yes," muttered Pukah. "I forgot."

"The guards would not search the women in the caravan—not their persons, at least—and so Mathew was able to conceal the fish. The slave trader said that he would take them back when they went into town. But then your master rescued Mathew and carried him away. And with him, the magical fish. . . ."

"How do you know they're magic? What do they do?" Pukah asked dubiously.

"Of course they're magic!" Asrial snapped irritably. "They live encased in a crystal globe that no force on this world can shatter. They do not eat. They are not bothered by heat or cold." Her voice lowered. "And one spoke to me."

"That's nothing!" Pukah scoffed. "I've talked to animals. I once shared my basket with a snake who worked for my former master. Quite an amusing fellow. Actually, it was the snake's basket, but he didn't mind a roommate after I convinced—"

"Pukah! This is serious! One fish—the gold one—told me to come with you to find the Lost Immortals. The fish referred to Mathew as the Bearer . . . and she said he was in dreadful danger. In danger of losing not only his life but his soul as well!"

"There, there, my dear. Don't get so upset. When we get back, you must show me these wonderful fish. What else do they— Oh, Sond! Where have you been?"

The elder djinn swam through the murky water, his strong arms cleaving it aside with swift, clean strokes. "I went ahead to Kaug's dwelling, to look around. The 'efreet's gone, apparently. The place is deserted."

"Good!" Pukah rubbed his hands in satisfaction. "Are you certain you want to continue on, Asrial? Yes? Actually, it's well that you are coming with us, beautiful angel, because neither Sond nor I may enter the 'efreet's dwelling without his permission. Now you, on the other hand—"

"Pukah, I need to talk to you." Sond drew the young

djinn to the far side of a large outcropping of rock covered with hollow, tubular plants that opened and shut with the flow of the water, looking like hundreds of gasping mouths.

"Well, what is it?"

"Pukah, a strange feeling came over me when I drew near Kaug's dwelling—"

"It's the stuff he cooks for his dinner. I know, I felt it, too. Like your stomach's trying to escape by way of your throat?"

"It's not anything I smelled!" Sond said angrily. "Quit being a fool for once in your life. It's a feeling like . . . like . . . like I *could* enter Kaug's dwelling without his permission. In fact, it seemed as if I was being pulled inside!"

"Pulled inside an 'efreet's house! Who's the fool here now? Certainly not me!" Pukah appeared amused.

"Bah! I might as well be talking to the seaweed!" Shoving Pukah aside, Sond swam past him, diving down toward the cave on the ocean floor where the 'efreet made his home.

Pukah cast the djinn a scathing glance. "At least the seaweed would provide you an audience on your own mental level! Come on, Asrial." Catching hold of the angel's hand, he led her down to the very bottom of the sea.

Kaug's cave was hollowed out of a cliff of black rock. A light glimmered at the entrance, the eerie luminescence coming from the heads of enthralled sea urchins gloomily awaiting their master's return. The long greenish brown moss that hung from the cliff reminded Asrial of the squid's tentacles.

"I'm going in there alone," whispered the angel, reminding herself of Mathew's plight and trying very hard to be courageous. "I'm going in there." But she didn't move.

Sond, biting his lower lip, stared at Kaug's dwelling as though mesmerized by it.

"On second thought, Asrial," Pukah said in a bland and innocent voice, "I think it might be better if we *did* accompany you—"

"Admit it, Pukah! You feel it, don't you!" Sond growled.

"I do not!" Pukah protested loudly. "It's just that I don't think we should let her go in there alone!"

"Come on then," said Sond. "If we're not barred at the threshold, then we know something is wrong!"

The two djinn floated ahead to the entryway of the cave, their skin shimmering green in the ghostly light emanating from the sea urchins, who were staring at them with large, sorrowful eyes. Slowly Asrial swam behind. Her wings fanning the water, she paused, hovering overhead as the djinn stopped—one standing on either side of the entryway.

"Well, go on!" Sond gestured.

"And get a jolt of lightning through my body for breaking the rule. No thank you!" Pukah sniffed scornfully.

"This was your idea!"

"I've changed my mind."

"You're not going to be stopped and you know it. I tell you, we're being invited inside there!"

"Then *you* accept the invitation!"

Glaring at Pukah, Sond cautiously set his foot across the threshold of the 'efreet's dwelling. Cringing, Pukah waited for the blue flash, the crackle, and the painful yelp from Sond, an indication that the established rule among immortals was being violated.

Nothing happened.

Sond stepped across the threshold with ease. Pukah sighed inwardly. Despite what he'd told Sond, he, too, had the distinct feeling that he was being urged to enter the 'efreet's home. No, it was stronger than that. Pukah had the disquieting impression that he *belonged* inside the eerily lit cave.

"What nonsense, Pukah!" Pukah said to himself with scorn. "As if you ever belonged in a place where fish heads are an integral part of the decor!"

Sond was staring at him in grim triumph from the entryway. Ignoring him, Pukah turned to give Asrial his hand. Together, they entered the cave. The angel stayed quite near the djinn. The feathers of her wings brushed against his bare back, and despite his growing sense of uneasiness, Pukah felt his skin tingle and a pleasurable warmth flood his body.

Was Asrial right? he wondered for a moment, standing in the green-tinged darkness, the angel's hand held fast in his. Is this sensation something I've tricked myself into experiencing to become more like humans? Or do I truly enjoy her touch?

Leaning near him, looking around but not letting go of his hand, Asrial whispered, "What is it we're searching for?"

"A golden egg," Pukah whispered back.

"I doubt we'll find the egg," Sond muttered unhappily. "And if we did, my lovely djinniyeh would not be inside. Remember? Kaug said he had taken Nedjma to a place where I would never see her again until I joined her."

"Then what are we doing here?" Pukah demanded.

"How should I know? It was your idea!"

"Me? You were the one who said Kaug was holding Nedjma captive! Now you change your tune—"

The djinn sucked in a furious breath. "I'll change your tune!" Sond laid his hand on the hilt of his sword. "You will sing through a slit in your throat, you—"

"Stop it! Just stop it!" Asrial's tense voice hissed in the darkness. "Now that we're here, it can't hurt to look! Even if we don't find Nedjma, we may find something that would guide us to where this afright has taken her!"

"She's right," said Pukah hastily, backing up and stumbling over a sponge. "We should search this place."

"Well, we'd better hurry," Sond grumbled. "Kaug may be back any moment. Let's separate."

Repeating Mathew's name over and over to herself to give her courage, Asrial drifted deeper into the cave. Pukah slanted off to the right, while Sond took the left.

"Ugh! I just found one of Kaug's pets!" Rolling over a rock that the 'efreet used for a chair or a table or perhaps just liked to have around, Pukah grimaced as something black and ugly slithered out from underneath. "Or maybe it's a girlfriend." Setting the rock back hastily, he continued on, poking his long nose into a bed of lichen. "Asrial is right you know, Sond. *Hazrat* Akhran believes that Quar is responsible for the disappearance of the immortals, including his own. If that's true, then Kaug must know where they are."

"This is hopeless!" Asrial waved her hands helplessly. "There's nothing here but rocks and seaweed." Turning, she suddenly recoiled. "What's that?" She pointed to a huge iron cauldron standing in a recessed area of the cave.

"Kaug's stew pot!" Pukah's nose wrinkled. "Can't you smell it?" The djinn drifted over near the angel. "The place has changed," he admitted. "Last time I was here, there were all sorts of objects sitting about. Now there's nothing. It looks as if the bastard moved out. I think we've searched enough. Sond! Sond? Where are you!"

"But there must be something!" Asrial twisted a lock of her hair around her finger. "The fish said I should come with you! Maybe we could talk to your God. Perhaps he knows something?"

"No, no!" Pukah grew pale at the thought. "That wouldn't be wise. I'm sure if Akhran knew anything He would have informed us. Sond! Sond! I—"

A hoarse, ragged cry came from the inner depths of the cave.

"Sul's eyeballs! What was that?" Pukah felt the hair beneath his turban stand straight up.

"Promenthas be with us!" Asrial breathed.

The terrible cry rose again, swelled to a shriek, then broke off in a choking sob.

"It's Sond!" Pukah sprang forward, overturning rocks, shoving through curtains of floating seaweed. "Sond! Where are you? Did you step on a fish? Is it Kaug? Sond . . ."

Pukah's voice died. Rounding a corner, he came upon the elder djinn standing by himself in a small grotto. Sickly green light, oozing from slimy plants clinging to the walls, was reflected in an object Sond held in his hands. The djinn was staring at it in horror.

"What is it, my friend? What have you found? It looks like—" Pukah gasped. "Akhran have mercy!"

"Why? What's the matter?" Asrial tiptoed into the grotto behind Pukah and peered over his shoulder. "What do you mean scaring us half to death? It's only an old lamp!"

Sond's face was a pale green in the light of the plants. "Only an old lamp!" he repeated in an anguished voice. "It's my lamp! My *chirak*!"

"His what?" Asrial looked at Pukah, who was nearly as green as Sond.

"It is more than a lamp," Pukah said through stiff lips. "It is his dwelling place."

"And look, Pukah," Sond said in a hushed whisper. "Look behind me, at my feet."

"Mine, too?" Though Pukah's lips formed the words, no one could hear them.

Sond nodded silently.

Pukah sank slowly to the cave floor. Reaching out his hand, he took hold of a basket that stood behind Sond. Made of tightly wrapped coils of rattan, the basket was small at the bottom, swelled outward toward the top like the bulb of an onion, and curved back in toward the center. Perched atop it was a woven lid with a jaunty knob. Lovingly drawing the basket close, Pukah stroked its woven coils.

"I don't understand!" Asrial cried in growing fear, looking from one despairing djinn to the other. "All I see is a basket and a lamp! Why are you so upset? What does it mean?"

"It means," came a deep, booming voice from the front of the cave, "that now *I* am their master!"

# Chapter 3

The 'efreet's shadow fell over them, followed by the hulking body of the gigantic immortal. Water streamed from the hairy chest, the 'efreet's pugnacious face was split by a wide grin. "I took your homes several weeks ago, during the Battle at the Tel. A battle your masters lost, by the way. If that old goat, Majiid, is still alive, he now finds himself without a djinn!"

"Still alive? If you have murdered my master, I swear by Akhran that—"

"Sond! Don't! Don't be a—" Pukah bit off his words with a sigh. Too late.

Swelling with rage, Sond soared to ten feet in height. His head smashed into the cave ceiling, sending a shower of rock crashing to the floor below. With a bitter snarl, the djinn hurled himself at Kaug. The 'efreet was unprepared for the suddenness and fury of Sond's attack. The weight of the djinn's body knocked the hulking Kaug off his feet; the two hit the ground with a thud that sent seismic waves along the ocean floor.

Clutching at a rock to keep his balance on the heaving ground, Pukah turned to offer what comfort he could to Asrial, only to find that the angel had vanished.

A huge foot lashed out in Pukah's direction. Crawling up on the rock to be out of the way of the combatants thrashing about around him, Pukah considered the matter, discussing it with himself, whom he considered to be the most intelligent of all parties currently in the room.

"Where has your angel gone, Pukah?"

"Back to Promenthas."

"No, she wouldn't do that."

"You are right, Pukah," said Pukah. "She is much too fond of you to leave you."

"Do you really think so?" asked Pukah rapturously.

"I do indeed!" replied his other self, although his statement lacked a certain ring of conviction.

Pukah almost took himself to task over this, then decided, due to the serious nature of the current crisis, to overlook it.

"What this means is that Asrial is here and in considerable danger. I don't know what Kaug would do if he discovered an angel of Promenthas searching through his underwear."

Pukah glanced at the combatants irritably. The howling and gnarling and gnashing was making it quite difficult for him to carry on a normal conversation. "Ah, ha!" he said suddenly, hopefully, "but perhaps he didn't see her!"

"He heard her voice. He answered her question."

"That's true. Well, she's gone," said Pukah in matter-of-fact tones. "Perhaps she's just turned invisible, as she used to do when I first caught a glimpse of her in camp. Do you suppose she's powerful enough to hide herself from the eyes of an 'efreet?"

There was no answer. Pukah tried another question. "Does her disappearance make things better or worse for us, my friend?"

"I don't see," came the gloomy response, "how it matters."

Taking this view of the situation himself, Pukah crossed his legs, leaned his elbow on his knee and sat, chin in hand, to wait for the inevitable.

It was not long in coming.

Sond's rage had carried him further in his battle with the 'efreet than anyone could have expected. Once Kaug recovered from his surprise at the sudden attack, however, it was easy for the strong 'efreet to gain the upper hand, and Sond's rage was effectively punched and pummeled out of him.

Now it was the 'efreet who carried the djinn, and soon a battered and bloody Sond was hanging suspended by his feet from the cracked ceiling of the cave. Dangling head down, his arms and legs bound with cords of prickly green vine, the djinn did not give up, but fought against his bonds—struggling wildly until he began to revolve at the end of his tether.

"I wouldn't do that, Sond," advised Pukah from his seat

on the rock. "If you do free yourself, you will only come down on your head and you should certainly take care of what brains you have."

"You could have helped, you bastard son of Sul!" Sond writhed and twisted. Blood and saliva dripped from his mouth.

Pukah was shocked. "I would not think of attacking our new master!" he said rebukingly.

Turning from admiring his handiwork, Kaug eyed the young djinn suspiciously. "Such loyalty, little Pukah. I'm touched."

Sliding down from his rock, the young djinn prostrated himself on the cave floor before the 'efreet, his head brushing the ground.

"This is the law of the immortals who serve upon the mortal plane," recited Pukah in a nasal tone, his nose pressed flat against the floor. "Whosoever shall acquire the physical object to which the immortal is bound shall henceforth become the master of said immortal and shall be due all allegiance and loyalty."

Sond shrieked something vile, having to do with Pukah's mother and a male goat.

Pukah appeared pained. "I fear these interruptions annoy you, My Master. If I may be allowed—"

"Certainly!" Kaug waved a negligent hand. The 'efreet appeared preoccupied; his gaze darting here and there about the grotto.

Believing he knew the quarry the 'efreet was hunting, Pukah thought it best to distract him. He picked up a handful of seaweed, grabbed hold of Sond by his turban, and stuffed the pale green plant into the djinn's yammering mouth.

"His offensive outbursts will no longer disturb you, My Master!" Pukah threw himself on his knees before the 'efreet.

"Allegiance and loyalty, eh, little Pukah?" said Kaug. Stroking his chin, he regarded the djinn thoughtfully. "Then my first command to you is to tell me why you are here."

"We were drawn here, Master, by the physical objects to which we are bound according to the law that states—"

"Yes, yes," said Kaug irritably, casting another searching glance around the cave once more. "So you came here because you couldn't help yourself. You are lying to your master, little Pukah, and that is quite against the rules. You must be punished." Lashing out with his foot, the 'efreet kicked

Pukah under the chin, snapping the djinn's head back painfully and splitting his lip.

"The truth. You came here in search of Nedjma. And the third member of your party. What was her reason for coming?"

"I assure you, Master," said Pukah, wiping blood from his mouth, "there were only the two of us—"

Kaug kicked him in the face again.

"Come, come, loyal little Pukah! Where may I find the lovely body belonging to that charming voice I heard when I entered my dwelling this night?"

"Alas, My Master, you see before you the only bodies belonging to the only voices you heard in your dwelling place. It depends upon your taste, of course, but I consider *my* body the loveliest of the two—"

Nonchalantly, Kaug drove his foot into the young djinn's kidney. Real or imaginary, the pain was intense. Pukah doubled up with a groan.

"I heard a voice—a female voice, little Pukah!"

"I have been told I have a most melodious ring to my—ughh!"

Kaug kicked the djinn in the other kidney. The force of the blow rolled Pukah over on his back. Drawing his sword, the 'efreet straddled the young djinn, his weapon poised above a most vital and vulnerable area on Pukah's body.

"So, little Pukah, you claim the female voice was yours. It *will* be, my friend, if you do not tell me the truth and reveal the whereabouts of this trespasser!"

Covering himself with his hands, Pukah gazed up at the enraged 'efreet with pleading eyes. "O My Master! Have mercy, I beg of you! You are distressed by the unwarranted attack on your person by one who should, by rights, be your slave"—a muffled shriek from Sond—"and that has thrown a cog (ha, ha, small joke) in the wheel of your usually brilliant thought process! Look around, Great Kaug! Could anyone or anything remain hidden from your all-seeing gaze, O Mighty Servant of the Most Holy Quar?"

This question stumped the 'efreet. If he said yes, he admitted he wasn't all-seeing, and if he said no, he granted that Pukah was right and that he—Kaug—hadn't really heard the strange voice after all. The 'efreet sent his piercing gaze into all parts of the cave, dissecting every shadow, using all his senses to detect a hidden presence in the dwelling.

Kaug felt a thrill in his nerve endings, as if someone had

touched his skin with a feather. There *was* another being in his cave, someone who had the ability to enter his dwelling without permission, someone who was able to hide herself from his sight. A film of white mist blocked his vision. Kaug rubbed his eyes, but that did nothing to dispel the odd sensation.

What should he do? Castrate Pukah? The 'efreet pondered. Other than providing a bit of mild amusement, it would probably accomplish little else. Such an act of violence might actually frighten the creature into disappearing completely. No, she must be lulled into a sense of well-being.

I will give Pukah the hemp and watch him weave the rope that will go around his neck, said Kaug to himself. Aloud, he intoned, "You are right, little Pukah. I must have been imagining things." Sheathing his sword, the 'efreet kindly helped the djinn to his feet. Kaug wiped slime from Pukah's shoulder and solicitously plucked fronds of seaweed from the djinn's *pantalons*. "Forgive me. I have a quick temper. A failing of mine, I admit. Sond's attempt on my life upset me." The 'efreet pressed his hand over his huge chest. "It wounded me deeply, in fact, especially after all the trouble I went to in order to rescue both of you."

"Sond is a beast!" cried Pukah, casting Sond an indignant glance and congratulating himself on his cleverness. The young djinn's sharp ears pricked. "Uh, what do you mean . . . rescue us? If it's not asking too much of you in your weakened condition to explain, Most Beneficent and Long-Suffering Master."

"No, no. I'm just exhausted, that's all. And my head is spinning. If I could just sit down . . ."

"Certainly, Master. You do seem pale, sort of chartreuse. Lean on me."

Kaug draped his massive arm over Pukah's slender shoulder. Groaning, the young djinn staggered beneath the weight.

"Where to, Master?" he gasped.

"My favorite chair," said Kaug with a weak gesture. "Over there, near my cooking pot."

"Yes, Master," Pukah said with more spirit than breath left in his body. By the time the two reached the huge sponge that the 'efreet indicated, the young djinn was practically walking on his knees. Kaug sank into his chair.

Pukah, suppressing a groan, slumped down on the floor at his feet. Sond had lapsed into silence, whether in order to hear better or because he was unconscious the young djinn didn't know and, at this point, didn't care.

"You were not present at the battle that took place around the Tel, were you, little Pukah?" said Kaug, settling his massive body in his chair. Leaning back, he regarded the young djinn with a mild-eyed gaze.

"You mean the battle between Sheykhs Majiid and Jaafar and Zeid?" questioned Pukah uneasily.

"No," said Kaug, shaking his head. "There was no battle between the tribes of the desert."

"There wasn't?" Pukah appeared much amazed, then recovered himself. "Ah, of course, there wasn't! Why should there be? After all, we are all brothers in the spirit of Akhran—"

"I mean the battle between the tribes of the desert and the armies of the Amir of Kich," continued Kaug coolly. Pausing a moment, the 'efreet added, "Your mouth is working, little Pukah, but I hear nothing coming out of it. I didn't accidentally hit something vital, did I?"

Shaking his head, Pukah found his voice, somewhere down around his ankles. "My . . . my master and the . . . the armies of—"

"Former master," amended Kaug.

"Certainly. Former m-master," Pukah stammered. "Forgive me, noble Kaug." Prostrating himself, he hid his burning face against the floor.

The 'efreet smiled and settled himself more comfortably in his spongy soft chair. "The outcome of the battle was never in question. Riding their magical steeds, the troops of the Amir easily defeated your puny desert fighters."

"Were . . . were all . . . killed?" Pukah could barely force himself to say the word.

"Killed? No. The objective of the Imam was to bring as many living souls to Quar as possible. The orders of the Amir, therefore, were to capture, not kill. The young women and children we brought to Kich to learn the ways of the One, True God. The old people we left in the desert, for they can be of no use to us in building the new world Quar is destined to rule. Your master and his *spahis* we left there, also. Soon, bereft of their families, broken in spirit, weak in body, they will come to us and bow before Quar."

A strangled sound from Sond was expressive of defiance.

Kaug gazed at the elder djinn sadly. "Ah, he will never learn gratitude, that one. You are intelligent, Pukah. The

winds of heaven have switched direction. They blow, not
from the desert, but from the city. The time of Akhran is
dwindling. Long did Majiid call for his djinn to come to his
aid, but there was no answer."

Glancing through his fingers at Sond, Pukah saw that the
older djinn had ceased struggling. Tears flowed from Sond's
eyes, dripping into the puddles of sea water on the floor
beneath him. Pukah turned his head from the distressing
sight.

"The Sheykh's faith in his God is beginning to weaken.
His djinn will not come at his command. His wife and children were taken captive. His eldest son—the light of his
eyes—is missing and all assume him to be dead—"

Pukah lifted a strained face. "Khardan? Dead?"

"Isn't he?" Kaug's eyes stabbed at him.

"Don't you know?" Pukah parried the thrust.

They stared at one another, mental swords clashing, then
Kaug—falling back—shrugged. "The body was not discovered, but that means little. It is probably in the belly of a
hyena—a fitting end to a wild dog."

Lowering his head again, Pukah endeavored to gather up
his widely scattered wits. "It *must* be true! Khardan *must* be
dead! Otherwise, he would have called on me to come to his
aid!"

"What are you mumbling about, little Pukah?" Kaug nudged
the djinn with his foot.

"I was . . . er . . . remarking to myself that I am most
fortunate to be your slave—"

"Indeed you are, little Pukah. The Amir's men were going
to burn your basket and sell that lamp but I—recognizing
them as the dwellings of fellow immortals—was quick to
rescue you both. Only to be set upon in my own home—"
The 'efreet glowered at Sond.

"Forgive him, Master. He thinks with his pectorals."
Where is Asrial? Pukah wondered. Much like Kaug, he was
darting glances here and there in an effort to locate her. Has
she heard? A sudden thought occurred to him. If she has, she
must be frantic with worry.

"I—I don't suppose, Kind Kaug, that you could reveal to
me the fate of my mast—former master's—wives?" Pukah
asked warily.

"Why do you want to know, little Pukah?" Kaug yawned.

"Because I pity those who must try to console them for

the loss of such a husband," Pukah said, sitting back on his heels and regarding the 'efreet with a face as bland as a pan of goat's milk. "The Calif was deeply in love with his wives and they with him. Their sorrow at his loss must be terrible to witness."

"Now, as a matter of fact, it is a great coincidence, but Khardan's two wives have disappeared as well," Kaug said. Leaning back in his chair, the 'efreet regarded Pukah through narrowed eyelids.

It may have been his overwrought imagination, but Pukah thought he heard a smothered cry at this. The 'efreet's eyes opened suddenly. "What was that?" Kaug glanced about the cave.

"Sond! Moan more quietly! You disturb the Master!" Pukah ordered, leaping to his feet. "Allow me to deal with him, O Mighty 'Efreet. You rest."

Kaug obediently leaned back and shut his eyes. He could sense Pukah hovering over him, staring at him intently. Then he heard the djinn padding away on his bare feet, hastening toward Sond. The 'efreet heard something else, too—another grieving moan. Opening his eyes a slit, he saw a most interesting sight. Pukah had tucked his hands beneath his armpits and was flapping his elbows frantically.

Sond stared at him, bewildered, then suddenly took the hint—for that's what it obviously was—and began to groan loudly.

"What do you mean by that dismal howling?" Pukah shouted. "My Master is in enough pain as it is. Shut up this instant!" Whirling about to face the 'efreet, Pukah grabbed hold of a largish rock. "Allow me to knock him senseless, My Master!"

"No, that will not be necessary," Kaug muttered, shifting in his chair. "I will deal with him myself."

Pukah flapping his arms. Pukah with wings? The trail had taken an unusual turn and the 'efreet, in trying to follow the path, had the distinct impression he'd become lost en route. He knew he was getting somewhere, but he needed time to find his way.

"Sond, I confine you to your *chirak*!" The 'efreet snapped his fingers and the djinn's body slowly began to dissolve, changing to smoke. The smoke wavered in the air; two eyes could be seen, fixed in malevolent fury on Kaug. A simple

gesture from the 'efreet caused the lamp to suck the smoke
out of the air, and Sond was gone.

"And what is your will concerning me, My Master?"
Pukah asked humbly, bowing low, his hands pressed against
his forehead.

"Return to your dwelling. Remain there until I call for
you," Kaug said absently, preoccupied with his thoughts. "I
am going to pay my homage to Quar."

"A safe and pleasant journey, Master," said Pukah. Bowing his way across the floor, the djinn retired precipitously to
his basket.

"Ugggh," grunted Kaug, heaving his bulk up out of the
chair.

"Ugggh," Pukah mimicked, his ears attuned to ascertain
the 'efreet's departure. "One of his more intelligent noises.
The great oaf! Pukah, my friend, you've fooled him completely. He has neglected to confine you to your dwelling,
and while he is gone, you may leave it to search for your lost
angel."

Materializing inside his basket, Pukah found it in a state
of general disarray—the furniture overturned, crockery
smashed, food scattered about. Having previously shared his
dwelling with a snake, who had not been very neat in his
personal habits, the djinn was accustomed to a certain amount
of slovenliness. Ignoring the mess, Pukah set the bed to
rights, then lay down on it and waited, listening intently, to
make certain the 'efreet had really gone and that this wasn't
some sort of lamebrained trick to trap him.

Hearing nothing, Pukah was just about to leave his basket
and go search the cave when he was nearly suffocated by a
flurry of feathers. Silver hair obscured his vision and a warm,
soft body hurled itself into his arms.

"Oh, Pukah!" Asrial cried, clutching at him frantically.
"My poor Mathew! I have to find him! You must help me
escape!"

# Chapter 4

"This would seem to indicate that their Calif, this Khardan, is not dead," Quar mused.

Kaug found the God taking a stroll in His pleasure garden, Quar's mind occupied with the march of the Amir's army south. This *jihad* was a weighty matter, so much to do; making certain the weather was perfect, preventing rain so that the baggage trains did not founder in the mud; forcing Disease's deadly hand away from His troops; keeping the magic of Sul flowing into the horses, and a hundred other worries. Quar had frowned at Kaug's interruption but, since the 'efreet insisted it was important, magnanimously agreed to listen.

"That is what I think as well, O Holy One," said the 'efreet, bowing to indicate he was sensible of the honor of sharing like beliefs with his God. "The djinn, Pukah, has the brains of a mongrel, but even a dog knows when its master is dead and the news came as a complete surprise to Khardan's lackey."

"And this you tell me about the wives. It is certainly mysterious," Quar said offhandedly, sinking his white, perfectly shaped teeth into the golden skin of a kumquat. "What do you make of it?" A speck of juice dripped onto the costly silk robes. Irritably, the God dabbed at it with a linen napkin.

"Pukah brought up the matter, Magnificent One. When I asked him why he was interested, he lied, telling me that Khardan cared deeply for his wives. We know from the woman, Meryem, that the Calif hated his head wife and that his second wife was a madman."

"Mmmmm." Quar appeared entirely absorbed with removing the stain from his clothing.

"It was when I mentioned that the wives had disappeared that I heard the strange sound—as of someone stricken with grief, Holy One. I am convinced that there is someone else present in my dwelling." Kaug scowled, his brow furrowed in thought. "Someone with wings . . ."

Quar had been just about to take another bite of the fruit. His hand stopped midway to his mouth. "Wings?" he repeated softly.

"Yes, Holy One." Kaug described Pukah's peculiar behavior and Sond's reaction.

"Promenthas!" murmured Quar softly. "Angels in company with djinn of Akhran! So the Gods are fighting me on the immortal plane as well!"

"What is it you say, Holy One?" Kaug drew nearer.

"I said this strange winged intruder has probably taken advantage of your leaving and fled," Quar said coldly.

"Impossible, My Lord. I sealed my dwelling before I departed. I thought I should lose no time in bringing you this information," the 'efreet added deprecatingly.

"I do not see why you are so concerned with this Khardan!" said Quar, plucking another kumquat. "All my people have become obsessed with him! The Imam wants his soul. The Amir wants his head. Meryem wants his body. This Calif is human, nothing more—the blind follower of a dying God."

"He could be a threat—"

"Only if you make him one!" Quar rebuked sternly.

Kaug bowed. "And what are your instructions concerning the djinn, My Lord?"

Quar waved a delicate hand. "Do what you want. Keep them as your slaves. Send them where we send the others. It matters little to me."

"And the mysterious third party—"

"You have more important things to occupy your time, Kaug, such as the upcoming battles in the south. However, I give you leave to solve your little mystery, if you like."

"And would my Lord be interested in the outcome?"

"Perhaps some day, when I am bored with other foolishness, you may share it with me," Quar said, indicating with a cool nod that the 'efreet's presence was no longer wanted.

The 'efreet, bowing again, evaporated into the blossom-scented air.

As soon as Kaug was gone, Quar disgarded the semblence of negligence that he wore in the presence of the powerful 'efreet. Hastening back into his sumptuous dwelling, he entered a Temple, whose exact duplicate could be found in the world below, in the city of Kich. The God lifted a mallet and struck a small gong three times.

A wasted face appeared in Quar's mind, its eyes burning with holy ecstasy. "You have summoned me, *Hazrat* Quar?"

"Imam, among the people of the desert we captured must be some who are related to this Khardan, their Calif."

"I believe there are, Holy One. His mother and a half-brother . . . or so I am told."

"I want information regarding this man, this Calif. Attain it any way possible. It would be ideal, of course, if you could convert one or both to the true faith."

"I hope to convert all the desert nomads, Holy One."

"Excellent, Imam."

Feisal's face disappeared from Quar's sight.

Settling back on a silk brocade sofa, Quar noted that he still held the kumquat in his hand. Regarding it with complacence, he slowly closed his fist upon it and began to squeeze. The skin ruptured, the juice flowed over his fingers. When the fruit was reduced to an unrecognizable pulp, the God tossed it casually away.

# Chapter 5

"We must escape! We must get out of here, Pukah!" Asrial cried distractedly. "That terrible monster is right. Mathew has disappeared! I searched for his being in my mind and could not see him! A darkness shrouds him, hiding him from my sight. Some dreadful thing has happened to him!"

"There, there," murmured Pukah, too dazzled and confused to know what he was saying. The beautiful creature appearing out of nowhere, her soft hands clinging to him, her fragrance, her warmth. The djinn had just presence of mind enough to take hold of the soft hand and draw the angel down with him upon the bed.

"Let's relax and think about this calmly." Pukah brought his lips near the smooth cheek. How did one manage about the wings? They were bound to be in the way. . . .

"Oh, Pukah!" Asrial sobbed miserably, lowering her head. Pukah found himself kissing a mass of wet, silver hair. "It's all my fault! I should never have left him!"

Putting one arm around her waist (sliding it under the wings), Pukah held Asrial nearer. "You had no choice, my enchanter!" he whispered, brushing aside the hair. "The fish told you to come." His lips brushed her fevered skin.

"What if it was a trick!" Asrial sprang to her feet with such energy that her wings swept Pukah off the bed. "It could have been a ploy of Astafas's, an attempt for that Lord of Darkness to steal Mathew's soul! Oh, why didn't I think of this before! And your master, Khardan. He must be with

Mathew. He is undoubtedly in danger, too. Let's leave, Pukah, quickly!"

"We can't," said the djinn, picking himself up off the bottom of the basket.

"Why not?" Asrial stared at him, startled.

"Because"—Pukah, sighing, sat down upon the bed—"Kaug sealed the cave before he left."

"How do you know?"

Pukah shrugged. "See for yourself. Try going back out into the ocean again."

Asrial closed her eyes, her lips moved, her wings waved gently. Her eyes flew open, she looked about eagerly and her face crumpled in disappointment. "I'm still here!"

"Told you," said Pukah, lounging back on the bed. Reaching out, he patted a place beside him. "Come, beloved. Rest yourself. Who knows how long Kaug will be gone? We're trapped here together. We might as well make the best of it."

"I—I think I would prefer a chair," said Asrial. Her face flushing rosy red, she glanced about the djinn's dwelling in search of an article of furniture that was not smashed, missing a leg, or most of the stuffing.

"Not a whole piece of furniture in the place except the bed, I'm afraid," said Pukah cheerfully. He owed Kaug one. Two in fact. "Come, Asrial. Let me comfort you, distract your sorrowful thoughts, take your mind from your trouble."

"And how will you do that, Pukah?" Asrial asked coolly, the flush subsiding from her cheeks. "If I am not mistaken, you are attempting to seduce me, to . . . make love to me. That's completely ridiculous! We do not have bodies. We can't feel physical pleasure!"

"Tell me I didn't feel this!" Pukah said grimly, pointing to his swollen lip. "Tell Sond he didn't feel that drubbing he took!" Climbing out of bed, the djinn approached the angel, hands outstretched. "Tell me I'm not feeling what I feel now—my heart racing, my blood burning—"

"Sond didn't!" Asrial faltered, taking a step backward. "You don't! You've just tricked yourself—"

"Tell me you don't feel this!" Grabbing the angel around the waist, Pukah pressed her body close to his and kissed her.

"I . . . I didn't . . . feel a thing!" gasped Asrial angrily when she could breathe. Struggling, she tried to push Pukah away. "I—"

"Hush!" The djinn put his hand over her mouth.

Furious, Asrial clenched her fists and started to beat on the djinn's chest. Then she, too, heard the sound. Her eyes widening in fear, she went limp in Pukah's arms.

"Kaug's back!" whispered the djinn. "I've got to go!"

Pukah vanished so suddenly that Asrial, bereft of his support, nearly fell. Weakly, she sank down on the bed and crouched there, shivering, listening to what was happening outside the basket.

Slowly, unconsciously, her tongue moved across her lips, as though she could still taste a lingering sweetness.

"Master!" cried Pukah in a transport of joy. "You've returned!" He flung himself on the cave floor.

"Humpf," growled Kaug, glowering at the groveling djinn. "He doesn't pull the wool over my eyes!"

"Indeed, such a thing would take a great many sheep, Master," said Pukah, cautiously rising to his feet and padding after the 'efreet, who was stomping about the cave angrily.

"He fears Khardan!"

"Does he, Master?"

"Not because your former master is mighty or powerful, but because Quar can't rule him and, seemingly, he can't kill him."

"So my master—former master—is not dead?"

"Is that a great surprise to you, little Pukah? No, I thought not. Nor to your winged friend, either, eh?"

"Unless Sond has sprouted feathers, I have no idea to whom my Master is referring." Pukah prostrated himself upon the floor, extending his arms out in front of him. "I assure my Master of my absolute loyalty. I would do anything for my Master, even go in search of the Calif, if my Master commands it."

"Would you, Pukah?" Kaug, turning, eyed the djinn intently.

"Nothing would give me greater pleasure, My Master."

"I believe that for once you are telling the truth, little Pukah." The 'efreet grinned. "Yes, I think I will take you up on your offer, slave of the basket. You understand who it is you serve now, don't you, Pukah? By the laws of the djinn, I am your master, you are my servant. If I ordered you to bring Khardan sliced neatly into four equal parts, you would do so, would you not, slave?"

"Of course, My Master," said Pukah glibly.

"Ah, already I can see your mind turning, planning to find some way out of this. Let it turn all it wants, little Pukah. It is like a donkey tied to the waterwheel. Round and round he goes, never getting anywhere. I have your basket. I am your master. Do not forget that or the penalty if you disobey me."

"Yes, My Master," said Pukah in a subdued voice.

"And now, to prove your loyalty, little Pukah, I am going to send you on an errand before you go and search for the missing Khardan. I command you to take the *chirak* of Sond to a certain location. You will leave it there and you will return to me for my orders concerning the Calif."

"Where is this 'certain location,' My Master?"

"Not backing out already, little Pukah, are you?"

"Certainly not, My Master! It is just that I need to know where I am going in order to get there, you dundering squidhead." This last being muttered under Pukah's breath.

"Despite his harsh treatment of me, I am going to grant Sond his heart's wish. I am going to reunite him with his beloved Nedjma. You wanted to know where the Lost Immortals were, little Pukah?"

"I assure my Master that I have not the slightest interest—"

"Take the lamp of Sond and fly with it to the city of Serinda and you will discover what has become of the Vanished Ones."

"Serinda?" Pukah's eyes opened wide; he raised his head from the floor. "That city no longer exists, My Master. It vanished beneath the desert sands hundreds of years ago, so long past that I cannot even remember it."

Kaug shrugged. "Then I am asking you to deliver Sond's *chirak* to a dead city, little Pukah. Do you question my commands already?" The 'efreet's brow creased in a frown.

"No, Master!" Pukah flattened himself completely. "The wings of which you speak are on my feet. I will return to my dwelling—"

"No need to rush, little Pukah. I want you to take some time to look around this interesting city. For—if you fail me, djinn—your basket will find itself sitting in Serinda's marketplace."

"Yes, My Master. Now I'll just be getting back to my dwelling—"

"Not so fast. You must wear this." A black, three-sided rock attacked to a leather thong appeared in the 'efreet's hand. "Sit up." Pukah did as he was ordered and Kaug cast the thong around the djinn's neck. The rock—which came to a point at the top like a small pyramid—thumped against Pukah's bare chest. Pukah regarded it dubiously.

"It is kind of you to give me this gift, Master. What is this interesting looking stone, if I might ask?"

"Black tourmaline."

"Ah, black tourmaline," said Pukah wisely. "Whatever this is," he muttered.

"What did you say?"

"I will keep it always, Master, to remind me of you. It's ugly enough."

"You must learn to speak up, little Pukah."

"I was saying that if you don't need me, I will return to my dwelling and put this marvelous object somewhere safe—"

"No, no! You will wear it at all times, little Pukah. Such is my wish. Now, be gone!"

"Yes, Master." Rising to his feet, Pukah headed for his basket.

"What are you doing?" Kaug growled.

Pukah stopped, glancing over his shoulder. "I am returning to my dwelling, O Mighty Master."

"Why? I told you to take Sond's lamp and leave."

"And so I will, Master," said Pukah firmly, "after I have made myself presentable. These"—he indicated his *pantalons*—"are stained with blood and slime. You would not want me appearing before your friends in such a state, Master. Think how it would reflect upon you!"

"I have no friends where you are going, little Pukah," Kaug said with a grim smile. "And believe me, in Serinda, no one will remark on a few spots of blood."

"Sounds like a cheerful place," Pukah reflected gloomily. "Then I am *not* going to my dwelling. I am just going over to pick up Sond's lamp, Master," the djinn said loudly, sidling nearer and nearer his basket. "The floor of this cave is extremely wet. I hope I don't slip and fall— Ooops!"

The djinn sprawled headlong on the floor, knocking over the basket. As it hit the ground, the lid flew off and Pukah made a desperate attempt to slip inside, but Kaug was there ahead of him. Grabbing the lid, the 'efreet slammed it on top of the basket and held it there firmly with his huge hand.

"I hope you have not hurt yourself, little Pukah?" the 'efreet said solicitously.

"No, thank you, Master." Pukah gulped. "It is amazing how fast one of your bulk can move, isn't it, Master?"

"Isn't it, little Pukah? Now, you *will* be going!"

"Yes, Master." Sighing, Pukah leaned down and picked up Sond's lamp. Slowly and reluctantly, the young djinn began to dwindle away into the air until all that remained of him was his eyes, staring disconsolately at the basket. "Master!" cried his disembodied voice. "If you would only grant me—"

"Be gone!" roared Kaug.

The eyes rolled upward and disappeared.

Instantly the 'efreet snatched off the lid of the basket and thrust his huge hand inside.

# Book Two

# THE BOOK OF ZHAKRIN 1

# Chapter 1

The procession wound its way slowly across the plains toward the city of Idrith. It was a magnificent sight, and—as word of its approach spread through the *souks*—many Idrithians clambered up the narrow stairs and lined the city walls to see, exclaim, and speculate.

At the head of the procession marched two *mamalukes*. Gigantic men, both seven feet tall, the slaves wore red-and-orange feathered headdresses that added an additional three feet to their height. Short black leather skirts banded by gold encircled their narrow waists. Gold flashed from the collars they wore round their necks, jewels glittered on the headdresses. Their chests and legs were bare, their skin oiled so that it glistened in the noonday sun. In their hands, each *mamaluke* carried a banner with a strange device, the like of which had never before been seen in Idrith. On a background red as blood, there glistened a black snake with eyes of orange flame.

Now snake banners were common enough—every city had at least one minor or major potentate who thought himself wily enough to deserve such a symbol. But this particular insignia had something unusual—and sinister—about it.

The snake's body was severed in three places and still, from the portrayal of the forked tongue flicking from the silken mouth, it seemed that the snake lived.

Behind the *mamalukes* marched six muscular slaves clad in black leather skirts bound with gold but without the addi-

tional finery of the standard-bearers. These slaves bore between them a palanquin whose white curtains remained tightly
closed, permitting no one to catch a glimpse of the person
who rode inside. A troop of *goums* mounted on matching
black horses closely followed the palanquin. The soldiers'
uniforms were a somber black, with black short coats and
matching black, flowing pants that were tucked into knee-
high red leather boots. Each man wore upon his head a
conical red hat adorned with a black tassel. Long, curved-
bladed swords bounced against their left legs as they rode.

But it was that which came behind these *goums* in the
solemn processional that caught the attention of the crowd on
the walls of Idrith. Numerous slaves bore between them
three litters, each covered by white fabric. Several *goums*
rode at the side of the litters. The heads of these soldiers
were bowed, their black uniforms were torn, they wore no
hats.

Following the litters was another squadron of *goums*,
escorting three baggage-laden camels decked out in splendid
finery—orange-and-red feathered headdresses, long tassels of
black fringe that bounced about their spindly legs.

From the slow movement and sorrowful mien of those
marching across the plains, it was soon obvious to the people
of Idrith that this was a funeral cortege they were observing
from the walls. Word spread and more people pushed their
way through the crowds to see. Nothing attracts attention like
a funeral, if only to reassure the onlooker that he himself is
still alive.

About a mile from the city gates, the entire procession
came to a halt. The standard-bearers dipped their banners—a
sign that the party approached in peace. The slaves settled
the palanquin on the ground. The *goums* dismounted, the
camels sank to their knees, the rattan-covered litters were
lowered with great ceremony and respect to the ground.

Looking and feeling extremely important, aware of hundreds of envious eyes upon him, the Captain of the Sultan's
Guard led a squadron of his men out to meet and inspect
the strangers before permitting them to enter the city. Barking a sharp command for his men to keep in line and maintain
discipline, the Captain cast a glance toward the Sultan's palace that stood on a hill above Idirth. The Sultan could not
be seen, but the Captain knew he was watching. Bright
patches of color crowding the balconies gave indication that

the Sultan's wives and concubines were flocking to see the procession.

His spine might have been changed to iron, so stiff and straight was the back of the Captain as he walked his horse slowly and with great dignity past the standard-bearers, advancing upon the palanquin. A man had emerged from its white curtains and was waiting with every mark of respect to meet the Captain. Beside the man stood the leader of the *goums*, also on foot and also respectful. A slave held his horse some distance behind him.

Dismounting himself, the Captain handed the reins of his horse to one of his men and walked forward to meet the head of the strange procession.

The man of the palanquin was clothed almost completely in black. Black leather boots, black flowing trousers, a long-sleeved, black flowing shirt, a black turban adorning his head. A red sash and a red jewel in the center of the turban did nothing to relieve the funereal aspect of the man's costume. Rather, perhaps because of the peculiar shade of red that was the color of fresh blood, they enhanced it.

The skin of the man's face and hands was white as alabaster, probably why he took such precautions to keep himself out of the burning sun; Idrith being located just to the north of the Pagrah desert. By contrast, his brows were jet black, feathering out from a point above a slender, hawkish nose. The lips were thin and bloodless. Trimmed moustaches shadowed the upper lip, extending down the lines of the unsmiling mouth to join a narrow black beard that outlined a firm, jutting jawline.

The man in black bowed. Placing a white-skinned, slender hand over his heart, he performed the *salaam* with grace. The Captain returned the bow, far more clumsily—he was a big, awkward man. Raising his head, he met the gaze of the man in black and flinched involuntarily, as if the penetrating glance of the two dark, cold eyes had been living steel.

Instantly on his guard, the Captain cleared his throat and launched into the formalities. "I see by the lowering of your standards that you come in peace, *Effendi*. Welcome to the city of Idrith. The Sultan begs to know your names and your business that we may do you honor and lose no time in accommodating you."

The expression on the face of the man in black remained grave as he replied with equal solemnity and politeness. "My name is Auda ibn Jad. Formerly a trader in slaves, I am now traveling eastward to my homeland of Simdari. I wish only to stop over in your city for a day and a night to replenish my supplies and give my men some rest. Our journey has been a long and a sad one, and we have still many hundreds of miles to go before its end. I am certain that you must have surmised, Captain," the man in black said with a sigh, "that we are a funeral cortege."

Uncertain how to respond, the Captain cleared his throat noncommittally and glanced with lowering brows at the number of armed men he was being asked to let into his city. Auda ibn Jad appeared to understand, for he added, with a sad smile, "My *goums* would be most willing to surrender their swords to you, Captain, and I will answer for their good conduct." Taking hold of the Captain's arm with his slender hand, Auda led the soldier to one side and spoke in a low voice. "You will, however, be patient with my men, *sidi*. They have the gold of Kich in their purses, gold that melancholy circumstances prevented them from spending. They are excellent fighters and disciplined men. But they have suffered a great shock and seek to drown their sorrows in wine or find solace in the other pleasures for which this city is well-known. I myself have some business to do"—ibn Jad's eyes flicked a glance at several iron-bound wooden chests strapped to the camels—"with the jewel merchants of Idrith."

Feeling the cold sensation spread from the man's eyes to the fingers that rested on his arm, the Captain of the Sultan's Guard drew back from that icy touch. Every instinct that had made him a good soldier for forty years warned him to forbid this man with eyes like knives to enter his city. Yet he could see the heavy purses hanging from each *goum's* sash. The merchants of Idrith standing upon the city walls could not detect the money pouches from that distance, but they could see the heavy chests on the camels' backs, the gold that glittered around the necks of this man's slaves.

On his way out of the city gates, the Captain had seen the followers of Kharmani, God of Wealth, reaching for their tally-sticks, and he knew very well that the proprietors of the eating houses, the tea shops, and the *arwats* were rubbing their hands in anticipation. A howl of outrage would split the Sultan's eardrums if this woolly sheep all ready for the shearing were driven from the city gates—all because the Captain did not like the look in the sheep's eyes.

The Captain still had one more bone to toss in the game, however. "All those desirous of entering the city of Idrith must surrender to me not only their weapons but all their magic items and djinn as well, *Effendi*. These will be given as sacrifice to Quar," said the Captain, hoping that this edict—one that had come from the God and one that therefore not even the Sultan could lift—would discourage these visitors. His hope was a vain one, however.

Auda ibn Jad nodded gravely. "Yes, Captain, such a commandment was imposed on us in Kich. It was there that we left all our magical paraphernalia and our djinn. We were honored to do this in the name of so great a God as Quar and—as you see—he has in turn favored us with his blessing in our journeying."

"You will not be offended if I search you, *Effendi*?" asked the Captain.

"We have nothing to hide, *sidi*," said ibn Jad humbly, with another graceful bow.

Of course they don't, the Captain thought dowerly. They knew about this and were prepared. Nevertheless, he had to go through the motions. Turning, he ordered his men to commence the search, as Auda ibn Jad ordered the leader of the *goums* to unload the camels.

"What is in there?" The Captain pointed to the litters.

"The bodies, *sidi*," replied ibn Jad in low, reverent tones. "I did mention that this was a funeral cortege, didn't I?"

The Captain started. Yes, the man had said that they were a funeral procession, but the Captain had assumed it was an honorary one, perhaps escorting the icon of some deceased Imam back to his birthplace. It never occurred to the soldier that this Auda ibn Jad was carting corpses around with him. The Captain glanced at the litters and frowned outwardly, though inwardly sighing with relief.

"Bodies! I am sorry, *Effendi*, but I cannot allow those inside the city walls. The risk of disease—"

"—is nonexistent, I assure you. Come, Captain, look for yourself."

The Captain had no choice but to follow the man in black to where the litters rested on the sandy soil of the plains. Not a squeamish man—the Captain had seen his share of corpses in his lifetime—he nevertheless approached the litters with extreme reluctance. A body hacked and mangled on the field of battle was one thing. A body that has been traveling in the heat of early summer was quite another. Coming near the first litter, the Captain hardened himself for what was to come. It was odd, though, that there were no flies buzzing about. Sniffing, the Captain detected no whiff of corruption, and he glanced at the man in black in puzzlement.

Reading the Captain's thoughts, Auda ibn Jad smiled deprecatingly, as if denying credit for everything. He neared the litter, and his smile vanished, replaced by the most sorrowful solemnity. With a gesture, he invited the Captain to look.

Even as close as this, there was no hint of the nauseating odor of decay, nor could the Captain detect any perfume that might have covered it. His repugnance lost in curiosity, the Captain bent down and peered inside the first litter.

His eyes opened wide.

Lying in the most peaceful attitude of repose, his hands folded over the jeweled hilt of a splendid sword, was a young man of perhaps twenty-five years of age. He was handsome, with black hair and a neatly trimmed black beard. A helm carved to resemble the severed snake device lay at his feet, along with a broken sword that belonged—presumably—to the enemy who had vanquished him. Dressed in shining black armor, whose breastplate was decorated with the same design that appeared on the banners of Auda ibn Jad, the young man seemed by outward appearance to have just fallen asleep. So smooth and unblemished was the flesh, so shining black and lustrous was the hair, the Captain could not forbear stretching forth his hand and touching the white forehead.

The flesh was cold. The pulse in the neck was stilled, the chest did not move with the breath of life.

Stepping back, the Captain stared at the man in black in astonishment.

"How long has this man been dead?"

"About a month," ibn Jad replied in grave tones.

"That—that's impossible!"

"Not for the priests of our God, *sidi*. They have learned the secret of replacing the fluids of the body with fluids that can delay or completely arrest the natural process of decay. It is quite a fascinating procedure. The brains are taken out by drawing them through the nose—"

"Enough!" The Captain, paling, raised his hand. "Who is this God of yours?"

"Forgive me," said Auda ibn Jad gently, "but I have taken a sacred vow never to speak His name in the presence of unbelievers."

"He is not an enemy of Quar's?"

"Surely the mighty and powerful Quar can have no enemies?" Ibn Jad raised a black eyebrow.

This statement left the Captain somewhat at a loss. If he pursued the matter of this man's God, it would appear that the mighty and powerful Quar did indeed have something to fear. Yet the soldier felt uncomfortable in not pursuing it.

"Since your priests have conquered the effects of death, *Effendi*," said the Captain, hoping to gather more information, "why have they never sought to defeat Death himself?"

"They are working on it, *sidi*," said ibn Jad coolly.

Nonplussed, the Captain gave up and glanced back down at the corpse of the man lying in state in the litter. "Who is he and why do you carry him with you?"

"He is Calif of my people," answered ibn Jad, "and I have the sad task of bearing his body home to his grieving father. The young man was killed in the desert, fighting the nomads of Pagrah alongside the Amir of Kich—a truly great man. Do you know him, Captain?"

"Yes," said the Captain shortly. "Tell me, *Effendi*, why is a Prince of Simdari fighting in foreign lands so far from his home?"

"You do not trust me, do you, Captain?" said Auda ibn Jad suddenly, frowning, a look in the cold eyes that made the soldier—a veteran of many battles—shudder. The Captain was about to respond when ibn Jad shook his head, putting his hands to his temples as if they ached. "Please forgive me," he murmured. "I know you have your duty to uphold. I am short-tempered. This journey of mine has not been pleasant, yet I do not look forward to its ending." Sighing, he crossed his arms over his chest. "I dread bringing this news to my king. The young man"—with a nod toward the corpse—"is his only son, the child of his old age at that. And now"—ibn Jad bowed gracefully—"to answer your most reasonable question, Captain. The Calif was visiting the court of the Emperor in Khandar. Hearing of the fame of the Amir, the Calif rode to Kich to study the art of warfare at the feet of a master. It was by the vilest treachery that the savage nomads killed him."

Ibn Jad's story seemed plausible. The Captain had heard rumors of the Amir's attack on the nomads of the Pagrah desert. It was well-known that the Emperor of Tara-kan—a man who thirsted after knowledge as another thirsts for strong drink—encouraged visitors from strange lands who worshiped strange Gods. Yes, it was all nice and neat, so very nice and neat. . . .

"What do you carry in those other two litters, *Effendi?*"

"Ah, here you will see a sight that will move you profoundly, *sidi*. Come."

Walking over to the two litters that rested behind the first, the Captain saw—out of the corner of his eye—that his troops had almost completed their search of the caravan's goods. He would have to make a decision soon. Admit them into the city or keep them out. Every instinct, every twitching nerve fiber in his body warned him—keep them out. Yet he needed a reason.

Glancing inside the litter, expecting to see another soldier—perhaps a bodyguard who had sacrificed his life for his master—the Captain caught his breath. "Women!" he stated, looking from one litter to the other.

"Women!" murmured Auda ibn Jad in reproof. "Say rather 'Goddesses' and you will come nearer the truth, for such beauty as theirs is rarely seen on this wretched plane of mortal existence. Look upon them, Captain. You may do so now, though to have set eyes upon their beauty before the death of my Calif would have cost you your life."

A white gauze veil had been drawn over the face of each woman. With great respect and reverence, ibn Jad removed the veil from the first. The woman had classic features, but there was something about the pale, still face that spoke of fierce pride and stern resolution. Her long black hair glistened blue in the sun. Bending near her, the Captain caught the faintest smell of jasmine.

Auda ibn Jad turned to the other woman, and the Captain noticed that his touch grew more gentle. Slowly he drew back the veil from the motionless body. Gazing at the woman lying before him, the Captain felt his heart stirred with pity and with admiration. Ibn Jad had spoken truly. Never had the soldier seen a woman more beautiful. The skin was like cream, the features perfect. Hair the color and brilliance of dancing flame tumbled down over the slender shoulders.

"The wives of my Calif," Auda said, and for the first time the Captain heard grief in the voice. "When his body was brought into the palace at Kich where they were staying, awaiting my lord's return, they hurled themselves upon him, weeping and tearing their clothes. Before any could stop them, the one with the red hair grabbed the Prince's sword. Crying that she could not live without him, she drove the blade into her own fair body and dropped dead at his feet. The other—jealous that the red-haired wife should reach him first in the Realm of Our God—drew a dagger she had hidden beneath her gown and stabbed herself. Both are the daughters of Sultans in my land. I bear them back to be buried with honor in the tomb of their husband."

His head whirling from his glimpse of the beauty of the women, combined with a story of such tragedy and romance, the Captain wondered what to do. A Prince of Simdari, a friend of both the Emperor and the Amir, the body of this young man should be rights be escorted into the city. The Sultan would never forgive his Captain if, on his yearly visit to the court of Khandar, he was asked by the Emperor if he had received the funeral cortege of the Calif with honor and the Sultan was forced to reply that he knew nothing of any such cortege. In addition, was the Captain to deny his Sultan— who was always on the verge of perishing from boredom—the opportunity of meeting exotic guests, of hearing this sad tale of war and love and self-sacrifice?

The only metal the Captain had to set against all this glittering gold was plain, solid iron—an instinctive feeling of dislike and distrust for this Auda ibn Jad. Still pondering the matter, the Captain turned to find his lieutenant hovering at his elbow, the leader of the *goums* standing at his side.

"We have completed the search of the caravan, sir," the lieutenant reported, "with the exception of those." He pointed at the litters.

The leader of the *goums* gave a shocked yelp that was answered swiftly and sternly in their own language by Auda ibn Jad. Even so, the leader of the *goums* continued to talk volubly until Auda silenced him with a sharp, angry command. Red-faced and ashamed, the *goum* slunk away like a whipped dog. Auda, pale with fury, yet with his temper under control, turned to the Captain.

"Forgive the outburst, *sidi*. My man forgot himself. It will not happen again. You mentioned searching the corpses. By all means, please proceed."

"What was all that about, *Effendi*?" the Captain asked suspiciously.

"Please, Captain. It was nothing."

"I insist on knowing—"

"If you must." Auda ibn Jad appeared faintly embarrassed. "The priests of our God have placed a curse upon these bodies. Any who disturb their rest will die a most horrible death, their souls sent to serve the Calif and his wives in heaven." Ibn Jad lowered his voice to a confidential whisper. "Accept my apologies, Captain. Kiber, the leader of my *goums*—while he is a good soldier—is a superstitious peasant. I beg you to pay no heed to him. Search the bodies."

"I will," said the Captain harshly.

Turning to his lieutenant to issue the order, the Captain saw by the carefully impassive, frozen expression on the soldier's face that he had heard ibn Jad's words quite clearly. The Captain opened his mouth. The lieutenant gave him a pleading look.

Angrily, the Captain marched over to the body of the Calif. "May Quar protect me from the unknown evil," he said loudly, reaching forth his hand to search the mattress upon which the corpse rested. Any number of objects could be concealed in it, or beneath the silken sheet that covered the lower half of the body, or even inside the armor itself. . . .

An eerie murmur, like the low whistle of a rising windstorm, caused the Captain's hair to bristle. Involuntarily, his hand jerked back. Looking up swiftly, he saw the sound had come from ibn Jad's *goums*. The men were backing away, their horses—affected by the fear of their masters—rolled their eyes and danced nervously. The slaves huddled together in a group and began to wail piteously. Auda ibn Jad, with a scowl, rounded upon them and shouted at them in his own language. From the motion of his hand, the Captain gathered he was promising them all a sound thrashing. The wailing ceased, but the slaves, the *goums*, the horses, and even, it seemed, the camels—beasts not noted for their intelligence—watched the Captain with an eager, anticipatory thrill of horror that was most unnerving.

Ibn Jad's face was tense and strained. Though he was endeavoring hard to conceal his emotions, apparently he, too, was a superstitious peasant at heart. Abruptly, the Captain withdrew his hand.

"I will not disturb the honored dead. And you, Auda ibn Jad, and your men have leave to enter Idrith. But these"—he gestured at the rattan litters—"must remain outside the city walls. If they are indeed cursed, it would not do to bring them into the sacred precincts of Quar." At least, the Captain thought grimly, he had solved *that* dilemma! Perhaps Auda ibn Jad and his men will take offense at this and leave.

But the man in black was smiling and bowing graciously, his fingers going to heart, lips, and forehead in the graceful *salaam*.

"I will order my men to guard the dead," the Captain offered, though—glancing at his troops—he knew such an order would be unnecessary. Word of the curse would spread like the plague through the city. The most devout follower of Benario, God of Thieves, would not steal so much as a jeweled earring from the corpses.

"My grateful thanks, Captain," said Auda, bowing again, hand pressed over his heart.

The Captain bowed awkwardly in return. "And perhaps you would do me the very great honor of accompanying me to the Sultan's palace this evening. Affairs of state prevent His Magnificence from seeing the world, and he would be much entertained by the stories you have related to me."

Auda ibn Jad protested that he was not worthy of such attention. The Captain patiently assured him that he was. Auda insisted that he wasn't and continued to demur as long as was proper, then gave in with refined grace. Sighing, the Captain turned away. Having no legitimate reason to keep this man and his *goums* out of Idrith, he had done what he could. At least the corpses with their unholy curse would not pollute the city. He would himself take personal charge of Auda ibn Jad and order his men to keep a watchful eye upon the *goums*. After all, they numbered no more than thirty. The Sultan's wives alone outnumbered them two to one. Amid the thousands of people jammed into Idrith, they would be as a single drop of rain falling into a deep well.

Telling himself that he had the situation under control, the Captain started to remount his horse. But his uneasiness persisted. His foot in the stirrup, he paused, hands on the saddle, and looked for one last time at the man in black.

Beneath hooded lids, the eyes of Auda ibn Jad were

glancing sideways into the eyes of Kiber, leader of the *goums*. Much was being said in that exchange of glances, though probably nothing that was not of the most innocent nature. The Captain shivered in the noonday sun.

"I am," he said grimly, "a superstitious peasant."

Pulling himself up into the saddle, he wheeled his horse and galloped off to order the city gates be opened to Auda ibn Jad.

# Chapter 2

The Sultan was—as the Captain had foreseen—charmed with Auda ibn Jad. Nothing would do but that the Sultan and his current favorites among his wives and concubines must leave the palace and traipse outside the city walls to pay homage to the dead. The women cooed and sighed over the handsome young Prince. The Sultan and the nobles shook their heads over the wasted beauty of the women. Auda ibn Jad told his story well, bringing tears to many eyes in the royal court as he related in heartfelt tones the final words of the red-haired wife as she fell dead across her husband's body.

Following this, there was a sumptuous dinner that lasted long into the night. The wine flowed freely, much of it into the Captain's mouth. Ordinarily, the Captain did not take to strong drink, but he felt he had to warm himself. There was something about Auda ibn Jad that chilled his blood; but what it was, the Captain couldn't say.

Deep into his sixth cup of the unwatered vintage that came from the grapes grown in the hills above Idrith, the Captain stared at the man, seated cross-legged on silken cushions opposite him. He couldn't take his eyes off ibn Jad, feeling himself caught by the same terrible fascination a cobra is said to exert over its victims.

It is Auda ibn Jad's face, the Captain decided muzzily. The man's face is too smooth. There are no lines on it, no traces of any emotion, no traces of any human feeling or passion—either good or evil. The corners of the mouth turn neither up nor down. The cold, hooded eyes narrow in neither laughter nor anger. Ibn Jad ate and drank without enjoyment. He watched the sinuous twistings of the dancing girls without lust. A face of stone, the Captain decided and drank another cup of wine, only to feel it sit in his stomach like a lump of cold clay.

At last the Sultan rose from his cushions to go to the bed of his chosen. Much pleased with his guest, he gave Auda ibn Jad a ring from his own hand. Nothing priceless, the Captain noted, staring at it with bleary eyes—a semiprecious gem whose glitter was greater than its worth. Auda ibn Jad apparently knew something of jewels himself, for he accepted it with a flicker of sardonic amusement in the cold eyes.

In answer to the Sultan's invitation to return to the palace tomorrow, ibn Jad replied regretfully that he must not tarry in his sad journey. His king had, as of yet, no knowledge of the death of his son and Auda ibn Jad feared lest it should reach his ears from some stranger, rather than a trusted friend.

The Sultan, yawning, was very understanding. His Captain was overwhelmed with relief. In the morning they would be rid of this man and his well-preserved corpses. Stumbling to his feet, the Captain—accompanied by a cold sober ibn Jad—made his way through the winding passages of the palace and stumbled drunkenly down the stairs. He narrowly missed tumbling headfirst into a large ornamental pool that graced the front of the palace—it was ibn Jad's hand that pulled him back—and finally weaved his way through the various gates that led them by stages back into the city.

Once in the moon-lit streets of Idrith, Auda ibn Jad glanced about in perplexity.

"This maze of alleys confuses me, Captain. I fear I have forgotten the way back to the *arwat* in which I am staying. If you could guide me—"

Certainly. Anything to get rid of the man. The Captain lurched forward into the empty street; ibn Jad walking at his side. Suddenly, inexplicably, the man in black slowed his pace.

Something inside the Captain—some old soldier's instinct—screamed out a desperate warning. The Captain heard it, but by then it was too late.

An arm grabbed him from behind. With incredible strength, it wrapped around his neck, choking off his breath. The

Captain's fear sobered him. His muscles tensed, he raised his hands to resist. . . .

The Captain felt the stinging pain of the knife's point entering his throat just beneath his jaw. So skilled was the hand wielding the blade, however, that the Captain never felt the swift, slicing cut to follow.

There was only a brief tremor of fear . . . anger. . . .

Then nothing.

The Captain's body was discovered in the morning—the first in a series of grisly discoveries that left the city of Idrith in the grip of terror. Two streets over, the body of an old man was found lying in a gutter. Ten blocks to the north, a father woke to find his young, virgin daughter murdered in her sleep. The body of a virile, robust man turned up floating in a *hauz*. A middle-aged mother of four was discovered lying in an alley.

The disciplined guards surged outside the city walls to question the strangers, only to find that the funeral cortege of Auda ibn Jad had disappeared. No one had heard them leave. The sunbaked ground left no trace of their passing. Squadrons of soldiers rode out in all directions, searching, but no trace of the man in black, his *goums*, or the bodies in the rattan litters was ever found.

Back inside the city, the mystery deepened. The dead appeared to have been chosen at random—a stalwart soldier; a decrepit old beggar; a beautiful young virgin; a wife and mother; a muscular young man. Yet the victims had one thing in common—the manner of their dying.

The throat of each person had been slit, neatly and skillfully, from ear to ear. And, most horribly, by some mysterious means, each body had been completely drained of blood.

# Book Three

# THE BOOK
# OF QUAR 1

 # Chapter 1

It was the noise—the noise and the stench of the prison that disturbed the nomads most. Accustomed to the music of the desert—the song of the wind over the dunes, the hum of the tent ropes stretched taut in a storm, the barking of camp dogs, the laughter of children, the voices of the women going about their daily chores, the cry of a falcon making a successful kill—the sounds of the prison tore at the young men until they felt as if every inch of their skins had been flayed from their bodies.

The soldiers of the Amir did not mistreat the desert dwellers, who had been captured in the raid on the camp around the Tel. Far from it. Although the nomads had no way of knowing, they were being accorded better treatment than any other prisoners. Physicians had been sent to treat their wounds, and they were allowed exercise and a small amount of time each day to see their families. But to the imprisoned Akar, Hrana, or Aran tribe members, being deprived of their freedom was the most excruciating torture the Amir could have devised.

When the captives were first brought in, they were assembled in the prison yard and the Amir spoke to them.

"I watched you in battle," he said, sitting astride his magical, ebony horse, "and I will not hide from you the fact that I was impressed. All my life I had heard the stories of the bravery and skill of the followers of Akhran."

The nomads, who had previously been standing sullenly,

eyes on the ground, looked up at this, pleased and startled
that Qannadi should know the name of their God. The Amir
made it a point to keep such details in his mind, often
surprising his own men by speaking to each by name, recalling some act of bravery or daring. An old soldier, he knew
such small things touched the heart and won undying loyalty.

"I did not believe it," he continued in his deep baritone,
"until I saw it for myself." He paused here dramatically, to
let his words slide like oil upon the troubled waters.
"Outnumbered, taken by surprise, you fought like devils. I
needed every soldier in my command to defeat you and even
then I began to fear that the might of my army was not strong
enough."

This was not exactly true; the outcome had never been in
doubt and—considering the strength of the army the Amir
had built up to conquer the south—Qannadi had thrown only
a token force at the nomads. He could afford to lie at his own
expense, however, being ten times rewarded by seeing the
sullen eyes gleam with pride.

"Such men as you are wasted out there." Qannadi gestured dramatically toward the Pagrah desert. "Instead of stealing sheep, you could be capturing the wealth of cities. Instead
of knifing each other in the dark, you could be challenging a
brave foe in glorious combat on an open field. I offer you this
and more! Fight with me, and I will pay you thirty silver *tumans*
a month. I will give your families free housing in the city, the
opportunity for your women to sell their wares in the *souks*,
and a fair share in the spoils of any city we conquer."

Most of the nomads growled and shook their heads, but
some—Qannadi noted—dropped their eyes, shuffling their
feet uneasily. Many here had ridden with their Calif in the
raid on the Kich. Qannadi skillfully conjured up visions in
their minds of galloping their horses through rich palaces,
snatching up gold and jewels and Sultans' beautiful daughters. The Amir did not delude himself. He did not think it
likely he would gain any recruits this moment. After all, the
men had just seen their families carried off, they had seen
some of their own die in battle. But he knew that this arrow
he had fired would pierce their imaginations and stick there,
festering, in their minds.

Sayah, Zohra's half brother, stepped forward. "I speak for
the Hrana," he cried, "and I tell you that we serve no man
except our Sheykh!"

"The same for the Akar!" came a voice and, "The same for the Aran," came another.

Without responding, Qannadi turned and galloped out of the prison yard. The nomads thought he rode off in anger and congratulated themselves on having tweaked the Amir's nose. So rowdy were they that the guards thought it best to beat soundly the most vocal before driving them back to their cells.

Qannadi was not angry, however. The true, underlying meaning of what these men said struck the Amir with such force it was a wonder he didn't fall from his saddle. Absorbed in thought, he returned to the palace and sent at once for the Imam.

"Bringing their Sheykhs in is out of the question," the Amir said, pacing back and forth the length of the room that had once been the Sultan's private study and was now his, never noticing that his boots were tracking mud and manure on the handwoven, priceless carpets covering the floor. "They are old dogs who will bite any hand other than their master's. But these young pups are different. They might be taught to jump through the hoops of another, especially if it is one of their own. We need to raise up a leader in their midst, Feisal, someone they trust and will follow. But someone who, in turn, must be under our complete control. Is that possible, do you think, Imam?"

"With Quar, all is possible, O King. Not only possible, but probable. It is too bad," Feisal added, with a subtle change of expression in his voice, "that their Calif, this Khardan, should have vanished so mysteriously."

Qannadi glanced at the priest sharply. "Khardan is dead."

"His body was not discovered."

"He is dead," the Amir said coldly. "Meryem reported to me that she saw him fall in battle, mortally wounded. As for why the corpse was not discovered, it was probably hauled off by some wild beast." Qannadi fixed Feisal with a stern, black-eyed gaze. "We both want these nomads on our side, Imam!"

"There is one difference, O King," said Feisal, not at all discomfited by the Amir's baleful gaze. "*You* want their bodies. *I* want their souls."

The following day, and many days after that, the Imam visited the prison. Though he would never admit as much to the Amir, Feisal realized Qannadi had grasped hold of the tail of a valuable idea. It would be up to the Imam to soothe the beast attached to that tail and make it work for them. Consequently, he talked to the young men, bringing them news of their families, assuring them that their mothers, wives, and children were being well cared for, and extolling the virtues of settled city life, drawing subtle differences between it and the harsh life of the wanderer. Wisely, the Imam never mentioned Quar. He never mentioned Akhran, either, but left the young men to draw their own conclusions.

One person in particular drew his attention. Sitting alone in the tiny, narrow, windowless cell in the Zindan, Achmed, Khardan's half brother, foundered in a despair so black and murky he felt as though he were drowning in it.

The smell in the prison was poisonous. Once a day, the prisoners were allowed outside to walk around the compound and to perform their ablutions, but that was all. The remainder of the time they had to make do with a corner of the cell, and though it was cleaned out daily by slaves, the stench of human excrement, as well as that of sickness, was always in the air.

Achmed could not eat. The stink penetrated the food and tainted the water. He could not sleep. The noise, that spoke of pain and suffering and torture, was dreadful. In the cell next to his, an unlucky follower of Benario's had been captured inside one of the bazaars after curfew, making away with stolen goods. The wretch's hands had been cut off, to teach him a lesson, and he moaned and howled with the pain until he either lapsed into unconsciousness or one of the guards—irritated at the clamor—clouted him over the head.

In the other side cell, a debtor to the followers of Kharmani, God of Wealth, had developed an insidious cough and lay hacking his life away while bemoaning the fact that he couldn't raise the money to pay off his debts while confined in prison.

Across from Achmed, a beggar caught exhibiting fake sores to a gullible audience was developing real ones. Two cells down a man condemned to be hurled from the Tower of Death for raping a woman pounded on the walls and pleaded with an unhearing Amir for another trial.

At first, getting out of the cell was a welcome release, but after a few days Achmed grew to dread the time they were allowed to walk in the compound. No loving wife came to stretch her hand out to him through the bars of the gate, no mother came to weep over him. His own mother—one of Majiid's many wives—had been captured in the raid on the camp. She was in the city, but too ill to come and see him. This Achmed heard from Badia, Khardan's mother, the only one who occasionally visited the young man.

"The soldiers did not hurt her," Badia hastened to assure Achmed, seeing by the dark, violent expression on the young man's face that he might commit some foolish act. "They were really very kind and gentle and took her to a house of one of their own Captains, whose wives are caring for her like a sister. The Imam himself has been to see her and said a prayer for her. But she was never strong, Achmed, not since your baby sister was born. We must put our trust in Akhran."

Akhran! Alone, despairing, Achmed cursed the name of the God. Why have You done this to me, to my people? the young man questioned, head in his hands, tears creeping through his clenched fingers. This day would have been my birthday. Eighteen years. There would have been a *baigha* held in my honor. Khardan would have seen to that, even if Majiid—Achmed's father and Sheykh of the Akar—forgot. Majiid very likely would have forgotten; he had many sons and took pride in only one—his eldest, Khardan.

Achmed didn't mind. He, too, admired Khardan with all his heart and soul, feeling—in many ways—that Khardan was more of a father to him than the rough, bellowing, quick-tempered Majiid. Khardan would have seen to it that this day was special for his younger half brother. A present—perhaps one of the Calif's very own jeweled daggers. A dinner just for the two of them in Khardan's tent, drinking *qumiz* until they couldn't stand and listening to Pukah's tales of bloodsucking ghuls, the flesh-eating *delhan*, or the alluring and deadly *ghaddar*.

The thief in the next cell began to rave deliriously. A sob burst from Achmed's throat. Slumping down onto the straw spread over his floor, he hid his face in the crook of his arm and wept in lonely, bitter anguish.

"My son."

The soft, sympathetic voice spread over Achmed's bleeding soul like a soothing balm. Startled—the young man had been so lost in his grief he had not heard the sound of the key in the door or the door being opened—Achmed sat up and hastily wiped away the traces of his tears. Glancing suspiciously at the slender figure of the priest entering his cell,

Achmed crouched down on the dirty mattress that was his bed and affected to be intently interested in a crack in the wall.

"I hear that you suffered a wound in the battle. Are you in pain, my son?" the Imam inquired gently. "Shall I send for the physicians?"

Sniffing, Achmed wiped his nose on the sleeve of his robe and stared fiercely straight ahead.

The priest smiled inwardly. He felt instinctively he had arrived at precisely the right moment, and he thanked Quar for having been led to the suffering lamb in time to save it from the wolves.

"Let me examine your injury," said the Imam, although he knew well that it was not the wound on the head but the wound in the heart that brought the tears to the young man's eyes.

Achmed ducked his head, as though he would have refused, but Feisal pretended not to notice. Removing the *haik*, he examined the cut. During the battle, Achmed had been struck by the flat of a sword blade. The blow had split the skin and knocked him unconscious, leaving him with a terrible headache for a day after but doing no serious injury.

"Tsk," the Imam made a clucking sound, "you will have a scar."

"That is good!" Achmed said suddenly, huskily. He had to say something. The attention the priest paid him and the gentle touch of his fingers had come dangerously near to making him start to cry again. "My brother has many such scars. It is the mark of a warrior."

"You sound like the Amir," said Feisal, his heartbeat quickening in secret delight. Many times he had looked in on Achmed and the young man had never spoken to him, never even looked at him. The Imam smoothed back the black hair. "To me, such scars are the mark of the savage. When man is truly civilized, then all wars will cease and we will live in peace. There." He handed back the headcloth. "The wound is healing cleanly. It will leave a white mark on your scalp, however. The hair will not grow back."

Holding the cloth in his hands, Achmed twisted it with his fingers. He did not put it back on. "Civilized? You're one to talk. This"—he pointed to his head—"was the work of your 'savages'!"

The Imam carefully concealed his joy by glancing around

the cell. It was impossible to talk here. Next door the mutilated thief was screaming feverishly. "Will you come outside and walk with me, Achmed?"

The young man glowered at him suspiciously.

"It is a fine day," the Imam said. "The wind blows from the east."

The east. The desert. Achmed lowered his eyes. "Very well," he said in a low voice. Rising to his feet, he followed Feisal out the door of his cell, trudging down the long, dark corridor. The guard started to follow, but the Imam shook his head and warned him away with a gesture of his thin fingers. As they passed the cells, those inside stretched out their hands to the priest, begging for his blessing, or tried to snatch up and kiss the hem of his robe. Stealing a glance from the corner of his eye, Achmed saw the Imam react to all this with extraordinary patience, murmuring the ritual words, reaching through the bars to touch a bent head, offering comfort and hope in the name of Quar.

Achmed recalled the first time he had seen the priest, when Khardan had come to the palace to try to sell horses to the Amir. Achmed had been frightened of the Imam then and he was frightened of him now. It was not that the priest's physical presence was formidable. Days and nights of fasting and praying had left the Imam's body so slender and delicate that Achmed could have picked the man up and broken him in two with his bare hands. The fear did not generate from the gaunt and handsome face.

It was the eyes, aflame with holy zeal, whose fire could burn holes through a man as a hot iron burns through wood.

Emerging into the sunshine, Achmed lifted his face to the heavens, reveling in the welcome warmth on his skin. He drew a deep breath. Though the air smelled of city, at least it was better than the stench in the prison. And, as the Imam had said, the wind was from the east and Achmed could swear he caught the faintest breath of the desert's elusive perfume.

Glancing about, he saw Feisal watching him intently. Shoulders slumping, Achmed dove back into sullen uncaring like a startled djinn diving back into his bottle.

"Your mother's health is improving," said the Imam.

"She wouldn't have fallen sick if you'd left her alone," Achmed returned accusingly.

"On the contrary, my son. It was well for her that we

brought her to Kich. Our physicians have undoubtedly saved her life. Out there, in that wretched land"—the Imam looked to the east—"she would surely have perished." Seeing stubborn disbelief on the young face, the priest turned the conversation. "Of what were we speaking?" he asked.

"Savages." Achmed sneered.

"Ah, yes. So we were." Feisal gestured to what little shade existed in the compound. "We are alone. Shall we sit down to talk more comfortably?"

"You'll soil your robes."

"Clothes can be cleansed, just like the soul. I see that no one has brought you a clean robe. Disgraceful. I will speak to the Amir."

The Imam settled himself comfortably on the hard rock pavement. Leaning against the prison wall, the priest appeared as much at home as if he had been lounging on a sofa in the finest room in the palace. Awkwardly, Achmed squatted down beside him, the young man flushing in embarrassment at the deplorable condition of his clothes.

"You have a younger sister," the Imam said.

Achmed—all his suspicions aroused once more—scowled and did not answer.

"I have seen her, when I visited your mother," Feisal continued, gazing unblinking out over the compound that was bathed in brilliant sunlight. "Your sister is a beautiful child. How old is she? Two?"

Still no reply.

"An interesting age. So full of curiosity and testing one's limits. I suppose that, like all children, she put her hand into the cooking fire, didn't she?"

"What?" Achmed stared at the priest in puzzlement.

"Did she ever put her hand into the fire?"

"Well, yes, I guess so. . . . All little kids do."

"Why?"

Achmed was confused, wondering why they were discussing small children. He shrugged. "They're attracted to it—the bright light, the colors, the warmth."

"They don't understand that it will hurt them?"

"How could they? They're too little."

"What did your mother do when she caught your sister starting to put her hand in the dancing flames?"

"I don't know. Smacked her, I guess."

"Why didn't your mother reason with the child, tell her that the fire will hurt her?"

"You can't reason with a two-year-old!" Achmed scoffed.

"But the child understands a slap on the wrist?"

"Sure. I mean, I guess so."

"Did she understand it because it gave her pain?"

"Yes."

"And did your mother enjoy hurting her child?"

"We're not barbarians, no matter what you think!" Achmed answered hotly, thinking this was a slur on his people.

"I am not saying that. Why does your mother choose to hurt her child?"

"Because she's afraid for her!"

"A slap on the wrist hurts, yet not like the fire."

"This is a stupid conversation!" Moodily, Achmed picked up small pieces of loose rock and began tossing them into the compound.

"Be patient," the Imam counseled softly. "We see the road beneath our feet, not the end. But we walk it still or we would get nowhere. So—the child reaches for the fire. The mother slaps the child's wrist and tells her no. Until the child is capable of understanding that the fire will burn her, the lesser hurt protects the child from the greater. Is this true?"

"Something like that, I suppose." Achmed had always heard priests were crazy. Now he had proof.

Reaching out his hand, the Imam touched the young man upon his forehead. "Now do you understand?" Feisal asked, his fingers gliding gently over the wound.

Turning, pausing in midthrow, Achmed stared at the priest in astonishment. "Understand what?"

Feisal smiled, his eyes were brighter than the sun of *dohar*.

"In spiritual matters, you are the child. Your God, the false God, Akhran, is the fire—bright colors and dancing light. Like the fire, he is a dangerous God, Achmed, for he will burn up your soul and leave it nothing but ashes. The Amir and myself are the parents who must protect you from everlasting harm, my son. We tried to reason with you, but you did not understand our words. Therefore, in order to save you from the inferno, we had to strike out, to slap your hand. . . ."

"And what about those you hit a little too hard?" Achmed cried angrily. "Those who died!"

"No one regrets loss of life more than I," the Imam said, his almond-shaped eyes burning into Achmed's. "It was your people—most notably your headstrong brother—who attacked us. We defended ourselves."

Jumping to his feet, Achmed began to walk away, heading back for the cells.

"Believe me, Achmed!" The Imam called after him. "The Amir could have destroyed your tribes! He could have wiped you out. It would have been far less trouble. But such was not his intent, nor mine!"

"You take us hostage!" Achmed tossed the words over his shoulder.

Rising gracefully, the Imam walked after the young man, talking to a steel-stiffened back.

"Hostage? Where is the demand for ransom? Have you been put up on the slave blocks? Tortured, beaten? Has one of your women been violatéd, molested?"

"Perhaps not." Achmed slowed his furious pace across the compound, his head half-turned. "Cream floating on soured milk! What do you want from us?"

Coming to a halt before the young man, the Imam spread his hands. "We want nothing *from* you. We want only to give."

"Give what?"

"The cream, to use your words. We want to share it with you."

"And what is this cream?" The young man was scornful.

"Knowledge. Understanding. Faith in a God who truly loves and cares for you and for your people."

"Akhran cares for His people!"

Achmed's tone was defiant, but Feisal knew it to be the defiance of a small child striking back at the hand that had hurt him, not the defiance of a man firm in his convictions. Coming up behind the young man, the priest rested his hands upon Achmed's shoulders. The Imam felt the young man flinch, but he also felt that the touch of friendship was not unwelcome to the lonely youth. Feisal said nothing more to challenge the young man's faith, wisely knowing that this would only force him to strengthen his defenses. It was Feisal's plan to slip quietly into the carefully guarded fortress of Achmed's soul, not attack it with a battering ram.

"There is someone who wants to see you, Achmed—a member of your tribe. May I bring him tomorrow?"

"You can do what you like. What choice do I have? I am your prisoner, after all."

"We keep you in your cells only as the mother keeps her babe in a cradle, to protect it from harm."

Tired of hearing about children—or perhaps tired of being constantly referred to as a child—Achmed made an impatient gesture.

"Until tomorrow, then?" the Imam said.

"If you like," Achmed said sullenly, but the priest had seen the flash of the eyes, the heightened color in the averted face at the mention of a visitor.

"The peace of Quar be with you this night," the Imam said, gesturing to a guard, who arrived to take Achmed back to his cell.

Twisting his head, the young man watched the priest leave, the spare body moving gracefully beneath the white robes that were now stained with the filth and muck of the prison. Yet Feisal didn't appear disgusted. He hadn't tried to brush it off or keep himself away from it. He had touched the beggars, the condemned, the diseased. He had given of his God to them. *Clothes can be cleansed,* the Imam had said. *Just like the soul.*

The peace of Quar or any other God was a long way from Achmed that night.

# Chapter 2

Achmed waited impatiently the next morning to learn the identity of this mysterious visitor. He hoped it might be his mother, but the morning hour for the meeting of the prisoners and their families at the iron gates came, and she was not there. Khardan's mother was there to visit, however, and Badia told Achmed that what the Imam had said was true. Sophia was improving. Although she was not strong enough to make the journey to the prison, she sent her love to her son.

"What the Imam said about my mother, that she would have died out there in the desert. Is that true?"

"Our lives are in the hands of Akhran," said Badia, averting her eyes and turning to leave. "Pray to him."

"There is something wrong!" cried Achmed, catching hold of the woman's hand through the gate. "What is it? Badia, you have always been a second mother to me. I see trouble in your face. Is it my mother? Tell me what is the matter!"

"It is not your trouble, Achmed," the woman said in a broken voice. "It is my own." She pressed her hand over her heart. "Our God gives me strength to bear it. Farewell. I leave you with this"—she kissed him on the forehead—"and your mother's blessing."

Turning, she hurried away, disappearing into the crowd of the nearby *souks* before Achmed could question her further. A bell sounded. The guards came out to lead the prisoners back to their cells amid the wailing and parting cries of their mothers, wives, and children.

Badia surely hadn't been the visitor the Imam meant, Achmed thought as he walked with slow and shuffling step across the compound. Lost in his thoughts, he started when he felt an elbow dig into his side. Glancing up, he saw Sayah, a Hrana.

"What do you want, shepherd?" Achmed asked rudely. noting that Sayah's expression was grim and dark.

"Just wondering if you'd heard the news."

"What news?" Achmed appeared uninterested. "Has one of your women given birth to a goat that you fathered?"

"It is you who has bred the goat and it is in your own tribe."

"Bah!" Achmed tried to move away, but Sayah caught hold of the sleeve of his robe.

"One of your own, an Akar, has renounced our holy Akhran and gone over to the God of this city," he hissed.

"I don't believe you!" Achmed glared at Sayah defiantly.

"It is so. Look there!" Sayah gestured toward the gate.

Achmed turned his head reluctantly, knowing what he would see even before he glanced around, for he had instantly guessed the identity of the Imam's visitor. Standing at the bars, dressed in clean, fresh white robes, looking both defiant and extremely nervous was Saiyad, one of Majiid's most trusted men. Next to Saiyad stood the Imam.

From the sound of the low growl that rumbled around him, Achmed knew that the other members of the Akar had heard Sayah's words and seen Saiyad standing by the gate next to the priest. Looking about the crowd for advice, Achmed was amazed to find that all the men of the Akar were staring expectantly at him! It suddenly occurred to the young man that they were assuming he would take the role of leadership! He was Majiid's son, after all. . . .

Confused and overwhelmed by this unexpected responsibility, Achmed muttered something about "talking to him myself and clearing up this mistake," then walked back toward the gate. The guards leaped after him, but a gesture from the Imam sent them about their duties. Gathering together their other prisoners, the guards marched them back to the cells, taking out their frustrations on the nomads when they were certain that the Imam wasn't watching.

Drawing nearer, a stern, unwavering gaze fixed on Saiyad,

Achmed saw that the man's eyes looked everywhere but at him—the ground, the sky, the prison, the Imam. Saiyad's fingers worked busily, folding and pleating, then drawing smooth, then folding and pleating a handful of the white cotton of his flowing robes.

"So it is no mistake," Achmed said beneath his breath, his heart dragging in the sand.

He reached the gate. The Imam did not enter, keeping both himself and Saiyad outside, perhaps afraid for his visitor's life. A glance at Achmed's dark and foreboding expression must have made the priest thankful for his precaution.

"Saiyad," said Achmed coolly. "*Salaam aleikum.*"

"And . . . and greetings to you, Achmed," answered Saiyad, his eyes meeting the young man's for the first time. He was obviously sorry they did so, for his gaze darted away the next instant. His fingers clenched around the fabric of his robe.

"What brings you here?" Achmed asked, attempting to conceal his rising fury. Why had Saiyad done this foul act? Worse, why did he feel it necessary to come and rub their noses in his dirt?

"Saiyad has come to check on your welfare, Achmed," said the Imam smoothly, "and to make certain that you and the others are being well treated."

"Yes, that is the reason I have come!" Saiyad said, his bearded face splitting into a grin.

Liar! thought Achmed, longing to shove the man's teeth down his throat. "So it is true what they say," the young man's voice was low. "You have converted to Quar."

The man's grin vanished instantly, to be replaced by a sickly smile. Shrugging his shoulders, he glanced deprecatingly at the Imam, and still working the fabric that was now dirty from the misuse, he drew near the iron gates and motioned for Achmed to come closer.

Feeling his skin crawl as though he were approaching a snake, the young man did as he was asked. The Imam, half turning, affected to be absorbed in the beauty of the palace that was nearby.

"What could I do, Achmed?" Saiyad whispered, his fingers leaving his robes and gripping the young man's through the bars. "You don't know what it's like out there in the desert!"

"Well, what is it like?" Achmed asked, trying to maintain his composure, yet feeling himself go cold all over.

"We are starving, Achmed! The soldiers burned everything, they left us with nothing—not even a goatskin in which to put the water! We have no shelter. By night we sleep in the sand. During the day, we fight for the shade of a palm tree! There are many sick and injured and only a few old women with magic enough to tend them. My wife, my children were carried away. . . ."

"Stop whining!" Achmed snapped. Unable to help himself, he drew back from Saiyad's touch in disgust. "You are not the only one to suffer! And at least you are free! Look at us, locked in here, worse than animals!" Lowering his voice, glancing at the Imam, he added softly, "Surely my father must be planning some way to get us out of here. Or Khardan—"

"Khardan!" Saiyad spoke too loudly. Both saw the thin shoulders of the Imam jerk, the turbaned head move ever so slightly. Hunching around so that his back was to the priest, Saiyad faced Achmed. The eyes that had been cast downward in guilt suddenly met his in contempt; the young man was disquieted to see the older man's lip curl in a sneer.

"Haven't you heard about your precious brother?"

"What? What about Khardan?" Achmed's heart stopped beating. "What's happened to him?" Now it was he who grabbed hold of the older man's robes.

"Happened? To him?" Saiyad laughed unpleasantly. "Nothing! Nothing at all, the filthy coward!"

"How dare you!" Achmed dragged the man closer with a jerk of his hands, banging Saiyad's head against the bars. One of the guards took a step toward them, but the Imam, supposedly neither hearing nor seeing what was going on, made a quick, imperceptible gesture, and—once again—the guard retreated.

"It's true, and all your ill usage of me won't change it! Our Calif fled the battlefield, disguised as a woman!"

Achmed stared at the man, then suddenly began to laugh. "Liar as well as a traitor! At least you could have come up with something more believable." Releasing his hold of the older man, Achmed wiped his hands on his robes, like one who has come into contact with a leper.

"Yes, couldn't I?" Saiyad retorted angrily. "Think, Achmed! If I was lying, wouldn't I have made up a better tale? What reason would I have to lie anyway?"

"To get me to join him!" Achmed made a furious gesture at the priest.

"I don't give a damn whether you join us or not!" Saiyad snarled. Realizing he was losing control and hurting his own cause, the older man drew himself up with an air of shabby dignity. "I came here to explain why I did what I did, hoping you and the others would understand. What I told you about Khardan is the truth, I swear by—" Saiyad hesitated. He had been about to say "Akhran," but seeing the silent figure of the Imam standing some distance away, he choked on the word "—by the honor of my mother," the older man concluded lamely. "All in the desert know it is true."

"Not my father!"

"Your father more than any of them!" Saiyad waved his hands. "Here!" Reaching into his sash, he fumbled for something, then withdrew a sword, "Majiid bade me give this to Khardan's mother, but I did not have the heart. You do with it what you want."

Seeing the flash of steel passing between the visitor and the prisoner, the guard leaped to intervene—Imam or no Imam.

"You dogs!" the guard swore at them. "I'll have you both whipped—"

Hastily, the Imam stepped in front of the guard, extending a slender arm between him and the nomads. "It is nothing of importance, I assure you!"

"Nothing! I saw that man give the boy a sword—"

"True," the Imam interrupted. Reaching through the bars, he grasped Achmed's limp hand and held the weapon up for inspection. "It is a sword. But can this be of harm?"

Looking at the weapon intently, the guard scowled, then gave a brief laugh and turned away, shaking his head over the stupidity of those who cooked their brains in the sun.

The sword's blade was broken; only the hilt and three inches of steel remained.

"Your father himself did that with an axe," Saiyad hissed, when the Imam had once again turned away.

Achmed held the broken sword—Khardan's sword—in a nerveless grasp, staring at it with anguished eyes. "I . . . I don't understand. . . ." he said thickly.

"Your father proclaimed Khardan dead." Saiyad sighed. Reaching through the bars, he patted Achmed's arm, giving awkward, embarrassed comfort. "Majiid is a broken man. We are leaderless now. Day after day, he sits doing nothing but staring into the east, where it is said Khardan vanished!"

"But how could he know? Did he see Khardan . . . ?"

"No, but there was one who did. Fedj, the djinn."

"Jaafar's servant? A Hrana djinn?" Fire scorched the tears that had glimmered in Achmed's eyes. "No one would believe that—"

"He swore the Oath of Sul, Achmed," Saiyad said quietly. "And he walks among us still."

The young man stared. He could not speak, his tongue seemed to have swollen, his throat gone dry. The Oath of Sul was the most terrible, the most binding oath an immortal could take.

*If what I now repeat is not the truth, may Akhran take me now, as I stand here, and lock me in my dwelling, and drop that dwelling into the mouth of Sul, and may Sul swallow me and hold me in the darkness of his belly for a thousand years.*

Thus ran the Oath. Many times Achmed had seen the djinn (most notably Pukah) threatened with the Oath, and each time he had seen them back down, refusing to take it. This was the first he had ever heard of one actually swearing by it.

Dazed, blinded by his tears, he could only whisper, "How?"

"Fedj was not present at the battle. He was detained by Raja, Zeid's djinn, who attacked him. Fearing for his master, Fedj left the contest as speedily as he could, only to find the battle ended. He discovered Jaafar lying among the wounded. Seeing his master to safety, Fedj then went to see if there was anyone else who needed his aid. The Amir's soldiers were burning the camp, and all was in disorder. Dusk had fallen, smoke filled the air. Fedj heard a noise and saw three women taking advantage of the confusion to flee the soldiers. Thinking he would lend them his assistance, Fedj flew toward them. Just as he started to speak, he saw the veil covering the face of one of the women slip down— "

Seeing the pain in Achmed's eyes, Saiyad stopped speaking and stared at his feet.

"Khardan?" the young man murmured almost inaudibly, more of a sigh than a spoken word.

Saiyad nodded.

Clutching the broken sword, Achmed slumped against the bars of the gate. Then, angrily, he cried, "I don't believe it!

Maybe he was injured, unconscious, and they were helping him!"

"Then why hasn't he come back? He knows his people need him! Unless . . ."

"Unless what?" Achmed glanced up swiftly.

"Unless he is truly a coward—"

Grabbing hold of Saiyad, Achmed slammed the man's face up against the bars. "Swine! Who is the coward? Who has come crawling on his belly? I will kill you, you—!"

The Imam could see that Saiyad was in trouble this time. Together he and the guard managed to free the nomad from Achmed's strangling grip.

"The bearer of bad news is always treated as though he were the cause of it," Saiyad muttered, breathing heavily and twitching his robes back into place. "Others feared telling you, but I thought you should know."

"The bearer of bad news is treated thus only when he takes pleasure in the telling!" Achmed retorted. "You have hated Khardan ever since he made you look a fool over the madman!" The last words were so choked that they were practically indistinguishable. "Get out of my sight, dog!" Achmed waved the broken sword. "My father is right! Khardan is dead!"

Saiyad's face flushed in anger. "For his sake and for yours, I hope so!" he snarled.

Half-blind with rage, Achmed hurled himself again at the bars, thrusting at Saiyad with the broken sword as though it had a blade still.

Alarmed at this sight, afraid that the young man would hurt himself, the Imam shoved Saiyad away from the gate. "Go back to your home!" the priest instructed in a low voice. "You can do nothing more here!"

Guards came running from across the compound. Grabbing hold of Achmed by both arms, they wrestled the young man away from the gate. Glowering at the priest defiantly, Saiyad moved closer. "Listen to me, Achmed! We are finished as a people and a nation. Akhran has abandoned us. You and the rest of them in there"—he nodded at the prison—"must face that. Now you know why I turned to Quar. He is a God who protects and rewards His own."

With his last strength, Achmed hurled the broken sword at Saiyad.

"You have done enough, my friend," the Imam said coldly. "Go back to your home!"

Gathering the remnants of his dignity about him, Saiyad turned and headed for the *souks*.

"Take the young man back to his cell," the Imam ordered. "Treat him well," the priest added, seeing glances pass among the guards and guessing that they intended to use this display of defiance as an excuse to punish their prisoner. "Any marks on his body and you will answer to Quar!"

The guards dragged their prisoner away and deposited him in his cell without a bruise on him. But they grinned at each other as they left the young man, rubbing their hands in satisfaction. The Imam had much to learn. There are ways and methods that leave no marks.

In the darkness and stench of the cell, Achmed lay upon his bed, doubled up with a pain that twisted his soul more than the beating had twisted his body.

Khardan was dead. And so was his God.

# Chapter 3

Leaving the prison, Feisal walked slowly through the crowds that parted at his coming, many sinking to their knees, hands outstretched to seek his blessing. He granted it reflexively, absentmindedly touching the foreheads with his thin fingers, murmuring the ritual words as he passed. Absorbed in his thoughts, the Imam was not even consciously aware of where he was until the incense-scented, cool darkness of the inner Temple washed over his skin, a relief from the noonday heat.

Pacing back and forth before the golden ram's-head altar of his God, Feisal considered all that he had heard.

Believing that Achmed was wavering in his faith, the Imam had brought the nomad, Saiyad, to the prison with the simple intent of showing the young man that his people remaining in the desert were scattered and despairing and that those who came to Quar were finding a chance for better lives. That was all. The Imam had been as shocked as Achmed to hear this news of Khardan, and now Feisal considered what to make of it.

The Imam had his spies—exceedingly good ones, devoted to him and to Quar. The priest knew how many segments of orange the Amir ate for breakfast in the morning; he knew the woman the Amir chose to sleep with at night. Qannadi had kept his voice low—but not low enough—when he gave his favorite Captain, Gasim, secret orders to make certain that Khardan's soul was one of the first to be dispatched to Quar. The Imam had been angry at the flouting of his God's

74

wishes, at Qannadi thus acting against the Imam's expressed command that the *kafir*, the unbelievers, be brought to Quar alive. Nevertheless, anger did not draw the veil of folly over Feisal's eyes. The priest detested bloodshed, but he was wise enough in his knowledge of man's stubborn nature to know that there were some who would see Quar's light only when it gleamed through the holes in their flesh. Qannadi was a skillful general. He would be needed to bring the southern cities to their knees in both surrender and worship. Feisal knew he must occasionally toss a bone to this fierce dog to keep him friendly, and therefore he said nothing about his knowledge that Khardan's death had been a deliberate act of murder.

But now—was Khardan dead? Apparently Quar did not think so. If not, how had the Calif escaped? Feisal could hardly credit this strange tale about the Calif disguising himself as a woman. And, more important, where was he?

One person might know the answer to this. The one person who had been acting very mysteriously since the Battle at the Tel.

Ringing a tiny silver bell, the Imam summoned a half-naked servant, who flung himself upon the polished marble floor at his master's feet.

"Bring me the concubine, Meryem," ordered Feisal.

Leaving the inner Temple, Feisal walked a short distance down a corridor to the chamber where he held audience. Like the inner Temple, the room gave the appearance of being closed off from the outside world. It had no windows and the only doorways were reached by means of circumnavigating long and winding corridors. The floor was made of black marble. Tall marble columns supported a ceiling of carved ivory that had been shipped in squares from the Great Steppes of Tara-kan and whose ornate figures represented the many blessings that Quar bestowed upon his people. Lit by huge charcoal braziers that stood on tripods in each corner of the square room, the Imam's audience chamber was otherwise empty, with the exception of a single, marvelous wooden chair.

Sent from Khandar, the chair was probably worth more than the entire Temple, complete with furnishings, for it was carved of *saksaul*. Found only in the salt-impregnated sand of the eastern Pagrah desert, the *saksaul* tree had been long venerated for its unusual properties. The black wood was extremely hard, yet—when carved—it splintered and broke like glass. Thus the craftsman needed to exert extraordinary care, and even small carvings could take many months of work. The wood was heavy and sank in water. When burned, the *saksaul* gave off spicy, fragrant fumes that induced a kind of intoxication. The ash left behind was often carefully preserved and used by physicians for various medicines. Most curious of all, the tree grew beneath the sand, its snakelike trunk—stretching over thirty feet or more—lying buried ten to twelve inches below the surface.

Seated in the *saksaul* chair, the ornate carving of which had reputedly taken several craftsmen many years of painstaking labor, Feisal began collecting in his mind all the reports he'd received and everything he had himself observed about Meryem. One by one he considered them, fingering each as a beggar fingers gold coins.

Qannadi's soldiers had discovered the Amir's concubine and spy lying unconscious in the nomads' camp. Most of her clothes and all her possessions had been stripped from her body, including all of her powerful magical paraphernalia. When the Amir questioned her, Meryem told him that one of his soldiers had mistaken her for a filthy *kafir* and had tried to rape her. She was able to point out the man and watched in offended innocence while he was flogged nearly to death in punishment.

The Amir had not believed her and neither had Feisal. Qannadi's soldiers had been ordered under penalty of castration not to molest any woman. They had been given orders to watch for Meryem, to rescue her from the nomads if it appeared she was in danger. The idea that one of his men would risk his life harming the Amir's concubine was ludicrous. But the Amir had no proof, other than that the soldier volubly protested his innocence, and so he had no choice but to have the wretch punished. Qannadi did not carry out his threat to castrate the man, but a flogging on occasion was useful in maintaining discipline, and if the soldier didn't deserve punishment for this infraction, he undoubtedly deserved it for something else.

The matter was closed, and Meryem was sent back to the *seraglio* where, according to Yamina, the girl waited in dread for the Amir to fulfill his promise and make her one of his wives. Feisal knew that two months ago this had been the dearest dream of Meryem's heart. Not that Qannadi was any great prize in the bedroom. He was nearly fifty, his warrior's body grotesquely scarred, his hands rough and callused, his breath often sour with wine. It was not, therefore, for the pleasure of his company that the women vied with each other to be his chosen favorite, but for the pleasure of the rich rewards of such a distinction.

The status of wife in the Amir's harem meant that a woman joined the ranks of the powerful sorceresses who worked the palace magic. Any children born of this union were legitimate sons and daughters of the Amir and, as such, were often granted high places in court, to say nothing of the fact that any one could be chosen as Qannadi's heir. A concubine might be loaned out or even given as a gift to a friend or associate. Not so a wife, who was kept in well-guarded seclusion.

Such isolation did not mean that the wives were not a force in the world. Yamina, Qannadi's head wife, was known to every grandee, noble, priest, and lowly citizen to be the true ruler of the city of Kich. The Imam had, more than once, seen Meryem watching and listening when he and Yamina were involved in political discussions. There was no doubt that it was her ambition to gain as much power as she was able.

But Qannadi never sent for her.

"I think the time she spent living in the desert has driven her insane," Yamina had confided during one of the many private and confidential talks with the Imam she always managed to arrange in his chambers in the Temple. "Before she left, she did everything possible to catch Qannadi's eye— dancing naked in the baths, flaunting her beauty, appearing unveiled. . . ."

Yamina always went into details describing such things to the Imam; her hand—by accident—touching the priest's thin leg or gliding gently along his arm. Sitting alone in his marvelous chair, Feisal remembered Yamina's words and remembered her touch as well. He frowned to himself in displeasure.

"Since her return," Yamina had continued somewhat coldly, the priest having sidled farther away from her on the sofa on which they both sat, "Meryem bathes in the morning when she knows the Amir is away reviewing his troops. She hides whenever the eunuch appears to select Qannadi's choice for the night. If the Amir asks for dancers, she pleads that she is unwell."

"What is the reason for this strange behavior?" Feisal asked. He recalled that he had not been particularly interested, other than keeping himself aware of all that concerned the Amir. "Surely she knows the risk she is taking? She is already in disfavor. Qannadi is convinced she lied about what happened to her in the nomads' camp."

"I think she is in love," Yamina said in a throaty, husky whisper, leaning nearer Feisal.

"With the nomad?" Feisal appeared amused. "A wild man who smells of horse."

"A wild man? Yes!" Yamina breathed, running her fingers along the Imam's arm. Her veil had slipped from her face, her hand artfully displaced the filmy fabric covering her neck and breasts, allowing the priest to see a beauty still considered remarkable after forty years. "A wild man with eyes of flame, a body hard and muscular, a man accustomed to taking what he desires. A woman in love with such a man will risk everything!"

"But this Khardan is dead," Feisal said coolly, rising to his feet and walking around to the back of the sofa.

Biting her lip in frustration, Yamina stood up. "Like other men I could mention!" she hissed. Covering herself with her veil, she left his chambers in an angry rustle of silk.

Feisal had not paid much heed to Yamina's words. She frequently used gossip such as this in her attempts to arouse him to a passion that his religious soul viewed as onerous and disgusting, his common sense viewed as highly dangerous. Now, however, he began to wonder. . . .

"The concubine, Meryem," said the servant, startling Feisal out of his reverie.

The Imam looked up and saw a lithe, slender figure clothed in a pale blue *paranja* standing, hesitating, inside the chamber's doorway. The light from the flaming brazier glistened on golden hair, just barely visible beneath the folds of her veil. Bright blue eyes watched the Imam with what the priest noted was an almost feverish luster.

Dismissing the servant, Feisal beckoned.

"Come nearer, child," he said, assuming a paternal tone, though he himself was only a few years older than the woman.

Meryem crept forward and threw herself on the floor before him, her arms extended. Gazing down at her, the Imam saw that the girl was terrified. She trembled from head to toe, the fabric of her gown shivered as in a breeze, her earrings and bracelets jingled in nervous agitation. Feisal smiled to himself in inward satisfaction, all the golden coins of his thoughts falling together in one bag. Bending down, he took hold of her hand and raised her to her knees, drawing her close.

"Meryem, my child," he began softly, his almond eyes catching hers and holding them fast, "I have received reports saying that you are unwell. Now that I see you, I know they are true! I am deeply concerned, both as your spiritual adviser and, more importantly, as your friend."

He could not see her face, hidden behind her veil. But he saw the fear in the eyes waver, the feathery brows come together in confusion. This wasn't what she had expected. The Imam grew more and more certain of himself.

"What have you heard, Imam?" she asked, casting out her line, fishing for information.

Feisal was quick to take the bait. "That you imagine someone is trying to poison you, that you refuse to eat or drink unless a slave tastes your portion first. That you sleep with a dagger beneath your pillow. I realize that your experiences in the desert among the nomads must have been quite frightening, but you are safe from them now. There is no way they can harm you—"

"It isn't the nomads!" The words burst from Meryem's lips before she could stop them. Realizing too late that the fish had just landed the fisherman, she turned deathly white and covered her veiled mouth with her hand.

"It isn't the nomads you fear," Feisal said with increasing gentleness that brought tears to the blue eyes. "Then it must be someone in the palace."

"No, it is nothing! Only my foolishness! Please, let me go, Imam!" Meryem begged, trying to free her hand from the priest's grasp.

"Qannadi?" Feisal suggested. "Because you lied to him?"

Meryem made a choked sound. Almost strangling, she sank down onto the floor, cowering in terror. "He will have me killed!" she wailed.

"No, no, my child," the Imam said. Slipping out of the chair, the priest knelt beside the girl and gathered her into his arms, rocking her and talking to her soothingly. Yamina, had she been there, would have writhed in jealousy completely misplaced. The only desire Feisal felt was the intense

desire to drain this girl of the vital information she had
hidden in her heart.

"On the contrary," the Imam said to Meryem when her
sobs grew calmer, "the Amir has completely forgotten the
incident. Of course he knew you lied. More than one of his
men had reported seeing Gasim fighting Khardan hand to
hand. Qannadi thought it very strange, then, to hear that his
best Captain died of a knife wound in the back!" Meryem
groaned, shaking her head. "Hush, child. Qannadi guessed
only that you were trying to save your lover. With the war in
the south, he has more things on his mind than concern over
a concubine's infidelity."

The blue eyes looked up at him over the edge of the veil.
Shimmering with tears, they were wide and innocent and
Feisal wasn't fooled by them in the least.

"Is . . . is that truly what he believes, Imam?" Meryem
asked, blinking her long lashes.

"Yes, my dear," said Feisal, smiling. Reaching up, he
smoothed back a lock of blond hair that had slipped from
beneath the head-covering. "He doesn't know you were plotting to overthrow him."

Meryem gasped. Her body went rigid in the Imam's
arms. She stared at him wildly, and suddenly Feisal had
another golden coin to add to his growing accumulation of
wealth. "No," he said softly. "That's not quite true. Not *were*
plotting to overthrow him. You *are* plotting to overthrow
him!"

The tears in the blue eyes vanished, burned away by
shrewd, desperate calculation. "I will do anything!" Meryem
said in a tight, hard voice. "Anything you ask of me. I will be
your slave!" She tore the veil from her face. "Take me now!"
she said fiercely, pressing her body against Feisal's. "I am
yours— "

"I want nothing from you, girl," the priest said coldly,
pushing her away from him, sending her sprawling onto the
marble floor. "Nothing, that is, except the truth. Tell me
everything you know. *Everything!*" he added, speaking the
word slowly and with emphasis. "And remember. I know
much already. If I catch you in another lie, I will turn you
over to Qannadi. Then you can tell your story to the Lord
High Executioner under much less pleasant circumstances!"

"I will tell you the truth, Imam!" Meryem said, rising to
her feet and regarding Feisal with cool dignity. "I will tell

you that the Amir is a traitor to Quar! Because of his sacrilege, the God himself has ordained his downfall. I am but His humble instrument," she added, lowering her eyes modestly.

Feisal found it difficult to maintain his countenance during this sudden, newfound religious fervor on Meryem's part. Placing his fingers over his twitching lips, he motioned with the other hand for her to speak.

"It is true that I love Khardan, Imam!" Meryem began passionately. "And because I love him I wanted more than anything else to bring him to the knowledge of the One, the True God. I knew that the Amir planned to attack the camp, of course, and I feared for Khardan's life. From some words of Yamina's, I came to realize that Qannadi is afraid of Khardan and with reason," the girl added loftily, "for he is strong and brave and a fierce warrior. I guessed that the Amir might try to have Khardan assassinated.

"Before the battle, therefore, I gave Khardan a charm to wear around his neck, Imam. He thought it an ordinary amulet of good luck, such as are made by the backward women of his tribe."

"But it wasn't, was it?" said Feisal grimly.

"No, Imam," Meryem answered with some pride. "I am a skilled sorceress, almost as powerful as Yamina herself. When I spoke the word, the charm cast an enchantment over the nomad, sending him into a deep sleep. It also acted as a shield, preventing any weapon from harming him. It was well I did so," she said, her voice hardening, "for it was as I suspected. Going against your express command that the nomads were not to be harmed, Qannadi attempted to have Khardan murdered. I caught Gasim in the act."

She paused, glancing at the Imam from the corner of her eye, perhaps hoping to see the priest fly into a rage at this news. Having been aware of it, Feisal showed no emotion whatsoever, and Meryem was forced to continue without having any idea how the priest might be reacting. "I carried Khardan from the battle on Gasim's horse. I intended to bring him to Kich and place him in your care, Imam, so that the Amir would not have him killed. Between the two of us, I knew we could convert Khardan's soul to Quar!"

"I doubt you were interested in his soul so much as his body," the Imam said dryly. "What happened to spoil your little plan?"

Meryem's face flushed in anger, but she carefully controlled herself and went on smoothly with her story, as though there had been no interruption. "I was waiting for Kaug, the 'efreet, to extend his hand and take us up into the clouds when I saw, out of the corner of my eye, that madman coming up behind me and—"

"Madman?" Feisal questioned curiously. "What madman?"

"Just a madman, Imam!" Meryem said impatiently. "A youth Khardan rescued from the slave traders here in Kich. Khardan thought the boy was a woman, but he wasn't; he was a man without hair on his face or chest who had dressed up in woman's clothing. The other nomads wanted to execute him, but Khardan wouldn't let them, saying that the youth was mad because he claimed to have come from over the sea and to be a sorcerer. Then the witch woman—Khardan's wife— said that the youth should be taken into Khardan's harem, and that is why Khardan couldn't marry me!"

Feisal didn't hear half of this involved and somewhat incoherent explanation. The words "over the sea" and "sorcerer" had completely overwhelmed his mind. It was only with a violent effort that he managed to wrench his thoughts back to what Meryem was saying.

"—the madman pulled me from the horse and struck me savagely over the head. When I woke up," she concluded pitifully, "I was as they found me—half-naked, left for dead."

"Khardan?"

"Gone, apparently, Imam. I don't know. I didn't wake up until I was in the palace. But when I questioned the soldiers, they had seen no sign of him."

"And his body was never discovered," the Imam mused.

"No, it wasn't," Meryem muttered, drawing her veil over her face once more, keeping her eyes lowered.

"And why do you think this . . . this madman would strip off your clothes?"

"Isn't that obvious, if you will forgive me, Imam? To have his way with me, of course."

"In the midst of a raging battle? He must have been mad indeed!"

Meryem kept her gaze on the floor. "I—I suppose, Imam, that he was interrupted in his foul deed—"

"Mmmm." Feisal leaned forward. "Would it surprise you to hear that Khardan was seen fleeing the field of battle, dressed in women's clothes?"

Meryem looked up, blue eyes open wide. "Of—of course!" she stammered.

"Don't lie!"

"All right!" she cried wildly, stamping her small foot. "I didn't know, but I suspected. It would have been the only way to escape the soldiers! There were a lot of old hags left behind in the camp. If the soldiers saw Khardan dressed as a woman, they would probably just let him go."

"And Khardan is still alive!" Feisal said softly. "You know it and you are hoping he will come back!"

"Yes!"

"How do you know?"

"The enchantment will continue working to keep him from harm as long as he wears the necklace. . . ."

"But someone may have removed it, taken it off. Perhaps the madman." Feisal sank back into the chair, his brows knotted. "If he is truly a sorcerer—"

"That is nonsense!" Meryem said spiritedly. "Only women have the magic. All know that!"

"Still . . ." Feisal seemed lost in thought. Then, shrugging, he returned to the matter at hand. "You do not speculate that he may be alive, Meryem! You *know* he is alive! You know where he is, and that is why you have been afraid. Because you think that he will turn up any moment and challenge the Amir, who will then begin to suspect there is a snake hiding in his fig basket—"

"No! I swear—"

"Tell me, Meryem. Or"—Feisal caught hold of her hand—"would you prefer to tell the Lord High Executioner as he flays the skin from these delicate bones. . . ."

Meryem snatched her hand away. The veil, stained with sweat and tears, clung damply to her face. "I—I looked into the scrying bowl," she murmured. "If . . . if he was dead, I would see his . . . his body."

"But you didn't?"

"No!" Her voice was faint.

"You saw him alive!"

"No, not that either. . . ."

"I grow tired of these evasions!" The Imam's voice cracked, and Meryem shuddered, the words flicking over her like a whip.

"I am not lying now, Imam!" she cried, casting herself upon the floor and looking up at him pleadingly. "He is alive, but he is covered by a cloud of darkness that hides him from my sight. It is . . . magic, I suppose. But like no magic I have ever seen before! I do not know its meaning!"

There was silence in the Temple chamber, a silence so deep and thick and reverent that Meryem stifled her sobs, holding her breath so as not to disturb it or the Imam, whose almond eyes stared unseeing into the shadows.

Finally, the Imam stirred. "You are right. You are in danger in the palace."

Lifting her head, Meryem gazed at him with incredulous, unbelieving hope dawning in her eyes.

"What's more, you are being wasted. I am going to suggest to the Amir that you be sent to live in the city with the nomads. Khardan's mother, I believe, is one who was captured and brought to Kich."

"But what will I tell them?" Meryem sat back on her knees. "They think I am the Sultan's daughter! They would expect the Amir to execute me!"

"An expert on lying such as yourself should have no trouble coming up with a story that will melt their hearts," Feisal remarked. "The Amir was going to have you thrown from the Tower of Death but then he succumbed to your charms. He begged you to marry him, but you—loyal to your nomadic prince—refused. Qannadi hurled you in the dungeon and fed you only on bread and water. He beat you. Still you remained true. Finally, knowing he could never have you, he cast you into the streets. . . ."

Meryem's lips came together, the blue eyes glistened. "Lash marks and bruises," she said. "The guards must throw me out at midday, when there is a crowd—"

"Anything you want," the Imam interrupted, suddenly impatient for the girl to be gone and leave him to his thoughts. Clapping his hands, he caused the servant to appear. "Return to the *seraglio*. Make your preparations. I will speak to the Amir this evening and convince him of the necessity of replanting our spy among the nomads." He waved his hand. "Get up. Your thanks are not necessary. You are serving Quar, as you said. And Meryem— "

This to the girl as she was rising to her feet.

"Yes, Imam?"

"Anything you discover concerning Khardan—anything at all—you will inform me."

"Yes, Imam," she said glibly.

Too glibly. Feisal leaned forward in the *saksaul* chair. "Know this, my child. If I hear his name on the tongue of another before I hear it on yours, I will have that tongue torn from your mouth. Do you understand?"

"Yes, Imam." All glibness disappeared.

"Very well. You may go. Quar's blessing attend you."

When the girl and the servant were gone, Feisal sank back into the chair. His elbow resting on the hard, carved surface of the chair arm, the Imam allowed his head to sink into his hand as though the weight of his contemplations was too much for his neck to bear. The nomads . . . Khardan . . . the Amir . . . Achmed . . . His thoughts tumbled about in his mind like rocks in a jeweler's polishing wheel. One only he found rough, uncut, disturbing.

The madman . . .

# Chapter 4

The prison guards sat hunched in the meager shade afforded by the squat, square gatehouse, their backs pressed against the cool wall that had not yet been baked by the sun. It was nearly noon and the shade was dwindling rapidly. Soon the heat of afternoon would drive them inside the gatehouse itself. They avoided that as long as possible. Entering the clay-brick dwelling was tantamount to entering an oven. But though the heat inside was intense, it had at least the advantage of providing shelter from the sweltering sun. As the last vestige of shade was vanishing, the guards, grumbling, rose to their feet. One of the younger nudged an older man, his superior, and pointed.

"Soldiers."

Squinting into the sunlight, the commandant peered out toward the *souks,* always thankful for some change in the monotony of his watch. Several of the Amir's soldiers, splendid in their colorful uniforms, were urging their horses through the crowds in the bazaar. The people scattered before them, mothers grabbing up small children, the merchants quickly removing their most valuable items from display and shoving their daughters behind the curtained partitions. If the crowd was too thickly packed together, and the horses could not get through, the soldiers cleared a path, lashing out efficiently with their riding sticks, ignoring the cursing and the angry shouts that died away to a hushed awe when the crowd caught sight of the man riding behind the soldiers.

"The Amir," the commandant muttered.

"I think he's coming here," said the young guard.

"Pah!" The older guard spat on the ground, but his gaze was fixed warily on the retinue that was making its way through the bazaars. "I think you're right," he said slowly, after a moment's pause. Whirling around, he began bellowing orders that brought other sleepy guards to their feet, hastily stumbling across the compound at the commandant's call.

"What's the matter with Hamd?" he bellowed, noting that one of the guards was not responding. "Drunk again? Drag him inside the gatehouse! Quickly! And look to your uniforms! What's that? Blood? Yours, too? Tell him it's from the thief. What's that? The man died two days ago? Worse luck! Keep out of sight, then! The rest of you—try to look alert, if that's possible, you sons of pigs. Now go on! Back to your places!"

Muttering imprecations on the heads of everyone from the Amir to the comatose Hamd, whose limp, flabby body was being dragged unceremoniously across the ground to the gatehouse, the commandant began pushing and shoving his bleary-eyed men toward their assigned positions, some of the slower being assisted on their way by sound thwacks from the commandent's thick cudgel.

The clattering of horses' hooves drew nearer. Gulping for breath, sweating profusely, the commandant cast one final glance around his prison. At least, he thought thankfully, the prisoners had been put back in their cells following the midday exercise period. In the darkness of the Zindan, swollen cheeks, split lips, and blackened eyes were not readily apparent. Neither were blood stains on tunics, for that matter. Just to be safe, however, the commandant's dull mind was fumbling with excuses for going against the Amir's express orders that the prisoners—particularly the nomads—were not to be physically abused. The commandant was just fabricating a full-scale riot that had forced him to resort to the use of force when the younger guard interrupted his lumbering thoughts.

"Why is the Amir coming here? Is this customary?"

"No, by Sul!"

The two were standing at some semblance of attention in front of the gatehouse and the commandant—keeping eyes forward with a grin of welcome plastered across his face—was forced to talk out of the side of his mouth.

"The old Sultan never came within a thousand paces of

the place, if he could help it. And when he was forced to ride past, he did so in a covered sedan chair with the curtains pulled tightly shut, holding an orange stuck all over with cloves to his nose to ward away the smell."

"Then why do you suppose the Amir's coming?"

"How in Quar's name should I know?" the commandant grunted, surreptitiously mopping his face with his sleeve. "Something to do with those damn nomads no doubt. It's bad enough we have the priest skulking about, sticking his nose into everything. Quar forgive me." The commandant glanced warily up at the heavens. "I'll be glad when the lot of them are out of here."

"When will that be?"

"When they convert, of course."

"They'll die first."

"All the same to me." The commandant shrugged. "Either way, it shouldn't take very long. Shhh!"

The men fell silent, the commandant shifting uneasily, longing to turn his head and look behind him to see that everything was in order but not daring to allow his nervousness to show. Behind him, he could hear Hamd's drunken voice suddenly raise in a bawdy song. The commandant's blood began throbbing in his temples, but then came a sound as of someone thumping an overripe melon, a muffled groan, and the singing ceased.

The soldiers on horseback trotted up to the gate. At their leader's command, they spread out in a straight line, sitting stiffly at attention in their saddles, their magical horses standing as still as if they had turned back to the wood out of which they were created. The Captain raised his sword with a flourish. Qannadi, who had been riding a short distance behind his troops, cantered forward. Returning his Captain's salute, he dismounted. Eyes flicking here and there over the prison and its yards, he slowly approached the sweating commandant. The Captain followed.

In the old days, if the Sultan had taken it into his head to visit the prison—which was about as likely as if he had taken it into his head to fly to the moon—such a visit could never have been accomplished without hundreds of guards surrounding his sacred person; slaves carrying his chair and rolling out velvet carpets so that he might not soil his silken shoes upon the unworthy ground; several other litters bearing his favorite wives, who would be peeping out between the

curtains and holding their veils over their mouths; more
slaves carrying huge feathered fans to keep away the flies that
found the prison a veritable feasting ground.

The Sultan would have stayed four minutes, five at the
most, before the hot sun and the stench and the general
unpleasantness of the place drove him back into the per-
fumed silken shelter of his palanquin. Watching the Amir
walk with long, purposeful strides over the hard-baked ground,
appearing cool and calm, his nose not even wrinkling, the
commandant heartily missed the old days.

"O Mighty King!" The commandant dropped to his belly
on the blisteringly hot ground, looking—in this undignified
attitude—very much like a toad and adding nothing to the
already deplorable state of his uniform. "Such an honor—"

"Get up!" Qannadi said with disgust. "I've no time for
that. I'm here to see one of your prisoners."

The commandant scrambled to his feet but left his heart
lying on the pavement. Which prisoner? Hopefully not one
who had been chastised too severely.

"Filthy wretches, O King. Unworthy of such attention! I
beg of you—"

"Open the gate."

The commandant had no choice except to obey. His hands
shook so that he could not fit the key into the latch, however,
and Qannadi made a sign. The Amir's Captain stepped forward, took the keys from the shaken guard, and opened the
gate that rotated on its hinges with a shrill squeak. Thrusting
his way past the stammering commandant, the Amir entered
the prison compound.

"Where is the cell of Achmed, the nomad?"

"On . . . on the lower level, third to your left. But do not
offend your spirit by entering the House of the Damned,
Your Majesty!" Panting, the commandant waddled about six
steps behind the swiftly walking general. "My eyes are accustomed to the sight of these dregs of humanity. Allow me to
bring the *kafir* into your Exalted Presence, O King."

Qannadi hesitated. He had intended to enter the prison
and talk to Achmed in his cell. But now that he stood before
the ugly, windowless building, now that he could smell the
smell of human refuse and despair, now that he could hear
faintly the moans of hopelessness and pain coming from inside, the general's courage—whose flame had never once
died on the field of battle—wavered and dimmed. He was

accustomed to death and misery in war, he would never grow accustomed to death and misery where men were caged like beasts.

"The gatehouse is quite comfortable this time of day, O Magnificent One," the commandant suggested, seeing the Amir hesitate.

"Very well," Qannadi said abruptly, turning his steps and attempting to ignore the audible whoosh of relief that escaped the commandant.

"Go ahead!" the commandant shouted at the young guard, who was standing rooted to the spot, staring at the Amir in awe. "Make the gatehouse ready for His Majesty!"

By dint of several frantic hand motions behind the Amir's back and a series of threatening grimaces, the commandant managed to convey the message to the dumbfounded young guard that he was to make certain the drunken Hamd was out of sight. Catching on, the young man bolted away, and Qannadi entered the sultry shadows of the bare brick room just in time to hear a scuffling sound and see the soles of the boots of the unfortunate Hamd disappear into a back room. A door slammed shut.

Picking up an overturned chair, the Captain of the Amir's guard placed it at a crude table for Qannadi who, however, seemed to prefer pacing about the small dwelling. The commandant appeared, gasping for breath, in the doorway.

"Well?" said Qannadi, glaring at the man. "Go get the prisoner!"

"Yes, O King!" The commandant had completely forgotten this small matter. He vanished precipitously from the doorway. Glancing out a small window, Qannadi saw the man running across the compound, headcloth flapping in the wind of his exertions. Glancing at the Captain, the Amir raised his eyebrows. The Captain silently shook his head.

"Clear everyone out," Qannadi ordered, motioning toward the back room.

The Captain acted immediately on his orders and by the time Qannadi saw the commandant returning across the compound, shoving a reluctant and unwilling Achmed along in front of him, the building had been emptied of all its occupants, including a dazed and bloody Hamd. The Captain of the guard took up his post outside the door.

The puffing and panting commandant appeared in the entrance. Dragging the young man by the arm, he thrust

Achmed inside the gatehouse. The nomad stood in the cool shadows, dazed, blinking his eyes, glancing around in confusion.

"Bow! Bow to the Amir, dog of an unbeliever!" the commandant shouted angrily.

It was obvious to Qannadi that the sun-blinded young man had no idea an Amir or anyone else was in the room. But when Achmed did not respond fast enough to suit the commandant, he kicked the youth painfully in the back of the knees, causing his legs to buckle. Gripping him by the back of his tunic, the commandant bashed the young man's head on the floor.

"I apologize for the dog's ill manners, O Exalted One—"

"Get out!" said Qannadi coldly. "I want to speak to the prisoner in private."

The commandant glanced uneasily at Achmed, lying prostrate on the floor, and spread his hands in a deprecating manner. "I would not be so bold as to disobey an order of my king but I would be remiss in my duties if I did not inform His Majesty that these *kafir* are wild beasts—"

"Are you saying that I—General of the Armies of Quar's Chosen—cannot deal with one eighteen-year-old boy?" Qannadi inquired smoothly.

"No! No! Assuredly not, O King!" babbled the commandant, sweating so it appeared he might melt into a puddle on the spot.

"Then leave. The Captain of my guard will be posted outside. In case I find myself in any danger, I can always yell for him to come rescue me."

Not knowing exactly what to make of this speech, the dull-witted commandant stammered out that this knowledge would be of great comfort to him. Disgusted, Qannadi turned his back upon the prison guard and gazed out a square window at nothing with magnificent aplomb. The folds of the *haik* hiding his face, the Amir was able to turn his head slightly to see what was happening behind him out of the corner of his eye. The commandant, casting a swift, fearful glance at his king, administered a swift, savage kick to Achmed, catching the boy painfully in the crook of his knee. His face dark, the commandant raised a fist at his prisoner threateningly, then, bobbing up and down like a beggar's monkey, backed out the door, fervent in his praise of the Amir, the Emperor, Quar, the Imam, the Amir's wives, and anyone else he could think of.

His hand itching to draw his sword and rid the world of this specimen of humanity, Qannadi kept his back turned until a scuffle, the sound of his Captain's voice, and a whine assured him that the commandant had been hustled off the premises.

Still Qannadi did not turn around.

"Get up," he ordered the young man gruffly. "I detest seeing a man grovel."

He heard the sharp intake of breath as Achmed stood upon his injured leg but even that indication of weakness was quickly choked off by the young man. Qannadi turned around just in time to see the nomad draw himself up, standing straight and tall and facing the Amir with defiance.

"Sit down," said Qannadi.

Startled, seeing only one chair and realizing—barbarian though he was—that no one ever sat in the presence of the king, Achmed remained standing.

"I said sit down!" Qannadi snapped irritably. "That was a command, young man, and—like it or not—you are in no position to disobey my commands!"

Slowly, his face carefully impassive, Achmed sank down into the chair, gritting his teeth to keep the gasp of pain from slipping out.

"Are the guards mistreating you?" Qannadi asked abruptly.

"No," lied the young man.

The Amir turned his head back to the window again to hide the emotion on his face. The "no" had not been spoken out of fear. It had been spoken in pride. Qannadi remembered suddenly another young man who had nearly died of a festering arrow wound because he was too proud to admit he'd been hit.

The Amir cleared his throat and turned back again.

"You will address me as 'King,' or 'Your Majesty,' " he said. Walking over to the door, he glanced outside to see his men, mounted on their horses, waiting patiently in line in the hot sun. He knew his men would remain there uncomplaining until they dropped but—magic or not—the animals were beginning to suffer. Cursing himself, aware that in his preoccupation he'd forgotten them, the Amir ordered the Captain to disperse the guard and see that the horses were watered. The Captain left, and the Amir and the young man were alone.

"How long have you been confined here?" Qannadi asked, coming over to gaze down upon the young man.

Shrugging, Achmed shook his head.

"A month? Two? A year? You don't know? Ah, good. That means we are starting to break you."

The young man looked up swiftly, eyes glittering.

"Yes," Qannadi continued imperturbably. "It takes spirit, an effort of will, to keep track of the passing of time when one is in a situation where each day of misery blends into a night of despair until all seem alike. You've seen the wretches who've been here for years. You've seen how they live only for the moment when they receive their wormy bread and their cup of rancid water. Less than animals, aren't they? Many forget how to talk." Qannadi saw fear darken the young man's eyes and he smiled to himself in inner satisfaction. "I know, you see. I was in prison myself for a time. I wasn't much older than you, fighting the warriors of the Great Steppes.

"They are fierce fighters, those men of Hammah. Their women fight alongside them. I swear by Quar that is the truth," Qannadi added gravely, seeing Achmed's stare of disbelief. "They are a large, big-boned race—the women as big as the men. They have golden hair that, from birth, is never cut. Men and women both wear it in braids that hang down below their waists. When they fight, they fight in pairs—husband and wife or couples betrothed to be married. The man stands upon the right to wield sword and spear, the woman stands to his left, holding a great, huge shield that protects them both. If her husband is killed, the wife fights on until either his death is avenged or she herself falls beside his body." Qannadi shook his head. "And woe betide the man who takes the life of a shieldmaid."

Pain forgotten, Achmed listened with shining, wondering eyes. Gratified, Qannadi paused a moment to enjoy this audience. He had told this story to his own sons and received only stifled yawns or bored, glazed stares in return.

"I was lucky." Qannadi smiled wryly. "I didn't have a chance to kill anyone. I was disarmed the first pass and knocked unconscious. They took me prisoner and cast me into their dungeons that are carved out of rock into the sides of mountains. At first, I was like you. My life was over, I thought. I cursed my bad luck that I hadn't fallen among my comrades. The Hammadians are a just people, however. They offered all of us the chance to work out our servitude, but I was too proud. I refused. I sat in my cell, wallowing in my misery, day after day, blind to what was happening to me. Then something occurred that opened my eyes."

"What?" Achmed spoke before he thought. Face flushed, he bit his lip and looked away.

Qannadi kept his own face carefully smooth and impassive. "When the Hammadi first captured me, they beat me every day. They had a post planted in the center of the prison yard and they would put a man up against it like so"—the Amir demonstrated— "and chain his hands to the top. Then they stripped the clothes from my back and struck a leather thong across my shoulders. To this day I bear the scars." Qannadi spoke with unconscious pride. He wasn't watching Achmed now, but was looking back, into his past. "Then one day they didn't beat me. Another passed, and another, and they continued to leave me alone. My comrades—those that still lived—were being punished. But not me. One day I overheard another prisoner demand to know why I alone was spared this harsh treatment.

"Can you guess their answer?" The Amir looked at Achmed intently.

The young man shook his head.

" 'We do not beat the whipped dog.' "

There was silence in the gatehouse. Because it had been many years since he had thought of this incident, Qannadi had not realized that the pain and shame and humiliation was still within him, festering like that arrow wound of long ago.

" 'We do not beat the whipped dog,' " he repeated grimly. "I saw then that I had let myself become nothing but an animal—an object of pity, beneath their contempt."

"What did you do?" The words were forced through clenched teeth. The young man stared at hands clasped tightly in his lap.

"I went to them and I offered myself as their slave."

"You worked for your enemy?" Achmed looked up, his black eyes scornful.

"I worked for myself," the Amir replied. "I could have proudly rotted to death in their prison. Believe me, young man, at that point in my life, death would have been the easy way out. But I was a soldier. I reminded myself that I had been captured, I had not surrendered. And to die in their foul prison would be to admit defeat. Besides, one never knows the paths God has chosen one to walk."

The Amir glanced surreptitiously at Achmed as he said this last, but the young man's head was bowed again, his gaze fixed upon his clenched hands.

"And, as it turned out, Quar chose wisely. I was sent to work on the farm of a great general in the Hammadi army. Their armies are not as ours," Qannadi continued. Staring out his window, he saw not the crowded *souks* of Kich but the vast, rolling prairies of the Great Steppes. "The armies are under the control of certain rich and powerful men, who hire and train their soldiers at their own expense. In time of war, the king calls these armies to come fight for the defense of the land. Of course, there is always the chance that the general might become too powerful and decide that he wants to be king, but that is a danger all rulers must face.

"I was put to work in the fields of this man's farm. At first, I regretted that I had not died in the prison. I was thin, emaciated. My muscles had atrophied during my long confinement. More than once, I sank down among the weeds with the thought that I would never rise again. But I did. Sometimes the overseer's lash helped me up. Sometimes I myself struggled to my feet. And, as time passed, I grew strong and fit once more. My interest in life and, more importantly, my interest in soldiering returned. My master was constantly exercising his troops, and every moment I could escape from my labors I spent watching. He was an excellent general, and the lessons I learned from him have helped me all my life. Particularly, I studied the art of infantry fighting, for in this these people were most skilled. At length, he noticed my interest. Far from being offended, as I feared, he was pleased.

"He took me from the fields and set me among his troops. My life was not easy, for I was different, a foreigner, and they did everything they could to test me. But I gave as good as I got, most of the time, and eventually earned their respect and that of my general. He made me one of his personal guard. I fought at his side for two years."

Achmed stared in blank astonishment at this, but Qannadi seemed no longer aware of the boy's presence.

"He was a great soldier, a noble and honorable man. I loved him as I have loved no other, before or since. He died on the field of battle. I, myself, avenged his death and was given the honor of placing the severed head of his enemy at his feet as he lay upon his funeral bier. I cast my lighted torch onto the oil-soaked wood and I bid his soul godspeed to whatever heaven he believed in. Then I left." Qannadi's voice was soft. The young man had to lean forward to hear him. "I walked for many months until I reached my homeland once more. Our glorious Emperor was only a king then. I came before him and laid my sword at his feet."

Sighing, the Amir withdrew his gaze from the window and turned to look at Achmed. "It is a curiosity, that sword. A two-handed broadsword it is called in the north. It takes two hands to wield it. When I first was given one, I could not even lift it from the floor. I still have it, if you would like to see it."

The young man glowered at him, dark eyes wary, sullen, suspicious.

"Why are you telling me this tale?" He rudely refused to use the proper form of address, and the Amir—though he noticed—did not press him.

"I came because I deplore waste. As for why I told you my story, I am not certain." Qannadi paused, then spoke softly. "You take a wound in battle and it can heal completely and never bother you again. Then, years later, you see a man hit in exactly the same place and suddenly the pain returns—as sharp and piercing as when the steel first bit into your flesh. When I looked into your face, Achmed, I felt the pain. . . ."

The young man's shoulders slumped. The pride and anger that had kept him alive drained from his body like blood from a mortal wound. Looking at Achmed, Qannadi had one of those rare flashes of illumination that sometimes, in the dark night of wandering through this life, lights the way and shows the soul of another. Perhaps it was seeing once again in his mind Khardan and Achmed together, standing before his throne—one brother proud and handsome, the other looking at him with complete and total adoration. Perhaps it was the Imam, telling him the strange tale of Khardan's alleged flight from the battle. Perhaps it came from within the Amir himself and the memory of his own starved childhood, the father who had abandoned him. Whatever it was, Qannadi suddenly knew Achmed better than he knew any of his own sons, knew him as well as he had come to know himself.

He saw a young man deprived of the light of a father's love and pride, growing in the shadow cast by an older brother. Instead of letting this embitter him, Achmed had simply transferred the love for his father to his older brother, who had—Qannadi knew—returned it warmly. But Khardan had betrayed him, if not by an act of cowardice (and the Amir found it difficult to believe such a wild tale) then at least by dying. The boy was left with no one—father, brother, all were gone.

Going up to the young man, Qannadi put his hand on his shoulder. He felt Achmed flinch, but the boy did not pull away from the Amir's touch.

"How old are you?"

"Eighteen," came the muffled response. "I—I had a birthday."

And no one remembered, Qannadi thought. "I was the same age myself when I was captured by the Hammadi." A lie. The Amir had been twenty, but that was not important. "Are you a whipped dog, Achmed? Are you going to lie down on your master's grave and die?" The boy cringed. "Or are you going to live your own life? I told you I deplore waste. You are a fine young man! I could wish my own sons to be more like you!"

A touch of bitterness crept into the voice. Qannadi fell silent, mastering his emotions. Achmed was too preoccupied with his own to notice, although he would recall it later.

"I came here to make you an offer," Qannadi continued. "I watched the Battle at the Tel. My men are good soldiers, but it took four of them to one of yours to conquer your people. It is not that you are more skilled in handling your weapons, I believe, but in handling your horses. Quar has given us magical beasts but, it seems, He has not seen fit to train them in the art of warfare. Instead of your people breaking your hearts in this prison, I give you the chance to earn your freedom."

Achmed's body held rigid for a moment. Slowly he raised his head to look directly into Qannadi's eyes.

"All we would do is train the horses?"

"Yes."

"We would not be forced to join your army? Forced to fight?"

"No, not unless you wanted."

"The horses we train will not fight our own people?"

"My son"—Qannadi used the word unconsciously, never realizing he had spoken it until he saw the eyes looking into his blink, the lids lower abruptly—"your people are no more. I do not tell you this to attempt to trick you or demoralize you. I speak the truth. If you cannot hear it in my voice, then listen to your own heart."

Achmed did not respond but sat, head down, his hands grasping spasmodically at the smooth top of the crude wooden table, seeking something to hold onto and not finding it.

"I will not make you convert to our God," the Amir added gently.

At this, Achmed raised his head. He looked, not at Qannadi, but eastward, into the desert that could not be seen for the prison walls.

"There is no God," the young man answered tonelessly.

# Chapter 5

The nomads of the Pagrah desert believed that the world was flat and that they were in its center. The huge and splendid city of Khandar—as far distant, in their minds, as a remote star—glittered somewhere to the north of them and beyond Khandar was the edge of the world. To the west was the city of Kich, the mountains, the great Hurn Sea, and, finally, the edge of the world. To the south was more desert, the cities of the land of Bas in the southeast, and the edge of the world. To the east was the Sun's Anvil—the edge of the world.

It was rumored among the nomadic tribes that the city dwellers spoke of the existence of another great sea to the east, beyond the Sun's Anvil, and had even given it a name—the Kurdin Sea. The nomads scoffed at this belief—what could one expect of people who built walls around their lives—and spoke scornfully of the Kurdin Sea, referring to it in ironic terms as the Waters of Tara-kan and considering it the biggest lie they had heard since some insane *marabout* of Quar's had ventured into the desert a generation ago, babbling that the world was round, like an orange.

There was also rumored to be a lost city somewhere in the Sun's Anvil—a city of fabulous wealth, buried beneath the dunes. The nomads rather liked this idea and kept the tradition of Serinda alive, using it to illustrate to their children the mutability of all things made by the hands of man.

The djinn could have told their masters the truth of the matter. They could have told them that there *was* a sea to the

99

east, that there *had* been a city in the Sun's Anvil, that
Khandar did *not* stand at the top of the world nor was the
Pagrah desert the world's center. The immortal beings knew
all this and much more besides but did not impart this
information to their masters. The djinn had one abiding rule:
When in the service of humans, you who are all knowing
know nothing and they who know nothing are all knowing.

To be fair to the nomads, the average city dweller of Kich
or Khandar or Idrith thought the world considerably smaller.
Let the *madrasahs* teach differently. Let the Imam preach
about bringing the *kafir* who lived in lands beyond to a knowledge of the True God. To the coppersmith, the weaver, the
baker, the fabric dyer, the lamp seller—the world's center
was the four walls of his dwelling, its heart the *souk* where he
sold his skill or his wares, its edge the wall surrounding the
city.

Born and bred in the court of an enlightened Emperor,
the Imam knew the truth about the world. So did the Amir,
who—though not an educated man—had seen too much of it
with his own eyes not to believe that there was always more
over the next hill. The learned scholars in the Emperor's
court taught that the world was round, that the land of
Sardish Jardan was just one of many lands floating atop the
waters of several great oceans, and that people of many kinds
and many different beliefs lived in these lands—people who
were to be drawn inevitably into the arms of Quar. Thus,
when the Imam heard from Meryem about a madman who
claimed to have come from over the sea, Feisal considered
this news worthy of being passed on to his God.

The Imam prepared for his Holy Audience by fasting two
days and a night, his lips touching only water and that spar-
ingly. Such a feat was no hardship for Feisal, who had fasted
whole months at a time in order to prove that the body could
be subdued and disciplined by the spirit. This short fast was
undertaken to purge the unworthy house of the spirit of all
outside influences. During this time, the Imam kept strictly to
himself, refusing contact with anyone from the outside (particularly Yamina), who might draw his thoughts from heaven.
He broke his self-imposed restriction only twice—once to talk
at length with Meryem, another to question the nomad,
Saiyad.

The night of the Audience came. Feisal bathed himself in
water made frigid by the addition of snow hauled from the

mountaintops; snow that was used in the palace to cool the wine, used by the Imam to mortify his flesh. This done, he anointed his unworthy body with scented oils, to make it more pleasing to the God. At the hour of midnight, when the weary minds and bodies of other mortals found solace from their sorrows in sleep, Feisal stripped himself of all his clothes except for a cloth wrapped about his thin loins. Trembling, in an ecstasy of holy fervor, he entered the Inner Temple. Carefully, reverently, he struck the copper-and-brass gong on the altar three times. Then he prostrated himself flat on the floor before the golden ram's head and waited, his skin shivering with excitement and the chill of the air.

"You have called, my priest, and I have come. What is it you want?"

The voice caressed him. The Imam caught his breath in rapture. He longed to lose himself in that voice, to be lifted from this body with its weak need for food and water, its unclean habits, its impure lusts, its unholy longings. It was with an effort that the Imam reminded himself of what Quar had told him when the priest was young—it was through this unworthy body that the Imam could best serve his Master. He must use it, though he must fight constantly never to let it use him.

Knowing this and knowing, too, that he had to wrench his soul from the peace it longed to attain in heaven back to the travails of the world, the Imam lifted a silver dagger and thrust the knife blade with practiced skill into his ribs. There were many such scars on the Imam's body; scars he kept hidden from view, for knowledge of such self-inflicted torture would have shocked the High Priest himself. The pain, the knowledge of his mortality, the blood running down his oiled skin—all brought Feisal crashing down from heaven and enabled him to discuss the concerns of humans with his God.

Pressing his hand over his side, feeling the warm blood well between his fingers, Feisal slowly drew himself to a kneeling position before the altar.

"I have been in contact with the nomads and I have heard, O Most Holy Quar, a very strange thing. There is or was a man living among the followers of Akhran who claimed to have come from over the sea and—what's more—who claimed to possess the magic of Sul."

The very air around the priest quivered with tension. Feeling now no pain from his wound, Feisal reveled in the sensation of knowing that, as he had believed, this information was welcome to his God.

"Is your informant reliable?"

"Yes, Holy One, particularly because she considers this to be of little importance. The man is dismissed as mad."

"Describe him."

"The man is a youth of about eighteen years with hair the color of flame and a hairless face and chest. He goes about disguised in women's clothes to hide his identity. My informant did not see him practice magic, but she sensed it within him—or thought she did."

"And where is this man?"

"That is the strange part, *Hazrat* Quar. The man escaped capture by the soldiers when they raided the camp. He interfered with plans to bring that most dangerous of the nomads—Khardan—into our custody. Both the madman and Khardan have disappeared under mysterious circumstances. Their bodies were not found, yet—according to those I have questioned—neither has been seen. What is stranger still is that my informant, a skilled sorceress, knows Khardan to be alive, yet, when using her magic to search for him, she finds her mystic vision obscured by a cloud of impenetrable darkness."

The God's silence hummed around the Imam, or perhaps it was a buzzing in his ears. Feisal was growing dizzy and light-headed. Grimly, he clung to consciousness until his God should have no further need of him.

"You have done well, my servant, as usual," spoke Quar finally. "Should you hear or discover anything further about this man from across the sea, bring it to my attention at once."

"Yes, Holy One," murmured Feisal ecstatically.

The darkness was suddenly empty and cold. The God's presence in the Inner Temple was gone. The bliss drained from the Imam's body. Shivering with pain, he rose unsteadily to his feet and crept over to where his pallet lay on the cold marble floor. Knees weak, he sank down onto it and groped with a shaking hand for a roll of soft cloth he had hidden beneath it. Pulling it out, Feisal—with his fading strength—bound the bandage tightly about his wound.

His consciousness slipped from him and he slumped down upon the bloodstained pallet. The ball of cloth fell from his hand and rolled, unwinding, across the black, chill floor.

# Chapter 6

*We do not beat the whipped dog. . . . Are you going to lie down on your master's grave and die?*

Crouched in his dark cell, Achmed repeated the Amir's words to himself. It was true. Everything the Amir said was true!

"How long have I been in prison? Two weeks? Two months?" Despairing, Achmed shook his head. "Is it morning or night?" He had no idea. "Have I been fed today, or was that yesterday's meal I remember eating? I no longer hear the screams. I no longer smell the stench!"

Achmed clutched at his head, cowering in fear. He recalled hearing of a punishment that deprived a man of his five senses. First the hands were cut off, to take away the sense of touch. Then the eyes were gouged out, the tongue ripped from the mouth, the nose cut off, the ears torn from the head. This place was his executioner! The death he was dying was more ghastly than any torture. Misery screamed at him, but he had lost the ears to hear it. He had long ago ceased being bothered by the prison smell, and now he knew it was because the foul stench was his own. In horror, he realized he was growing to relish the guards' beatings. The pain made him feel alive. . . .

Panic-stricken, Achmed leaped to his feet and hurled himself at the wooden door, beating it with his fists and pleading to be let out. The only response was a shouted curse from another cell, the debtor having been rudely awakened from a nap. No guards came. They were used to such disturbances. Sliding down the doorway, Achmed slumped to the floor. In his half-crazed state, he fell into a stupor.

He saw himself lying on a shallow, unmarked grave, hastily dug in the sand. A terrible wind came up, blowing the sand away, threatening to expose the body. A wave of revulsion and fear swept over Achmed. He couldn't bear to see the corpse, decaying, rotting. Desperately, he shoveled the sand back over the body, scooping it up in handfuls and tossing it onto the grave. But every time he lifted a handful, the wind caught it and blew it back into his face, stinging his eyes, choking him. He kept working frantically, but the wind was relentless. Slowly, the face of the corpse emerged—a man's face, the withered flesh covered by a woman's silken veil. . . .

The scraping sound of the wooden bar being lifted from the door jolted Achmed out of his dream. The shuffling footsteps of prisoners being herded outside and the distant cries of women and children told the young man that it was visiting time.

Slowly Achmed rose to his feet, his decision made.

Emerging into the bright sunlight, Achmed squinted painfully against the brilliance. When he could see, he scanned the crowd pressed against the bars. Badia was there, beckoning to him. Reluctantly, Achmed crossed the compound and came to stand near her.

The woman's eyes, above the veil, were shadowed with concern.

"How is my mother?" Achmed asked.

"Sophia is well and sends her love. But she has been very worried." Badia examined the young man intently. "We heard that the Amir sent for you. That he spoke to you . . . alone."

"I am all right." Achmed shrugged. "It was nothing."

"Nothing? The Amir sends for you for nothing? Achmed"—Badia's eyes narrowed—"there is talk that the Amir offered you a place in his army."

"Talk! Talk!" Achmed said impatiently, turning from the woman's intense gaze. "That is all."

"Achmed, your mother—"

"—should not worry. She will make herself ill again. Badia"—Achmed changed the subject abruptly—"I heard about Khardan."

Now it was the woman's dark eyes that lowered, the long

lashes brushed the gold-trimmed edge of the veil. Achmed saw Badia's hand steal to her heart, and he knew now what sorrow she had hidden from him the last time she had visited.

"Badia," the young man asked hesitantly, swallowing, "do you believe—"

"No!" Badia cried stubbornly. Raising her eyes, she looked directly at Achmed. "The rumor about him is a lie—a lie concocted by that swine Saiyad. Meryem says so. Meryem says Saiyad has hated Khardan ever since the incident with the madman and that he would do anything—"

"Meryem?" Achmed interrupted in amazement. "Wasn't she captured? The Sultan's daughter— Surely the Amir would have done away with her!"

"He was going to, but he fell in love with her and couldn't bear to harm her. He begged her to marry him, but Meryem refused. Don't you see, Achmed," Badia said eagerly, "she refused because she knows Khardan is alive!"

"How?"

Achmed was skeptical. Meryem was certainly lovely. The young man could remember watching the lithe, graceful body gliding like the evening breeze through the camp, going about her chores, long lashes modestly downcast until you came close to her then, suddenly, the blue eyes were looking right into your heart. Khardan had fallen headlong into the pool of those blue eyes. Achmed tried to visualize the stern-faced, gray-haired, battle-scarred Qannadi floundering in the same water. It seemed impossible. But, Achmed was forced to admit, what a man does in his tent in the night is best covered by the blanket of darkness.

"—she gave Khardan a charm," Badia was relating.

Achmed scoffed. "Women's magic! Abdullah's wife gave him a charm, too. They buried it with what was left of him."

Badia drew herself to her full height, which brought her about to Achmed's chin, staring at him with the sharp-edged gaze that had often cut the tall Majiid off at the knees. "When you have known a woman, then mock her magic and her love if you dare. But do not do so while you are still a boy!"

Wounded, Achmed lashed out. "Don't you understand, Badia? If Khardan is alive, then what Saiyad said is true! He fled the battle—a coward! And now he hides in shame—"

Thrusting her arm through the prison gate, Badia slapped him. The woman's blow, hampered as it was by the iron bars, was neither hard nor painful. Yet it brought bitter tears to the young man's eyes.

"May Akhran forgive you for speaking of your brother so!" Badia hissed through her veil. Turning on her heel, she walked away.

Achmed sprang at the bars, shaking them with such violence that the guards inside the compound took a step toward him.

"Akhran!" Achmed laughed harshly. "Akhran is like my father—a broken old man, sitting in his tent, mourning a way of life that is as dead as his son! Can't you understand, woman? Akhran is the past! My father is the past! Khardan is the past!" Tears streaming down his cheeks, Achmed clutched the bars, rattling them and shouting. "*I*—Achmed! *I* am the future! Yes, it is true! I am joining the army of the Amir! I—"

A hand caught hold of his shoulder, spun him around.

Achmed saw Sayah's face, twisted with hatred.

"Traitor!" A fist slammed into Achmed's jaw, knocking him backward against the bars. The faces of other tribesmen loomed close. Glittering eyes floated on waves of hot breath and pain. A foot drove into his gut. He doubled over in agony, slumping to the ground. Hands grabbed him roughly by the collar of his robes and dragged him to his feet. Another blow across the mouth. A flaring of fire in his groin, burning through his body, forcing a scream from his lips. He was on the ground again, covering his head with his arms, trying to shield himself from the eyes, the hands, the feet, the hatred, the word . . .

"Traitor!"

# Chapter 7

Qannadi sat late in his private chambers. He was alone, his wives and concubines doomed to disappointment, for none would be chosen this night. Dispatches had arrived by courier from the south, and the Amir had informed his staff that he was not to be disturbed.

By the light of an oil lamp burning brightly on his desk, Qannadi read the reports of his spies and double agents—men he had planted in the governments of the cities of Bas who were working for their overthrow from the inside. Studying these, he compared them to the reports of his field commanders, occasionally nodding to himself in satisfaction.

The ripples created by the rock thrown at the nomads were still spreading across the pond. Qannadi had made certain his agents proclaimed publicly that the Amir had done Bas a tremendous favor by ridding them of the spear that had long been pointed at their throats. Never mind that centuries had passed since the nomads had attacked Bas and that the attack had come at a time when the newly arising cities were seen as a distinct threat to the nomads and their way of life. So devastating had been the battles fought then that they lived in legend and song, and it took only the mention of the fearsome *spahis*—the cruel desert riders in their black robes and black masks—to drain the blood from the plump cheeks of many a Senator.

Governed by democratic rule that permitted all men of property (excluding women, slaves, laborers, soldiers, and

foreigners) to have an equal vote, the people of Bas had lived
in relative peace for many years. Once they had established
their city-states, they devoted themselves to their favorite
occupation—politics. Their God, Uevin—whose three pre-
cepts were Law, Patience, and Reality—delighted in all that
was new and modern, despising anything that was old or
outdated. His was a materialistic outlook on life. What counted
was the here and now—that which could be seen and that
which could be touched. The people of Bas insisted on having
every moment of their lives controlled, and there existed so
many ordnances and laws in their cities that walking on the
wrong side of the road on an odd-numbered calendar day
could land one in prison for a month. The great joy in their
lives was to crowd the Senate chambers and listen by the
hour to endless harangues over trivial points in their numerous constitutions.

Uevin's followers' second greatest joy was to create mar-
vels of modern technology to enable them to better the
quality of their lives in this world. Huge aqueducts criss-
crossed their cities, either bringing water into the homes or
carrying waste away from them. Their buildings were massive, and of modern design with no frivolous adornments,
filled with mechanical devices of every conceivable shape and
description. They had developed new methods of farming—
terracing the land, using irrigation, rotating crops to rest the
soil. They invented new ways to mine gold and silver and, so
it was rumored, had even discovered a black rock that burned.

Though the majority of people in Bas believed in Uevin,
they considered themselves enlightened, and encouraged be-
lievers in other Gods to settle in their cities (mostly, it was
believed, for the sake of the debates it stirred up). Followers
of both Kharmani and Benario were numerous in Bas, and an
occasional temple could be found to Zhakrin and Mimrim and
Quar. Life was good in Bas. The people exported their crops,
their technological devices, their ores and metals, and were
generally well off. Their faith in Uevin had never wavered.

Until now.

In determining how his immortals should best serve both
himself and his followers, Uevin rejected the notion of djinn
and angels that were used by other Gods and Goddesses. He
designed a more modern system, one that could be completely controlled and was not subject to the whim of change-
able humans. Delineating his immortals as "minor dieties," he

put each in charge of one specific area of human life. There was a God of War, a Goddess of Love, a God of Justice, a Goddess of Home and Family, a Goddess of Crops and Farming, a God of Finance, and so forth. Small temples were built wherein each of these minor dieties and their human priests and priestesses dwelt. Whenever a human had a problem, he or she knew exactly what deity to consult.

This worked well until, one by one, Uevin's immortals began to disappear.

First to vanish had been the Goddess of Crops and Farming. Her priestesses went to her one day with a question and did not hear her voice in response. A drought struck. The wells ran dry. The water in the lakes and ponds dwindled. Crops withered and died in the fields. Uevin ordered the God of Justice to salvage the desperate situation, but his God of Justice was nowhere to be found. The system of government fell apart. Corruption was rife, the people lost faith in their Senators and threw them out of office. At this critical juncture, Uevin lost his God of War. Soldiers deserted or rioted in the streets, demanding more pay and better treatment. With the God of War went the Goddess of Love. Marriages fell apart, neighbor turned against neighbor, entire families split into quarreling factions.

At this critical juncture, Quar's followers lifted their voices. Look to the north, they said. Look to the city of Kich and see how well the people are living. Look to the rich and powerful city of Khandar. See her Emperor and how he brings peace and prosperity to the people. See the Amir of Quar, who has saved you from the savage nomads. Discard your useless beliefs, for your God has betrayed you. Turn to Quar.

Many of Uevin's followers did just that, and Quar took care to see to it that those who came to worship at his temples were blessed in all their endeavors. Rain fell on *their* fields. *Their* children were polite and did well in school. *Their* gold mines were prosperous. *Their* machines worked. Consequently *they* were elected to the Senate. *They* began to gain control of the armies.

Uevin attempted to fight back, but without his immortals he was losing the faith of his people and therefore growing weaker and weaker.

The Amir knew little and cared less about the war in Heaven. That was the province of the Imam. Qannadi cared about the reports of a Bas general assassinated by undisciplined soldiers, a Governor deposed by the Senate, a student riot. Reading the missives of his spies, Qannadi deemed that the time was at hand to march south. Like rotten fruit, the city-states of Bas were ready to fall into his hand.

A knock at the door disturbed his thoughts.

Annoyed, Qannadi looked up from his reading. "I left orders not to be bothered."

"It is Hasid, General," came a rasping voice.

"Enter," said the Amir immediately.

The door opened. Qannadi could see his bodyguard on the other side and behind him an old man. Dressed in dirty rags, his body gnarled and twisted as a carob tree, there was a dignity and pride in the old man's bearing and his upright stance that marked him a soldier. The bodyguard stood aside to let the old man pass, then shut the door again immediately. The Amir heard the sentry's boots thud on the floor as he once more took up his position outside the door.

"What is it, Hasid? The young man—"

"I think you should send for him, O King." Hasid stumbled over the unfamiliar royal appellation.

"We have known each other long enough to dispense with formalities, my friend. Why should I send for the young man now?" Qannadi glanced at a candle marked off in hours whose slow-burning flame kept track of the time. It was well past the midhour of darkness.

"It must be tonight!" said the old soldier. "There will be no tomorrow for Achmed."

"What happened?" Frowning, the Amir laid the dispatch down on the desk and gave Hasid his complete attention.

"This noon, the young man lost control. He shouted out to the crowd at the gates his intention of joining your army."

"And?"

"There was a riot, General. I am surprised you didn't hear about it."

"That fat fool who runs the prison never reports to me. He is terrified that I will lock him in one of his own cells. He is right, but all in due time. Continue."

"The guards put the riot down, dragging off the other nomads, beating them and locking them in their cells. But not before Achmed's tribesmen had nearly killed him."

Startled to feel a pang of fear, like the thrust of cold iron through his bowels, Qannadi rose to his feet. "Is he all right?"

"I don't know, sir. I couldn't find out." Hasid shook his head.

"Why didn't you come to me sooner?" The Amir slammed his fist on the table, sloshing the oil in the lamp over the dispatches.

"If I am to remain valuable to you," the old soldier said shrewdly, "then I must keep up my appearance as an ordinary prisoner. I dared not leave until the guards had drunk themselves into their usual nightly stupor. I think the young man is still alive. I went to his cell and I could hear his breathing, but it is very rapid and shallow."

Buckling on his sword, Qannadi flung open the door. "I want an escort of twenty men, mounted and ready to ride within five minutes," he said to the sentry.

Saluting, the guard turned and ran to a balcony overlooking the soldiers' quarters. His voice rang out through the night, and within moments the Amir heard the clatter and clamor below that told him his orders were being obeyed with alacrity.

"Wait here," the Amir told the old soldier. "I have further need of you, but not in that prison."

Hasid saluted, but his king was already out of the room.

# Chapter 8

Achmed wakened and this time managed to hold onto awakening. Until now, consciousness had slithered away from him—a snake sliding through the hands of the dancer in the bazaars. Now he gazed about him, able to bring reality and dreams together, for he vaguely remembered coming to this place, except that he visualized it in his mind as being dark and shadowy, lit with soft candles and peopled with veiled women whispering strange words and touching him with cool hands.

Now it was daylight. The women were gone. There was only an old man, sitting beside him, looking at him with a grave face. Achmed gazed at him and blinked, thinking he might be a trick of his aching head and vanish. He knew the old man, but not from the shadowy dreams. He remembered him from . . . from . . .

"You were in the prison," Achmed said and was startled at the sound of his own voice. It seemed different, louder.

"Yes." The old man's grave expression did not alter.

"I'm not there now, am I?"

"No. You are in the palace of the Amir."

Achmed looked around. Yes, he had known that. There had been flaring torchlights and strong arms lifting him from the pallet. The Amir's voice, thick with anger. A ride on horseback and jolting pain. Warm water washing over him, the hands of men—gentle as women—cleansing his battered body..

112

Then this room . . .

His hand smoothed silken sheets. He was lying on thick, soft mattresses resting on a tall, ornately carved wooden frame. He was clad in clean clothes. The filth had been washed from his body, he smelled the sweet fragrance of rose and orange blossom, mingled with pine and other, more mysterious perfumes.

Look up, Achmed saw silken drapes swooping gracefully over the tall wooden pillars of the bed to fall in folds around him. The curtains had been pushed aside, to permit him a view of his room—magnificent and beautiful beyond fantasy—and the wizened old man, sitting unmoving beside him.

"You very nearly died," said the old man. "They sent for the physicians, who did what they could, but it was the magic of Yamina that brought you back."

"You were one of the prisoners. Why are you here?"

"I was in the prison," corrected the old man. "I was not one of the prisoners."

"I don't understand."

"I was placed in the prison by the gener—the Amir—to watch over you. I am called Hasid and I was Captain of the Body Guard under Abul Qasim Qannadi for twenty years, until I grew too old. I was pensioned honorably and given a house. But I told him when I left—'General,' I said, 'there's going to come a time when you'll need an old soldier. Not these young men, who think all battles are won with trumpet calls and shouts and dashing here and there. You'll need someone who knows that sometimes victory comes only by stealth and long waiting and keeping the mouth shut.' And so he did." Hasid nodded gravely. "So he did."

"You went into prison . . . voluntarily?" Achmed sat up in his bed, staring at the old soldier in amazement. "But—they beat you!"

"Hah!" Hasid looked amused. "Call that a beating? From those dogs? My mother gave me worse, to say nothing of my sergeant. Now there was a man who could lay it on! Broke three of my ribs once," the old soldier said, shaking his head in admiration, "for drinking on watch. 'Next time, Hasid,' the sergeant told me, helping me to my feet, 'I'll break your skull.' But there wasn't a next time. I learned my lesson."

Achmed paled. Memory leaped out at him. The angry, frightened faces, the flailing fists and feet, punching and kicking . . .

"They hate me! They tried to kill me!"

"Of course! What do you expect? But not for the reason you think. You spoke the truth, and it was the truth they were trying to beat down—not you. I know. I've seen it before. There isn't much," Hasid said on reflection, scratching himself beneath his rags, "that I haven't seen."

"What happened to them?" Achmed asked in a strained voice.

"The Amir released them."

"What?" Achmed stared. "Freed?"

"He opened the prison gates wide. Sent them slinking back out into the streets, crawling on their bellies like whipped curs."

*Lying on your master's grave . . .*

"Why is he doing this?" Achmed muttered, restlessly shoving aside the silken sheets.

"He's smart, is the Amir. Let them go. He's keeping their mothers, their wives, their families here in the city. They can go home to them—if they choose—or they can make their way across the desert and find that their tribe is nothing but a few old men, beating their toothless gums, yammering about a God who no longer cares—"

Achmed cringed. "I understand that!" he said hurriedly. Glancing at the luxury and finery about him, he gestured. "I meant why is the general doing *this*. You . . . watching over me. Bringing me here. Saving my life . . . All to train horses." His face grew dark with suspicion. "I don't believe it."

"You believed it in prison."

"In that pit of Sul, it made sense. Maybe because I wanted it to." Achmed tossed the blankets aside and swung his bare legs over the edge of the mattress. Ignoring the sharp pain in his head, he struggled to rise. "I see it now. He's been lying to me. Maybe he's using me, holding me hostage." A sudden dizziness assailed him. Pausing, he put his hand to his head, fighting it off. "Where are my clothes?" he demanded groggily.

"Hostage? And what ransom would your father pay? He has nothing left."

Achmed closed his eyes to keep the room from spinning. A bitter taste filled his mouth; he was afraid he would be sick.

*Nothing left.* Not even a son. . . .

Cold water splashed in his face. Gasping, Achmed opened his eyes, staring at Hasid.

"Why—" he sputtered.

"Thought you were going to faint." Hasid returned the water carafe to a nearby table. "Feel better?"

A nod was all Achmed could manage.

"Then get dressed," the old soldier ordered. "Your old clothes have been burned, as mine will be once I can get rid of them." He scratched himself again. "There are your new ones."

Wiping his dripping face, Achmed glanced at the foot of his bed to see a simple white cotton caftan lying there, not unlike that which Qannadi himself wore.

"I can't tell you why he's doing this—not in words. That would be betraying a friend's trust. But, if you feel up to walking a bit," Hasid continued, "I've got something to show you that might answer your questions"—he peered at the young man out of the corner of his eye—"if you're as smart as he says you are, that is."

Wordlessly, moving slowly and carefully to avoid jarring his aching head, Achmed drew on soft undergarments, then the caftan. He hoped that they wouldn't have to walk far. Despite the magical healing, his legs felt weak and wobbly as a newborn colt's.

"Come on!" Hasid prodded him in the ribs. "I marched five miles once on a broken ankle, and no woman's hands tended me either!"

Gritting his teeth against the pain, Achmed followed the old soldier across the room that was as large as Majiid's tent. Carpets of intricate and delicate weave covered the floor, their shimmering colors so beautiful that it seemed a desecration to walk on them. Lacquered wood furniture, decorated with gold leaf and adorned with objects rare and lovely, stood beside low sofas whose overstuffed, silken cushions invited the young man to sink down and lose himself amid their embroidered leaves and flowers. Feeling clumsy and awkward, fearful of knocking some precious vase to the floor, Achmed tried to imagine walking on a broken ankle. Finally, he decided the old man was lying. Later, when Achmed asked the Amir if Hasid's claim was true, Qannadi grinned. Hasid *was* lying. It hadn't been five miles he walked. It had been ten.

Approaching a window, the old soldier pressed his face against the glass and indicated that Achmed was to do the same. The room stood on the ground floor of the palace. The windows opened onto the lush garden through which he and Khardan had escaped only months ago. The bright sunlight sent a stabbing throb through his eyeballs, memories sent a pain through his heart. Achmed couldn't see anything for long moments.

"Well?" Hasid prodded him again.

"I—I can't . . . That is, what am I—"

"There, the man right across from us. By that fountain."

Blinking his eyes rapidly, not daring to wipe his hand across them for fear of rousing Hasid's contempt, Achmed at last focused on a man standing not five feet from them, tossing grain to several peacocks that had gathered around him.

The sight of the man was interesting enough to dry Achmed's tears and make him forget the pain of both body and soul. The man was young—perhaps twenty-five—tall and slender with skin as white as the marble fountains. A turban swathed his head, its silken fabric glittering with jewels and golden baubles. His clothing was equally sumptuous. Full-cut silken *pantalons* in colors of blues and greens and gold rippled about his legs as he moved among the peacocks. A golden sash encircled his slim waist, golden shoes with turned-up toes graced his feet. A billowing sleeved shirt, open at the throat, was covered by a vest made of golden fabric decorated with green embroidered curlicues and knots, finished off by a row of silken fringe that swung when he made the slightest move.

The man's eyelids were painted green and outlined in kohl. Jewels sparkled on the fingers that tossed the grain to the birds, gold dangled from his earlobes.

Achmed gasped. He had never seen anyone so truly magnificent. "Is that the Emperor?"

"Hah!" Hasid began to wheeze with laughter, causing the man outside to turn his head and glance at them with disapprobation. Brushing the grain from his hands, he walked away, moving past the splashing fountain with studied grace and elegance, the peacocks walking with mincing step behind him.

"The Emperor!" Hasid struggled to catch his breath. "If the Emperor came, where do you think we'd be, boy? Turned out in the streets, most likely. This place wouldn't be big enough to hold all his wives, let alone his wazirs and priests and grandees and scribes and slaves and cupbearers and platebearers and footwashers and asslickers that surround him from the moment he wakes up in the morning to when he enters one of his hundred bedrooms in the night. The Emperor!" The old soldier chuckled, shaking his head.

"Then who is it?" Achmed demanded irritably, feeling the pounding in his head once more.

"The answer to your question." Hasid eyed him shrewdly. "The eldest son of Abul Qasim Qannadi."

Achmed gaped. Turning to look outside, he saw the man pluck an orchid and begin ripping the petals from it in bored fashion, tossing them idly at the birds. "He was raised in the Emperor's court and lives in the palace in Khandar. Yamina, his mother, is one of the Emperor's sisters, and she saw to it that her son had all the advantages of being brought up in the royal household. Qannadi rarely saw the boy." Hasid shrugged. "His own fault, perhaps. He was always away somewhere, conquering more cities in the Emperor's name. He sent for his son a month ago, to teach him the art of warfare. He was going to take him south. His son said he would be honored to attend his father, but he would need a covered litter in which to travel since he couldn't for the life of him ride a horse and he dare not remain out in the sun long—it would ruin his complexion—and was it possible to bring several of his own friends, as he could not stand to be in the company of vulgar soldiers, and he wanted his own personal physician as well since it was quite likely that he would faint at the sight of blood.

"The young man," Hasid added dryly, "is returning to Khandar tomorrow."

Achmed's breath was gone from his body. He felt like the man who commanded his djinn to bring him a silver ball and found himself holding the gleaming moon. As the man said to the djinn, "It is beautiful and of exceeding value, but I'm not certain what to do with it." The garden dissolved before the youth's eyes. Gazing out the window, he did not see the ornamental trees and the hanging orchids and the blood red roses. He saw the desert—the vast, empty dunes beneath a vast, empty sky; the tall tasseled grass bending in the everlasting wind; the scraggly palms clinging to life around a bracken puddle of water; the shriveled, stinking plant whose name now held for the young man a terrible, bitter irony—the Rose of the Prophet.

"You were right," Hasid said softly. "This has nothing to do with the training of horses. Qannadi has asked to see you. Will you come to him?"

Achmed turned away from the window.

"Yes," he said. "I will come."

# Chapter 9

The God Quar stood in the incense-sweetened darkness of his Temple in the City of Kich, his hand resting upon the golden ram's head of his altar. The God was obviously waiting and doing it with an obvious ill grace. Occasionally his fingers drummed nervously upon the ram's head. More than once, his hand lifted a mallet to strike a small gong which stood on the altar, but he always—after a moment's hesitation and an impatient snarl—withdrew it.

Lying on a pallet on the cold marble floor opposite Quar, the God's Imam muttered and moaned, tossing in a feverish sleep. His self-inflicted wound had not healed cleanly, the flesh around it was swollen and hot to the touch, streaks of fiery red were spreading outward from it. Yamina had attempted to tend to the priest, as had all the court physicians, but Feisal refused all help.

"This is . . . between my God . . . and myself!" he gasped, clutching Yamina's hand with painful intensity, his other hand pressed against the bandages that were wet with blood and pus from the oozing wound. "I have done . . . something to . . . displease Him. This . . . is my punishment!"

Pressing Feisal's wasted hand against her lips, Yamina pleaded, calling him every endearing name that came to mind. Gently, firmly, he told her to leave. Sorrowfully, she did as he asked, secretly intending to sneak back in when he was asleep and use her magic to heal him without his knowledge.

To Feisal, Yamina was transparent as the water in the palace *hauz*. Feeling his strength dwindle, knowing that consciousness would soon leave him, the Imam commanded his servant to permit no one to enter, binding the man with the most terrible of oaths to insure his obedience. The servant was to shut the inner Temple doors and seal them. Not even the Amir himself would be allowed entry. The last sound Feisal heard before he sank into fever-ridden, insane dreams, was the hollow booming of the great doors coming together, the crashing fall of the iron bar across them.

Drifting in and out of delirium, the Imam was vaguely aware of the arrival of the God in his Temple. At first Feisal doubted his senses, fearing that this was a fever dream. Battling pain and the fire that was consuming his body, he struggled to hold onto consciousness and knew then that Quar was truly with him. His soul radiant with joy, the priest attempted to rise to do Quar homage, but his body was weaker than his spirit, and he fell back, gasping for breath.

"Tell me . . . what I have done . . . to incur your wrath, O Holy One," murmured Feisal weakly, extending a trembling hand to his God.

Quar did not respond or even look in the direction of his suffering priest. Pacing about near the altar, he peered with markedly growing irritation into the darkness. Feisal lacked the breath to repeat his question. He could only stare with adoring eyes at his God. Even the pain and torment he was enduring seemed blessed—a flame cleansing soul and body of whatever sins he had committed. If he died in the fire, then so be it. He would stand before his God with a spirit purged of infection.

The gong spoke suddenly, sounding three times. Quar turned toward it eagerly. The gong was silent for the count of seven, then rang three times again. A cloud of smoke took human shape and form around the gong, coalescing into a ten foot tall 'efreet.

Clad in red silken *pantalons* girded with a red sash around its massive stomach, the 'efreet performed the *salaam*, its huge hands pressed against its forehead. Feisal watched silently, without wonder.

"Well, where is he?" Quar demanded.

"I beg your pardon, *Effendi*," said the 'efreet in a voice like the low rumbling of distant thunder, "but I have not found him."

"What?" The God's anger stirred the darkness. "He cannot have gone far. He is a stranger in this land. Bah! You have lost him, Kaug!"

"Yes, *Effendi*, I have lost him," replied Kaug imperturbably. "If I may be permitted to tell my tale?"

Turning his back upon the 'efreet, the God made an irritated gesture.

"As you surmised, My Holy Master, the so-called madman was one of the *kafir* who came by ship across the Hurn Sea and landed near the city of Bastine. Immediately on their arrival, the priests and sorcerers of Promenthas—"

"—were met by a group of my zealous followers and slaughtered," interrupted the God impatiently. "I know all this! What—"

"I beg your pardon, *Effendi*," interrupted the 'efreet, "but it seems we were misled. It was not your followers who murdered the *kafir*."

The God was silent for long moments, then said skeptically, "Go on."

"Consider, Majesty of Heaven—if the unbelievers had been killed in your name, you should have had some claim to their souls."

"They were protected by guardian angels—"

"I have fought the angels of Promenthas before, *Effendi*, as you well know," the 'efreet stated.

"Yes, and this time you fought them and lost and did not tell me," Quar remarked coldly.

"This time, I did *not* fight them. I never saw them. I was not called to fight the angels."

Quar half turned, regarding Kaug through narrowed eyes. "You are speaking the truth."

"Certainly, *Effendi*."

"Then it is Death who has failed us."

"No, *Effendi*. The angels of Promenthas whisked their charges away without contest. According to Death, the *kafir* were killed in the name of a God of Evil—a God too weak to claim them."

Quar sucked in his breath, the skin with which he adorned his ethereal being paled.

"Zhakrin!"

"Yes, *Effendi*. He has escaped!"

"How is that possible? He and Evren were being held in

the Temple of Khandar, my most powerful priests guarding
them. No one knew the Gods were being held there—"

"Someone knew, *Effendi*. At any rate, neither Zhakrin
nor Evren are there now. One of your powerful priests, it
now appears, was in reality in the service of Zhakrin. By
some means not known to us, he managed to free the Gods
and carry them away."

"What do we know about him? Where has he gone?"

"I believe him to be the same man who slaughtered the
worshipers of Promenthas. He passes himself off as a slave
trader, but he is in reality a Black Paladin, a devoted follower
of Zhakrin. He first appeared in Ravenchai, where he captured a number of the natives and brought them to sell in
Kich. He has a troop of *goums* in his command, and it was
they who killed the priests and the magi of Promenthas. But
one person was left alive. A young man of extraordinary
beauty who was mistaken for a woman. Thinking to fetch a
high price for such a prize, the slave trader took her to Kich.
The young man—maintaining his disguise as a woman—was
put upon the block just as Khardan and his nomads were
terrorizing the city. Khardan took it into his head to rescue
the beautiful 'woman.' "

"Took it into his head! Hah!" Quar snarled. "I see the
guiding hand of Promenthas in this. He has joined with
Akhran to fight me!"

"Undoubtedly, Holy One." Kaug bowed. "The young man
was taken to the camp of the nomads. Here, according to the
woman, Meryem, he was nearly executed by the enraged
man who sought to take the lovely 'woman' as his concubine.
Khardan saved the young man's life, proclaiming him mad.
Meryem believes that it was this young 'madman' who thwarted
her plans to bring Khardan to Kich."

"Then the two are together."

"Presumably, *Effendi*."

"Presumably!" Quar's rage beat upon the walls of the
Temple. Feisal, in his fevered imaginings, thought he saw
the marble blocks start to melt beneath the heat. "I am
divine! I am all-knowing, all-seeing! No mortal can hide himself from my sight and the sight of my servants!"

"Not a mortal, Holy Master." Kaug's voice lowered. "Another God. A dark cloud hides them from my sight and the
sight of your sorceress."

"A dark cloud. Slowly, inexorably, the power of my enemies grows." Quar fell silent, musing. The 'efreet's hulking body wavered in the air, or perhaps it was Feisal's dimming vision that caused the immortal to appear as if he were a mirage, shimmering against empty sand. "I dare not wait longer."

The God turned his attention to his dying priest. Gliding across the black marble floor, his silken slippers making no noise, his silken robes shining a cold and brilliant white in the darkness, Quar came to stand by Feisal's pallet.

Unable to move, the Imam gazed up at the face of the God with an adoration that banished all pain and fever from his body. The Imam saw his soul rise to its feet, leaving the frail husk of its flesh behind, holding out its hands to the God as a child reaches for its mother. Content, blissful, Feisal felt life ebbing away. The name of the God was on his lips, to be spoken with his last breath.

"No!" said Quar suddenly, and the Imam's soul—caught between two planes—shrank back in bewilderment. Kneeling beside Feisal, the God tore off the bloodstained bandages and laid his hand upon the wound. His other hand touched the priest's hot forehead. "You will live, my faithful Imam. You will rise up from your bed of pain and suffering and know that it was I who saved you. You will remember my face, my voice, and the touch of my hands upon your mortal flesh. And the lesson you will have learned from the agony you have undergone is this.

"You have placed too great a value on human life. As you have seen, it is a thing that can be taken from us as easily as thieves robbing a blind man. The souls of men are what is truly important and they must be rescued from stumbling about in the darkness. Those who do not believe in me must die, so that the power of their false gods dies with them."

Feisal drew a deep breath and another and then another. His eyes closed in a peaceful sleep, his soul reluctantly returned to the fragile body.

"When you awaken," Quar continued, "you will go to the Amir and tell him it is time. . . ."

"Time?" Feisal murmured.

*"Jihad!"* whispered Quar, bending low over His priest, caressing him, smoothing the black hair with His hand. "Convert or die!"

# Book Four

# THE BOOK OF ZHAKRIN II

# Chapter 1

"In the name of Zhakrin, God of Darkness and All That Is Evil, I command you, wake!"

Mathew heard the voice as if it were coming from far away. It was early morning in his homeland. The sun shone brightly, joyous bird song greeted the new day. A spring breeze, laden with the scent of pine and rain-damp earth blew crisp and chill in his window. His mother stood at the foot of the long, stone stairs, calling her son to come break his nightlong fast. . . .

"Wake!"

He was in a classroom, after luncheon. The wooden desk, carved with countless names and faces long since gone out into the world, felt cool and smooth beneath lethargic hands. The old Archmagus had been droning on and on for an eternity. His voice was like the buzzing of flies. Mathew closed his eyes, only for a moment while the instructor turned his back. . . .

"Wake!"

A painful tingling sensation was spreading through Mathew's body. The feeling was distinctly unpleasant, and he tried to move his limbs to make it cease. That only made it worse, however, sending small needles of agony darting through his body. He moaned.

"Do not struggle, Blossom. Lie still for an hour or so and the sensation will pass."

Something cold brushed across his forehead. The cold touch and the colder voice brought back terrifying memories.

Forcing his eyes open—the lids feeling as if they'd been covered with some sort of sticky resin—Mathew gazed upward to see a slender hand, a face masked in black, two cruel and empty eyes.

"Lie still, Blossom. Lie very still and allow your body to resume its functioning once more. The heart beats rapidly, the sluggish blood now runs free and burns through the body, the lungs draw in air. Painful? Yes. But you have been asleep a long time, Blossom. A long, long time."

Slender fingers brushed his cheek.

"Do you still have my fish, Blossom? Yes, of course you do. The city guards do not search the bodies of the dead, do they, my Blossom?"

Mathew felt, cool against his skin, the crystal globe that was hidden in the folds of the woman's gown he wore; the globe filled with water in which swam two fish—one golden, one black.

The sound of boots crunching on sand came to Mathew's ears. A voice spoke respectfully, "You sent for me, *Effendi?*" and the hand and eyes withdrew from Mathew's sight.

The young wizard's vision was blurred. The sun was shining, but he could see it only as if through a white gauze. It was hot and stuffy where he lay, the air was stale. He was smothering and he tried to suck in a deep lungful of breath. His flaccid muscles refused to obey his mind's command. The attempt was more of a wheeze or a gulp.

The tingling sensation in his hands and legs increased, nearly driving him wild. Added to this was a panicking feeling that he was suffocating, the inability to draw breath. His sufferings were acute, yet Mathew dared not make so much as a whimper. Death itself was preferable to those cruel eyes.

"Blossom is coming around. What about the other two?" queried the cold voice.

"The other woman is conscious, *Effendi*. The bearded devil, however, will not awaken."

"Mmmm. Some other enchantment, do you think, Kiber?"

"I believe so, *Effendi*. You yourself mentioned the possibility that he was ensorcelled when we first captured him, if I recall correctly?"

"You do so. Let us take a look at him."

The booted feet—now two pairs of them—moved somewhere to Mathew's right.

Bearded devil. The other woman. Khardan! Zohra! Mathew's body twitched and writhed in agony. Memory returned. . . .

Escaping the Battle at the Tel; Khardan, unconscious, bound by some enchantment. Zohra and I dressed him in Meryem's rose-colored, silken *chador*. The veil covered his face. The soldiers stopped us!

"Let the old hags go!"

We escaped and crouched down in the mud near the oasis, hidden in the tall grass. Khardan, wounded, spellbound; Zohra, exhausted, sleeping on my shoulder.

"I will keep watch."

But tired eyes closed. Sleep came—to be followed by a waking nightmare.

*"A black-haired beauty, young and strong," the cold voice had spoken. "And what is this? The bearded devil who stole the Blossom and put me to all this trouble! Truly, the God looks down upon us with favor this night, Kiber!"*

*"Yes, Effendi!"*

*"And here is my Blossom with the flame-colored hair. See, Kiber, she wakes at the sound of my voice. Don't be frightened, Blossom. Don't scream. Gag her, Kiber. Cover her mouth. That's right."*

*I looked up, bound and helpless, to see a black jewel sparkling in the light of the burning camp.*

*"In the name of Zhakrin, God of Darkness and All That Is Evil, I command you all—Sleep. . . ."*

And so they had slept. And now they woke. Woke . . . to what? Mathew heard the voices again, coming from a short distance away.

"You see, Kiber? This silver shield that hangs round his neck. See how it glows, even in daylight?"

"Yes, *Effendi.*"

"I wonder at its purpose, Kiber."

"To protect him from harm in the battle, surely, *Effendi.* I have seen such before, given to soldiers by their wives."

"Yes, but why render him unconscious as well? I begin to see what must have happened, Kiber. These women feared their man would come to harm. They gave him this shield that not only would protect him from any blow, but would also cause him to fall senseless during the battle. Then they dragged him away, dressed him in women's clothes—as we found him—and escaped the field."

"One of them must be a powerful sorceress, then, *Effendi*."

"One or both, although our Blossom did not exhibit any magical talents when in our company. These nomads are fierce and proud warriors. I'll wager this one did not know he was being saved from death by his womenfolk, nor do I think he will be at all pleased to discover such a fact when he awakes."

"Then why bring him out of the enchantment, *Effendi?*" It seemed to Mathew that Kiber sounded nervous. "Let him stay in stasis, at least until we reach Galos."

"No, we have too much work to do to load the ships without hauling him on as well. Besides, Kiber"—the cold voice was smooth and sinuous as a snake twisting across the sand—"I want him to see, to hear, to taste, to feel all that is yet to come to him. I want the poison to seep, little by little, into the well of his mind. When his soul goes to drink, it will blacken and die."

Kiber did not appear so confident. "He will be trouble, *Effendi*."

"Will he? Good. I would hate to think I had misjudged his character. Remove the sword from his hands. Now, to break this enchantment—"

"Let one of the women, *Effendi*. It is never wise to interfere with wizardry."

"Excellent advice, Kiber. I will act upon it. When Blossom is able to speak and move about, we will question her concerning this. Now, remove the baggage from the *djemel* and line it up along the shore. We must be ready to load the ships when they land, for they will not be able to stay long. We do not want to be caught here in the heat of the afternoon."

"Yes, *Effendi*."

Mathew heard Kiber move away, his voice shouting orders to his men. Closing his eyes, the wizard could once again see the colorful uniforms of the *goums*, the horses they rode. He could see the slaves, chained by the feet, shuffling across the plains. He could see the white-curtained palanquin. . . .

White curtains! Mathew's eyes opened, he looked about him. His vision had cleared. Gritting his teeth against the pain, concentrating every fiber of his being on the effort, he managed to move his left hand enough to draw aside the fold in the fabric and peer out at his surroundings.

The sight appalled him. He stared, aghast. He had thought

the desert around the Tel, with its undulating dunes of sand stretching to the far distant mountains, empty and forbidding. There was life around the oasis, certainly. Or at least the nomads considered it life. The tall palm trees, their brown-tipped fronds—looking as if they had been singed—clicking in the everlasting wind. The lacy tamarisk, the sparse green foliage, every blade and leaf precious. The waving stands of brown, tasseled grass that grew near the water's edge. The various species of cacti that ranged from the wiggly-armed burn plant—so called because of its healing properties —to the ugly, sharp-needled plant known by the incongruous, romantic appellation of the Rose of the Prophet. Coming from a world of ancient, spreading oaks, stands of pine forests, wild mountain flowers, Mathew had not considered this desert life life at all—nothing more than a pathetic mockery. But at least, he realized now, it had been life.

He looked out now on death.

The land was dead and the death it had died had been a tortured one. Flat and barren, the earth was white as bone. Huge cracks spread across its surface, mouths gaping open in thirst for the rain that would never fall. Not far from where he lay, Mathew could see a heap of black, broken rock, and near that a pool of water. This was no oasis, however. Nothing grew near that pool. Steam rose from its surface, the water bubbled and churned and boiled.

The sun had just lifted into the eastern sky. Mathew could see, from where he lay, the tip of a red, fiery ball appearing over the horizon. Yet already the heat was building, radiating up from the parched ground. There was a gritty taste in his mouth and he suffered from a terrible thirst. Mathew ran his tongue across his lips. Salt. Now he knew why the land was this strange, glaring white. It was covered with salt.

His strength gave out. Mathew's hand fell limp at his side, the curtain hid the vision. No wonder they had to be gone before afternoon. Nothing could live in this desert in the noonday sun. Yet the man had spoken of ships. Mathew feebly shook his head, hoping to clear it. He must be hallucinating, imagining things. Or perhaps he meant camels, the young wizard thought weakly. Weren't they sometimes called the ships of the desert?

But where would they go? Mathew had seen nothing in that picked-clean corpse of a world. And his thirst was growing unbearable. Cruel eyes or not, he was desperate for

water. Just as his parched lips shaped the word and he tried
to force sound from his dry throat, Kiber thrust aside the
curtains of the litter. He held a waterskin in his hand.

"Drink!" he commanded, glowering sternly at Mathew,
perhaps remembering the days in the slave caravan when
he'd caught the young wizard refusing to eat.

Mathew had no intention of refusing water. By a supreme
effort he raised his arms, grasped the neck of the *girba*,
aimed a stream of the warm, stale liquid into his mouth and
drank thirstily. Some splashed on his neck and face, cooling
him. All too soon, Kiber snatched the waterskin away and
disappeared. Mathew heard the *goum's* boots crunching on
the salt-covered ground and, in a few moments, a throaty
murmur, probably Zohra.

Mathew lay back on the litter. The water gave him strength;
he seemed to feel it spreading energy through his body. He
longed to sit up and his hand itched to draw the curtains
aside. But to do so was to risk attracting the attention of the
man with the cruel eyes to himself.

Thrusting his hand into the folds of the woman's clothing,
Mathew touched the crystal globe containing the fish. It was
cold and smooth against his hot skin. He was suddenly possessed by a desperate desire to examine the fish, to see if
they were all right. Fear stopped him. The slaver might
chance to look inside and Mathew did not want to seem to be
paying too much attention to the magical globe. He wondered what the man had meant by the curious statement,
"The city guards do not search the bodies of the dead."

The smothering sensation increased, that and an almost
overwhelming urge to move his body. Finally Mathew sat up
and was almost immediately seized with a sudden dizziness.
Starbursts exploded before his eyes. Weakly, he propped
himself up on his arm and, hanging his head, waited until his
vision cleared and the terrible light-headed feeling passed.
Cautiously pushing aside the curtain a crack, he peered out,
further examining his surroundings. The litter, he discovered, was sitting on stilts about four feet off the floor of the
salt flats. Keeping a wary eye out for the slave trader, Mathew
looked to the front of the litter and blinked in astonishment.

Before him stretched a vast body of water—wide as an
ocean—its deep blue color like nothing he had ever seen
before. A cool breeze, blowing off the sea, drifted in a

whisper past his face, and he thankfully gulped in the fresh air.

The slave trader stood at the water's edge, facing out into it. Lifting his arms above his head, he cried in a loud voice, "It is I, Auda ibn Jad! In the name of Zhakrin, I command you. Send my ship!"

So he *had* meant ships! But what sea could this be? It didn't look like the Hurn. No waves crashed against the shore. It wasn't the greenish color of the ocean he had crossed. The water lapped gently about the feet of the slave trader, Auda ibn Jad (it was the first time Mathew recalled ever hearing the man's name). Staring intently out into the sea in the same direction as ibn Jad, Mathew thought he could detect a shadow on the horizon—a dark cloud in an otherwise cloudless sky.

Turning abruptly, the slave trader caught Mathew staring out of the curtains.

"Ah, Blossom! You are enjoying the fresh air."

Mathew did not answer. He could not speak a word. The cold eyes had snatched out all the wits in his head, leaving behind nothing but empty fear.

"Come, Blossom. Stand up. That will help get the blood circulating again. I need you."

Walking over to Mathew, ibn Jad reached out his slender hand and grasped hold of the young wizard's right arm. The man's touch was as cold and unfeeling as his eyes and Mathew shivered in the hot sun.

Rising to his feet, he thought at first he was going to faint. His knees gave way, the sunbursts flared again in his vision. Falling back, he caught hold of one of the supports of the litter's roof with his hand and hung onto it grimly; Auda propping him up. The slave trader gave Mathew a few moments to recover, then dragged the groggy wizard across the sand to another litter. Mathew knew who lay inside, just as he knew the question he was going to be asked. Shoving aside the curtains of the palanquin, ibn Jad pushed Mathew forward.

"The charm the bearded devil wears around his neck? Did you make it? Are you the sorceress who laid the enchantment upon him?"

We plan and work for years to chart our life's course, and then sometimes one instant, one word will irrevocably alter our destiny.

"Yes," said Mathew in a barely audible whisper.

He could not have told the conscious reasoning behind his lie. He had the distinct feeling it was motivated by fear; he did not want to appear completely defenseless and helpless in the eyes of this man. He knew, too, that if he answered no, ibn Jad would simply question Zohra, and he would not believe either of them if both denied it.

"I made . . . the charm," Mathew said hoarsely.

"A fine piece of work, Blossom. How do you break the spell?"

"By taking it from around his neck. He will immediately begin to come out of the enchantment." That was a guess, but Mathew felt fairly certain it was a good one. Generally, that was how charms such as this one worked. There wouldn't have been any reason for Meryem to have created a delayed effect.

"Break it," commanded ibn Jad.

"Yes, *Effendi*," Mathew mumbled.

Leaning over Khardan, the young wizard stretched forth a trembling hand and took hold of the silken ribbon from which hung the softly glowing silver shield. Mathew noticed, as he did so, the unusual armor in which Khardan had been dressed. It was made of metal—black and shining. A strange design was inset into the breastplate—a snake whose writhing body had been cut into several pieces. It was a gruesome device, and Mathew found himself staring at it, unmoving, his hand poised in midair above Khardan's neck.

"Go on!" grated ibn Jad, standing over him. "Why do you delay?"

Starting, Mathew wrenched his gaze from the grotesque armor and fixed it on the silver shield. Cupping his hand beneath the talisman, he closed his fingers over it gingerly, as though fearing it would be hot to the touch. The silver metal felt warm, but only from the heat of Khardan's body. Clasping the shield, Mathew gave the ribbon a sharp tug. It snapped. The charm came off in Mathew's hand. Almost instantly the metallic glow began to fade. Khardan moved his head, groaning.

"Give that to me."

Wordlessly, Mathew handed ibn Jad the charm.

The man studied it carefully. "A delicate bit of craftsmanship." He glanced from the charm to Mathew to Khardan. "You must care about him very much."

"I do," Mathew said softly, keeping his eyes lowered.

"A pity," said Auda ibn Jad coolly.

Mathew looked up in alarm, but at that moment, movement seen out of the corner of his eye distracted him.

Zohra, stumbling with faltering footsteps but managing to walk nonetheless, was approaching their group. Mathew saw the set of her jaw, the fire in the black eyes, and tried to call out, to speak, to warn her, but the words caught in his dry throat. Seeing his fixed gaze, the slave trader turned.

The wind from the sea was rising. Small waves were washing up on the shore now. Behind Zohra, Mathew saw the cloud on the horizon growing larger and darker.

The wind whipped Zohra's veil from her face. She caught hold of it and covered her nose and mouth. Coming to stand before Auda ibn Jad, she drew herself weakly to her full height, regarding him with flashing black eyes.

"I am Zohra, Princess of the Hrana. I do not know where I am or why you have brought me here, dog of a *kafir*! But I insist that you take me back!"

# Chapter 2

An angry shout from Kiber, who was lashing out at one of his own men with his camel stick, attracted Auda's attention, and he did not immediately answer Zohra's demand. Kiber was busy supervising the unloading of several *djemel*, baggage camels. Under their leader's direction, the *goums* and the slaves placed the wooden boxes, rattan baskets, and other items in the sand near the water's edge. It was the mishandling of several large, carved ivory jars with sealed lids that brought down Kiber's wrath on his *goum*. The slaves were not allowed to touch these jars, Mathew noted. Several hand-picked *goums* were lowering the jars from the *djemel* to the sand with extreme care and caution, treating them with almost reverential respect. When one of the *goums* nearly dropped his end of the jar. Kiber was on him in a flash, and ibn Jad frowned darkly.

Mathew wondered what could be in the jars—possibly some rare incense or perfume. Whatever it was, it was heavy. It took two of Kiber's strongest *goums* to lift a jar by its ivory handles and stagger across the sand to place it with the other merchandise stacked along the shoreline.

The men carrying the jars passed quite close to where Mathew stood in the hot sun near Khardan's litter. The young wizard would have liked to have examined the jars more closely, for he thought he detected magical runes among the other designs carved on the sides, and his skin prickled with a tingle of fear and curiosity when he observed that the lid was decorated with the carved body of a severed snake—the same device that appeared on Khardan's black armor. But Mathew did not have time to investigate or even give more than a moment's passing thought to the ivory jars. His attention was focused on Zohra, and he stared at the woman with mingled anger, frustration, fear, and admiration.

She must be as bewildered and confused as I am, Mathew thought. No, more so, because he at least knew the slave trader and knew why Auda ibn Jad wanted him—the fish, obviously, although that didn't begin to answer all the questions. Zohra had wakened in a strange place from some sort of enchanted sleep, experienced all the same uncomfortable sensations Mathew had experienced—even now she swayed slightly on her feet and he could tell that it was taking every ounce of will she possessed to remain standing. She had, apparently, no idea where she was (This disappointed Mathew. He had hoped she would recognize this place.) and yet she was regarding the formidable Auda ibn Jad with the same scornful gaze she might have fixed upon poor Usti, her djinn, for bungling a command.

Auda's attention continued to remain focused on the unpacking of the ivory jars. Mathew saw Zohra's dark eyes above the veil flare with anger, her black brows draw together. He knew he should stop her. In his mind he saw the slave girl falling to the sand, ibn Jad's knife in her ribs. But the intense heat of the sun radiating up from the salt floor was sapping Mathew's strength. Clinging to one of the poles supporting the litter where Khardan lay, Mathew could only try to warn Zohra to keep still with a gesture of his hand. Zohra saw him and she saw Khardan, who was groaning, shaking his head muzzily, and making feeble, futile attempts to sit up.

"I asked you a question, swine!" Zohra said, stamping her slippered foot on the cracked ground, her jewelry jingling, her body quivering with anger.

Dog of a *kafir*! Swine! Mathew cringed.

"I am a Princess of my people. You will treat me as such," Zohra continued, holding the veil tightly over her face, the rising wind whipping the silken folds of her *chador* around her legs. "You will tell me where I am and you will then return me to my people."

Seeing the nine ivory jars safely stacked up on the shoreline with four *goums* posted guard around them, Auda ibn

Jad turned his attention to the woman standing before him. A glint of amusement flickered in the hooded eyes. Weakly Mathew sank down onto the hot ground, huddling in a small patch of shade cast by Khardan's litter. Almost immediately, however, a new fear arose when the young wizard saw Khardan's eyes open to stare about his surroundings in confused astonishment.

A waterskin lay nearby. Catching it up, Mathew held the mouth out to Khardan to drink, trying as best he could to warn him to keep silent. The Calif thrust the waterskin aside. Gritting his teeth against the pain, Khardan propped himself up on one elbow and stared intently at Auda ibn Jad.

"You stand, Princess, on the shores of the Kurdin Sea—"

"The Waters of Tara-kan?" Zohra cut in scornfully. "Do you take me for a fool?"

"No, my lady." Respect coated the surface of Auda's voice.

He was toying with her, amusing himself because he had no other entertainment. The slaves and the *goums* had completed unloading the camels. The slaves sank, panting, down onto the ground, trying desperately to find some modicum of shade by crouching beside the kneeling camels. The *goums* stood in disciplined silence, sipping water and keeping watch over the baggage and the slaves. They appeared immune to the heat, though Mathew could see huge patches of sweat darkening their black uniforms. And he noted, as he glanced at them, that more than one turned his gaze out to sea, nodding in relief and satisfaction at the sight of the shadow growing larger upon the water.

"All know the Waters of the Tara-kan do not exist," said Zohra, dismissing the vast sea that stretched before her with decisive finality. So calmly and firmly did she speak that it seemed the sea itself must realize its mistake and take itself out of her presence at once.

"I assure you, madam, that these are the waters of the Kurdin Sea. We have reached them by traveling north from the Tel in the desert of Pagrah to the city of Idrith, then due east across the southernmost border of the Great Steppes."

Zohra gazed at Auda pityingly. "You are mad. Such a journey would take months!"

"Indeed it has, my lady," ibn Jad replied softly. "Look at the sun."

Zohra looked upward at the sun. So did Khardan. Mathew watched the Calif carefully, searching for clues in the expres-

sion on the man's face. The young wizard himself did not
bother to study the orb's position in the sky. In this strange
part of the world, he was barely able to judge the passing of
day into night much less the passing of weeks into months. It
seemed to him to have been only last night that they had
escaped the Battle at the Tel. Had it truly been months ago?
Were they truly far from their homeland?

*Our* homeland! Mathew shook his head bleakly. What am
I thinking about? My homeland . . . So much farther away
than that . . . Farther away than the blazing sun . . .

He saw Khardan's eyes widen, the man's face grow pale
beneath the growth of heavy black beard, the lips part, the
tongue attempt to moisten them. The Calif looked down now
upon the strange armor that he wore, noticing it for the first
time. His hand ran over it, and Mathew saw the fingers
tremble. Wordlessly the young wizard held out the waterskin
again. This time Khardan accepted it, drinking a small amount,
his brow furrowed, his black eyes fixed upon Auda ibn Jad
with a dark expression Mathew could not fathom.

Zohra's cool demeanor, too, was shaken. She darted a
swift, fearful glance at Mathew from above her veil—the
glance of one who has ventured blithely onto smooth,
hardpacked sand, only to discover herself being sucked beneath the shifting surface.

Mathew quickly averted his eyes. She had thrown herself
into this, she must get herself out. He could say or do
nothing that would help her, and he dared not attract the
attention of the slave trader to himself. By the looks of it,
Auda ibn Jad was telling the truth. They had undertaken a
long journey, apparently traveling under some sort of spell
that feigned death yet kept them very much alive.

*The city guards do not search the bodies of the dead.*

That statement was beginning to make sense. Mathew's
hand stole surreptitiously to the globe containing the fish.
Ibn Jad had given it to him originally to sneak it past the
guards in the city of Kich. Now Mathew had been instrumen-
tal, apparently, in doing the same thing with the guards of
Idrith. That was the reason ibn Jad had taken Mathew captive
instead of killing him and retrieving the fish. Mathew recalled the moment of terror when he had awakened in the tall
grass near the oasis. Seeing the slave trader standing above
him, he had supposed the man meant to murder him. Instead, ibn Jad had cast him into a deep sleep.

But why take Khardan? Why take Zohra? Why bring them here? Why the ships? Where were they being taken? Surely, if he had brought them this far, ibn Jad did not intend to kill them now.

Looking at Auda's smooth, impassive face, the unblinking eyes; looking at the waters of the sea that were growing rougher by the moment; looking at the shadow covering the water and realizing that it was the darkness of a rapidly approaching storm—a strange storm, a storm that seemed to rage only on a small part of the ocean—Mathew wondered despairingly if death coming to them this minute might not be a blessing.

"I do not like this place," said Zohra coolly. "I am leaving."

Mathew raised his eyes, staring at her in astonishment.

Gathering the folds of her wind-whipped clothes around her with one hand, holding her veil over her nose and mouth with the other, Zohra turned her back upon Auda ibn Jad and began walking due west over the cracked, tortured earth.

Shrugging, ibn Jad moved over to the shoreline and stood there, gazing intently out eastward into the storm. The *goums,* watching Zohra, nudged each other, many pointing at the sun and laughing. Kiber said something to Auda ibn Jad, who glanced at Zohra out of the corner of his eye and shrugged again.

Mathew stared at her, aghast. She knew, far better than he, having lived in the desert, that she would not last more than a few hours out there before the merciless heat blistered her skin and boiled her blood, before the lack of water drove her to madness. The storm wind blowing off the sea tore the silken veil from her head, her long black hair streamed into her face, nearly blinding her. Still weak from the effects of the spell, Zohra stumbled over the cracked, uneven ground, slipped and fell. Pausing a moment to catch her breath, she staggered back up to her feet and continued on, limping.

She's twisted her ankle. She won't get a hundred yards! Mathew realized. Half-heard words spoken by the *goums* indicated they were placing bets on how far she could go before collapsing. Of all the stupid, meaningless gestures! Mathew fumed. Why didn't she just drive a knife into her heart? Was her pride that important? More important than her life?

And these people considered *him* mad!

Struggling to his feet, Mathew cast a wary glance at ibn

Jad. Seeing him apparently absorbed in watching for the ship, the young wizard started after Zohra. She was weakening fast. Her limp was more pronounced, every movement must be causing her agony. Mathew quickly caught up with the woman and grabbed hold of her arm.

Turning, she saw who it was held her and immediately jerked away.

"Let me go!" she ordered

At the sight of her pain-twisted face, the parched lips already cracked and bleeding from the salt-laden air, and the fierce pride and determination masking the terror in the black eyes, Mathew felt tears well up in his throat. Whether they were tears of pity, tears of admiration, or tears of exasperated rage, he wasn't certain. His instinct was to take her in his arms and comfort her, let her know she wasn't alone in the fear and despair she was trying desperately to hide. Yet the wizard had the distinct feeling that once he got his hands on the obstreperous woman, he'd shake her until her teeth rattled in her head.

"Zohra! Stop! Listen to me!" Mathew caught hold of her again and this time held on firmly. Unable to free herself, she glared at him in fury. "You're only making things worse! Do you know what kind of death you'll die out there?"

The black eyes stared at him unwaveringly.

She knows, Mathew thought, swallowing the lump in his throat. "Zohra"—he tried again—"whatever we face can't possibly be as bad as that! Don't leave me! Don't leave Khardan! We've got to get through this together. It's our only chance!"

Her eyes blinked, her gaze shifted from Mathew to Khardan, a slight smile twisted the cracked lips. Not liking the looks of that smile, Mathew glanced swiftly around.

Auda ibn Jad had his back turned, staring out to sea. Unarmed, with no weapon but his bare hands, Khardan had risen from the litter and was running across the sand toward the slave trader.

Gnashing his teeth in frustration, his heart stopped in fear, Mathew watched helplessly, expecting to see the *goums* rush the Calif, Kiber draw his shining sword and cut Khardan down. Instead, no one made a move. No one even shouted a warning to ibn Jad, who still had his back to his rapidly approaching enemy.

Khardan hurled himself at the slave trader, his hands outstretched.

The end came swiftly, occurring so fast that Mathew wasn't certain what happened. He saw Auda ibn Jad sidestep ever so slightly. Khardan leaped on his back, his arms closing around the slave trader's throat. Auda's hands grabbed hold of Khardan's arms and in the same, fluid movement, bent forward, pulling the Calif with him. Propelled by his own momentum, Khardan was flipped over the slave trader's shoulder. The Calif flew through the air and splashed into the shallow water at the shore's edge. He lay there, dazed and stunned, staring up at the sky.

"Has everyone gone insane? Are all you nomads intent on delivering yourselves as quickly as possible into the arms of Death?" Mathew demanded bitterly.

"We are not cowards!" Zohra hissed, struggling feebly to escape his grip. "Not like you! I will die before anyone keeps me captive, for whatever reason!"

"Sometimes it takes more courage to live!" Mathew responded, his voice thick and choked.

Zohra stared at him, the women's clothes he wore, and made no answer.

Auda ibn Jad was shouting orders. *Goums* came running across the sand toward them. Catching hold of both Zohra and Mathew, they dragged them back to the slave trader. Other *goums*, supervised by Kiber, were lifting Khardan out of the sea. They shoved Mathew down into the sand near the baggage that was to be loaded onto the approaching vessels. Zohra fell down next to him, Kiber dropped Khardan, breathing heavily, at their feet. Bending over the Calif, ostensibly to see if he was hurt but in reality hiding his face, Mathew saw Zohra looking at him, her dark eyes unusually thoughtful.

He turned his head, not wanting to meet her gaze, afraid that if she should be able to see inside him, she would see there the sick fear that shamed him and made a mockery of his words.

# Chapter 3

Bruised and aching, Khardan was content for the moment to catch his breath and consider the situation. His attack on Auda ibn Jad had not been as rash and ill considered as it appeared to Mathew. The Calif knew that the fall of a leader can never fail to throw even the best disciplined army into confusion and disarray. There was every possibility this slave trader ruled by fear alone and his followers might be exceedingly grateful to the man who removed the sword from their throats.

That man is not likely to be me—at least not at this moment, Khardan thought, glancing at ibn Jad with grudging respect. The slave trader had tossed him around with the ease of a father playing with his children! Looking at the long, curved sword ibn Jad wore at his side, the Calif guessed that the man was undoubtedly equally skilled with it, as well. And the longer Khardan watched Kiber and his *goums*, the more obvious it became to him that they served ibn Jad with unshakable, unswerving loyalty—the type of loyalty that is not and never can be generated by fear.

What I need now are answers, Khardan thought upon reflection. Of course, these had to come from the red-haired youth, the one whose life he had saved. The Calif had recognized the slave trader as the man in the white palanquin who had stared at Khardan with such malevolence in the city of Kich. More than once Khardan had wakened in the night, sweating and shaking, remembering the dreadful promise of revenge in those cold, flat eyes—the eyes of a snake.

Khardan could understand ibn Jad's anger—the Calif had stolen one of his salves, after all. But Khardan had known at the time, when those deadly eyes first pierced his soul, that there was more to it than that. It was as if the Calif had snatched up the one thing in this world that gave ibn Jad reason to live. And Auda had promised, in that look, that he would have it back.

What was the young man's name, anyway? Khardan tried to remember through the haze of pain and confusion. Mathew. Something like that. He'd heard Zohra pronounce it. Thinking of his wife, who wasn't a wife to him any more than the young man was a wife to him, Khardan glanced at her. Zohra sat on the other side of Mathew, and unlike the young man, who was looking at him with a worried expression, she didn't appear to be the least interested in Khardan's welfare. He couldn't see her face; the black hair, blown by the wind, covered it like a veil. Nursing her sore ankle, rubbing it with her hand, she stared straight out to sea and was seemingly lost in her thoughts.

Khardan wondered what she knew about the young man. It was too late to ask. Bitterly he regretted not questioning this man about his past, about where he'd come from, why he had chosen to hide his sex from the world in women's clothes. It occurred to Khardan that he hadn't spoken more than twenty words to the youth the entire time he'd been in the nomad's camp.

Who could blame me? Khardan reflected grimly, looking up at the young man with the flame-colored hair and the face as smooth and delicate as that of any woman. Kneeling beside Khardan, Mathew was making a clumsy attempt to loosen the fastenings of the breastplate clamped over the Calif's chest.

A man who disguises himself as a woman! A man who lets himself be taken into another man's harem! Bad enough I had to live with such disgrace—but to be seen taking an interest in him!

There was too much on my mind to worry over a boy— Sheykh Zeid, Meryem . . . Khardan's heart jumped. Meryem! She'd been in danger! The battle . . . he remembered seeing her face just before he lost consciousness. What had happened to her? What had happened to all of them—his people? Why was he here? He stared again at the sun whose position in the sky meant the passage of two months at least.

From Idrith to the Kurdin Sea . . . Answers! He needed answers!

Reaching out, he caught hold of the young man's arm. "What is going on?" he asked softly.

Startled, Mathew glanced at Khardan uneasily, then shook his head and averted his face. He was attempting to untie a knot in one of the leather thongs holding the sides of the breastplate together. Khardan's hand closed over his, halting his work with its firm pressure.

"What is your name?"

"Mathew," was the barely audible reply. The young man kept his eyes lowered.

"Mat-hew," repeated Khardan, stumbling over the strange-sounding word and coming out with it finally in a manner and accent similar to Zohra's. "Mat-hew, it is obvious that we are here because of you. Why does this man want you?"

Mathew lowered his head. Locks of the flaming red hair slid out from beneath the woman's veil he wore, partially hiding his face. But Khardan saw a flush stain the fair cheeks, he saw the curved lips tremble, and he could guess at the answer the youth was too embarrassed to give.

"So, he does not know you are a —" Khardan paused.

The crimson in the cheeks deepened. Mathew shook his head. Khardan felt the young man's hands shake; the fingers were icy to the touch, despite the terrible heat.

Letting loose the boy's hand, Khardan glanced around cautiously. Auda ibn Jad and Kiber stood together on the beach, conferring in low tones, occasionally glancing out to sea. The goums' attentions were focused on the sea as well. The slaves sat huddled together near the camels, heads bowed, no interest in anything.

"That's not the truth, Mat-hew," Khardan said slowly, turning his gaze back to the youth. "He doesn't want you for his bed. He would have sold you in Kich if I hadn't stolen you away. There is another reason he wants you and it is the reason we are here. Tell me."

Raising his head, Mathew looked at Khardan. The young man's eyes were wide and in them was a look of such pleading and terror that Khardan was taken aback.

"Don't ask me!" The words came out a gasp.

Khardan's lips tightened in anger and frustration. The boy's fear was contagious. Khardan felt it chill his own blood and the feeling irritated him. He'd never experienced fear like this before, and he had faced death in battle since he was seventeen years old. This fear was like a child's fear of the dark—irrational, illogical, and very real.

Mathew gave up on the knot; his hands were shaking too violently. He started to turn away, to go sit with Zohra, who was crouched on the hot ground near Khardan's feet. The Calif caught hold of him again.

Slowly, reluctantly, Mathew glanced back at him. The face was terror stricken, the eyes begged Khardan to release him. Khardan bit back the words he'd been going to say. He wanted to sit up; the heavy metal of the armor was poking him uncomfortably in the back. But moving about might attract the attention of ibn Jad, and Khardan wanted to talk undisturbed for as long as possible.

"What happened at the Tel, then," Khardan said gruffly, frowning. "Surely you can tell me that! How did we come to fall into the hands of this slave trader?"

As he had hoped she would, Zohra turned her head at his question. She stared at her husband, exchanged a swift, grim glance with Mathew, then turned back to gaze out at the sea in silence once more.

"The Amir's forces raided the camp. Everyone—women and children—were taken prisoner—" Mathew answered softly, warily.

"I know that," Khardan snapped impatiently. "I saw. I mean after."

"We—Zohra and I—escaped by hiding in a tent." Mathew's eyes, as he spoke, were focused on the snake on Khardan's armor. "You . . . fell in battle. We . . . uh . . . found you on the battlefield. The Amir's men were taking prisoners, you see, and we feared that they would take you, so we carried you off the field of battle—"

"—disguised as a woman."

The cold, smooth voice broke in on the conversation. Intent upon Mathew's story, Khardan had not heard the man approach. Twisting, he looked up into the black masked face of Auda ibn Jad.

The man was talking nonsense! Khardan sat up, chafing beneath the hot, heavy armor. Ignoring ibn Jad, the Calif looked to Mathew to continue his story and was astounded to see that the boy had gone deathly white and was biting his nether lip. Khardan's gaze went to Zohra. She kept her back turned to him, but that back was rigid, her neck stiff, her head held high in a manner quite well-known to him.

"Is this true?" Khardan demanded angrily.

"Yes, it's true!" Zohra whirled to face him, her hair whipping about her in the wind blowing off the sea. "How do you think you would have escaped otherwise? Is the Amir such a kindly man that he would say, 'Ah, poor fellow, he's hurt. Take him away and tend him'? Hah! More likely a sword through the throat and the jackals feasting off your brains, much food they would find there!"

A smile twitched at the corner of the mouth of Auda ibn Jad.

"You have . . . shamed me!" Khardan's face burned an angry red. Sweat beaded his brow. His hands clenched and he struggled for breath. "I am . . . dishonored!"

"It was all we could think of to do!" Mathew faltered. Glancing up, he saw the reptile eyes of ibn Jad watching with interest. The youth laid a placating, trembling hand on Khardan's arm. "No one saw us, I'm certain. There was so much smoke and confusion. We hid in the tall grass, near the oasis. . . ."

"The young woman tells the truth, Nomad," said ibn Jad. "It was there I found you, in the oasis, dressed in rose-pink silk. You don't believe me?" Crouching down opposite Mathew, the slave trader reached out his slender hand and caught hold of the youth by the chin. "Look at that face, Nomad. How can such beauty lie? Look into the green eyes. See the love they hold for you? Blossom here did it for love, Nomad." Ibn Jad released Mathew roughly, the marks of the man's fingers showing clearly on the youth's livid face. "Now this one." The slave trader turned to look admiringly at Zohra, who was pointedly ignoring him. "This one, I'd say, did it for spite." Auda ibn Jad rose to his feet. "Not that it matters, where you are going, Nomad," he added casually.

"Where *are* we going?" Zohra asked with disdain, as though inquiring of a slave what they might be having for dinner.

"Across this—the waters of the sea whose existence you refuse to acknowledge, Princess," said Auda ibn Jad with a smile and a gesture of his hand. "We go to the island fortress of Galos, where dwells the last remnant of those who worship Zhakrin, God of the Night."

"I have never heard of this God," Zohra stated, dismissing Zhakrin as she dismissed the ocean.

"That is because he has been deposed from his heavenly throne. Some think him dead—a costly mistake. Zhakrin lives, and we gather now in his palace to prepare for his return."

"We?" Zohra's lip curled in scorn.

Auda ibn Jad's voice became cool, reverent. "The Black Paladins, the Holy Knights of Evil."

# Chapter 4

Black Paladins, Zhakrin . . . The words meant nothing to Zohra. None of this meant anything to Zohra, except that she was here where she did not want to be, she was being held captive by this man, and her attempt to escape had been stopped by Mathew. Zohra did not believe ibn Jad's wild tales about traveling to Idrith and beyond to a sea that did not exist. The Tel was nearby. It had to be. He was lying to prevent them from attempting to escape, and Mathew had swallowed that lie. And so had Khardan, apparently. As for the odd position of the sun in the sky, a summer sun—it had been spring when she closed her eyes to sleep the sleep of exhaustion in the oasis—that could be explained. She knew it could, if only she could get away from this man with the disturbing eyes and discover the truth.

What they needed was action, to fight, to do something instead of just sit here like . . . like old women! Zohra glanced at the two men with her and her lips twisted in derision. At least Khardan had tried to fight. She had been proud of him at that moment. But now the man's anger and hurt pride had overthrown his reason, casting him into some sort of stupor. He stared at his hands, his fists clenching and unclenching, his breath coming in short gasps. As for the young wizard— Zohra glanced at him in scorn.

"He has already exhibited *his* worth!" the woman muttered beneath her breath. "I could measure it in goat droppings!"

She herself was at a disadvantage now, with her injured ankle. At a disadvantage, but not helpless. Her hand went to her breast. The dagger she had grabbed during the onset of the raid was hidden in her bosom. Pressing against her flesh, the metal felt warm and reassuring. She would never be taken aboard a ship, if such was truly the intent of this man. She would never be taken to any palace of a dead God.

Mathew's voice, speaking to the Paladin, disturbed her thoughts.

"So that is how you did it?" The young man was staring up at Auda ibn Jad with awe; fear made his voice crack. Zohra glanced away from him in disgust. "That is how you cast the enchanted sleep over us. You are not a wizard—"

"No, Blossom." Ibn Jad frowned at the idea. "I am a true knight and my power comes from Zhakrin, not from Sul. Long ago, in my youth, I learned the might of Zhakrin. I accepted him as my God and pledged to him my life, my soul. I have worked—all those of my Order have worked—unceasingly to bring about our God's return into this world."

"A priest!" Zohra sneered. She did not see the cruel eyes, gazing at her, narrow dangerously.

"No!" said Mathew hastily. "Not a priest. Or rather a priest who is a warrior. One who can"—the young man paused, then said heavily—"kill in the name of the God."

"Yes," said the Black Paladin coolly. "I have laid many souls upon the altar of Zhakrin." The toe of his boot idly scraped the salty soil from around the base of one of the ivory jars that stood near them. "We kill without mercy, yet never without reason. The God is angered by senseless murder, since the living are always more valuable in his service than the dead."

"That's why you've kept us alive," Mathew said softly. "To serve your God. But . . . how?"

"Haven't you figured that out yet, Blossom?" Auda ibn Jad looked at him quizzically. "No? Then I prefer to keep you ignorant. Fear of the unknown is much more debilitating."

The storm was worsening. Water that had previously been calm now crashed on the shore. Everyone's clothing was wet through with salt spray. The sun had disappeared behind the storm clouds, casting a dark shadow over them.

Kiber's voice called out urgently. The Black Paladin turned to look to sea. "Ah! The ship is in sight. Only a few more moments before it lands. You will excuse me, I am certain." Ibn Jad bowed. "There are matters to which I must attend."

Turning, he walked over to Kiber. The two conferred briefly, then Kiber hurried over to his *goums*, gesturing and shouting orders. The soldiers sprang into action, some running over to the camels, others taking up positions around the baggage, others hauling the slaves to their feet.

Curious, Zohra looked out to sea.

She had heard tales of the *dhough*, the vessels made of wood that floated upon the water and had wings to drive them before the wind. She had never seen one before. She had never, in fact, seen a body of water as large as this one and was secretly in awe of it, or would have been, if such an emotion would not have betrayed weakness. Looking critically at the ship as it approached, Zohra felt at first disappointment.

The *meddah*, the storyteller, had said these vessels were like white-winged sea birds, swooping gracefully over the water. This *dhough* resembled a gigantic insect, crawling over the ocean's surface. Oars stuck out from either side, scrabbling over the waves like feet, propelling the insect forward into the teeth of the wind. Ragged black wings flapped wildly.

Zohra knew nothing about ships or sailing, but she found it impossible to see how this one stayed afloat. Time and again she expected to see it perish. The vessel plunged in and out of the tall waves, its prow sliding down an incline that was steep and smooth as polished steel. It disappeared, and it seemed it must have vanished forever beneath the churning waters. Then suddenly it came in sight, springing up out of the watery chasm like a many-legged bug scrabbling to regain its footing.

Zohra's disappointment turned to uneasiness; her uneasiness darkened and deepened the nearer the ship approached.

"Mat-hew," she said softly, moving nearer the young wizard, whose gaze was fixed, like hers, upon the ship. "You have sailed in these *dhough*?"

"Yes." His voice was tight, strained.

"You have sailed across a sea?" She had not believed his story before. She wasn't certain she believed it now, but she needed reassurance.

He nodded. His eyes, staring at the ship, were wide.

"It looks so frail. How does it survive such a beating?"

"It shouldn't." He coughed, his throat was dry. "It"—he hesitated, licking his lips—"it isn't an . . . ordinary ship, Zohra. Just like that isn't an ordinary storm. They're supernatural."

He used the term from his own language and she stared at him, uncomprehending.

Mathew groped for words. "Magic, enchanted."

At that, Khardan lifted his head, his fog of rage blown away by the cold, biting wind of Mathew's words. The Calif stared out at the ship that was so close now they could see figures walking across its slanting deck. A jagged bolt of lightning shot from the churning black clouds, striking the mast. Flame danced along the yardarms, the rigging caught fire and burned, the sails became sheets of flame whose garish light was reflected on the water-slick deck and flickered in the rising and falling oars. The vessel had become a ship of fire.

Catching her breath, Zohra looked hurriedly at Auda ibn Jad, expecting some outcry, some angry reaction. The man paced the shore and appeared disturbed, but the glances he cast the ship were of impatience, not dismay.

Mathew's hand closed over hers. Looking back out to sea, Zohra shrank close to the young man. The flames did not consume the vessel! Burning fiercely, the ship surged across the storm-tossed waves, being driven to shore by buffeting winds. Thunder boomed around it, a black banner burst from its masthead. Outlined in flame was the image of a severed snake.

"They would put us aboard that!" Zohra's voice was low and hollow.

"Zohra," Mathew began helplessly, hands on her shoulders, "it will be all right. . . ."

"No!" With a wild shriek, she broke free of him. Leaping to her feet, fear absorbing the pain of her injured ankle, Zohra ran wildly away from the sea, away from the blazing ship. Her flight caught everyone off guard; the Black Paladin fuming at the slowness of the ship in docking was staring out to sea, as were all those not involved with more pressing tasks, A flutter of silk seen out of the corner of the eye caught Kiber's attention. He shouted, and the *goums* guarding the captives and the baggage set off instantly in pursuit.

Fear lends strength, but it saps strength, too, and when panic subsides, the body is weaker as a result. The fire from the ship seemed to shoot through Zohra's leg; her ankle could no longer bear her weight and gave way beneath her. Away from the water's edge and the cooling winds of the storm, Zohra felt the heat that was rising from the salt flats suck out her breath and parch her throat. The glare of the sun off the crystalline sand seared through her eyes and into her brain. Behind her, she could hear panting breath, the pounding of booted feet.

Staggering blindly, Zohra stumbled and fell. Her hand closed over the hilt of the hidden dagger and, when rough hands grabbed hold of her, she struck out at them with the knife. Unable to see through her tangled hair, she lashed wildly at the sound of their voices or their harsh, rasping breath. A grunt and a bitter curse told her she'd drawn blood and she fought ever more furiously.

A cold voice barked a command.

Hands closed over her wrist, bones cracked, pain burned in her arm. Gagging, choking, she dropped the dagger.

Gripping her firmly by the arms, the *goums*—one of them bleeding from a slash across the chest—dragged her back across the sand. The ship had dropped anchor some distance from the shore and stood burning in the water like a horrible beacon. The sight of small boats, black against the flames, crawling slowly toward land, renewed Zohra's terror.

She struggled against her captors, pulling backward with all the weight of her body.

Sweating profusely, the *goums* hauled her before the Black Paladin. Zohra shook the hair out of her eyes, her sun-dazzled vision had cleared enough to see him. He was regarding her coolly, thoughtfully, perhaps wondering if she was worth the trouble.

Decision made, ibn Jad lifted his hand and struck.

# Chapter 5

"Bind his hands and arms!"

Rubbing his knuckles, Auda ibn Jad glanced from the comatose body of Zohra lying at his feet to the insane struggles of Khardan, battling with the *goums*. "If he persists in causing trouble, render him unconscious as well."

"Khardan!" Mathew was pleading, "be calm! There's nothing we can do! No sense in fighting! We must just try to survive!"

Soothingly, timidly he touched the muscular arm that was being wrenched behind Khardan's back and bound tightly with cords of braided hemp used to hold the baggage in place upon the camels. Glaring at him in bitter anger, Khardan drew away from the young man. His struggles ceased, however, but whether from seeing the logic in Mathew's words or because he was bound, helpless and exhausted, the young wizard did not know.

His body shivering, like that of a horse who has been run into the ground, Khardan stood with head bowed. Seeing him calm for the moment at least, Mathew left the Calif to tend to Zohra, who lay in a heap on the ground, her long black hair glistening with the salt spray from the pounding waves.

Mathew glanced warily at the *goums*, but they made no attempt to stop him. The flat, cruel eyes turned their gaze on him, however, and Mathew faltered, a bird caught and held by the mesmerizing stare of the cobra.

Kiber spoke, ibn Jad's gaze turned to his Captain, and Mathew—with a shivering sigh—crept forward again.

"These two are trouble," the leader of the *goums* grumbled. "Why not leave them as payment, along with the slaves."

"Zhakrin would not thank us for wasting such fine, healthy bodies and souls to match. This woman"—ibn Jad bent over to caress a strand of Zohra's black hair—"is superb. I like her spirit. She will breed many strong followers for the God. Perhaps I will take her myself. As for the bearded devil" —ibn Jad straightened and glanced over at Khardan, his eyes coolly appraising the young man's muscular build—"you know what awaits him. Will that not be worth some trouble in the eyes of Zhakrin?"

Auda ibn Jad's tone was severe. Kiber cringed, as though the knight's stern rebuke cut his flesh. The *goum's* "Yes, *Effendi*" was subdued.

"See to the landing party," ibn Jad ordered. "Keep your men occupied in loading the baggage aboard. Send the sailors to me. I will take charge of them."

Kiber, bowing, scurried away. It seemed to Mathew that, at the mention of the sailors, Kiber's tan face became unusually pale, strained, and tense.

Zohra moaned, and Mathew's attention turned to her.

"You had best rouse her and get her on board the boats as quickly as possible, Blossom," said the Black Paladin carelessly. "The sailors will be coming to me for their payment and you are both in danger here."

Payment? Mathew saw the Black Paladin's reptile eyes go to the slaves, who crouched together in a miserable huddle, chained hand and foot by the *goums* as soon as their labors were finished. Pitifully thin and emaciated, their bones showing beneath their whip-scarred skin, the slaves stared in wild-eyed terror at the fiery ship, obviously fearing that they would be forced to board it.

Mathew had a sudden, chilling premonition that the poor wretches' fears were groundless—or rather, misplaced. Hastily he helped Zohra to her feet. Draping one of her arms over his shoulder, he put his arm around her waist and half carried, half dragged her across the sand, over to where the *goums* were keeping a wary eye on Khardan. Groggy but conscious, Zohra clung to Mathew. The right side of her face was bruised and swollen. Blood trickled from a split lip. She must have had a blinding headache, and a tiny gasp of pain escaped her every time her injured foot touched the ground.

She made no complaint, however, and did her best to keep up with Mathew, whose own growing fear was lending impetus to his strides. He was facing the incoming boats now, and his gaze went curiously to the crew who sailed a ship of flame across storm-blasted water and who were now coming to shore to demand payment for their services.

There seemed nothing unusual about them. Human males, they shipped their oars with disciplined skill. Jumping over the side into the shallow water, they dragged the boats onto the shore, leaving them under Kiber's command. At his orders, the *goums* immediately began to stow the baggage on board, Kiber personally supervising the loading of the large, ivory jars. Though all did their work efficiently, Mathew noted that every *goum*—Kiber included—kept his eyes fearfully upon the sailors.

They were all young, muscular men with blond hair and fair, even features. Coming ashore, they paused and looked long and hard at the *goums*, their blue eyes eerily reflecting the orange glow of the fire that blazed in the water behind them. Kiber gave them a swift, hunted glance. His eyes darted to Auda ibn Jad, then back to his men, who weren't moving fast enough to suit him. Shouting at the *goums*, Kiber's voice cracked with fear.

"In the name of Zhakrin, God of Night and Evil, I bid you greeting," called Auda ibn Jad.

The eyes of the sailors reluctantly left the *goums*. As one man, they looked to the Black Paladin standing, facing them, some distance up the beach from the shoreline. Mathew caught his breath, his arms went limp, he nearly let loose his hold on Zohra. He couldn't move for astonishment.

Each of the sailors was identical to every other. The same nose, same mouth, same ears, same eyes. They were the same height, the same weight. They moved the same, they walked the same, they were dressed the same—in tight-fitting breeches, their chests bare, gleaming with water.

Zohra sagged wearily in Mathew's arm. She did not look up and something warned Mathew to make certain that she didn't. Snatching the veil from his hair, he cast it over her head. The sailors' eyes swept over both of them like a bone-chilling wind. Mathew knew he should move, should take the few steps—all that was required to bring them back under the protection of Kiber and his *goums*. But Mathew's feet were numb, his body paralyzed by a fear that came from deep inside the part of his mind where nightmares lurked.

"We answered your summons and sailed our ship to do your bidding," spoke one of the sailors—or perhaps it was all the sailors; the fifty mouths moved, but Mathew heard only one voice. "Where is our payment?"

"Here," said Auda ibn Jad, and pointed at the slaves.

The sailors looked and they nodded, satisfied, and then their aspect began to change. The jaws thrust forward, the lips parted and drew back, gleaming teeth lengthened into fangs. The eyes burned, no longer reflecting the fire of their ship, but with insatiable hunger. Voices changed to snarls, fingernails to ripping talons. With an eager howl, the sailors swept forward, the wind of their passing hitting Mathew with a chill, foul-smelling blast, as if someone had opened the doors of a desecrated and defiled tomb.

He did not need to look at the prints left behind by the creatures in the sand to know what these monsters were. He knew what he would see—not a human track, but the cloven hooves of an ass.

"Ghuls!" he breathed, shuddering in terror.

The slaves saw death running toward them. Their shrieks were heartrending and piteous to hear. Zohra started to lift her head, but Mathew—clasping her close to him—covered her eyes with his hand and began to run, dragging her stumbling and blinded along with him.

"Don't look!" he panted, repeating the words over and over, trying not to hear what was happening behind him. There was the clanking of chains—the slaves trying desperately to escape. He heard their wails when they realized it was hopeless and then the first horrible scream and then more screams and the dreadful ripping, tearing sounds of teeth and talons sinking into and devouring living flesh.

Zohra became dead weight in Mathew's arms. Overcome by her pain, she had lost consciousness. Shaking, unable to take another step, he lowered her onto the ground. Kiber himself ran forward to lift up the woman's body and carry her into the waiting boats. The *goum* kept his eyes averted from the grisly massacre, driving his men to their work with shouts and curses.

"*Hazrat* Akhran, have mercy on us!" The voice was Khardan's, but Mathew barely recognized it. The Calif's face was livid, his beard blue against the pallid skin. His eyes were white-rimmed and staring, purple shadows smudged the skin. Sweat trickled down his face; his lips trembled.

"Don't watch!" Mathew implored, trying to block the man's vision of the gruesome carnage.

Khardan lunged forward. Bound or not, he obviously intended to try and help the doomed slaves.

Mathew caught hold of him by the shoulders. Struggling wildly, Khardan sought to free himself, but the youth held onto him tightly, with the strength of desperation.

"Ghuls!" Mathew cried, his voice catching in his burning throat. "They feed on human flesh. It will be over soon. There's nothing you can do!"

Behind him, he could hear screams of the dying, their still living bodies being rended from limb to limb. Their wails tore through head and heart.

"I can't stand it!" Khardan gasped.

"I know!" Mathew dug his nails into the man's flesh. "But there is nothing you can do! Ibn Jad holds the ghuls in thrall, but just barely. Interfere, and you kill us all!"

Wrenching himself free from Mathew's hold, Khardan lost his balance, stumbled, and fell to his knees. He did not get up, but remained crouched on the ground, sweating and shivering, his breath coming in painful sobs.

The screams ceased suddenly. Mathew closed his eyes, going limp in relief. Footsteps crunched in the sand near him, and he looked up hurriedly. Auda ibn Jad stood beside him, staring down at Khardan. The Calif heaved a shuddering sigh. Wiping his hand across his mouth, he lifted his head. His face was white, the lips tinged with the green of sickness. Dark, bloodshot eyes, shadowed with the horror of what they had witnessed, stared up at the Black Paladin.

"'What kind of monster are you?" Khardan asked hoarsely.

"The kind you will become," answered Auda ibn Jad.

# Chapter 6

It was well Mathew had others to worry about during the
journey across the Kurdin Sea on the demon-driven vessel,
or he might have truly succumbed to madness. They had no
more set foot on board when the ghuls returned from their
feast. Once more in the guise of handsome young men, their
bodies daubed with blood, they silently took their places at
the oars below and on the decks and in the rigging above.
A word from Auda ibn Jad set the black sails billowing.
The anchor was weighed, the ghuls heaved at the oars, the
storm winds howled, lightning cracked, and the ship clawed
its way through the foaming water toward the island of
Galos.

Khardan had not spoken a word since ibn Jad's strange
pronouncement on shore. He had suffered himself to be
hoisted roughly aboard ship without a struggle. The *goums*,
under Kiber's orders, lashed the nomad to a mast and left
him there. Sagging against his bindings, Khardan stared around
him with dull, lusterless eyes.

Thinking the sight of Zohra might rouse the Calif from the
stupor into which he had fallen, Mathew brought the limp
and lifeless form to lie on the deck near where her husband
stood, tied to the mast. Soaked through to the skin from the
rain and the sea water breaking over the heaving deck, the
young wizard did what he could to keep Zohra warm and dry,
covering her with a tarp, sheltering her amid the tall ivory
jars and the rest of the baggage that the ghuls had secured as

best they could on the slippery deck. Khardan did not even glance down at the unconscious woman.

After he had done what he could for Zohra, Mathew wedged himself between two carved wooden chests to keep himself from sliding around with the yawing of the ship. Wet and miserable and extremely frightened, the young man glared up at the stupefied Khardan with bitter anger.

He can't do this to me! Mathew thought, shivering from cold and fear. He's the one who's strong. He's the warrior. He's supposed to protect us. I need *him* now. He can't do this to me!

What's the matter with him anyway? Mathew wondered resentfully. That was a horrible sight, but he's been in battles before. Surely he's seen things just as gruesome. I know I have. . . .

The memory of John, kneeling on the sand, Kiber's shining sword flashing in the sunlight, the warm blood splashing on Mathew's robes, the head with the lifeless eyes rolling across the sand. Tears blinded Mathew. He hung his head, clenching his hands.

"I'm frightened! I need you! You're supposed to be strong! Not me! If I can cope with this . . . this horror, why can't you?"

If Mathew had been older and able to think rationally, he would have been able to answer his own despairing question. He had *not* seen the ghuls attack and devour the helpless slaves. Khardan had, and though to Mathew there was not much difference between driving a sword into a man's gut and sinking fangs into his neck, the warrior's mind and heart reacted differently. One was a clean death, with honor. The other—a horrifying death brought about by creatures of evil, creatures of magic.

Magic. If Mathew had considered it, magic was the key—a key that unlocked the box of Khardan's innermost fears and let them loose to terrorize and overthrow his mind.

To the nomad, magic was a woman's gift—a tool used to quiet teething babies, to soothe horses during a sandstorm, to make the tent fast against wind and rain, to heal the sick and injured. Magic was the magic of the immortals, which was the magic of the God—the earth-shaking, wind-roaring magic of Akhran's 'efreets; the miraculous comings and goings of Akhran's djinn. This was the magic Khardan understood, much as he understood the rising of the sun, the falling of the rain, the shifting of the dunes.

The dreadful evil magic Khardan had just witnessed was beyond his comprehension. Its terror slammed into the mind like cold steel, shattering reason, spilling courage like blood. Ghuls to Khardan were creatures of the *meddah*'s creation, beings ruled by Sul who could take any human form but were particularly fond of turning themselves into young, beautiful women. Wandering lost and alone in the desert, they would trap unwary travelers into helping them, then slay their rescuers and devour them.

To Mathew, ghuls were forms of demons studied in textbooks. He knew the various means by which they could be controlled, he knew that for all services rendered the living, these undead demanded payment and this must be made in the form of that which they constantly craved—warm, sweet human flesh. The magic of the ghuls, the storm, the sea, the enchantment that had kept him asleep for two months, all of this was familiar to Mathew, and understandable.

But he was in no condition to consider any of this rationally. Khardan was slipping under very fast, and the young wizard had to find some means of rousing him. Had he been stronger, had he been Majiid or Saiyad or any of Khardan's fellow tribesmen, Mathew would have clouted the Calif in the jaw—it being well-known that bloodletting cleared the brain. Mathew considered it. He pictured himself hitting Khardan and discarded the idea with a rueful shake of the head. His blow would have all the force of a girl slapping an over-eager suitor. He lashed out with the only other weapon he had available.

"It seems we should have left you in women's clothing!" Mathew cried bitterly, loud enough to reach Khardan through the pounding of the rain and the howling wind and the blackness that was engulfing him.

The verbal thrust stung. "What did you say?" Khardan turned his head, bleary eyes staring at Mathew.

"Your wife has more courage than either of us," Mathew continued, reaching out a gentle hand to wipe away water that had dripped onto Zohra's bruised face. "She fought them. They had to strike her down."

"What was there to fight?" Khardan asked in a hollow voice, his gaze going to the ghuls sailing their enchanted ship through the storm. "Demons? You said yourself there was nothing to be done against them!"

"That is true, but there are other ways to do battle."

"How? Disguise yourself and run away? That isn't fighting!"

"It's fighting to survive!" Mathew shouted angrily, rising to his feet. His red hair, wet and matted, poured like blood over his shoulders. The wet clothing clung to his slim body, the heavy folds of the soaked fabric kept his secret, hiding the flat chest and the thin thighs that would never be mistaken for a woman's. His face was pale, his green eyes glinted in the glare of the flame and the lightning.

"Survive through cowardice?"

"Like me?" Mathew questioned grimly.

"Like you!" Khardan glared at him through the water streaming down his face. "Why did you save me? You should have let me die! Unless"—he cast a scathing glance at Zohra—"it was her intent to humiliate me further!"

"Me! Me! Me! That's all you think about!" Mathew heard himself screaming, knew he was losing control. He could see several of the *goums*, clinging to the rigging for balance, look in their direction, but he was too caught up in his anger to speak calmly. "We didn't save you! We saved your people. Zohra had a magical vision of the future—"

"Magic!" Khardan shouted in fury and derision.

"Yes, magic!" Mathew screamed back, and saw that here would be the end of it. Khardan would never listen to the telling of Zohra's vision, much less credit it. Angry and exasperated, frightened and alone in his fear, Mathew slumped back down on the slick, wet deck and prepared to let misery engulf him.

"Akhran, save us!" Khardan cried to the heavens, struggling against his bonds. "Pukah! Your master is in need! Come to me, Pukah!"

Mathew didn't even bother to lift his head. He hadn't much faith in this God of the nomads, who seemed more a megalomanic child than a loving father. As for the djinn, he was forced to believe that they *were* immortal beings, sent from the God, but beyond that he hadn't seen that they were of much use. Disappearing into the air, changing themselves to smoke and sliding in and out of lamps, serving tea and sweet cakes when guests arrived . . .

Did Khardan truly expect his God to rescue him? And how? Send those fearsome beings called 'efreets to pluck them off the deck of the ship and carry them, safe and sound, back to the Tel? Did he truly expect to see Pukah—white *pantalons*, turban, and impish smile—trick Auda ibn Jad into setting them free?

"There is no one who can help you!" Mathew muttered bitterly, hunching himself as far back into the shelter of the baggage as possible. "Your God is not listening!"

And what about you? came the voice inside Mathew. At least this man prays, at least he has faith.

I have faith, Mathew said to himself, leaning his head wearily on the side of a basket, cringing as the sea broke over the ship and deluged him with chill water. He closed his eyes, fighting the nausea that was making his head whirl. Promenthas is far away from this land. The powers of darkness rule here. . . .

The powers of darkness . . .

Mathew froze, not daring to move. The idea came to him with such vivid clarity that it seemed to take material form on the deck. So powerful was the impression in his mind that the young wizard opened his eyes and glanced fearfully around the ship, certain that everyone must be staring at him, divining his thoughts.

Auda ibn Jad paced the foredeck, hands clasped behind his back, his eyes looking straight ahead, unseeing, into the storm. His body was rigid, his hands clenched so tightly that they were white at the knuckles. Mathew breathed easier. The Black Paladin must be exerting all his power to maintain control over the ghuls. He wouldn't waste a scrap of it on his captives. And why should he?

We're not going anywhere, Mathew thought grimly. He looked swiftly at the *goums*. Kiber, green around the mouth and nose, clung to the rigging, looking nearly as bad as Mathew felt. Several of the other *goums* were also seasick and lay upon the deck moaning. Those who had escaped the sickness eyed the ghuls warily, shrinking away whenever one of the sailors drew too close. The ghuls, their hunger assuaged, were occupied with outsailing the storm.

Sick and despondent, Khardan slumped against his bonds. The Calif's head hung limply. He had ceased to call upon his God. Zohra, unconscious, was probably the most fortunate person on the ship.

Hunching down amidst the jumble of baskets and chests and the tall ivory jars, Mathew doubled over as though clenched by sickness. Unfortunately, the play-acting became reality. The nausea, forgotten in his initial excitement, rose up and overwhelmed him. His body went hot, then cold. Sweat rolled down his face. Panting, refusing to give way, Matthew closed his eyes and waited grimly for the sick spell to pass.

At last he felt the nausea ease. Reaching into the folds of the caftan, he drew out a small pouch that he'd hurriedly tied around the sash at his waist. He cast a swift, furtive glance over his shoulder. Fingers trembling, he yanked open the pouch and carefully shook the contents out in his lap.

When he and Zohra had accosted the sorceress Meryem—fleeing the battle with the enchanted Khardan—Mathew had taken from her all the magical paraphernalia he could find. Surrounded by soldiers, smoke, and fire, he hadn't bothered to examine them other than a cursory glance before he thrust them into a pouch and concealed the pouch in the folds of his clothing.

That they were objects empowered to work black magic, Mathew hadn't a doubt. He guessed Meryem was devoted to the dark side of Sul since she had used her skill in the arcane arts to attempt murder. Looking at the various articles, unwilling even to touch them, he was overwhelmed with revulsion and disgust—feelings that ran deeper than his sickness; the feelings all wizards of conscience experience in the presence of things of evil.

Mathew's first impulse—and one so strong it nearly overpowered him—was to cast the ensorceled items into the sea. This is what he should do, this is what he had been taught to do.

This was what he could not afford to do.

Feverishly, between bouts of sickness, he examined each object.

There weren't many. Counting on her beauty and charm and the naïveté of the nomads to succumb to these, Meryem hadn't considered herself in any real danger. She had carried a small wand, about six inches in length, designed to be easily concealed in a pouch or tucked into the bosom of a gown. Mathew studied it intently, trying, as he had been taught, to understand its use by analyzing the material out of which it was made. The base of the wand was formed of petrified wood. Set atop that was a piece of black onyx in the form of a cube with the corners ground down. It was a remarkable example of workmanship and obviously the most powerful of the arcane treasures Mathew held. His fingertips tingled when he touched it, a numbing sensation spread up his arm. The wand slipped from his nerveless grasp.

This won't do! Mathew said to himself angrily, beginning to see hope's light flicker and dim. I can overcome this natural aversion, any disciplined wizard can. It's mental, not physical, after all. I've seen the Archmagus demonstrate the use of objects far darker and more foul than these!

Resolutely, he picked up the wand from where it lay on the deck and held it tightly in his hand. The chill sensation spread instantly from his palm up to his elbow, then into his shoulder. His arm began to ache and throb. Biting his lip, fighting the pain, Mathew held onto the wand. He saw, in his mind, Khardan's face and the look of scorn in the man's eyes. I will prove myself to him! I will!

Slowly the chill wore off. Sensation returned to his hand and Mathew discovered he'd been gripping the wand so tightly that the cube's sharp edges had cut into his flesh. Carefully, he dropped it back into the pouch.

Now, if he only knew what it did. . . .

He mentally recounted all the possible enchantments that could be laid upon wands; he considered also the natural powers of black onyx itself. Mathew attempted to come up with the answer as he hurriedly sorted through the other objects. But his mind was clouded with sickness and terror. Every time he heard a footstep on the deck, he started and glanced fearfully over his shoulder, certain he'd been discovered.

"Black onyx," he mumbled to himself, leaning back against a wooden chest, another wave of sickness breaking over him. Closing his eyes, he saw himself in the classroom—the wooden desks with their high stools, meant for copying; the smell of chalk dust; the clatter of the slates; the monotone voice of an aged wizard reciting the text.

*Black onyx. Black for self-protection, the power of disciplined thought. Onyx, possessor of an energy that can be used to control and command, frequently useful in direct intercession with those who dwell on Sul's plane of existence. Petrified wood—that which was once alive, but which is now dead, devoid of life, mocking its form. Often used as base for wands because the wood has the ability to absorb the life of the wielder and transfer it to the stone.*

Add to this the strange design of the wand's onyx tip—not spherical, which would have indicated a harmony with nature, not even a perfect cube that would have represented order. A cube with the corners ground off—order turned to chaos?

So what did it all mean? Mathew shook his head weakly. He couldn't guess. He couldn't think. He gagged and wretched, but there was nothing in his stomach to purge. His body, under the spell of the Black Paladin, had apparently not required food. Knowing he was growing weaker and fearful of discovery, Mathew began to thrust the remaining magical objects, one by one, back into the pouch. They seemed relatively worthless anyway. A couple of healing scrolls, a scroll of minor protection from pointed objects (so much for Zohra and her dagger. Meryem had protected herself against that.), a charm carved in the shape of a phallus that affected male potency (to be used for or against Khardan?), and finally a ring.

Mathew stopped to study the ring. It was made of silver, not very elegant craftsmanship. The stone was a smoky quartz and was obviously designed to be functional rather than ornamental. Of all the objects, this was the only one that did not make the young wizard holding it feel unease or disquiet. He guessed it was the only object whose magic was not harmful. Smoky quartz—protection from harm—*by showing us the dark, we are drawn toward the light.*

It wouldn't help him. If he went through with his plan, it might hinder him. He turned to Zohra, lying near him. They hadn't taken her jewelry from her. Lifting a limp left hand, Mathew slid the ring onto her finger. It looked plain and poor near the other more beautiful jewels. Mathew hoped she wouldn't notice it, at least until he found a chance to whisper some quick word of explanation.

The young wizard closed the pouch and thrust it into the bodice of his gown, near the globe containing the fish. Then he gave himself up to feverish consideration.

This plan is sheer folly. It will end in disaster. What I contemplate risks not only my life, but my immortal soul! No one expects that of me. Not Zohra. Certainly not Khardan. Not even myself.

I am helpless, just as I was when I came to this accursed land and ibn Jad slaughtered my comrades and took me captive.

I stand blindfolded upon the edge of a cliff. Perhaps if I keep perfectly still and do not move, nothing will happen to me! If I start to walk, I will surely fall, for I cannot see where I am going! I am helpless! Helpless!

But that wasn't quite true, and Mathew's soul squirmed uncomfortably. Months ago, when he'd first been cast up onto the shore where the bones of his friends now lay buried in the blood-drenched sand, he *had* been helpless. He'd had no magic, the only weapon with which he could defend himself.

Mathew rested his hand over the pouch, concealed in his clothes. Now he had the power to act. He had the power to take a step that might lead him—lead them all—safely to the bottom of the cliff.

He had the power.

If only he could find the courage.

# Book Five

# THE BOOK
# OF THE
# IMMORTALS II

# Chapter 1

"Poor Sond," commiserated Pukah, flitting through the ethers, the djinn's lamp clasped firmly in his hands. "You're going to be incarcerated in a dark dungeon, in a town that has been dead and buried for centuries. Chained hand and foot, water dripping on your head, rats nibbling your toes—if rats are able to live in such a desolate place, which I hope, for your sake, poor Sond, that they cannot. I truly feel for you, my friend. I truly do. Of course"—Pukah heaved a sigh—"it is nothing, absolutely nothing compared to the torture *I'm* going to be forced to endure as slave to that oyster-headed monster. Oh, granted I'll be free to come and go pretty much as I choose. And it's undoubtedly true that since Kaug has clam shells for brains it is I myself, Pukah, who will likely end up the master and he, Kaug, my slave. Plus, I'll have my beautiful angel with me.

"Ah, Sond! She adores me!" Pukah heaved another sigh, this time a rapturous one. "You should have seen us together in my basket before squid-lips returned. She pulled me down on the bed and began to fan me with her wings. She kissed me again and again and . . . well . . . we are both men of the world aren't we, poor Sond? I dare say you know what she wanted of me.

" 'Ah, my dear,' I said sadly, 'I would more than gladly oblige you, here and now, but this is hardly a romantic setting. That crustacean who calls himself an 'efreet may return at any moment. And then there is my poor friend, Sond, who is in a most dire predicament,' I continued, trying manfully to break free of her embrace. But she continued to have her way with me and what could I do? The basket is only so big, you know, and I didn't want to make too much noise.

I believe I'll tell Kaug I am indisposed tonight. He can find someone else to cook his flounder. As soon as I discover where my white-winged dove is hiding, we will have leisure to finish what we began."

Pausing for breath, Pukah peered through the swirling mists of the immaterial plane.

"Dratted stuff. It's as thick in here as Jaafar's wits. I can't see a thing! Ah, wait. It's clearing. Yes, this is it. I do believe, my poor Sond, that we have arrived."

Setting the *chirak* down at his feet, Pukah looked around with wonder.

"This is Serinda? This is where the immortals are being held . . . prisoner?"

Long ago, so many centuries past that it was not worth remembering, when the great and glorious city of Khandar was nothing but a camel-watering hole, a beautiful city named Serinda flourished.

Few people living now remembered Serinda. Those who did so were generally scholars. The city was marked on the Emperor's maps, and many were the evenings in the Court of Khandar when learned minds debated long and ardently over the mystery of Serinda—a city that existed, supposedly thrived—in the middle of a desert.

Kuo Shou-ching, a man of vast wisdom who had traveled to the Emperor's court from the far eastern lands of Simdari, maintained that the Pagrah desert was not always a desert. It was a known fact in Simdari that the volcano, Galos, erupted about this time, spewing out deadly ash, belching tons of rock into the air, and sending lava—the hot blood of the world's heart—pouring forth.

The eruption was so powerful, claimed Kuo Shou-ching, that a black cloud of ash hung in the sky for a year, obliterating the sun, turning day to night. It was during this time that the city of Serinda died a horrible death, its people perishing from the volcano's foul breath, their bodies and their city buried in ash. Galos continued to belch forth fire and smoke sporadically for years, forever changing the face of the land of Sardish Jardan.

One who disputed the theory of Kuo Shou-ching was Hypatia, a wise woman from the land of Lamish Jardan. She maintained that the city of Serinda was founded *after* the eruption of Galos, that the natives—who were extremely advanced in the ways of science and technology—brought the water of the Kurdin Sea into the desert through a remarkable system of aqueducts and that they literally made the desert bloom. She stated further that they built ships to sail the inland sea, formed by the volcano's eruption, and that they traded with the peoples of the Great Steppes and the populace of Lamish Jardan.

According to Hypatia, the fall of Serinda was brought about by the desert nomads, who feared the city was growing too powerful and would attempt either to absorb them into it or to drive them from their lands. Consequently, the fierce tribes fell upon peaceful Serinda, putting every man, woman, and child to the sword.

Needless to say, this was the theory that found favor with the Emperor, who had become increasingly irritated by reports he had been receiving of the nomads in the Pagrah desert, and who began to think that it might be an excellent thing for the world if the nomads were obliterated from the face of it.

There was likewise the theory of Thor Hornfist, from the Great Steppes, who stated that the city of Serinda and its inhabitants had been eaten by a giant bear. Almost no one paid attention to Thor Hornfist.

The immortals, of course, knew the truth, but being highly diverted by the theories of the mortals, they kept it to themselves.

The history of the dead city of Serinda was not in Pukah's mind as he stared about the place, however. What was in the young djinn's mind was the fact that—for a dead city—Serinda was certainly lively!

"Market day in Khandar is nothing to this!" Pukah gaped.

The streets were so crowded it was difficult to walk through them. They reverberated with noise—merchants extolling, customers bargaining, animals bleating. *Arwats* and coffee houses were doing a thriving business, so packed that their patrons were literally tumbling out the doors and windows. No one seemed to be making any attempt to keep order. Everyone was intent on doing whatever he or she pleased, and pleasure seemed to be Serinda's other name.

Pukah stood in a dark alley between the weapons dealers' and the silk merchants' bazaars. In the length of time it took him to orient himself, the djinn saw two fistfights, a drunk get his face slapped, and a couple kissing passionately in a garbage-infested corner.

Raucous laughter echoed through the streets. Women hanging out of silk curtained windows called out sweet enticements to those below. Gold and silver flowed like water, but not so freely as the wine. Every mark and feature of every race in the world of Sularin was visible—straight black hair, curly golden hair, slanted dark eyes, round blue eyes, skin that was white as milk, skin tanned brown by wind and sun, skin black and glistening as ebony. All jostled together; greeted each other as friend, fell upon each other as enemy; exchanged wine, laughter, goods, gold, or insults.

And every one of them was an immortal.

"Poor Sond!" snarled Pukah, giving the lamp a vicious kick. "Poor Sond! Sentenced to a life of constant merrymaking, lovemaking, drinking, and dicing! While I'm chained, day and night, to a beast of an 'efreet who will no doubt beat me regularly—"

"If he does, it will be no more than you deserve," cried an indignant, feminine voice.

Smoke poured forth from the lamp's spout, coalescing into the handsome, muscular Sond. Bowing gallantly, the djinn extended his hand and assisted another figure to step from the lamp—this one slender and lovely with flowing silver hair and feathery white wings, who glared at Pukah with flashing blue eyes.

"What do you mean—I fanned you with my wings?" Asrial demanded angrily.

"What were you two doing in there?" Pukah demanded back.

"Precisely what we did in your basket!" retorted Asrial.

"Aha!" Pukah cried, raising clenched fists to Sond.

"Nothing!" Asrial shrieked, stamping her bare foot.

"A fight! A fight!" cried several onlookers. Immortals swarmed into the alley, pressing eagerly around Sond and Pukah.

"My money on the big handsome one!"

"Mine on the skinny one with the shifty eyes. He probably has a dagger in his turban."

"You're fools, both of you. My money for the enchanting creature with the wings. My dwelling place is near here, my sweet. A little wine to cool you after your journey—"

Steel flashed in Pukah's hands. "I do have a dagger, and you'll feel it if you don't let go of her!" He caught hold of

Asrial, dragging her out of the arms of a bearded, red-haired barbarian dressed in furs and animal skins.

"There's not going to be any fight," Sond added, his strong hand closing over the arm of the barbarian, who was hefting a wicked-looking, two-handed sword. A handful of gold coins materialized in the djinn's palm. "Here, go have a drink on us. Pukah, put that knife away!" Sond ordered out of the corner of his mouth.

Swearing fealty forever, the barbarian threw his arms around Sond and gave him a hug that nearly squeezed the djinn in two. Then, weaving drunkenly, he and his companions staggered back down the alley and out into the street. Seeing that there was, after all, not going to be a fight, the other onlookers dwindled away in disappointment.

"Well, what *were* you doing in there?" Pukah asked sullenly.

Asrial removed herself from the djinn's grasp. "It was obvious that the 'efreet must have guessed where I was hiding. When I heard him coming, I had no choice but to flee into Sond's lamp. Your friend"—she smiled sweetly and demurely at Sond— "was a perfect gentleman." The blue eyes turned to Pukah, their gaze cool. "More than I can say for you."

"I'm sorry," Pukah said miserably. Suddenly contrite, he cast himself bodily at the angel's feet. "I'm a wretch! I know! So do you, I've mentioned it before!" He groveled in the alley. "Trod on me! Grind me into the dust! I deserve no less! I'm dog meat! The hind end of a camel! The tail of the donkey—"

"I'd enjoy taking you up on that offer," said Sond, kicking at Pukah with his foot. "But there isn't time. We have to find Nedjma and get out of here. After all," added the djinn smoothly, "soon Kaug will command *you* to return!" Grinning, the djinn reached down to pick up his lamp, only to see it vanish beneath his hand. Kaug's laughter could be heard echoing above the noise.

For an instant, Sond paled. Then he shrugged. "It doesn't matter. I'll escape him somehow."

"And how do you think you're going to get free?" Pukah cast a bitter glance at the djinn.

"Do you see any guards?" Sond countered, sauntering down the alley.

"No, but we've only been here a quarter of an hour."

Emerging out of the shadows of the alley, the three blinked in the bright sunlight pouring down upon Serinda.

"I don't think we'll find any guards," said Sond quietly, after a moment's study of their surroundings.

The only ruler in the city of Serinda appeared to be Chaos, with Disorder as his Captain. A victorious army invading a conquered city could have created no greater turmoil in the streets. Every conceivable vice known to mortal flesh was being plied in the streets and houses, the alleys and byways of Serinda.

"You're right," Pukah admitted glumly. "Why don't they all leave, then?"

"Would you?" Sond asked, pausing to watch a dice game.

"Certainly," said Pukah in lofty tones. "I hope *I* know my duty—"

Sond made an obscene noise.

"Pukah!" gasped Asrial, grabbing the djinn, digging her nails into his arm. "Pukah, look!" She pointed. "An . . . an archangel!" Her hand covered her mouth.

"Arch who?"

"Archangel! One . . . one of my superiors!"

Turning, the djinn saw a man, dressed in white robes similar to Asrial's, standing in a doorway. His wings quivering, he was enjoying the favors of a giggling, minor deity of the goddess Mimrim.

Forgetting himself, Pukah sniggered. Asrial flashed him a furious glance.

"He . . . he shouldn't be doing . . . such things!" the angel stammered, a crimson flush staining her cheeks. "Promenthas would be highly displeased. I'll . . . I'll go and tell that angel so, right now!"

Asrial started to push her way through the milling, jostling crowd.

"I don't think that's such a good idea!" Pukah snatched her out from under the nose of a horse whose rider—another barbarian—was urging the animal into the very heart of the mob, heedless of those he knocked down and trampled.

"You told me you angels didn't indulge in that sort of thing," Pukah teased, sweeping Asrial into the shelter of an ironmonger's stand.

"We don't!" Asrial blinked her eyes rapidly, and Pukah saw tears glimmering on her long lashes.

"Don't cry!" Pukah's heart melted. Wiping her tears with

one hand, he took advantage of the situation to slide the other around the angel's slim waist, congratulating himself on dealing adroitly with the wings. "You're too innocent, my sweet child. Knowing their God disapproves, I imagine your higher-ranking angels have learned to keep their love affairs private—"

"Affairs? There are no love affairs! None of us would ever even think of doing . . . such . . . such . . ." Glancing back at the couple in the doorway, her eyes widened. She flushed a deep red, and hastily turned away. "Something's wrong here, Pukah!" she said earnestly. "Terribly wrong. I must leave and tell Promenthas—"

Pukah's heart—that had melted and run through his body like warm butter—suddenly chilled into a lump. "No, don't leave me!" he pleaded. "I mean, don't leave . . . us. What will you tell your God, after all? I agree with you. Something is wrong, but what? There are no guards. It doesn't look like anyone's being held here against his will. Help us find Nedjma," continued Pukah, inspired. "She'll tell us everything, and then you can take that information to Promenthas, just as I'll take it to Akhran."

The thought of being the bearer of such news to his own God considerably lightened the lump that was Pukah's heart. He envisioned Akhran listening in profound admiration as his djinn described the numerous harrowing dangers he—Pukah—faced in the daring rescue of Nedjma and the discovery of the Lost Immortals. He could picture Akhran's reward. . . .

"How can you go to Akhran if you belong to Kaug?" Asrial asked thoughtfully.

"Fish-face?" Pukah was amused. "His brain can deal with only so much at one time. When I'm not in his direct line of sight, he probably doesn't remember that I exist. I'll be able to come and go as I please!"

Asrial appeared dubious. "I'll come with you to find Sond's friend and hear what she has to say. Then I must return to Promenthas. Although I don't quite understand," she added with a tremor in her voice, "how this is going to help Mathew."

"Your protégé is with my master," Pukah said, hugging her comfortingly. "Khardan will protect him. When you have reported to your God and I to mine, then you and I will go find both of them!"

"Oh, Pukah!" Asrial's eyes gleamed through her tears, the light within making them glitter more beautifully than the stars in the heavens, at least to the djinn's enraptured mind. "That would be wonderful! But . . ." The light dimmed. "What about Kaug?"

"Oh damn and blast Kaug!" Pukah snapped impatiently. He was not, in fact, quite as confident as he sounded about the 'efreet's thickness of skull and dullness of wit and did not want to be reminded of him at every turning. "Come on, Sond! Are you going to stand here for the next millennium?"

"I was just considering the best way to search for her." Sond looked bleakly at the hundreds of people milling about in the street. "Perhaps we should split up?"

"Since neither Asrial nor I know what she looks like, that is hardly a good idea," remarked Pukah acidly. "From what you've told me about her, I suggest we just listen for the sound of *tambour* and *quaita* and look for the dancing girls."

Sond's face darkened with anger, and he began to swell alarmingly.

"I'm only trying to be helpful," said Pukah in soothing tones.

Muttering something that fortunately never reached the angel's ears or Asrial might have left them then and there, Sond began to shove his way through the crowd.

Pukah, with a wink at the angel, followed along behind.

# Chapter 2

As it turned out, Pukah's suggestion led them straight to Nedjma. Unfortunately, the djinn never had a chance to gloat over it.

It was with some difficulty that they made their way through the dead city of Serinda—now possibly the liveliest city in this world or the next. The two djinn and the angel were continually accosted by merrymakers seeking to draw them into their revels.

"Thank you," said Pukah, disentangling himself from a throng of Uevin's Gods and Goddesses who were weaving through the streets. Clothed in nothing but grape leaves, they carried jars of wine that they lifted to purple-stained mouths. "But we're a girl short, you see. We're looking for one for my _friend!_" he explained to the countless pairs of glazed eyes focused—more or less—on him. "Yes, that's right. Now if you'd just let us past. . . . No, no! Not you, I'm afraid, my dear. We're hunting a _specific_ girl. But if we don't find her, I'll bring him right back."

"I'm not 'your girl,'" said Asrial coldly, attempting to pry her hand loose from Pukah's.

"Fine!" returned the djinn, exasperated. "When I've rescued my master and your madman from whatever difficulty they've managed to land in without me, then I'm coming straight back here!"

"Mathew isn't mad!" Asrial cried indignantly. "And I don't care where you go—"

"Shhh!" Pukah held up his hand for silence, something practically impossible to achieve amidst the hubbub around them.

"What?"

179

"Listen!"

Rising above the laughter and the giggles and the shouts and the singing, they could hear—very faintly—the shrill, off-key, sinuous notes of the *quaita*, accompanied by the clashing jingle of the *tambour*.

Sond glared at Pukah.

"Very well!" The young djinn shrugged. "Ignore it."

Without saying a word, Sond turned and crossed the street, heading for a building whose shadowy arched doorways offered cool respite from the sun. Roses twined up ornate lattice work, decorating the front. Two djinn in silken caftans lounged around outside the doorways, smoking long, thin pipes. Sond looked neither to the right nor the left, up nor down, but pushed his way past the djinn, who stared after him in some astonishment.

"Eager, isn't he?" said one.

"Must be a newcomer," said the other, and both laughed.

Raising his gaze to the upper levels of the building, Pukah saw several lovely djinniyeh leaning seductively over the balconies, dropping flowers or calling out teasingly to the men passing by in the street below.

Pukah shook his head and glanced at a grave and solemn Asrial. "Are you sure you want to come in here?" he whispered.

"No. But I don't want to stay out here either."

"I guess you're right," Pukah admitted, scowling at the red-bearded barbarian who appeared to be following them. "Well"—he grasped her hand again, smiling as her fingers closed firmly over his—"just keep close to me."

Tugging Asrial after him, Pukah stepped between the two djinn lounging in the doorway.

"Say, friend, bring your own?" commented one, tapping Pukah on the shoulder.

"I know that voice!" Pukah said, studying the other djinn intently. "Baji? Yes, it is!" Pukah clapped the djinn on his muscular forearm. "Baji! I might have known I'd find you here! Didn't you recognize Sond, who just walked past you?"

"Friend, I don't even recognize you," said the djinn, eyeing Pukah calmly.

"Of course, you do! It's me, Pukah!" said Pukah. Then, frowning, "You aren't trying to get out of paying me those five silver *tumans* you owe me, are you, Baji?"

"I said you're mistaken," returned the djinn, a sharp edge

to his voice. "Now go on in and have your fun before things turn ugly—"

"Like your face?" said Pukah, fists clenching.

The shrill, anguished bleep of a *quaita* being cut off in midnote and the clattering of a *tambour* hitting the floor mingled with a female scream and angry, masculine voices raised in argument.

"Pukah!" Asrial gasped. Peering into the shadows of the entryway, she tugged on the djinn's hand. "Sond's in trouble!"

"He's not the only one!" said Pukah threateningly, glaring at his fellow djinn.

"Pukah!" Asrial pleaded. The voices inside were growing louder.

"Don't leave!" Pukah growled. "This will only take a moment."

"Oh, I'll be right here," said the djinn, leaning back against the archway, arms folded across his chest.

"Pukah!" Asrial pulled him along.

Crystal beads clicked together, brushing against Pukah's skin as he passed through them into the cool shadows of the *arwat*. A wave of perfume broke over him, drenching him in sweetness. Blinking his eyes, he tried to accustom himself to a darkness lighted only by the warm glow of thick, jojoba candles. There were no windows. Silken tapestries covered the walls. His foot sank into soft carpeting. Luxurious cushions invited him to recline and stretch out. Flasks of wine offered to make him forget his troubles. Dishes heaped high with grapes and dates and oranges and nuts promised to ease his stomach's hunger, while the most enticing, beautiful djinniyeh he'd ever seen in his life promised to ease any other hungers he might have.

An oily, rotund little djinn slithered his way through the myriad cushions that covered every inch of the floor and, glancing askance at the angel, offered Pukah a private room to themselves.

"A charming little room, *Effendi,* and only ten silver *tumans* for the night! You won't find a better price in all of Serinda!" Catching hold of Pukah's arm, the chubby djinn started to draw him across the room to a bead-curtained alcove.

Pukah jerked his arm free. "What's going on here?" He glanced toward the center of the room, where the shouting was the loudest.

"Nothing, *Effendi*, nothing!" assured the rotund djinn, making another attempt to capture Pukah's arm, urging him onward. "A small altercation over one of my girls. Do not trouble yourself. The *mamalukes* will soon restore peace. You and your lady friend will not be disturbed, I assure you—"

"Pukah! Do something!" Asrial breathed.

Pukah quickly assessed the situation. A flute player sat gagging and coughing on the carpeted floor; it appeared he'd had his *quaita* shoved down his throat. The *tambour* player lay sprawled amid the cushions, unconscious; one of the drummers was attempting to bring him around. Several patrons were gathered together in a circle, shouting and gesticulating angrily. Pukah couldn't see between their broad backs, but he could hear Sond's voice, bellowing from their midst.

"Nedjma! You're coming with me!"

A shrill scream and the sound of a slap was his answer, followed by laughter from the patrons. Irritably shoving away the grasping hands of the rotund *rabat-bashi*, Pukah ordered, "Stay here!" to Asrial and shoved his way through the circle.

As he had expected, Sond stood in the center. The djinn's handsome face was twisted with anger, dark with jealousy. He had hold of the wrist of a struggling djinniyeh with the apparent intent of dragging her out of the building.

Pukah caught his breath, forgetting Asrial, forgetting Sond, forgetting why they were here, forgetting his own name for the moment. The djinniyeh was the most gorgeous creature he'd ever laid eyes on, and there were parts of her on which he longed to lay more than his eyes. From her midriff up, only the sheerest of silken veils covered her body, sliding over her firm, high breasts, slipping from around her white shoulders. Honey gold hair had come loose in her struggle and tumbled about a face of exquisite charm that, even in her indignation, seemed made to be kissed. Numerous long, opaque veils hanging from a jeweled belt at her waist formed a skirt that modestly covered her legs. Noticing several of these veils wound around the heads of the onlookers, Pukah guessed that the djinniyeh's shapely legs, already partially visible, wouldn't be covered long.

"Nedjma!" said Sond threateningly.

"I don't know any Nedjma!" the djinniyeh cried.

"Let go of her! On with the dance! Pay your way like everyone else!"

Pukah glanced behind him and saw the *rabat-bashi* make

a peremptory gesture. Three huge *mamalukes* began to edge their way forward.

"Uh, Sond!" Shoving the unsteady-footed patrons out of his way, Pukah tripped over a cushion and tumbled onto the cleared area of the dance floor. "I think you've made a mistake!" he said urgently. "Apologize to the lady and let's go!"

"A mistake? You bet he's made a mistake." A huge djinn that Pukah didn't recognize and thought must be one of Quar's immortals thrust his body between Sond and the djinniyeh.

"The girl doesn't know you and doesn't want to," the djinn continued, his voice grating. "Now leave!" Pukah saw the djinn's hand go to the sash he wore round his waist.

Sond, his gaze fixed on the djinniyeh, saw nothing. "Nedjma," he said in a pleading, agonized voice, "it's me, Sond! You told me you loved—"

"I said leave her alone!" The large djinn lunged at him.

"Sond!" Pukah leaped forward, trying to deflect the knife. Too late. A quick hand movement, the flash of steel, and Sond was staring down at the hilt of a dagger protruding from his stomach. The huge djinn who had stabbed him stepped back, a look of satisfaction on his face. Slowly, disbelievingly, Sond clutched at the wound. His face twisted in pain and astonishment. Red blood welled up between his fingers.

"Nedjma!" Staggering, he extended the crimson-stained hand to the djinniyeh.

Crying out in horror, she covered her eyes with her jeweled hands.

"Nedjma!" Blood spurted from Sond's mouth. He crashed to the floor at her feet and lay there, still and unmoving.

Pukah sighed. "All right, Sond," he said after a moment. "That was very dramatic. Now get up, admit you were wrong, and let's get out of here."

The djinn did not move.

The patrons were gathering around the djinniyeh, offering comfort and taking advantage of the opportunity to snatch away more of the veils. The huge djinn put his arm around the weeping Nedjma and drew her away to one of the shadowy alcoves. The other patrons, wailing in protest, demanded that the dance continue. Other djinniyeh soon appeared to ease their disappointment.

Clucking to himself about blood ruining his best carpets,

the *rabat-bashi* was pointing at Pukah and demanding payment for damages. The tall *mamalukes*, faces grim, turned their attention to the young djinn.

"Uh, Sond!" Pukah knelt down beside him. Placing his hand on the djinn's shoulder, he shook him. "You can quit making a fool of yourself any time now! If that was Nedjma, she's obviously enjoying herself and doesn't want to be bothered. . . . Sond." Pukah shook the unresponsive body harder. "Sond!"

There was a flutter of white wing and white robes, and Asrial was beside him. "Pukah, I'm frightened! Those men are staring at me! What's Sond doing? Make him get up and let's leave— Pukah!" She caught sight of his face. "Pukah, what's wrong!"

"Sond's dead," said Pukah in a whisper.

Asrial stared at him. "That's impossible," she said crisply. "Is this more of your antics, because—" The angel's voice faltered. "Promenthas have mercy! You're serious!"

"He's dead!" Pukah cried. Almost angrily, he grabbed Sond's shoulder and rolled the body of the djinn over on its back. An arm flopped limply against the floor. The eyes stared at nothing. Pulling the dagger from the wound, the djinn examined it. The blade was smeared with blood. "I don't understand!" He glared around the room. "I want answers!"

"Pukah!" Asrial cried, trying to comfort him, but the *mamalukes* shoved the angel aside. Grasping the young djinn by the shoulders, they dragged him to his feet.

Pukah lashed out furiously. "I don't understand! How can he be dead?"

"Perhaps I can explain," came a voice from the beaded-curtained entryway. "Let him go."

At the sound, the *mamalukes* instantly dropped their hold on the djinn and stepped back from him. The proprietor ceased his lamentations, the patrons swallowed words and wine, several nearly choking themselves, and even this sound they did their best to stifle. No one spoke. No one stirred. The light of the candles flickered and dimmed. The fragrant air was tinged with a sweet, cloying smell.

A cold whisper of air on the back of his neck made Pukah's skin shiver. Reluctantly, unwillingly, but completely unable to help himself, the djinn turned to face the doorway.

Standing in the entrance was a woman of surpassing beauty.

Her face might have been carved of marble by some master craftsman of the Gods, so pure and perfect was every feature. Her skin was pale, almost translucent. Hair, thin and fine as a child's, fell to her feet, enveloping her slender, white-robed body like a smooth satin cape of purest white.

Pukah heard Asrial, somewhere near him, moan. He couldn't help her, he couldn't even see her. His gaze was fixed upon the woman's face; he felt himself slowly strangling.

The woman had no eyes. Where there should have been two orbs of life and light in that classic face were two hollows of empty blackness.

"Let me explain, Pukah," said the woman, entering the room amid a silence so deep and profound that everyone else in the room seemed to have suffocated in it. "In the city of Serinda, through the power of Quar, it is at last possible to give every immortal what he or she truly desires."

The woman looked expectantly at Pukah, obviously waiting for him to question her. "And that is?" he was supposed to say. But he couldn't talk. He had no breath.

Yet his words echoed, unspoken, through the room.

"Mortality," the woman replied.

Pukah shut his eyes to blot out the sight of the empty eye sockets.

"And you are—" he blurted out.

"Death. The ruler of Serinda."

# Chapter 3

In the *arwat*, the immortals resumed their pleasure-taking, giving the body of Sond nothing more than a cool, casual glance or—at most—a look of bitterness for having bled all over the carpet (this from the *rabat-bashi*).

"Get him out of here!" the proprietor muttered to two *mamalukes*, who bent down and—lifting the dead djinn by his flaccid arms—appeared prepared to drag him unceremoniously out the door.

"The back door," specified the *rabat-bashi*.

"No one's taking Sond anywhere," declared Pukah, drawing a dagger from the sash around his slim waist. "Not until I have some answers."

Dropping Sond's arms, which fell with a lifeless thud on the floor of the *arwat*, the two immortal *mamalukes* drew their daggers, eager grins on their faces.

"Pukah, no!" cried Asrial, hurling herself at the young djinn.

Gently he pushed her away, his eyes on the knife-wielding slaves who were circling, one to either side of him, steel flashing in their hands.

"You there!" cried the proprietor distractedly, gesturing to another *mamaluke*, "roll up that other carpet! It's the best one in the house. I can't afford to have it ruined as well. Quickly! Quickly! Excuse me, sir"—this to Pukah—"if you could just lift your foot for a moment? Thank you. It's the blood, you see, it doesn't wash—"

"Blood!" Asrial put her hands to her head in an effort to concentrate. "This is impossible. Our bodies are ethereal. They cannot bleed, they cannot die!" Lowering her hands, she looked at Death. "I don't believe this," the angel stated

186

flatly. "Sond is *not* dead! Not even you can make the immortal mortal. Pukah, stop that nonsense."

Somewhat startled, Pukah glanced at her, then at Sond lying on the floor. Slowly he lowered his dagger. "That's true," he said. "Sond can't be dead."

"You are both young," said Death, turning the empty eye sockets toward them, "and you have not lived long among humans—especially you," she said to Asrial. "You are right, of course. Sond is not dead—at least not as mortals would term it. But he might as well be. When the sun dawns tomorrow, this djinn will regain his life—but nothing else."

"What do you mean?" Pukah glared at the cold and lovely woman suspiciously. "What else is there?"

"His identity. His memory. He will have no knowledge of who he is, whom he serves. He will be—as it were—newborn and will take on whatever identity occurs to him at the moment. He will forget everything. . . ."

"Even the fact that he is immortal," said Asrial slowly.

Death smiled. "Yes, child, that is true. He will have the mortal hunger to live life to the fullest. As are mortals, he will be driven—blessed and cursed with the knowledge that it must all come to an end."

"This is why the immortals are lost to the world," realized Pukah, staring at Sond. "They no longer remember it. And that is why Nedjma did not know my poor friend."

"She is no longer Nedjma, nor has she been for a long time now. Only a few nights ago she died at the hands of a jealous lover. Days before that, she was accidentally killed in a street brawl. No one in this city"—the hollow eyes turned to Asrial—"remains alive from dusk to dawn."

A hoarse cry interrupted them. The djinn who had stabbed Sond staggered out of the inner room, clutching his throat with one hand, a half-emptied goblet of wine in the other. Falling to the floor, he writhed in agony for a few seconds, then his body went rigid. The cup fell from his hand, rolling across the carpet, leaving a trail of spilled wine. Nedjma swept out from the room. Standing above the body, she deliberately brushed a fine, white powder from her delicate fingers. "Let this be a lesson to all who think they own me!" Tossing her honey-colored hair, she vanished behind another beaded curtain.

"Wine . . . it stains are almost as bad as blood," whined the proprietor, wringing his hands.

Death watched appreciatively, her lips slightly parted as though she were sipping the dead djinn's life.

"So," said Pukah to himself. "I am beginning to understand. . . ." His hand went to the tourmaline amulet Kaug had given him. As he touched it, he thought he saw Death flinch. The hollow eyes met his, a fine line marring the marble smoothness of the white brow.

Tucking his dagger into his sash, Pukah crossed his arms and rocked back on his heels. "There is one who will leave this city at dusk or dawn or whenever I choose. Me." He held up the amulet that he wore around his neck. "My master cannot do without me, you see, and so has insured my return."

"What is this?" Death peered closely at the tourmaline, the coldness of her eyeless gaze causing Pukah's flesh to shiver and crawl. "This goes against our agreement! I am to have all who come here! Who is this master of yours?"

"One Kaug, an 'efreet, in the service of Quar," answered Pukah glibly.

"Kaug!" Death's brow furrowed. The shadow of her anger descended upon the *arwat*, causing the *rabat-bashi* to hush his complainings, and the guests to hastily withdraw to whatever dark, obscure corners they could find.

Pukah saw Asrial staring at him pleadingly, begging him to take her from this place. The thought that she might die and forget her protégé must be terrifying to her. What she didn't realize—and Pukah had—was that *he* could leave, but she couldn't. Death would never allow it. *I am to have all who come here*. The only way for them to escape, the only way for all the immortals trapped here to escape was Pukah's way. Pukah had a plan.

Not only will *Hazrat* Akhran reward me, Pukah thought blissfully. All the Gods in the Jewel of Sul will be forever indebted to me! I will be an immortal among immortals! Nothing in this world or in the heavens will be too good for me! One palace—hah! I will have twenty palaces—one given by each God. I will spend the heat of the summer in a vast stone fortress on the Great Steppes. I will winter in a grass hut of thirty or forty rooms on one of those little tropical islands in Lamish Aranth, sleeping on the feathery wings of a grateful, loving angel . . .

Seeing Death's pallid hand reaching for the amulet, Pukah hastily clamped his fingers over it and took a step backward.

"Rest assured my master reverences you most highly, my lady," Pukah said humbly. " 'Death is second to Quar in my esteem.' Those were the 'efreet's very words."

" 'Second to Quar!' " Death's eyeless sockets grew dark as endless night.

"Quar is becoming the One, the True God," Pukah said apologetically. "You must concede that. The number of humans worshiping Him grows daily."

"That may be true," Death said sharply, "but in the end their bodies are mine! That is the promise of Sul!"

"Ah, but didn't you hear?—" Pukah stopped, biting his tongue, lowering his eyes, and glancing at Death from beneath the lids—"but then I guess you didn't. If you'll excuse me, my lady, I really should be getting back. Kaug is dining on boiled ray tonight, and if I'm not there to remove the sting, my master will—"

"Hear what?" questioned Death grimly.

"Nothing, I assure you, my lady." Grabbing hold of Asrial's hand, Pukah began to sidle past Death toward the door. "It is not my place to reveal the secrets of the Most Holy Quar—"

Death raised a pale, quivering finger and pointed at Asrial. "You may have an Amulet of Life, djinn, but this feathered beauty here does not! Tell what I need to know, or she will be struck down before your eyes this instant!"

Death gestured, and the two *mamalukes*, their daggers still in hand, looked with eager, burning eyes at the angel. Asrial caught her breath, pressing her hands over her mouth and shrinking next to Pukah. The djinn put his arm around her reassuringly. The foxish face was pale, however, and he was forced to swallow several times before he could speak.

"Do not be hasty, my lady! I will tell you everything, for it is obvious to me now that you have been the victim of a trick played upon you by the God. I assume that it was Quar who schemed to trap the immortals by laying this spell upon the city of Serinda?"

Death did not reply, but Pukah saw the truth in the face whose marble facade was beginning to crack. Hurriedly he continued, "Quar gave you the delightful task of casting this spell over the city, knowing—as He did—that your greatest pleasure in life comes from watching others leave it?"

Again, though Death did not answer, Pukah knew he was right and spoke with increasing confidence, not to mention a hint of smugness. "Thus, Lady, Quar rid the world of the immortals—*all* the immortals, if you take my meaning. Your grave and lovely self included."

"Pukah! What are you saying?" Asrial glanced up at him in alarm, but the djinn hugged her into silence.

"For you see, O Sepulchral Beauty, Quar has promised all who follow him *eternal life!*"

Death sucked in a deep breath. Her hair rose around her in a wrathful cloud, a cold blast of fury hit those in the *arwat*, causing the strongest slave to tremble in fear. Asrial hid her face in her hands. Only Pukah remained confident, sure of himself and his glib tongue.

"I have proof," he said, forestalling what he was certain would be Death's next demand. "Only a few months ago, Quar ordered the Amir of Kich to attack bands of nomads living in the Pagrah desert. Were you present at the battle, Lady?"

"No, I was—"

"Busy here below," Pukah said, nodding knowingly. "And your presence was sorely missed, Lady, I can tell you, particularly by the jackals and hyenas who count upon your bounty. For hardly anyone died in that battle. The Imam of Quar ordered them taken alive! Why? So that his God could grant them eternal life and thereby be assured of eternal followers! Before that was the battle in Kich—"

"I was present then!" Death said.

"Yes, but whom did you take? A fat Sultan, a few of his wives, assorted wazirs. Piffle!" Pukah said with a disdainful sniff. "When there was an entire city filled with people who could have been raped, murdered, burned, stoned—the survivors left to fend off disease, starvation—"

"You are right!" said Death, her teeth clenching in a skull-like grimace.

"Far be it from me to betray *Hazrat* Quar, for whom I have a high respect," added Pukah humbly, "but I have long been one of your most ardent admirers, my lady. Ever since you took my former master—a follower of Benario—in the most original fashion—his body parts cut off one at a time by the enraged owner of the establishment my poor master took it into his head to rob without first checking to make certain that no one was at home. That is why I have revealed to you

Quar's plot to remove you forever from the world of the living and keep you here below, playing games."

"I will show you how games are played!" Seething, Death approached Pukah, the hollow of her empty eyes seeming to grow larger, encompassing the djinn.

"Show me?" Pukah laughed lightly. "Thank you, but I really don't have time for such frivolities. My master cannot do without—" It suddenly occurred to the djinn that Death was drawing uncomfortably near. Letting go of Asrial, he tried to back up and tumbled over a hubble-bubble pipe. "What have I to do with this? Nothing!" He scrambled to his feet. "If I were you, now, Lady, I would leave this city immediately and fly to the world above. No doubt the Amir is riding to battle this very instant! Spears through chests, sword slicing through flesh. Arms ripped from their sockets, entrails and brains on the ground! Tempting picture, isn't it?"

"Yes indeed! So Quar has sent you here to frighten me—" Death stalked him.

"F-frighten you?" Pukah stammered, knocking over a table and small chair. "No, Lady," he said with complete honesty, "I assure you, that frightening you is the furthest thing from my— his mind!"

"What does He want? His immortals returned? Eternal life! We'll see what Sul has to say about this!"

"Yes, yes!" gabbled Pukah, backed up against a wall, his hand clutching the amulet. "Go talk to Sul! Wonderful person, Sul. Have you ever met Him?"

"I intend to speak with Him," said Death, "but first I will send Quar his messenger back in the form of a skeleton to remind him of whom he is trying to cheat!"

"You can't touch me!" said Pukah quickly, raising the amulet in front of Death's baleful, empty eyes.

"No," said Death softly, "but I can her!"

Death vanished and reappeared. The pale, cold hands were suddenly clasped around Asrial's shoulders, the angel caught fast in Death's grip.

The djinn stared into the angel's blue, despairing eyes and wondered what had gone wrong. It had been such a simple, beautiful plan! Get Death out of the city. Set her on Quar. . . . "I'll make a bargain with you," offered Pukah desperately.

"A bargain?" Death stared at him suspiciously. "I have had enough of your Master and His bargains!"

"No," said Pukah solemnly, "this would be . . . just between you and me. In exchange for her"—he looked at Asrial, his soul in his eyes, his voice softening—"I will give you my amulet—"

"No, Pukah, no!" Asrial cried.

"—and I will remain in the city of Serinda," the djinn continued. "You boast that no one lives from dawn to dusk in this city. I challenge that claim. I say that I am cleverer than you. No matter what form you choose to take, I can avoid falling your victim."

"Ha!" snorted Death.

"No one shall goad *me* into any quarrel," averred Pukah. "No woman will slip poison into *my* drink!"

"And if I win, what do I get out of this bargain, beyond the pleasure of seeing you stretched lifeless at my feet?"

"I will give you not only myself, but my master as well."

"Kaug?" Death sneered. "Another immortal? As you can see, I am well supplied with those already."

"No." Pukah drew a deep breath. "You see, Kaug is not my master so much as he is my jailer. Sond and I were captured by the 'efreet and forced to do his bidding. My true master is Khardan, Calif of the Akar—"

"Pukah, what are you saying?" cried Asrial, appalled.

"Khardan!" Death appeared interested. "Akhran holds that particular mortal in high favor. He keeps close watch upon him. I cannot get near. You are saying that if I win—"

"—the eyes of Akhran will be looking elsewhere."

"You know that now your mortal, Khardan, stands in dire peril?" Death inquired coolly.

"No," said Pukah, looking somewhat uncomfortable, "I didn't. It's been some time, you see, since I was captured, and I—"

"Not only him, but those with him," said Death, her eyes on Asrial.

Clasping her hands, the angel gazed at the pale woman beseechingly. "Mathew?" she whispered.

"We will speak of this later, you and I," said Death soothingly, running her cold hand over Asrial's silver hair. "Very well," she added, "I accept your bargain, Pukah. Hand me the amulet."

"But you haven't heard the rest of the deal," protested the young djinn in offended dignity. "The part about what *you* give me if I win."

Death glanced around the *arwat*. "If he wins!" she repeated. Everyone burst into shouts of laughter, the proprietor guffawing until he lost his breath and had to be pounded on his back by one of the slaves. "Very well," said Death, wiping tears of mirth that sprang horribly from the empty sockets. "If you win, Pukah, I will give you—what? Your freedom, I suppose. That's what all you djinn want."

"Not only my freedom," said Pukah cunningly. "I want the freedom of every immortal in the city of Serinda!"

The laughter in the *arwat* suddenly ceased.

"What did he say?" puffed the *rabat-bashi*, who—between trying to breathe and getting thumped on the back—hadn't been able to hear clearly.

"He says he wants us freed!" growled an immortal of Zhakrin's, eyeing Pukah grimly.

"Freed!" said a cherubim, staggering out of a bead-curtained room, a goblet in her hand. "Free to go back to a life of drudgery!"

"A life of slavery," slurred one of Quar's 'efreets from where it lay comfortably beneath a table.

"Death take him!" cried Uevin's God of War.

"Death! Death!" chanted everyone in the *arwat*, rising to their feet, fingering their weapons.

"Free? Did I say free?" Sweat trickled down from beneath Pukah's turban. "Look, we can discuss this—"

"Enough!" Death raised her hands. "I agree to his terms. Pukah, if you are alive by sunset tomorrow"—hoots and howls of derision greeted this. Clenching her raised fists, Death commanded silence—"then I swear by Sul that the spell over the city of Serinda will be broken. If, however, the failing light of the sun casts its rays over your body as it lies upon its bier, Pukah, then your master, Khardan, is mine. And his end will be truly terrible"—Death looked at Asrial—"for he will be slain by one whom he trusts, one who owes him his life."

Asrial stared at Death in horror. "Not—" She couldn't finish.

"I fear so, child. But—as I said—we will discuss that

later. Hear me!" Death lifted her voice, and it seemed that the entire city of Serinda fell silent. "I owe allegiance to no God or Goddess. I have no favorites. Whatever else may be said of me, I am impartial. I take the very young. I take the very old. The good cannot escape me, neither can the sinner. The rich with all their money cannot keep me from their doors. The magi with all their magic cannot find a spell to defeat me. And so I will have no favorites here. Pukah will have this night to prepare his defense. The people of Serinda will have this night to prepare their attack.

"Pukah, this night you may keep your amulet and freely walk the city. Whatever weapon you find will be yours. Tomorrow, at the Temple in the city plaza, at the dawning of the new day, you will deliver to me the amulet and the contest will begin. Is this agreed?"

"Agreed," said Pukah through lips that, despite his best efforts, trembled. He couldn't meet Asrial's despairing eyes.

Death nodded, and the people resumed their frenetic activities, everyone making eager preparations for tomorrow's deadly contest.

"And now, child, you want to see what is happening in the world of humans?" asked Death.

"Yes, oh yes!" cried Asrial.

"Then come with me." Death's hair lifted as though stirred by a hot wind. Floating around her, it enfolded the angel like a shroud.

"Pukah?" Asrial said, hesitating.

"Go ahead," said the djinn, trying to smile. "I'll be fine, for a while at least."

"You will see him again, child," Death said, putting her arm around Asrial and drawing her away. "You will see him again. . . ."

The two vanished. Pukah slumped down into a nearby chair, ignoring the snarls, the hostile stares. Gulping slightly at the sight of daggers, knives, swords, and other cutlery that was making a sudden appearance, he turned his head to look out the window. He was not cheered by the sight of an imp pushing a grindstone down the street; the demon was besieged by a mob of immortals brandishing weapons to be sharpened.

Seeing his reflection in the window, Pukah found it more comforting to look at his own foxish face. "I'm smarter than Death," he said, seeking reassurance.

The unusually gloomy reflection made no answer.

# Book Six

# THE BOOK
# OF QUAR II

# Chapter 1

Far from the Kurdin Sea, where the ship of ghuls sailed amid its own storm; far from where Mathew struggled against inner darkness; far from Serinda, where a djinn battled against Death; another young man fought a battle of his own, though on much different ground.

Quar's *jihad* had begun. In the first light of dawn, the city of Meda, in northern Bas, fell to the troops of the Amir without putting up more resistance than was necessary for the citizens to be able to meet each other's eyes and say, "We fought but were defeated. What could we do? Our God abandoned us."

And it did seem as if this were true. In vain the priests of Uevin called for the God of War to appear in his chariot and lead the battle against the armies of the Emperor. In vain the priestesses of the Earth Goddess called for the ground to open and swallow the Amir's soldiers. There came no answer. The oracles had been silent many months. Uevin's immortals had disappeared, leaving their human supplicants to cry their pleas to deaf ears.

Uevin's ears were not deaf, though he often wished they were. The cries of his people rent his heart, but there was nothing he could do. Bereft of his immortals, losing the faith of his people, the God grew weaker by the day. Ever before him was the vision of Zhakrin and Evren, their shriveled and starved bodies writhing upon the heavenly plane, then blowing away like dust in the wind. Uevin knew now, too late, that the Wandering God, Akhran, had been right. Quar was intent on becoming the One, the Only. Uevin hid inside his many-columned dwelling, expecting every moment to hear Quar's voice summon him forth to his own doom. The God, quaking and trembling, knew there was nothing he could do to stop Quar.

The army of Meda—outnumbered, beset by dissension within their ranks, aware that their Governor was hastily packing his valuables and fleeing through the back wall of the city as they prepared to defend its front—fought halfheartedly and, when called upon to surrender, did so with such promptness that the Amir remarked to Achmed drily that they must have ridden forth to battle with white flags in their saddlebags.

Achmed never had a chance to fight—a fact that made him burn with disappointment. Not that he would have seen battle this day anyway. The young man rode with the cavalry and they would not be used today unless the Medans proved more stubborn than was expected. Chafing with inaction, he sat his magical horse high on a ridge overlooking the plains on which the two armies rushed together like swarms of locusts.

Achmed shifted in his saddle, his gaze darting to every boulder and bush, hoping to see some daring Medan raise up out of the cover with bow poised and arrow at the ready, endeavoring to end the war by killing the general. Achmed saw himself hurling his own body protectively in front of the Amir (the king's bodyguards having fled, the cowards!). He saw the arrow fly, he felt it graze his flesh (nothing serious). He saw himself draw his sword and dispatch the Medan. Cutting off the man's head, he would present it to the Amir. Refusing all assistance, he would say, with eyes modestly downcast, "The wound? A scratch, my lord. I would gladly be pierced by a thousand arrows if it would serve my king."

But the Medans selfishly refused to cooperate. No assassin crouched in the bushes or crept among the rocks. By the time Achmed saw himself, in his vision, carried away on a shield, the Medans were throwing their own shields on the ground and handing over their weapons to the victors.

When the battle had ended, the Amir rode up and down the long line of prisoners that were drawn up outside the city walls. Most of the Medans stood with heads bowed, in sullen or fearful silence. But occasionally Achmed—riding at Qannadi's side—saw a head raise, a man glance up at the king out of the corner of an eye. The Amir's stern and rigid face never changed expression, but his eyes met those of the prisoner, and there was recognition and promise in that glance. The man would look back down again at his feet, and Achmed knew he had seen someone in Qannadi's pay—a worm the Amir had purchased to nibble at the fruit from the inside.

Achmed heard mutterings of disgust from the Amir's body-guards, who rode behind him. They, too, knew the meaning of that exchange of glances. Like most soldiers, they had no use for traitors, even when the traitors were on their side.

The young man's face burned, and he hung his head. He felt the same stirrings of disgust for the treacherous who had betrayed their own people, yet all he could ask himself was, "What is the difference between them and me?"

The inspection came to an end. Qannadi announced that the Imam would speak to the prisoners. The Amir and his staff rode off to one side. Achmed, still brooding, took his place beside and a few steps behind Qannadi.

A creaking of the Amir's leather saddle and a slight cough caused Achmed to raise his head and look at the man. For a brief moment a warm smile flickered in the dark eyes.

"You came to me out of love, not for money," was the silent message.

How had Qannadi divined what he was thinking? Not that it mattered. This wasn't the first time their thoughts had ridden together over the same path. Feeling comforted, Achmed allowed himself to accept the answer. Knowing it was true in part, he could feel satisfied with it and firmly shut out any efforts by his conscience to question it further.

In the past month that they had been together, Achmed had come to love and respect Qannadi with the devotion of a son—giving to the Amir the affection he would have been glad to give to his own father, had Majiid been the least bit interested in accepting it. Each filled perfectly the void in the other's heart. Achmed found a father, Qannadi the son he'd been too busy fighting wars to raise.

The Amir was careful not to let his growing affection for the young man become obvious, knowing that Yamina watched her husband jealously. Her own child stood to inherit the Amir's position and wealth, and neither she nor her mincing peacock of a son would hesitate to send a gift of almonds rolled in poisoned sugar to one who might pose a threat. Long ago, a pretty young wife of whom Qannadi had been especially fond and who was to have delivered a baby near the same date as Yamina's had died in a similar manner. Such things were not unusual in court, and Qannadi accepted it. But it was one reason, perhaps, that he afterward exhibited no great affection for any of his wives.

The Amir gave Achmed the rank of Captain, put him in charge of training both men and horses in the cavalry, and took care—while they were in court—to speak to him as he would any other soldier in his army. If he spent a lot of time with the cavalry, it was only natural, since they were the key to victory in many instances and required much training in advance of the war against Bas. Yamina's single, jealous eye saw nothing to give her concern. She sent her son back to the glittering court in Khandar, both of them happy in the knowledge that generals often met with fatal mishaps.

Qannadi himself had no illusions. He would have liked to make Achmed his heir, but he feared that the young man would not last even a month in the palace of the Emperor. Honesty, loyalty—these were qualities a king rarely saw in those who served him. Qualities the Amir saw in Achmed. The Amir didn't attempt to instruct the young man in the dangerous machinations of court intrigue. The nomad's blend of brute savagery and naive innocence delighted Qannadi. Achmed would not hesitate to hack to bits a rival in a fair fight, but he would allow himself to be devoured by ants before he would slyly murder that same rival. What was worse, Achmed fondly believed that every man worthy of being called a man abided by the same code of honor. No, he wouldn't last long in the court at Khandar.

Let my painted-eyed, painted-lipped son grovel at the Emperor's feet and smile when His Imperial Majesty kicks him. I have Achmed. I will make of him an honorable, dutiful soldier for Quar. For myself, I will have one person who will fight at my side, who will be near me when I die. One person who will truly mourn my passing.

But the ways of Quar are not the ways of Akhran. Qannadi himself was naive in thinking he could uproot the thorny desert Rose, bring it into the stifling atmosphere of court, and expect it to thrive. The cactus would have to send down tough new roots in order even to survive.

The Imam had watched the battle from the protection of a palanquin borne on the long journey from Kich to Meda by six sweating, struggling priests of Quar. At the Amir's signal, they hauled the covered litter out onto the plains before the city walls that were lined with Medans waiting in hushed, breathless silence to know their fate.

Feisal emerged from the palanquin, his thin hand pushing aside the golden curtains decorated with the head of the ram. A change had come over the Imam since his illness. No one knew what had happened to him, except that he had come very close to death and had been—according to his awestricken servant—healed by the hand of the God. Feisal's body, always slender from fasting, now appeared emaciated. His robes hung from his spare frame as they might have hung from a bare-limbed tree. Every bone, every vein, every muscle and tendon was visible in his arms. His face was skull-like, with cadaver-ous hollows in the cheeks, the sunken eyes appeared huge.

These eyes had always glowed with holy zeal, but now they burned with a fire that appeared to be the only fuel the man needed to keep the body functioning. The sun was blazing hot on the plains in midsummer. Achmed sweated in the leather uniform trousers worn by the cavalry. Yet he shivered when the Imam began to speak, and, glancing at Qannadi, he saw the black hair on the sunburned arms rise; the strong jaw—barely visible beneath the man's helm—tighten. The Imam's presence had always inspired discom-fort. Now it inspired terror.

"People of Meda!" Feisal's voice must have been ampli-fied by the God. It was hardly creditable that the lungs in that caved-in chest could draw air enough to breathe, let alone to shout. Yet his words could be clearly heard by all in Meda. It seemed to Achmed that they must be heard by every person in the world.

"You were not this day defeated by man," the Imam called out. He paused, drawing a deep breath. "You were defeated by Heaven!" The words rolled over the ground like thunder; a horse shied nervously. The Amir cast a stern glance behind him and the soldier quickly brought his animal under control.

"Do not grieve over your loss! Rather, rejoice in it, for with defeat comes salvation! We are children in this world and we must be taught our lessons of life. Quar is the father who knows that sometimes we learn best through pain. But once the blow has been inflicted, He does not continue to whip the child, but spreads His arms"—the Imam suited his action to his words—"in a loving embrace."

Achmed thought back to when he'd heard these—or similar—words, back to that dark time in prison. Clenching his hands over the saddle horn to keep himself calm, he wished desperately this would end.

"People of Meda! Renounce Uevin—the weak and imper-fect God who has led you down a disastrous path, a path that could have cost you your lives had not Quar been the merciful father that He is. Destroy the temples of the false God Uevin!

Denounce His priests! Melt down His sacred relics, topple His statues and those of the immortals who served Him. Open your hearts to Quar, and He will reward you tenfold! You will prosper! Your families will prosper! Your city will become one of the brightest jewels in the crown of the Emperor! And your immortal souls will be assured of eternal peace and rest!"

Growing light-headed in the heat, Achmed imagined the Imam's words leaping from the man's mouth in tongues of flame that set the dry grass ablaze. The flames spread from the priest to the prisoners lined up against the wall and lit them on fire. The blaze burned hotter and hotter until it engulfed the city. Achmed blinked and licked thirstily at a trickle of sweat that dropped into his mouth. The plains reverberated with the sound of cheering, started on cue by the Amir's forces and picked up eagerly by the defeated Medans.

Feisal had no more to say, which was well, since he could never have been heard. Exhausted, drained, he turned to make his way back to the palanquin, his faithful servant hurrying forward to assist the priest's feeble steps. At the city walls, enthusiastic crowds shoved open the wooden gates. Chants of "Quar, Quar, *Hazrat* Quar" reverberated across the plains.

Unexpectedly the Medan prisoners broke ranks and surged toward the Imam. Qannadi acted swiftly, sending his cavalry forward with a wave of his hand. Riding with the others, Achmed moved his horse in a defensive position around the priest's palanquin. Sword drawn, he had orders to hit with the flat of the blade first, the cutting edge second.

Achmed's horse was engulfed by a tide of humanity, but these men were not out for blood. Risking life and limb amid the horses of the cavalry, they sought only to touch the palanquin, to kiss the curtains. "Your blessing on us, Imam!" they cried, and when Feisal parted the curtains and extended his bony arm, the Medans fell to their knees; many had tears streaming down their dust-streaked faces.

Feisal's dark, burning eyes looked at Qannadi, giving a wordless command. The Amir, lips pressed grimly together, ordered his men to fall back a discreet distance. The Medans lifted the Imam's palanquin onto their own shoulders and bore him triumphantly through the city gates. The roar of the crowd must have been heard by the sorrowing Uevin as far away as heaven.

It's all over! thought Achmed with relief and turned to share a smile with his general.

Qannadi's face was stern. He knew what was coming.

# Chapter 2

Achmed crouched in the shadow of his tent, eating his dinner and watching the sun's last rays touch the grass of the prairie with an alchemist's hand, changing the green to gold. The young man ate alone. He had made few acquaintances among the Amir's troops, no real friends. The men acknowledged his skill in riding and his way with horses, even magical ones. They learned from him: how to sit a galloping horse by pressing the thighs against the flanks, leaving hands free to fight instead of clutching the reins; how to use the animals' bodies for cover; how to leap from the saddles of running horses and pull themselves back up again. They learned how to keep the horses calm before a battle, how to keep them quiet when slipping up on the enemy, how to hush them when the enemy is somewhere out there, preparing to slip up on you. They accepted Achmed's teaching, though he was younger than most of them. But they never accepted *him*.

Although accustomed to the close comradeship of the friends in his father's tribe, most of whom were not only friends but relatives in one way or another, Achmed was not bothered by the lack of friends among the troops. The month in prison had hardened him to isolation; cruel usage at the hands of his tribesmen had caused him to welcome it.

Few others were stirring about the camp. The guards walking the perimeter looked dour and put-upon, for they could hear the shouts and laughter drifting up over the city walls and knew that their comrades were enjoying themselves. The Amir had given each man a sackful of the Emperor's coins with orders to spend freely—the first sign that Quar was raining gold down upon Meda. The troops were commanded to be friendly and as well behaved as could be expected; dire punishments were threatened for those who raped, looted, or in any other way harmed a Medan. The Amir's household guards manned the streets to maintain order.

Achmed could have been among those disporting themselves in the city, but he chose not to. The Medans, who had surrendered their city to Heaven without a fight, disgusted him and, if truth be told, disturbed him more than he could admit.

The sun's gold was darkening to dross, and Achmed was thinking about rolling himself in his blanket and losing himself in sleep when one of Qannadi's servants appeared and told him that all officers were ordered into the Amir's presence.

Hurrying through the city streets, Achmed saw no signs of rising rebellion or any other threat, and he wondered what this was about. Perhaps nothing more than joining the Amir for a victory dinner. Achmed's heart sank. There was no way he could excuse himself, yet he didn't feel up to celebrating. The servant did not lead him to the Governor's Palace, however, but to an unexpected place—a large temple-like structure located in the center of a plaza.

A broken statue of Uevin lay on the paving stones. North of the plaza stood the columned building that was—Achmed realized from his talks with Qannadi—the seat of Medan government known as the Senate. Standing on top of the smashed remains of the God Uevin was a huge golden ram's head that had been carted from Kich for precisely this purpose. (When, days later, the Amir's troops moved on southward, the golden ram's head would be reloaded into the cart and hauled off to do similar service in future conquered cities.)

The plaza was crowded with Medans, talking in low voices. On its outer perimeter, the Amir's elite household guards stood stern-faced and implacable, the tips of their spears gleaming in the sun's afterglow. The crowd kept its distance from the soldiers, Achmed noticed. Taking advantage of this path that had formed between the people and the guards, the young man followed the servant to the steps leading up to a marble-columned portico.

A throne from the Governor's Palace had been carried

here by the Amir's servants and stood before the Senate's entryway. Qannadi sat on the throne, looking out onto the crowd gathered before him. He had changed from his battle armor into a white caftan, cloaked with a purple, gold-trimmed robe. His head was bare, except for a crown of laurel leaves, worn because of some silly custom of the Medans. It was already dark within the confines of the Senate porch. Torchbearers stood on either side of Qannadi, but they had, for some reason, not yet been given the order to light their brands. Looking intently at the Amir's face as he ascended the stairs, Achmed saw the firm set of the jaw, the shadows carved in the face, making Qannadi appear grim and unyielding in the fading light.

Next to Qannadi stood Feisal. No torchlight needed for him, the fire in the priest's eyes seemed to light the plaza long after the sun's glow had faded. Hoping to lose himself in the gathering gloom, Achmed took his place at the end of the line of officers who stood pressed against the Senate wall behind the Amir's throne. The young man wondered briefly how his absence had been noticed, when suddenly he felt the fiery gaze of the Imam sear his flesh. Feisal had been waiting for him! The priest raised his thin hand and beckoned for Achmed to approach.

Startled and unnerved, Achmed hesitated, looking to Qannadi. The Amir glanced at him from the corner of his eye and nodded slightly. Swallowing a knot in his throat, Achmed edged his way in front of his fellow officers, who stared straight out over the heads of the crowd. Why should I be afraid? he scolded himself, irritated at his clammy palms and the twisting sensation in his bowels. Perhaps it was the unusual silence of the people, who stood quietly as darkness washed slowly over them. Perhaps it was the unusually rigid stance and serious mien of the officers and guards. Perhaps it was the sight of Qannadi. Drawing closer, Achmed saw that the firmness of the man's jaw was being maintained by a strong effort of will, the merciless face beneath the leafy crown was the face of a man Achmed didn't know.

Feisal, though he had sent for the young man, took no further notice of him.

"Stand here," the Amir ordered coldly, and Achmed did as he was commanded, taking his place at Qannadi's right hand.

"Light the torches," was Qannadi's next order, and the

brands being held behind him sputtered into flame, as did other torches carried by those in the crowd in the plaza. "Bring forth the prisoners. You, guards, clear a space there." He gestured at the foot of the steps. The guards used the hafts of their spears to push back the Medans, forming an empty, circular area at the base of the Senate stairs. Facing the Medans, spears held horizontally before them, the guards kept the milling crowd at bay.

Achmed breathed easier. He'd heard it rumored that the Governor had been captured by the men-at-arms of those Medan Senators who had been in the Amir's pay. The wretched politician, bound hand and foot, was dragged forth, as were several other Senators and ministers who had remained loyal to their thankless citizens.

That this was to be a trial and execution, Achmed now recognized. He could view the deaths of these men with equanimity. In their gamble for power, the dice had turned against them. But they had lived well off the winnings up until this time; this was the chance they took when they first began to play the game. He found it difficult, therefore, to understand the unusual grimness of the Amir.

Perhaps he sees himself, standing there in chains, came the sudden, disquieting thought. No, that's impossible. Qannadi would never have run. He would have fought, even though he had been one against a thousand. What then?

More prisoners were being led by the guards into the doomed circle. One was a woman of about fifty, dressed in white robes, her gray hair worn in a tight braid around her head. Behind her stumbled four girls, younger than Achmed. They, too, were dressed in white, their gowns clung to bodies just swelling with the first buds of womanhood. Their hands were bound behind their backs, and they stared about with dazed, uncomprehending eyes. Following the four girls marched a man of rotund girth clad in red robes. From the expression on his face, he knew what was coming and yet walked with dignity, his back straight.

The voice of the crowd changed in regard to each prisoner. A guilt-laden murmur began when the Governor and the Senators were led in, many eyes looking up or down or anywhere but at the faces of the men for whom most of them had undoubtedly voted. The murmur changed to a whisper of pity at the sight of the young girls, and low mutterings of respect for the large man in red. The mutterings swelled to anger with the arrival of the last prisoner.

Beardless, with long brown hair, the prisoner was clad in black trousers tucked into the tops of black leather boots; a black silken shirt with flowing sleeves, open at the neck; and a crimson red sash around his waist. A curious device—that of a snake whose body had been cut into three pieces—was embroidered upon the front of his shirt.

Achmed stared at the snake in fascination. His skin prickled, his thumbs tingled, and from nowhere the image of Khardan came to him. Why should he think of his lost brother now, of all times? And why in the presence of this brown-haired man, who swaggered into the circle, closely followed by two guards carrying drawn swords. Achmed stared at the man intently, but found no answer to his question. The man in black started to move to the center of the circle. One of the guards put his hand on his arm to draw him back. The man turned on him with a vicious snarl, freeing himself of the guard's hold. The man in black walked where he was told, but of his own free will. He leered at the crowd, who swallowed their words at his baleful look. Those standing anywhere near the man fell backward in an attempt to get away from him—guarded as he was—an attempt that was thwarted by the press of the crowd.

The man looked up at the Amir and suddenly grinned, his white face skull-like in the light of the flaring torches. The vision of Khardan faded from Achmed's mind.

"Is this all?" demanded Feisal, the timbre of his voice quivering slightly with anger. "Where are the underlings for these two?" He gestured at the rotund man and the man in black.

The captain of the elite guard stepped forward, hand raised in salute, his gaze on the Amir. "Have I leave to report, My King?"

"Report," said Qannadi, and Achmed heard weariness and resignation in the reply.

"All the other priests of Uevin escaped, Highness, due to the cou—" he was about to say "courage" but a glimpse of Feisal's burning eyes made him change the word—"efforts of the High Priest." He gestured with a thumb toward the rotund man in red, who smiled serenely. "He held the doors with his own body, my lord. It took a battering ram to break them down, and due to the delay, the remainder of Uevin's priests escaped. We have no idea where they've gone."

"Secret passages underground," Qannadi growled.

"We searched, My Lord, but found none. That is not to say that they couldn't exist. The Temple of Uevin is filled with strange and unholy machines."

"Keep looking," Qannadi said. "And what about this one?" His gaze turned to the man in black, who stared boldly back.

"A follower of the god, Zhakrin, my lord," the captain said in a low voice. Qannadi frowned; his face grew, if possible, grimmer. Feisal sucked in a hissing breath.

"That God of Evil no longer has power in the world," the Imam said, speaking to the man in black. The thin hand clenched. "You have been deceived!"

"It is not we who have been deceived, but you!" The man in black sneered. Taking a step forward, before the guard could stop him, he spit at the Imam's face. The crowd gasped. The guard smote the bound man on the side of the head with the butt-end of the spear, knocking him to the ground. Feisal remained unmoving; the fire in his eyes burned brighter.

Slowly the brown-haired man regained his feet. Blood streamed down the side of his face, but his grin was as wide as ever.

"We found the rest of the scum in the temple dead, My Lord," the Captain reported. "They died by their own hands. This one"—he gestured at the man in black—"apparently lacked the courage to kill himself. The coward put up no resistance."

The follower of Zhakrin did not note or even seem to hear the condemnation. His eyes were focused now on Feisal, never leaving the priest.

"Very well," Qannadi said in disgust. "Are you satisfied, Imam?"

"I suppose I must be," said Feisal sourly.

Qannadi rose to his feet, facing the crowd that hushed to hear his words.

"Citizens of Meda, there stand before you those who refuse to accept the blessings of Quar, who spurn the mercy of the God. Lest their unbelief spread like a poison through the now healthy body of your city, we take it upon ourselves to remove the poison before it can do you further harm."

One of the young girls cried out at this, a piercing wail that was cut off by one of the guards clapping his hand over her mouth. Achmed's throat went dry, blood throbbed in his ears so that he heard the Amir's words as though through a hood of sheep's wool.

"It shall be done this night, before you all, that you may see Quar's mercy and His judgment. He is not a God of vengeance. Their deaths shall be quick"—the Amir's stern gaze went to the man in black—"even though some may not deserve such a fate. The bodies may be claimed by their relatives and buried in accordance with the teachings of Quar. Imam, have you words to add?"

The priest walked down the stairs to stand on the lowest step in front of the prisoners. "Are there any who would now convert to Quar?"

"I will!" cried a Senator. Flinging himself forward, the politician fell at the Imam's knees and began to kiss the hem of his robe. "I place myself and all my wealth into the hands of the God!"

Qannadi's mouth twisted; he regarded the wretched man with repugnance and made a motion with his hand for the Captain of the guard to come near. The Captain did so, silently drawing his sword from its sheath.

Feisal bent down, laying his hands upon the Senator's balding head. "Quar hears your prayer, my son, and grants you peace."

The Senator looked up, his face shining.

"Praise to Quar!" he shouted, a shout that ended in a shocked cry. The Captain's sword stabbed him to the heart. Staring at the Imam in amazement, the Senator pitched forward onto his stomach, dead.

"May Quar receive you with all blessing," the Imam said in a soft voice over the body.

"Carry on," ordered Qannadi harshly.

The guards surrounding the prisoners drew their swords. The rotund priest fell to his knees, praying to Uevin in a firm voice that ended only with his life. The Governor left the world in bitter silence, casting a scathing glance at those who had betrayed him. The priestess, too, met her end with dignity. But one of the young virgins—seeing the priestess fall lifeless, the bloody sword yanked from the body—twisted free of her guard and ran in panic-stricken terror to the stairs.

"Mercy!" she cried. "Mercy!" Slipping and falling, she looked up directly at Achmed, extending her hands pleadingly. "You are young, as I am! Don't let them kill me, Lord!" she begged him. "Please! Don't let them!"

Blonde hair curled about a pretty, terrified face. Fear made her eyes wild and staring. Achmed could not move or look away but regarded the girl with pity and dismay.

Hearing the guard's footsteps coming up behind her, too weakened by fear to stand, the girl tried pathetically to crawl up the stairs, her hands stretched out to Achmed.

"Help me, Lord!" she cried frenziedly.

Achmed took a step forward, then felt Qannadi's hand close over his forearm with a crushing grip.

Achmed halted. He saw the hope that had dawned bright in the girl's eyes darken to despair. The guard struck quickly, mercifully cutting short the girl's last moment of terror. The body sagged, blood poured down the stairs, the hand reaching out to Achmed went limp.

The torchlights blurred in Achmed's vision. Dizzy and sick, he started to turn from the gruesome sight.

"Courage!" said the Amir in a low voice.

Achmed lifted glazed eyes. "Is it courage to butcher the innocent?" he asked hoarsely.

"It is courage to do your duty as a soldier," Qannadi answered in a fierce, barely audible whisper, not looking at Achmed but staring straight ahead impassively. "Not only to yourself but to them." He cast a swift glance around the crowd. "Better these few than the entire city!"

Achmed stared at him. "The city?"

"Meda was lucky," the Amir said in flat, even tones. "Feisal chose it to set an example. There will be others, in the future, not so fortunate. This is *jihad*, a holy war. Those who fight us must die. So Quar has commanded."

"But surely He didn't mean women, children—"

Qannadi turned to look at him. "Come to your senses, boy!" he said angrily. "Why do you think *he* brought you here?" He did not look at Feisal, still standing at the bottom of the stairs, or motion toward him, but Achmed knew whom the Amir meant.

"My people!" Achmed breathed.

Nodding once, briefly, Qannadi removed his hand from the young man's arm and slowly and tiredly resumed his seat upon the throne.

His mind engulfed by the horror of what he had witnessed and the implication of what he'd just heard, Achmed stared blindly at the carnage when hoarse, triumphant laughter jolted him from his dark dream.

"The curse of Zhakrin upon the hand that kills Catalus!" cried the man in black.

He stood in the center of what had become a ring of bodies lying in the plaza. In his hand he held a dagger. Its blade, gleaming in the torchlight, twisted like the body of the snake on his shirt. So commanding was he and so forceful his presence that the guards of the Amir fell back from him, looking uncertainly at their Captain, all clearly loathe to strike him.

"I did not lack courage to die with my fellows!" cried the man, the dagger held level with his red sash, one hand extended to keep off the guards. "I, Catalus, chose to die here, to die now, for a reason."

Both hands grasped the dagger's hilt and plunged the weapon into his bowels. Grimacing in pain, yet forbearing to cry out, he drew the weapon across his gut in a slashing motion. Blood and entrails splashed out upon the stones at his feet. Sinking to his knees, he stared up at Feisal with that same ghastly grin on his face. The dagger slid from Catalus's grasp. Dipping his hands in his own blood, he lurched forward. His crimson fingers closed on Feisal's robes.

"The curse of Zhakrin . . . on you!" Catalus gasped, and with a dreadful gurgling sound that might have been laughter, he died.

# Book Seven

# THE BOOK OF ASTAFAS

# Chapter 1

The imp materialized within the darkness. It could see nothing, and the only part of the imp that could be seen were its bright red eyes and the occasional flick across the lips of an orange-red tongue.

"Your report astonishes me," said the darkness.

The imp was pleased at this and rubbed its long, skinny hands together in satisfaction. It could not see the speaker, not because the darkness hid the voice's source but because the darkness *was* the voice's source. The words reverberated around the imp as though spoken from a mouth somewhere beneath its feet, and the imp often had the impression, when summoned to appear before its God, that it was standing inside the brain of Astafas. It could sense the workings of the brain, and the imp occasionally wondered if it could grab a flash of intelligence as it whizzed past.

In order to prevent itself from touching that which was sacrosanct, the imp continued rubbing its hands, twining the large-knuckled fingers together in eager excitement.

"I begin to think the Wandering God was right after all," continued Astafas. "Quar played us all for fools. He intends to become the One, True God. The rival Gods of Sardish Jardan are falling to His might. I would not care so much, except that now His mask is off and I see His eyes turning to gaze greedily across the ocean."

The voice sank to the darkness and was silent. The imp

felt a tingling sensation in its feet—the God was thinking, musing. Fidgeting, the imp bit off a squeal.

"To think," muttered Astafas, "if it hadn't been for those wretched priests of my ancient foe, Promenthas, getting themselves involved, I might not have discovered Quar's intentions until it was too late. Strange are the ways of Sul."

The imp agreed heartily with this, but said nothing, thinking it best not to reveal that it had ever doubted its master. A sudden jolt in the vicinity of its arm sent the imp skittering across the darkness, its skin burning with the shock of the God's sudden anger.

"My immortals, too, have been disappearing! And, by your account, they are being held captive somewhere?"

"This is the reason the guardian angel, Asrial"—the imp spoke the name gingerly, as though it stung its tongue—"left her protégé, Dark Master. One of the fish of which I spoke in my report sent her, along with the two immortals of the Wandering God, to search for them."

"A guardian angel of Promenthas leaving her charge. I do not believe I have ever heard of such a thing." If Astafas had been Promenthas—instead of that God's evil opposite—he could not have been more shocked. "The natural order is falling apart!"

"Still," suggested the imp, nursing a singed elbow, "it does provide us with an opportunity. . . ."

"Yes," agreed the God thoughtfully. "But would it be worthwhile to gain one soul and lose thousands?"

The imp seemed to think it would—by the flicking of its hungry tongue across its lips.

The brain of the God hummed and buzzed around the imp. Its red eyes darted here and there nervously. It lifted up one foot and then the other, hopping back and forth in anticipation of some paralyzing shock. It still wasn't prepared for it, and when it came, the imp was knocked flat on its face.

"There is a way we can have both," said Astafas. "You are certain you know the young man's plans?"

"I see into his mind." The imp lifted its head, peering eagerly into the darkness, its red eyes shining like hot coals. "I read his thoughts."

"If he does what you anticipate, you will go along with him."

"I will?" The imp was pained. "I can't snatch him for you, then and there?"

"No. I need more information. I have an idea, you see, about these fish he carries. Humor the young man. He will not escape," said Astafas soothingly. "He will simply wind himself tighter and tighter in our coils."

"Yes, Dark Master." The imp did not sound overly enthusiastic. Scrambling to its splay-toed feet, it dejectedly asked if it was dismissed.

"Yes. Oh, one other thing—"

The darkness began to disappear; the imp had the uncomfortable sensation of falling.

"Dark Master?" it questioned.

"Do what you can to protect him."

"Protect him?" the imp wailed.

"For the time being," said the fading darkness.

# Chapter 2

The ghuls piloted their storm-driven ship through the murky waters of the Kurdin Sea. Whether the power of Sul kept the vessel afloat or the power of the evil God in whose service the ghuls sailed, Mathew had little idea. Fierce gusts ripped the sails into tattered black shreds that streamed from the yardarms like the banners of a nightmarish army. The rigging snapped and slithered to the deck, twisting and writhing like snakes. None except the ghuls and the Black Paladin, Auda ibn Jad, could stand on the pitching deck, swept constantly by battering waves. Kiber and his men huddled aft, crouched beneath whatever meager shelter they could find from the wind and wet. The faces of the *goums* were pale and strained; many were sick and they obviously liked this voyage as little as their captives.

Auda ibn Jad stood beside the wheel, staring intently ahead as though he could pierce the storm clouds and catch a glimpse of his destination. Where that destination was or what it might hold, Mathew had long ago ceased to care.

In his sickness, crazed thoughts came to his horror-numbed brain. The ghuls began to fascinate him; he could not take his eyes off the men who were not men but creatures of Sul held in thrall by the power of Zhakrin. The idea of leaping up and hurling himself into the arms of one of the ghuls came to his mind and the thought, in his weakness and terror, was a pleasant one. With the warm-blooded human in its grasp, the ghul would certainly kill him. Not even Auda ibn Jad—who was just barely holding them in check now—could prevent that. The ghuls suddenly became creatures filled with light, almost angelic in aspect. Benevolent, handsome, strong, they offered him escape, a way out.

"Come to me," the ghul seemed to whisper every time one looked his way. "Come to me and I will release you from this torment."

Mathew imagined the hands gripping him tightly, the teeth sinking into his flesh, the sharp, burning pain, and the swift fear that would soon mercifully end as the blood drained from his body, bringing blissful lethargy and, finally, welcome darkness.

"Come to me. . . ."

He had only to move, to stand, to run forward. It would all be over—the fear, the guilt.

"Come to me. . . ."

He had just to move. . . .

"Mat-hew!"

A thick, pain-filled call, heard over the terrible whispers, roused him. Reluctantly, he wrenched his mind from dreams of death and returned to the world of the living.

"Mat-hew!" Panic tinged the voice. Zohra could not see him, he realized. Her view was blocked by one of the heavy ivory jars. Slowly he made his way to her, crawling on hands and knees over the heaving deck.

At the sight of him, Zohra half raised, clutching at him desperately.

"Lie back down," he urged her, pressing her body gently back onto the deck.

But she sat up again, her eyes blinking against the pain that must be making her head throb. "Mat-hew, what is happening!" she demanded angrily.

Mathew sighed inwardly. First she acts, then she questions. Just like Khardan. Just like these nomads. Whenever anything out of the ordinary confronts you, don't think about it, don't try to understand it. Attack it. Kill it, and it will go away and not bother you anymore. If that doesn't work, perhaps ignoring it will. And if that doesn't work, then you cry and mope like a spoiled child. . . .

Mathew cast a bitter glance at Khardan. Lashed to the mast, the Calif sagged in his bindings, his head bowed. Occasionally a groan escaped his lips when the sickness took hold of him, but other than that—not a word. He has lost a battle and so considers that he has lost the war, Mathew thought, anger stirring in him again (completely ignoring that only moments before he himself had been courting death).

"Mat-hew!" Zohra tugged on his soaking-wet clothes. "Where are they taking us?" She looked fearfully about at the ship. "Why does that man want us?"

Mathew nudged his brain to function. Zohra had been unconscious when they brought her on board. She probably didn't even remember the ghuls attacking and devouring the helpless slaves. How could he hope to explain what he didn't understand himself?

"It's all . . . my fault," he said at last, or rather croaked, his throat sore from swallowing sea water and vomiting. Another wave of nausea swept over him, and he slumped down weakly beside Zohra, wondering, as he did so, why she wasn't deathly ill like the rest of them.

"Your fault!" Zohra frowned. Leaning over him, her wet black hair slapping against his face, she grabbed two handfuls of the wet silk of his caftan and shook him. "Get up! Don't lie there! If this is your fault, then you must do something!"

Closing his eyes, Mathew turned his head and did something.

He was sick.

Mathew lost all concept of time. It seemed they sailed forever before the storm winds began to abate and the black, lowering clouds that hung over the masts began to lift. Had he looked into a mirror at that moment and seen that his skin was wrinkled and aged, his eyes dim, his body bent, his hair white, he wouldn't have been much surprised. Eighty years might have passed on board that dreadful ship.

Eighty years . . . eighty seconds.

From his prone position on the deck, Mathew heard Auda ibn Jad's voice raised in command. He heard the sound of boots hitting wood and a few suppressed groans—the *goums* staggering to their feet.

Kiber's face—pale and green—loomed above him, the *goum* leader shouting something that Mathew could not hear over the crashing of the sea. Suddenly the young wizard wished the voyage would go on, that it would never end. The memory of his idea returned to him. He did not welcome it and wished heartily that the thought had never occurred to him. It was stupid, it was foolhardy. It was risking his life in what was undoubtedly a futile gesture. He had no notion of where his actions might lead him because he had no notion of where he was or what was going to happen to him. Conceivably, he could make matters worse.

No, he would not be like Khardan and Zohra. He would not leap forward in the darkness and grapple with the unknown. He would do what he had always done. He would let things take their course. He would ride the current in his frail craft and hope to survive. He would do nothing that might risk falling into the dark water where he would surely drown.

Kiber jerked him roughly to his feet. The motion of the ship, although not as violent, was still erratic, and sent Mathew stumbling back against the baggage. He caught himself and stood clinging to a large rattan basket. Kiber glanced at him, saw that for the moment he was standing, and turned to Zohra.

Seeing the *goum* approaching her, she repelled him with a flashing-eyed look and stood up on her own, backing out of the man's reach as far as she could before being brought up by several of the huge ivory jars.

Reaching out, Kiber grabbed hold of her arm.

Zohra struck the *goum* across the face.

Auda ibn Jad shouted again, sounding impatient.

Grim and tense, the red marks of the woman's hand showing clearly against his livid skin, Kiber caught hold of Zohra again, this time wrenching her wrist and twisting her arm behind her back.

"Why can't you be a woman like Blossom?" Kiber muttered, taking hold of Mathew, as well, and dragging him forward. "Instead of a wild cat!"

Zohra's eyes met Mathew's. A woman like you! Her contempt seared him. Despite that, his resolve was not shaken. He caught a glimpse of Khardan. The man didn't have strength enough left in his body to crush an ant beneath his heel, yet he had apparently roused himself from his stupor and was struggling feebly with the *goums* freeing him from his bonds. For what? Nothing but pride. Even if he did manage to overpower them, where could he go? Leap off the ship? Throw himself into the arms of the ghuls, who now watched the fight with intense, hungry interest.

That's what this plan of yours is—a feeble struggle against

overwhelming odds. And that's why it's forgotten, Mathew told himself, looking away from both Zohra and Khardan. His fingers brushed against the pouch that contained the magical objects, and he snatched his hand away as though it had burned him. He would have to get rid of them and quickly. They were a danger to him now. He cursed himself for having picked them up.

Fumbling at his belt, Mathew pulled out the pouch and instantly crumpled it in his hand, pressing it against his waist, concealing it in the folds of his wet clothes. He darted a furtive look from beneath his lowered eyelids, hoping to be able to drop the pouch to the deck without anyone noticing. Unfortunately, Auda ibn Jad turned from looking out over the sea, his snake-eyed gaze resting upon Mathew and Zohra and the grim-faced Kiber behind them.

"Trouble, Captain?" ibn Jad asked, noting with amusement Kiber's bruised cheek.

Kiber answered something; Mathew didn't know what. He froze beneath the piercing gaze. Panicked, he doubled over, digging the hand with the pouch into his stomach, hoping to seem to be still sick, although in reality his nausea was passing, either because the motion of the ship was settling down or his fear and worry had driven it from his mind.

Ibn Jad's gaze flicked over him, to rest more steadily at Zohra. There was neither lust nor desire in the man's dark eyes. He was regarding her with the same cool appraisal a man might regard a dog he was considering acquiring. When he spoke, his words were the embodiment of Mathew's thought, causing the young wizard to start guiltily, wondering if the Black Paladin had the power to read minds.

"The bitch will produce strong whelps," said ibn Jad in satisfaction. "Fine new followers for our God."

"Bitch!" Zohra's eyes flared.

Breaking free of the weakened Kiber, she hurled herself at ibn Jad. Kiber jumped after her and wrestled her back before she reached the Black Paladin—whose amusement seemed to grow. Auda made a sound in his throat that might have been a chuckle but caused Mathew to go cold all over. Obviously out of patience and in an ill humor, Kiber handed Zohra over to a couple of his men with orders to tie her hands and hobble her feet.

Ibn Jad's eyes were again on Mathew, and the young wizard cowered beneath their gaze, realizing too late that he could have dropped the pouch during the altercation and wondering, briefly, why he hadn't.

Ibn Jad ran his slender hand over Mathew's smooth cheek.

"A jackal, that one, compared to our fragile and delicate Blossom here who trembles beneath my fingers."

Mathew cringed and gritted his teeth, forcing himself to submit to the man's odious touch, slightly turning his body to keep the pouch in his hand concealed. He was vaguely aware of activity stirring around them, of the rumbling of a heavy chain, a splash, and the ship swinging slowly at anchor.

Brutal enslavement—this was to be Zohra's fate and his, too, undoubtedly, until ibn Jad discovered he had been deceived, that Mathew would never bear this God, Zhakrin, worshipers. It was happening all over, he realized in despair—the terrible waiting, the dread anticipation, the fear, the humiliation, and then the punishment. And there would be no one to save him this time. . . .

"These women . . . are my wives!" said a slurred voice. "You will die before you touch them!"

Mathew looked at Khardan and then averted his face, tears stinging his eyelids.

The Calif stood before ibn Jad. The bindings had cut deeply into the nomad's arms, fresh blood streamed from a gash on his swollen lip. The sickly pallor of his complexion was accentuated by the blue-blackness of his unkept beard. His eyes were sunken, encircled by shadows. He walked unsteadily; it took two *goums* to hold him upright. At a nod from ibn Jad, they let go. Khardan's knees buckled. He pitched forward, falling at the feet of the Black Paladin.

"A bold speech from a man on his knees, a man we found hiding from the soldiers of the Amir in a dress," said Auda ibn Jad coolly. "I begin to think I made a mistake with this one, Kiber. He is not fit for the honor I intended to bestow upon him. We will leave him to the ghuls. . . ."

Damn you, Khardan! Mathew cursed the Calif silently, bitterly. Why did you have to do that? Jeopardize your life for two people you detest—a woman who brought you to shame and a man who is shame personified. Why do this? Honor! Your stupid honor! And now they will rend your flesh, murder you before my eyes!

Putting his booted foot on Khardan's shoulder, ibn Jad gave the man a shove, and the Calif went over backward, landing heavily on the deck.

Mathew heard the splash of oars in the water. Small boats had set sail from land and were drawing near the ship. The ghuls, their ship at anchor, their task finished, were gathering around Khardan, eyes shining with an eager, eerie light. The Calif tried to rise, but Kiber kicked him in the face, knocking him back onto the deck. The ghuls drew nearer, their aspect beginning to undergo the hideous change from man to demon. Seeing them, Khardan shook his head to clear it and started to struggle once more to stand.

Stop it! Mathew cried in silent agony, fists clenching. Stop fighting! Let it end!

Auda ibn Jad was pointing toward the boats, issuing orders. Kiber, turning to obey, drove the toe of his boot deep into Khardan's gut. With a gasp of agony, the Calif sank back onto the deck and did not rise again.

The ghuls closed in, their teeth lengthening into fangs, their nails into talons.

"Bring the women," said ibn Jad, and Kiber motioned to the *goums* holding Zohra. She stared at the ghuls in dazed disbelief and horror, seeming not to comprehend what was happening. The *goums* dragged her forward to where the boats were pulling up beneath the ship's hull. She twisted around, straining to watch Khardan, who was pressing his body flat against the deck as though he might escape by crawling into the wood. Bending over him, their breath hot upon his skin, the ghuls began to howl, and Khardan's arms twitched, his hands clenched spasmodically. Then taloned fingers stabbed deep into his flesh, and the Calif screamed.

Mathew's hand was inside the pouch; he never remembered how. His fingers closed over the cold wand of obsidian. He had no clear conscious thought of what he was doing, and when he drew forth the wand, the hand holding it seemed to belong to someone else, the voice that spoke the words was the voice of a stranger.

"Creatures of Sul," he cried, pointing the wand at the ghuls, "in the name of Astafas, Prince of Darkness, I command you to withdraw!"

The world went completely black. During the breadth of a heartbeat, night engulfed those standing on the ship. Light returned in the blink of an eye.

A skinny, shriveled creature with skin the color of coal stood spraddle-legged over Khardan. Its eyes were red fire, its tongue flickering flame. Raising a splay-fingered hand, it pointed at the ghuls.

"Heard you not my master?" the imp hissed. "Be gone, lest he call upon Sul to cast you in the fiery depths where you will never more taste sweet flesh or drink hot blood."

The ghuls halted, some with their talons digging into Khardan's flesh, others with their teeth just inches from his body. They stared at the imp balefully. The imp stared back, its red eyes burning fiercely.

"Always hungry, always thirsting . . ."

One by one, the ghuls released their hold upon Khardan. Slowly—eyes on the imp—they moved away from the Calif, their aspect shifting from demon to man.

Its tongue flicking in and out of its mouth in pleasure, the imp turned to Mathew and bowed.

"Will there be anything more, My Dark Master?"

# Chapter 3

Mathew very nearly dropped the wand.

Of all the astonished people on the ship, the young wizard
was the most astounded of all.

Feeling the wand start to slip from his shaking fingers,
Mathew caught hold of it with a spasmodic jerk of his hand,
reacting more out of instinct than conscious thought. To drop
a wand during a spell casting was considered a grievous and
dangerous error on the part of any wizard. Almost every
nervous young student did it once, and Mathew could hear
the voice of the Archmagus dinning furiously in his ears. The
young wizard's training saved him. He gained additional
strength from the sudden frightening realization that if the
spell was broken, he was in far more danger than if all the
ghuls in the nether plane had ringed themselves round him.

An instant before the imp bowed, Mathew saw clearly in
the creature's eyes the burning desire to lay claim to his
immortal soul. Then it would be Mathew who was forever in
servitude to a Dark Master—Astafas, Prince of Darkness.
Why didn't the imp snatch him up? Mathew had put himself
in forfeit by speaking the name of Astafas. Why was the
creature obeying him? Only the most powerful of the wizard's
Order could summon and control immortals such as the imp.

The wand might have such powers, but Mathew doubted
it. Meryem was a skilled sorceress, but not even she could
have attained the high rank necessary to enable her to make a

Wand of Summoning. If she had possessed this kind of arcane power, she would not have needed to resort to anything as clumsy as murder. No, some strange and mystifying force was at work here.

Too late, Mathew regained control of his features. He had been staring blankly at the imp as these confused thoughts tumbled through his mind, and he hoped no one had noticed.

His hope was a vain one. Auda ibn Jad's cool composure had been disturbed by the appearance of the imp, still more by its referring to the beautiful red-haired young woman as Dark Master. Ibn Jad was quick to note Mathew's unnerved appearance, however, and—though the Black Paladin did not know what it portended as yet—he filed it away in memory for later consideration.

Mathew knew he had to act, and he tried desperately to think what was the next logical order a powerful, evil wizard might be likely to issue.

The command that was in his heart was to have the imp carry him, Khardan, and Zohra off this horror-filled ship, as far away from Auda ibn Jad as the creature could manage. But just as this thought traveled from heart to mind, the imp raised its head and looked at Mathew. Its red eyes flared fire, its mouth parted in a wicked grin, the tongue licked dry, cracked lips.

Mathew shuddered and banished the thought. The imp could read his mind, obviously. And while undoubtedly it would obey his command, Mathew knew exactly where the imp would take them—a place of eternal darkness whose Demon Prince made Auda ibn Jad seem saintly in comparison.

"Dark Master?" the imp prompted, rubbing its skinny hands together.

"I need you no more," Mathew said at last, a quaver spoiling the authoritative note he tried to instill in his voice. "Be gone until I call for you again."

Was this how one spoke to summoned creatures? Mathew couldn't remember; he'd had only the most cursory studies in Black Magic and the only object it accomplished was to fix in the minds of White Wizards that dabbling in this art would invariably lead to disaster. Mathew had the uncomfortable feeling, however, that no matter what he said, the imp would deal with the situation.

"I obey, My Dark Master," said the imp, and disappeared with a heart-stopping bang.

No one moved. Now that the imp was gone, all eyes turned to Mathew.

He had to keep going, keep performing. He gave them all what he hoped was a cold, threatening stare and made his way across the deck to Khardan. Raising the wand, he fixed his gaze upon the ghuls, and was relieved to see them step back respectfully at his approach.

Mathew knelt down beside Khardan. Wounded, shaken by the nearness he had come to a tortured death, the Calif barely had the strength to raise his head. Putting his arm around the man's shoulders, Mathew lifted him to a sitting position on the deck.

"Are you all right?" he asked in a low voice.

Khardan's teeth chattered, his lips were blue. "The scratches!" he gasped. "Burn . . . like . . . cold fire."

Mathew examined the places on his arms and torso where the ghuls had driven their talons into the flesh. The long tears in the skin were swollen and colored a bluish white. There was no blood visible, although the cuts were deep. Leaning against Mathew, Khardan shook as with a chill. He was in such agony that he seemed to have only the vaguest idea what had happened.

"The ghuls' poison has entered his blood. He is too ill to walk. Some of you carry him ashore." Looking up as he issued the command, Mathew's eyes met the eyes of Auda ibn Jad. He saw nothing in the black, reptilian flatness to give him a clue as to what the Black Paladin was thinking. If Auda challenged him, Mathew had no idea what he would do. Certainly not summon the imp again, if he could help it!

For long moments, the two stared at each other; the ship, the *goums*, the ghuls, the boats arriving beneath the ship's hull, voices shouting hails to the deck—all vanished from the mind of each man as he strove to see deep into the heart of the other.

Mathew came away with nothing. What Auda ibn Jad came away with—if anything—remained locked deep inside him.

"Kiber," said ibn Jad, "take three of your men and place the Calif in the bosun's chair, then lower him into the boats. Gently, Kiber, gently."

Kiber called out three *goums*, who left their duties tying the baggage that had been brought on board in huge nets to be swung out over the side and deposited in the waiting boats. Hurrying forward—with sidelong, distrustful glances at Mathew—the *goums* lifted Khardan by his knees and his arms and hauled him awkwardly over to the ship's rail.

Rising to his feet, Mathew followed them, thankful that the folds of the caftan hid the trembling of his legs and hoping he did not disgrace himself by collapsing in a heap upon the deck. He still clutched the wand in his hand and thought it best to keep it visible. So tightly were his fingers wrapped around it, he wasn't at all certain he could let loose of the thing.

"Approach me, Blossom," said Auda ibn Jad. "The rest of you"—he gestured at the *goums*—"continue your work. It is almost nightfall and we must be off this ship by then. Take her"—he indicated Zohra—"and put her in the same boat with her husband."

Mathew glanced at Zohra apprehensively; there was no telling what she might say, perhaps blurt out that the wand wasn't his at all or that he had told her the God he followed was called Promenthas not Astafas. Zohra said nothing, however; simply stared at him in wide-eyed astonishment. He managed to smile at her in what he hoped was reassurance, but she was apparently so completely shocked by what had happened that she couldn't respond. Zohra allowed her captors to lead her away, looking as though she were in a waking dream.

Sighing, Mathew came to stand before Auda ibn Jad, the two of them were alone in the center of the deck.

"Well, Blossom, it seems your face and lithe body and the sorcerer's robes you wore when I first saw you fooled me. It was not a woman I took into my slave caravan but a man. Of course, you thought I would kill you, and so you let me remain deceived. You might have been right, but then again, I am not so sure I would have had you murdered as I did the others. There are those who fancy a pretty boy above a pretty girl and who are just as willing to pay good money for such in the slave market. You might have spared yourself much humiliation and me much trouble had you told me the truth. Still, the water spilled into the sand cannot be drunk, and there is no going back. I think you should give me the fish, now, Blossom."

All this was spoken in cool, calm tones, even the last. But Mathew felt the steel-edged menace prick him sharply. Taking a moment to gather his thoughts and to grasp hold of his courage with the same desperate grip by which he held the wand, Mathew shook his head.

"No," he replied softly. "I will not do that. I know something of magic, as you have seen. You called me the Bearer and one so designated cannot be parted from that which he bears by any force in this world."

"I can kill you and take it from your corpse," said the Black Paladin with an easy, impersonal casualness that made Mathew blench.

"Yes," he answered, "you could kill me. But you won't, at least not until you know how much I know and—more importantly—how much my God"—the word came with difficulty—"knows."

"Astafas, our brother God in Evil." Auda ibn Jad nodded slowly, reflectively. "Yes, I must admit I am curious to know more about the Prince of Darkness. In fact, I am pleased at the opportunity for contact with our Brother. I will not sacrifice you in order to take the fish—not yet at least. There will come a time, Blossom—you don't mind me calling you this? I find I have grown accustomed to it—when your usefulness will be at an end, and then I will not hesitate to destroy you in a most unpleasant manner."

"I understand," said Mathew wearily. "You can do with me what you will—provided Astafas allows it—but I"—the young wizard drew a deep breath—"I insist that you let my friends go."

Auda ibn Jad smiled—so might a snake smile. Reaching out with his slender hand, he took hold of a strand of Mathew's wet red hair and drew it slowly and lingeringly through his fingers. The Black Paladin moved close to Mathew, his body touching that of the wizard's, his face and eyes filling Mathew's vision.

"I will let your friends go, Blossom," ibn Jad said gently. "Tell me where. Shall I leave them on this ship? Shall I drop them in the Kurdin Sea? Or perhaps you would prefer that I wait and set them free on the island of Galos? The Guardians of our castle find their work tedious sometimes. They would enjoy a chance for a little sport. . . ."

Ibn Jad wrapped the strand of hair tightly about his finger and pulled Mathew's head so near his own that the wizard could feel the man's breath upon his cheek. Involuntarily, Mathew closed his eyes. He felt suffocated, as if the Black

Paladin were breathing in all the air and leaving Mathew stranded in a vacuum.

"I was preoccupied, absorbed in keeping the ghuls in thrall. You took me by surprise, Blossom. You caught me off guard. Few have ever done that, and therefore I rewarded you by allowing your Calif to live." Ibn Jad gave a sharp tug on Mathew's hair, bringing tears to the young man's eyes and jerking his head nearer still. "But never again!" The Black Paladin breathed the words. "You are good, my dear, but young . . . very young."

Giving Mathew's hair a vicious yank, he sent the wizard sprawling face first on the deck. The wand flew from Mathew's hand, and he watched in agony as it slid across the sand-scrubbed wood. He made a desperate lunge for it, but a black-booted foot stepped on it.

Crouched on his hands and knees, Mathew cowered in chagrin and shame. He could feel Auda ibn Jad's smile shine upon him like the light of a cold, pale sun. And then he heard the boot scrape across the deck; the wand rolled toward Mathew and bumped against his hand.

"My regards to Astafas," said the Black Paladin. "I welcome his servant to the Isle of Galos."

# Chapter 4

The Isle of Galos was the peak of a huge volcano whose smoke-rimmed, storm-shrouded head reared up out of the murky waters of the Kurdin Sea. Like a fierce and ancient patriarch who sits motionless in his wheeled chair for days and at whom relatives glance fearfully and say, "Do you suppose he's still alive?" the volcano had done nothing in years. But, like the old man, the volcano lived still and occasionally gave evidence of this by a slight tremor or a small belch of noxious fumes.

It was here that the few followers of the dead Zhakrin chose to make what might very well be their final stand against the world and the Heavens. When it was known—almost twenty years ago—that their God was growing weaker, word went forth from the Lord of the Black Paladins, and those last remaining survivors of various purges and *jihads* and persecutions made their way to this place that seemed the embodiment of the dark horrors of their religion.

Carried across the Kurdin Sea by their few remaining immortals, the Black Paladins were left alone on the Isle when those immortals vanished. The knights' lives were harsh. Their God could no longer help them. They had nothing on which to live but faith and the code of their strict sect that bound them with undying loyalty to each other. Their single, unswerving goal was to bring about their God's return.

None but the members of that strict Order could have

survived the ordeal. Survive they did, however, and—not only that—they began to thrive and prosper, acquiring—by various means—new members for their Black Cause. The sorceresses of the Black Paladins were able to capture the ghuls and, by granting them human flesh in payment, they persuaded Sul's creatures to work a sailing vessel between the Isle and the mainland. Contact with the world was reestablished, and once more the Black Paladins went forth—always in secret—to bring back what was needed.

The knights imported slave labor and began building Castle Zhakrin—a place of refuge where they could live and a temple for their God when he should return. Castle Zhakrin was constructed of shining black obsidian, granite, magic, blood, and bones. Numerous unfortunate slaves either fell to their deaths from the towering battlements, were crushed beneath huge blocks of stone, or sacrificed to Zhakrin. The Black Paladins sprinkled the blood of the victims over the building blocks; their bones were mixed with the mortar. When the Castle was completed, the remaining slaves were put to death and their skeletons added to the building's decor. Human skulls grinned above doors, dismembered hands pointed the way down corridors, leg and foot bones were imbedded in the walls of winding staircases.

Riding in the stern of ibn Jad's boat, Mathew gazed in awe at the Isle that he had been too preoccupied to notice from the ship. A barren, windswept, jagged cone of rock jutted from the water, soaring up to lose itself in the perpetual clouds that shrouded the mountain's peak. Nothing grew on the rock's dead, rough-edged surface. The wind seemed the only living thing on the Isle, whistling through lips of twisted stone, howling bleakly when it found itself trapped in deep ravines, beating against blank canyon walls.

Castle Zhakrin stood against one side of the mountain, its sharp spires and gap-toothed battlements making it look like the mountain's offspring, something the volcano spewed forth in fire and smoke and ash. A great signal fire burning from atop one of the towers added to the illusion, reddish orange light poured from the windows like molten lava streaming down upon the black sand beach below.

Gathered upon that beach were the Black Paladins. Fifty men of ages ranging from eighteen to seventy stood in a single straight line upon the sand. They were dressed in

black metal armor that gleamed red in the rays of the setting
sun. Draped over their shoulders were vestments of black
cloth, each adorned over the left breast with the signet of the
severed snake. The knights wore no helms, their faces—
Mathew saw as the boat drew near—might have been carved
from the stone of their mountain, so cold and immovable
were they. Yet, when the boats were dragged ashore by the
rowers—young men of between fifteen and seventeen whom
Mathew judged, from what he overhead, to be knights-in-
training—he noticed that the faces of the Black Paladins
underwent a swift and subtle change. Greeting one of their
own, he saw true emotion light their eyes and soften their
features. And he saw this—astonishingly—reflected in the
usually impassive face of Auda ibn Jad.

Startled by the change in the man, Mathew watched in
wonder as the usually cold and taciturn Black Paladin leapt
from the boat into the water before the squires had a chance
to haul the boats ashore. Wading through the crashing waves,
Auda ran into the arms of an elderly man whose head was
ringed round by a crown shaped in the semblance of two
snakes, twined together, their heads joining at his forehead,
their red-jeweled eyes sparkling in the twilight.

"Ibn Jad! Zhakrin by thanked! You return to us safely,"
cried the man.

"And successfully, Lord of Us All," said Auda ibn Jad,
falling to his knees and reverently kissing the old man's
hands.

"Zhakrin be praised!" cried the Lord, lifting his hands to
the heavens. His words were echoed by the other knights in
a litany that reverberated from the mountainside and faded
away in the pounding of the surf.

Khardan cried out in pain, and Mathew's attention was
withdrawn from the Paladins. The Calif lay in the bottom of
Mathew's boat. He had lapsed into unconsciousness and
twitched and tossed and moaned in some horrid, fever-racked
dream.

"The Black Sorceress will care for him. Do not worry,
Blossom," Auda had told him. "He will not die. Don't be
surprised, however, if he doesn't thank you. You did him no
service in saving his life."

Mathew considered glumly that he had done none of
them any service by his foolhardy act and had undoubtedly
further compounded their troubles. Ibn Jad viewed him as a

threat. Worse still, Zohra saw him as a hero. Despite the fact that they were in separate boats—Zohra having been put into the custody of Kiber, who looked none too happy about the fact and watched her warily—Mathew could feel the woman's eyes on him, looking at him with admiration. This newfound regard for him only served to increase Mathew's unhappiness. She expected him to save them, now, and he knew it was impossible. Once again he found himself living a lie, trapped into pretending he was something he wasn't, with death the penalty for the tiniest mistake.

Or perhaps death was the reward. Mathew didn't know anymore. He'd lived with fear so long, lived with the twisting bowels and cold hands and chill sweat and thudding heart that he increasingly saw death as blissful rest. The irrational anger continued to burn inside him—anger at Khardan and Zohra for being dependent on him, for making him worry about them, for making him feel guilty over having plunged them into this danger.

The squires and *goums* carried Khardan to shore. Wading through the water beside him, Mathew looked down at the pain-racked body and tried to feel some pity, some compassion. But all was darkness inside him, darkness cold and empty. He watched them place Khardan upon a makeshift litter, watched them haul him slowly up stairs carved into the rock leading to the Castle, and felt nothing. Zohra floundered through the water, Kiber holding her arm. Raising her head, she gazed after her husband with lips that parted in concern. Fear and pity for him—not for herself—glimmered in her black eyes. Mathew saw then that Zohra's hatred of Khardan masked some type of caring—perhaps not love, but at least a concern for him. And Mathew, who had loved Khardan longer than he cared to admit to himself, was too frightened to feel anything.

The emptiness only angered him further. He thought, somewhere, he could hear the imp laughing, and he looked away from Zohra's smile of approval and expectation. Mathew was almost thankful when Auda ibn Jad beckoned peremptorily to the young wizard to attend him. Turning his back on Zohra—who was standing wet, haughty, and bedraggled in the black sand—Mathew walked over to where ibn Jad was exchanging warm greetings with his fellow knights.

"What dread brotherhood is this?" Mathew said to himself, glad to have something to which he could turn his thoughts. "This man sold humans into slavery with no more regard than if they had been goats. He murdered an innocent girl, driving a knife into her body with as little care as if she had been a doll. He cast men to ghuls and watched their terrible sufferings with equanimity. And I see nothing but the same cold, dispassionate cruelty in the faces of these men surrounding him! Yet tears shine in their eyes as they embrace!"

"But where is Catalus, my bonded brother?" Auda looked questioningly around the circle of knights surrounding him. "Why wasn't he summoned to join us for this, our greatest hour?"

"He was summoned, Auda," said the Lord in a gentle, sorrowful voice, "and it is sad news I must relate to you, my friend. Catalus was in the city of Meda, training priests in our new temple there when the city was attacked by troops of the Emperor of Tara-kan. Cowards that they are, the Medans surrendered and—to a man—pledged their allegiance to Quar!"

"So the war in Bas has begun," said ibn Jad, his brows drawing together, the cruel eyes darkening. "I heard rumors of it as I passed through the land. And Catalus?"

"Knowing the people would turn our followers over to the troops of the Amir, he commanded the priests to kill themselves before they could be offered up to Quar. When the troops came, they found the temple floor running with blood, Catalus standing in the middle, his sword red, having dispatched those who lingered overlong.

"The troops of the Amir laid hands upon him, calling him coward. He bore their taunts in silence, knowing that he would soon see them choke on their own poisoned words. They dragged him before the Amir and the Imam of Quar, who thought he now had possession of the soul of Catalus."

Shuddering himself at the terrible tale, Mathew saw Auda ibn Jad's face drain of its color. White to the lips, the Black Paladin asked softly, "And what did my bonded brother do?"

The Lord laid his hand upon Auda's shoulder. All the knights had fallen silent, their faces stern and pale, their lips compressed. The only sound was the breaking of the waves upon the shore, the mournful wailing of the wind among the rocks, and the deep voice of the Lord of Black Paladins.

"Catalus watched the other prisoners slaughtered around him. When it came his turn, he drew from his robes a dagger he had concealed there and sliced open his belly. He crawled forward and, with his dying breath, grasped hold of the

Imam's robes with his crimsoned hands and called down
Zhakrin's Blood Curse upon Feisal, the Imam of Quar."

Auda ibn Jad lowered his head. A sob tore through his
body; he began to weep like a child. Several of the knights
standing near rested their hands upon him in compassion,
many of them unashamedly wiping their own eyes.

"Catalus died in the service of our God. His soul is with
Zhakrin, and he will fight to help bring our God back to this
world," said the Lord. "We mourn him. We honor him. Next
we avenge him."

"Honor to Catalus! Praise to Zhakrin!" cried ibn Jad fiercely,
lifting his head, tears glistening on his cheeks.

"Honor to Catalus! Praise to Zhakrin!" shouted the knights,
and as if their call had summoned the darkness, the sun
vanished into the sea and only the red afterglow remained to
light the land.

"And now, tell us the name of this woman with hair the
color of flame who stands here with you," said the Lord, his
admiring gaze sweeping over Mathew. "Have you brought
her for one of the Breeders, or has your heart been touched at
last, Auda ibn Jad, and will you take her for wife?"

"Neither," said ibn Jad, his lips twisting in a smile. "No
woman, this one, but a man." There was laughter at this, and
several of the men flushed in embarrassment, their companions nudging them teasingly. "Do not be ashamed, my brothers, if you looked upon him with desire. His milk skin and
green eyes and delicate features have deceived more than
one, including myself. His story I will tell you in detail over
our evening repast. For now, know that he is the Bearer and
a sorcerer in the service of Astafas, our brother God."

A subdued, respectful murmur rippled through the Black
Paladins.

"A sorcerer!" The Lord looked at Mathew with interest. "I
have heard of men who were skilled in the art of magic, but
I have never before encountered one. Are you certain, ibn
Jad? Have you proof?"

"I have proof," said Auda with a touch of irony in his
voice. "He summoned an imp of Sul and kept the ghuls from
feasting upon that man whom you saw being carried into the
Castle."

"Truly a skilled magus! My wife will be pleased to meet
you," said the Lord to Mathew. "She is the Black Sorceress of
our people, without whose magic we could not have survived."

Ibn Jad's eyes still glistened with tears shed over the death of a comrade, yet their threat slid through Mathew's soul like sharp steel. The young wizard could not make a coherent response, his tongue seemed swollen, his throat parched and dry. Fortunately a bell began to toll from the Castle tower. The knights began to disperse, walking across the beach, their boots crunching in the sand. Several respectfully drew the attention of their Lord to themselves. Ibn Jad was carried off by friends demanding to hear the tales of his adventures. Mathew thought he was going to be left alone, forgotten on this dismal shore, when the Lord glanced around over his shoulder.

"Some of you squires"—he called to the young men unloading the ivory jars and other baggage from the boats—"take the sorcerer to the chambers of my wife. Bid her find him suitable clothing and prepare him for tonight's ceremony."

Two squires leaped to act on their Lord's command, taking charge of Mathew. Without speaking a word to him or paying him attention beyond a cool, curious glance at his sodden woman's clothes, they led him swiftly over the wet, packed sand to where Castle Zhakrin stood, its black shining surface tinged with the blood of the departed sun.

# Chapter 5

Climbing the black stairs carved into the side of the mountain, Zohra continued to maintain her haughty dignity and composure. Pride was, after all, the only thing she had left. Led by Kiber, who kept glancing at her as though she were a ghul and might eat him at a bite, Zohra set her face into a rigid mask that effectively hid her fear and confusion. It wasn't as difficult as might be expected. She seemed to have gone numb, as though she had been drinking *gumiz* or chewing the leaves of the plant that made city dwellers crazy.

She walked up the steep stairs without feeling the stone beneath her bare feet. At the top of the steps, a bridge known as the Dead March led the way across a deep ravine to the Castle. Made of wood and rope, the bridge swung between the sheer sides of the defile. Narrow, swaying dangerously whenever anyone stepped on it, the bridge could be crossed only by a few people at a time and was within easy arrow shot of the Castle's battlements. A hostile army attempting to use it was doomed—easy targets for the Castle's archers, who could also shoot flaming arrows that would set the ropes afire and send the entire structure plunging into the canyon below.

Human heads, mounted on poles, guarded the entrance to the Dead March. These were heads of prisoners, captured by the Black Paladins, and made to suffer the most dreadful tortures. By some arcane art, the flesh remained on the skulls and the agonized expressions on the dead faces served to warn all who looked on them what awaited an enemy of the Black Paladins in Castle Zhakrin.

Zohra glanced at the gruesome guardians with uncaring eyes. She navigated the perilously swinging bridge over the ravine with an appearance of calm that had Kiber shaking his head in admiration. Entering the gaping black archway of the Castle without faltering, she passed coolly beneath the red-tipped iron spikes that could be sent crashing down from the ceiling, impaling those who stood beneath them. The skulls grinning at her from the granite walls, the bony hands that held the flaring torches, didn't cause her cheeks to pale or her eyes to widen. Standing in the huge, torchlit hall, she watched the *goums* bear the litter on which Khardan shivered and moaned up a staircase. She had not spoken since they'd left the ship and asked only three questions upon entering the Castle.

"Where are they taking him? Will he recover?" and "What will become of him?"

Kiber glanced at the woman curiously. She certainly didn't sound the wife inquiring about the fate of a beloved husband. Kiber had seen many such in this hall, clinging to their men, being dragged away screaming and weeping. Of course, they had known or guessed what fate awaited their men. Perhaps this woman didn't . . . or perhaps she did and didn't care. Kiber suspected that it might not make much difference; she would never give way to weakness, no matter what she felt. Kiber had never met a woman like her, and he began to envy Auda ibn Jad.

"They are taking him to the Black Sorceress. She is skilled in healing the touch of the ghuls. If she chooses, he will recover. Beyond that his fate is up to my master," said Kiber gravely, "and will undoubtedly be determined at the Vestry"— he stumbled over the word, the only term comparable in her language was "conclave," but this did not give quite the correct nuance.

Her face did not change expression, and he doubted if she understood. Now she will ask about her fate or that of the other red-headed woman . . . man . . . whatever it was.

But she didn't; she didn't say a word. From the expression on her proud face it soon became clear to Kiber that the woman understood; she was simply refusing to speak to some-one she obviously considered far beneath her.

This irritated Kiber, who could have gone into detail concerning what would happen to this Zohra-woman, at least. The imagining of it excited him, and he considered telling her anyway, hoping to see her pride punctured by despair's sharp knife. But it wasn't his place to speak. The women brought to Castle Zhakrin either captive or voluntarily were the province of the Black Sorceress, and she would take it adversely if Kiber were to meddle in her affairs. Kiber—as did everyone else in the Castle—went out of his way to avoid offending the Black Sorceress.

Without saying anything further to Zohra, he led her up winding stairs to a spire known as the Tower of Women. There was no guard at the door; fear of the Black Sorceress was guard enough—the man who entered the Tower of Women at any other time except the scheduled hours would rue the day he had been born. So powerful was this influence that even though he was here on business, Kiber still felt uncomfortable. He opened the door and took a cautious step inside.

Silent figures shrouded in black robes glided away at his coming, melting into the shadows of the dark and gloomy hallway, their eyes darting frightened or curious glances at his prisoner. The air was heavy with perfume. The only sounds that broke the silence were the occasional cry of a baby or, far away, the scream of a woman giving birth.

Kiber hurried Zohra to a small room that stood just oppo-site the main entryway. Opening the door, he shoved her roughly inside.

"Wait here," he said. "Someone will come."

Hastily he shut the door, locking it with a silver key that hung from a black ribbon wrapped around a nail in the shining black wall. He returned the key to its place and started to leave, but his eyes were drawn to an archway that stood to his right. A curtain of heavy red velvet blocked the arch; he could not see beyond it. But from it wafted the scent of the perfume that hung in the air. The smell and the knowledge of what went on behind that curtain made his heart beat, his loins ache. Every night at midnight, the Black Paladins mounted the stairs and entered the Tower of Women. They and they alone had the right to pass beyond the red velvet curtain.

The sound of a door opening down the hall to his left

made Kiber start. Wrenching his gaze from the curtain, he yanked open the door leading out of the Tower with such haste that he very nearly hit himself in the head.

"Kiber?" said a dried, rasping voice.

Pale-faced and sweating, Kiber turned around, his hand still on the wrought iron handle of the door.

"Madam," he said faintly.

Facing him was a woman of such small stature she might have been mistaken for a frail girl of twelve years. In reality, she counted seven times that number, though no sign of those years could be seen upon her face. What arcane art she used to cheat age none could tell, although it was whispered she drank the blood of stillborn babes. Her beauty was undeniable, but it did not foster desire. The cheeks were free of wrinkles, but their smoothness—on close observation—was not the tender firmness of youth but that of the taut, stretched skin of a drum. The eyes were lustrous, it was the glow of power's flame that brightened them. The breasts, rising and falling beneath black velvet, were soft and ripe, yet no man sought to pillow his head there, for the heart that beat beneath them was ruthless and cold. The white hands that beckoned Kiber so gracefully were stained with the blood of countless innocents.

"You have brought another one?" the woman inquired in a low, sweet voice whose dread music stilled the heart.

"Yes, Madam," Kiber answered.

"Come into my room and give me your report." The woman vanished back into the fragrant shadows without waiting to see if her command was obeyed.

There was no question that it would be. Kiber, with a quivering sigh, entered the chambers of the Black Sorceress, wishing devoutly he was anywhere else, even setting foot upon the ghuls' ship instead. Far better his flesh be devoured than his soul, doomed to Sul's abyss—if the Sorceress chose—where not even his God would be able to find him.

Alone in the room, Zohra stood staring at nothing. There was no one to see her now. Pride, because it feeds on others, began to starve and waste away quickly, and hysteria was there to take its place. Zohra lifted her face to the Heavens, a cry burning in her throat.

"Free me, Akhran!" she screamed furiously, flailing her arms. "Free me from this prison!"

The frenzied excitement lasted only moments, draining her remaining strength. Zohra sank down to the floor and lay there in a kind of stupor, eventually slipping into exhausted sleep.

The cold woke her. Shivering, Zohra sat up. The nap had done her some good. She felt strong enough to blush with shame over the memory of her outburst. Anger returned, too, anger at Mathew for involving her in this and then abandoning her, anger at Khardan for his failures, anger at the God for refusing to answer her prayers.

"I am alone, as I have always been alone," Zohra said to herself. "I must do what I can to leave this horrible place and return to my people."

Rising to her feet, she walked over and tried to open the door. It was locked. She jerked on the handle several times, but it refused to give. Biting her lip in frustration, she turned and looked around the room, examining it for a way out.

An iron brazier standing on a tripod in a corner lighted the chamber, which was small and square and high-ceilinged. It had no windows and no other door except the one against which Zohra leaned. A handwoven carpet of extraordinarily beautiful design covered the floor, several black lacquer chairs were placed about the rug, small tables stood beside them.

Shivering in her wet clothes, Zohra walked the length and width of the room, searching for even the smallest crack. There was none, she realized, and the thought came to her, then, that she was trapped within these four walls. Never before had she been in any walled place. The yurts in which her people lived were temporary dwellings, made to let in air and light. They adapted to nature, permitted it entry. They did not shut it out and deny it.

The cold stone walls seemed to grow thicker the longer Zohra stared at them. Their solid structure and permanence weighted her down. The air was smoky and filled with dust that covered the furniture and the floor. She felt an increasing sensation of being unable to catch her breath and sank down into one of the chairs. The room was smaller than she'd noticed. What would happen when she used up all the air? She shrank back in the chair, panting, nervously twisting the rings on her fingers.

"Princess!" cried a distraught voice.

A puff of white smoke issued from a ring and hovered on the floor before her, swelling like a ball of flabby white dough. A turban, a pair of yellow silk *pantalons*, pointed shoes, and a fat face, squinched up in misery, gradually took form.

"Usti!" gasped Zohra.

Throwing himself at Zohra's feet, the djinn wrapped his fat arms around her legs and burst into tears.

"Save me, Princess!" he wailed. "Save me!"

# Chapter 6

"Save *you*?" repeated Zohra angrily, trying without success to free herself from the grip of the clinging, blubbering djinn. "I'll save you—in a goatskin!"

"Goatskin!" Usti hastily released his hold on Zohra. Sitting back on his heels, he groaned and mopped his eyes with the cloth of his turban that had come partially unwound and dangled down the side of his head. The djinn's clothes were torn and bedraggled, his face was grimy—now streaked with slobber, its expression woeful.

"I beg your pardon, Princess," whimpered the djinn. Every chin aquiver, he hiccuped. "But my life has been one of unendurable torment!"

"Your—!" Zohra began.

"For months," wailed Usti, placing his hands on his fat knees and rocking back and forth, "I've been sealed up inside . . . inside—"

He couldn't even say the word but pointed a trembling finger at the ring of smoky quartz on Zohra's hand.

"It was awful! When the 'efreet, Kaug, attacked the camp, my dwelling was destroyed. Fortunately I was outside of it at the time. I sought shelter in the first place I could find! That ring! And now, all these months, I've been trapped there! Nothing to eat and drink!" he sobbed wretchedly. "Nothing to do and no room to do it in. I've lost weight!" He gestured at his rotund stomach. "I'm skin and bones. And—"

Usti caught his breath in a gulp. Zohra had risen to her feet and was staring down at him with the formidable expression he knew so well.

"Skin and bones! You'll wish you were skin and bones, you bloated, oversized pig's bladder! I've been taken prisoner, brought to a sea that doesn't exist, carried across it on a ship filled with demons, and dragged to this awful place! Trapped in a ring!"

Glaring at the djinn, who was trying desperately to appear impressed and failing utterly, Zohra drew in a seething breath. Her hands flexed, her nails gleamed in the dim light. Usti's eyes flared wide in alarm, his visage began to waver.

The djinn was leaving!

She would be alone again!

"No! Don't go!" Zohra calmed herself. Sinking back into the chair, she held out a placating hand. "I didn't mean what I said. I—I'm frightened. I don't like this place or these people. You must free me! Get me out of here! You can do that, can't you, Usti?"

"Immortals, Princess, can do anything," said Usti loftily. "You will take me back to my brazier?"

"Yes, of course!"

"You won't make me return to that ring?"

"No!" Zohra snapped, exasperated, keeping a tight hold on the arms of the chair to prevent herself from grabbing hold of the djinn by the collar of his ripped silken shirt and shaking him until the remainder of his turban unrolled. "Hurry! Someone might come!"

"Very well," said Usti placidly. "First, I must know where we are."

"We're here!" Zohra cried, waving her hands.

"Unless the walls deign to speak, this tells me nothing," said the djinn coldly.

"Surely you were listening!" Zohra said accusingly. "You must know where we are!"

"Princess, how can you possibly have expected me, in my state of mental agony, to pay attention to the generally trite and uninteresting prattlings of mortals?" Usti was aggrieved.

Zohra's words came out strained through tightly clenched teeth. "We are being held captive by those who call themselves Black Paladins. They serve a God named Shakran or something—"

"Zhakrin, Princess?"

"Yes, that seems right. And we are on an island in the—"

"—middle of the Kurdin Sea," finished Usti crisply. "An island known as Galos. This, then, must be Castle Zhakrin." He glanced about with interest. "I have heard of this place."

"Good!" Zohra sighed in relief. "Now, hurry. You must take me"—she hesitated, thinking rapidly—"*us* out of here." Khardan would be forever in her debt. This would make twice she had saved his life.

"Impossible," said Usti. "Us? Who's us?"

"What do you mean—impossible!" Zohra's hands curled over the arms of the chair, her eyes glittered feverishly.

Usti blanched but did not quail before his mistress's anger. An expression of self-righteousness illumined his fat face. Clasping his fingers over his stomach, he said importantly, "I swore an oath."

"Yes, to serve your mistress, you—!"

"Begging your pardon, Princess, but this oath takes precedence and would be so adjudged in the Immortals' Court. It is a rather long story—"

"But one I am eager to hear!" Zohra's lip curled dangerously.

Usti gulped, but he had right on his side and so proceeded. "It involved my former master two masters ago, one Abu Kir, a man exceedingly fond of his food. It was he, the blessed Abu Kir, may Akhran himself have the pleasure of dining with him in heaven, who taught me the delights of the palate." Usti gave a moist hiccup. "And to think I should be forced to talk about him, I—who have not dined in months! Be still, poor shriveled thing"—he patted his stomach—"we shall dine soon, if there is anything fit to eat in this wretched place. Yes," he continued hastily, "begging your pardon, Princess. We were speaking of Abu Kir. One night, Abu Kir summoned me forth.

" 'Usti, my noble friend, I have a taste this evening for kumquats.'

" 'Nothing easier, My Master,' I said, being, of course, always willing to serve. 'I will send for the slave to run to the market.'

" 'Ah, it is not that easy, Usti,' said Abu Kir. 'The kumquats I fancy grow only in one place—the garden of the immortal Quar. I have heard that one taste of their sweet, thick lusciousness, and a human will forget all trouble and care.'

" 'Truly, Master, you have heard correctly. I myself have

tasted them, and that is no exaggeration. But acquiring the fruits of that garden is more difficult than inducing the mother of a beautiful young virgin to let her daughter spend the night in your bed. In fact, Master, if you but command it, I have a virgin in mind that will make you forget all about kumquats.'

" 'Women!' said Abu Kir in scorn. 'What are they compared to food! Fetch me the kumquats of Quar's garden, Usti, and I will—in turn—grant you your freedom!'

"I could not refuse such a generous offer; besides, I am—as you know, Princess—most devoted to those I serve and do my best to please them. A djinn of Akhran could not very well walk into the garden of Quar, however, and beg for kumquats, especially when Kaug—may his snout suck up sea water—is the gardener.

"Therefore I went to an immortal of Quar's and asked him if he would be so kind as to fetch me several kumquats from the garden of his master.

" 'Nothing would give me greater pleasure,' said Quar's djinn. 'And I would fly to do so right now except that my mistress has had her favorite jade-and-coral necklace stolen by one of the followers of Benario. I was currently on my way to try to persuade one of the God's light-fingered immortals to persuade his master to return it. Otherwise, dear Usti, I would bring you the kumquats.'

"He looked at me out of the corner of his slanted eye as he spoke, and I knew what I must do to obtain the kumquats.

"Off I went to the immortal of Benario, first taking care, as you might imagine, that I had left my purse safely in my charcoal brazier."

Zohra leaned her head on her hand.

"I told you it was a long story," Usti said deprecatingly.

"How long until we get to Zhakrin and your 'oath'?"

"Just coming to that, Princess. You see, the immortal of Benario promised to return the jade-and-coral necklace in exchange for an assassin's dagger made by the followers of Zhakrin. Therefore I went—"

"Shhh!" Sitting up, Zohra stared at the door. The sound of rustling could be heard outside, a strong scent of perfume drifted into the room.

"Musk," said Usti, sneezing.

"Shhh!" Zohra hissed.

A key rattled in the lock.

"Get back into the ring!" Zohra whispered.

"Princess!" Usti stared at her in horror.

"Do as I command!" Zohra said fiercely, holding out her left hand, the smoky quartz sparkling on her finger.

The lock on the door clicked. Usti cast a despairing glance at the ring. The door began to open. The djinn gasped, as though struck a physical blow. He gave the door a terrified glance. His eyeballs bulging in his head, he changed instantly into smoke, spiraled up to the ceiling, and dove headlong into the ring.

Zohra took a moment to glance at the ring as the djinn disappeared inside. It was a plain silver ring with its darkish gem. It was ugly, and it wasn't hers. Hurriedly, she clapped her hand over it and turned to face her visitor.

A woman stood in the doorway, delicately sniffing the air. Her face was not veiled; she wore no covering over her head. Thick hair, chestnut brown, was pulled back into a tight, intricately twisted coil worn on the back of her head. Her robes of black velvet swept the floor as she walked; the symbol of the severed snake that Zohra had seen both on Khardan's armor and fluttering from the mast of the ghuls' ship adorned her left breast. Her face was remarkable for its clear-cut beauty, but—in the light of the brazier standing near the door—the white skin took on a grayish cast, reminding Zohra of the ivory jars the goums had loaded aboard the ship.

"I demand that you release me." The words were on Zohra's lips, but they were never uttered.

The woman said nothing. She simply stood in the doorway, her hand on the handle, looking at Zohra intently with eyes whose color was indistinguishable. Zohra met and returned the gaze haughtily at first. Then she noticed that her eyes began to sting and water. She might have been looking directly into the sun. The sensation became painful. The woman had neither moved nor spoken; she stared straight at Zohra. But Zohra could no longer look at her. Tears blurred her vision; the pain grew, spreading from her eyes to her head. She averted her gaze, and instantly the pain ceased. Breathing hard, she stared at the floor, not daring to look back at the strange woman.

"Who has been here?" the woman asked.

Zohra heard the door shut, the rustle of black robes

whisper across the floor. The odor of musk was overpowering, choking.

"No one," said Zohra, her hand covering the ring, her eyes on the carpet at her feet.

"Look at me when you speak. Or do you fear me?"

"I do not fear anyone!" Zohra proudly lifted her head and glanced at the woman, but the pain returned and she started to turn away. Reaching out, the woman caught hold of Zohra's chin in her hand and held it firmly. Her grip was unusually strong.

"Look at me!" she said again, softly.

Zohra had no choice but to stare straight into the woman's eyes. The pain became excruciating. Zohra cried out, shutting her eyelids and struggling to free herself. The woman held her fast.

"Who was here?" she asked again.

"No one!" Zohra cried thickly, the pain throbbing in her head.

The woman held her long seconds. Blood beat in Zohra's temples, she felt nauseous and faint, then, suddenly, the hand released its hold, the woman turned away.

Gasping, Zohra slumped over in her chair. The pain was gone.

"Kiber said you were brave." The woman's voice touched her now like cool water, soothing her. Zohra heard the robes rustle, the soft sound of a chair being moved across the carpeting. The woman settled herself directly across from Zohra, within arm's reach. Cautiously Zohra lifted her eyes and looked at the woman once more. The pain did not return. The woman smiled at her approvingly, and Zohra relaxed.

"Kiber is quite an admirer of yours, my dear," said the woman. "As is Auda ibn Jad, from what I hear. I congratulate you. Ibn Jad is an extraordinary man. He has never before requested a specific woman."

Zohra tossed her head contemptuously. The subject of Auda ibn Jad was not worthy of being discussed. "I have been brought here by mistake," she said. "The one called Mat-hew is the one you want. You have him, therefore you must—"

"—let you go?" The woman's smile widened, a mother being forced to refuse a child some absurd demand. "No, my dear. Nothing ever happens by mischance. All is as the God desires it. You were brought here for a purpose. Perhaps it may be the very great honor of increasing the God's followers. Perhaps"—the woman hesitated, studying Zohra more intently—"perhaps there is another reason. But, no, you were not brought here by mistake, and you will not be released."

"Then I will go of my own accord!" Zohra rose to her feet.

"The Guardians of our Castle are called *nesnas*," said the woman conversationally. "Have you ever heard of them, my dear? They have the shape of a man—a man that has been divided in half vertically, possessing half a head, one arm, half a trunk, one leg, one foot. They are forced to hop on that one leg, but they can do so quite swiftly, as fast as a human can run on two. There have been one or two women who have managed to escape the Castle. We do not know what happened to them, for they were never seen again, although we heard their screams several nights running. We do know, however"—the woman smoothed a fold of her velvet robes— "that the *nesnas'* population increases, and we can only assume that, though they are half men in almost all aspects, there must be one aspect, at least, in which they are whole."

Slowly, Zohra sank back into her seat.

"I did not think you would want to leave us quite this soon."

"Who are you?"

"I am called the Black Sorceress. My husband is the Lord of the Black Paladins. He and I have ruled our people over seventy years—"

Zohra stared at the woman in astonishment.

"My age? Yes, I see you find that remarkable. I can promise you the same eternal youth, my dear, if you prove tractable."

"What do you want of me?"

"Now you are being reasonable. We want your body. That and the fruit it will bear. Have you ever borne children?"

Zohra shook her head disdainfully.

"Yes you are wife to the one who was attacked by the ghuls."

Zohra's face burned. Pressing her lips together, she stared into the flickering light of the brazier. She could feel the eyes of the sorceress on her and she had the uncomfortable sensation that the woman could see into the very depths of her soul.

"Extraordinary," the sorceress murmured. "Let me tell you, my dear, how the God chooses to honor women brought into this Castle. Those who are found worthy are selected to be the Breeders. It is they who are increasing the followers of Zhakrin so that our great God can return to us in strength and in might. Every night these women are placed into special rooms, and each midnight the Black Paladins enter this tower and go to the rooms. Here, each man honors the chosen woman by depositing his seed within her womb. When that seed takes, and the woman becomes pregnant, she is removed from the rooms and is well cared for until the babe is delivered. Then she is returned to the rooms to conceive another—"

"I would die first," stated Zohra calmly.

"Yes," remarked the sorceress, smiling. "I believe you would. Many say that, in the early days, and a few have attempted it. But we cannot afford to allow such waste, and I have means by which I make the most obdurate eager to obey my will."

Zohra's lip curled in scorn.

The sorceress rose to her feet. "I will have dry clothing brought to you, as well as food and drink. A room is being prepared for you. When it is ready, you will be taken there."

"You are wasting your time. No man will touch me!" Zohra said, speaking slowly and distinctly.

The sorceress raised an eyebrow, smiled, and glided toward the door, which opened at her approach. Two women, dressed in black robes similar to those of the sorceress, slipped noiselessly inside the room. One bore a bundle of black velvet in her arms, the other carried a tray of food. Neither woman spoke to Zohra or even looked at her, but kept their eyes lowered. Under the watchful gaze of the sorceress, they deposited the clothes upon a chair and set the tray of food upon a table. Then they silently departed. The sorceress, giving Zohra one final glance, followed them.

Zohra listened for the key but did not hear it. Swiftly, she ran to the door and pressed her ear against it. When all sounds had ceased in the corridor, she pulled on the handle. The door remained sealed fast. From far away, Zohra thought she heard a soft tinkle of laughter. Angrily, she whirled around.

"Usti!" she whispered.

Nothing happened.

"Usti!" she repeated furiously, shaking the ring.

Smoke drizzled out, coalescing into the form of a pale and shaken djinn.

"That woman is a witch!"

"To say the least. Oath or no oath, you must get me out of here!"

"No, Mistress!" Usti licked his lips. "She is a witch! A true witch! In all my lifetimes, I have never met such a powerful human. She knew I was here!"

"Impossible!" Zohra scoffed. "Quit making excuses and return Khardan and me to our desert this instant!" She stamped her foot.

"She spoke to me!" Usti began to tremble. "She told me what she would do to me if I crossed her. Princess"—he began to blubber—"I do not want to spend my eternal life sealed up in an iron box, wrapped round with iron chains! Farewell, Princess!"

The djinn leaped back into the ring with such alacrity that Zohra was momentarily blinded by the swirl of smoke. Enraged, she grabbed hold of the circlet of silver, and tried to yank it from her finger. It was stuck fast. She tugged and twisted, but the ring would not come off, and finally, her finger swollen and aching, she gave up.

She was shaking with cold. The smell of food made her mouth water.

"I must keep up my strength," she said to herself. "Since it seems I must fight this alone, it won't do to fall sick from a chill or hunger."

Her mind searching for some way out of this situation, Zohra stripped off her wet gown and replaced it with the black robes on the chair. Clothed and warm again, she sat down to dine. As she lifted the cover from the tray, her eyes caught the glimmer of steel.

"Ah!" Zohra breathed and swiftly picking up the knife, she tucked it into a pocket of her gown.

The food was delicious. All her favorites were on the various plates—stripes of *shiskhlick* grilled to her exact taste, succulent fruit, honey cakes, and candied almonds. A carafe was filled to the brim with clear, cold water, and she drank thirstily. Her strength returned and with it hope. The knife pressed reassuringly against her flesh. She could use it to force the door lock, then make her way out of the Castle. Dressed like all the others, she would simply be taken for one of the other women, and surely they must go about the castle on some errand or other. Once outside—Zohra thought of the *nesnas*.

Half men who hop on one leg! The sorceress must take her for a child to believe such stories. Zohra had a momentary regret in leaving Khardan; she recalled him lying in the litter, shivering and moaning in agony; she saw the bluish-purplish scratches on his arm and body, and she remembered guiltily that he had been willing to give his life to defend her.

Well, she told herself, it was all for his own honor, anyway. She cares nothing for me. He hates me for what Mathew and I did to him; humiliating him by taking him from the battlefield. I shouldn't have done it. That vision was stupid. Undoubtedly it was some trick of Mathew's to . . . to . . .

How hot it was! Zohra loosened the neck of the robe, unbuttoning the tiny buttons that held it together. It was growing unbearably warm. She seemed to smell again the stifling odor of musk. She was becoming sleepy, too. She should not have eaten so much. Blinking her heavy eyelids, Zohra struggled to her feet.

"I must keep awake!" she said aloud, tossing some of the cool water on her face. Standing up, she began to walk around the room, only to feel the floor slip away beneath her feet. She staggered into a chair and grabbed hold of it for support. The light coming from the brazier was surrounded, suddenly, by a rainbow of color. The walls of the room began to breathe in and out. Her tongue seemed dry, and there was an odd taste in her mouth.

Zohra stumbled back to the table, clinging to chairs, and grabbed hold of the water carafe. She lifted it to her lips. . . .

*"I have means by which I can make the most obdurate eager to obey my will."*

The carafe fell to the floor with a crash.

Two women, clothed in black, carried Zohra from the antechamber. Zohra's eyes were open, she stared at them dreamily, a vacant, vacuous smile on her lips.

"What do we do with her?"

The Black Sorceress looked down at the nomad woman, then raised her eyes to the red velvet curtain covering the archway. The two women holding Zohra by her arms and legs exchanged swift glances; one lowered her eyes to her own swelling belly, and a small sigh escaped her lips.

"No," said the Black Sorceress after a moment's profound

thought. "I am not clear in my mind about this one. The God's message is to wait. Take her to the chamber next to mine."

The women nodded silently and moved down the hall, carrying their burden between them.

The sonorous clanging of an iron bell, sounding from a tower high above them, caused the Black Sorceress to lift her head. Her eyes gleamed.

"Vestry," she murmured, and wrapping her fingers around an amulet she wore at her neck, she disappeared.

# Chapter 7

Auda ibn Jad had been at Mathew's side, step for step and almost heartbeat for heartbeat, as they made their way up from the beach to Castle Zhakrin. Mathew's sodden wet clothes clung to him. The mournful wind cut through his flesh like slivers of ice, but was nothing compared to the cold, glittering side-ways glances of the Black Paladin. Always the focus of that piercing gaze—even when ibn Jad was talking to a fellow knight—Mathew had a difficult time maintaining his composure when faced with the horrors of the Castle. A follower of Astafas, he was certain, would not stare fearfully at the gruesome heads that guarded the bridge, or shrink away from the human skeletons on the walls.

By the time ibn Jad had escorted him to an antechamber located on the ground level of the palace, and left him there alone with a flask of wine to ease the chill, Mathew thought that he had performed adequately. No credit to himself. After the long walk to the Castle in the company of the Black Paladin, the young wizard was so miserable and cold that he doubted if any emotion other than terror was left inside him.

Shivering so he could barely keep hold of the glass, Mathew drank a little wine, hoping to lift his spirits and warm his blood. All the wine squeezed from every grape in the world could not obliterate reality, however.

I may have deceived ibn Jad, he thought, but I can never hope to deceive the Black Sorceress. A skilled Archmagus would see through me as if I were crystal. Mathew had little doubt—from the obviously high regard in which this woman was held—that this Black Sorceress was, indeed, very skilled.

Hoping to distract himself from his mounting fear, Mathew listlessly examined his surroundings. The room was bleak and comfortless. A huge fireplace dominated almost one entire wall, but no fire burned there. Fuel must be difficult to obtain on this barren isle, Mathew realized, peering wistfully at the cold ashes upon the hearth. He knew now why everyone dressed in such heavy clothing and began to think with longing of soft black velvet draping him with warmth. Drawing back thick red curtains, he found a window. Made of large panes of leaded, stained glass bearing the design of the severed snake, it had no bars and looked as if it could be easily opened. Mathew had no wish to try it, however. Though he could not see them, he sensed the dark and evil beings that lurked outside. His life would not be worth a copper's purchase if he set foot beyond the Castle walls.

Turning back, leaning upon the mantelpiece above the chill fireplace, Mathew saw no hope for them—for any of them. Auda ibn Jad had described in a cold, dispassionate voice what fate awaited Zohra in the Tower of Women. The Black Paladin made it clear that he admired the nomad woman for the strong and spirited followers she would deliver to the God, adding that he planned to request her for his own private use, at least to father her first few children. Ibn Jad's talk of his intentions sickened Mathew more then the sight of the polished skulls adorning the stair railings. If the man had spoken with lust or desire, he would at least have demonstrated some human feeling, if only of the basest nature. Instead, Auda ibn Jad spoke as if he were discussing the breeding of sheep or cattle.

"What will happen to Khardan?" Mathew had asked, abruptly changing the subject.

"Ah, that I cannot say," was Auda's reply. "It will be up to the members of the Vestry this night. I can only make my recommendation."

Alone in the bitterly cold room, sipping the wine that tasted like blood in his mouth, Mathew wondered what this meant. Recalling the human heads mounted on the Dead March, he shuddered. But surely if they were intent only upon murdering Khardan they would not go through such ceremony. Ibn Jad had been ready to toss the Calif to the ghuls, but that had been done in anger or . . .

Mathew stared into the flame of a candle burning on the mantelpiece. Perhaps it had been a test. Perhaps ibn Jad had never intended to give Khardan to the ghuls.

A soft knock upon the door made Mathew start; his hand shook so that he sloshed wine on his wet clothes. He tried to bid the person enter, but his voice couldn't escape past the choking sensation in his throat. Not that it mattered; the door opened and a woman stepped inside.

She smote Mathew with the heat of the blazing desert sun, blinding him, burning him. Her evil was deep and dark and ancient as the Well of Sul. Her majesty overawed, her power overwhelmed, and Mathew bowed before her as he would have bowed to the head of his own Order. He was conscious of eyes studying him, eyes that had studied countless others before him, eyes that were old and wise in the knowledge of the terrible depths of the human soul.

There could be no lying to those eyes.

"You come from Tirish Aranth," said the Black Sorceress. The door shut silently behind her.

"Yes, Madam," answered Mathew inaudibly.

"That facet of the Jewel of Sul shared by Promenthas and your God, Astafas."

"Yes, Madam." Did she know he lied? How could she not? She must know everything.

"I have heard that in this part of the world men have the gift of magic. I have never met a male sorcerer before. You are man and not eunuch?"

"I am a man," Mathew murmured, his face flushing.

"How old are you?"

"Eighteen."

He was conscious of the eyes staring at him intently, and then suddenly he was enveloped by a fragrance of heady musk. The walls around him changed to water and began to slide down into some vast ocean that was rising up around him. Soft lips touched his, skillful hands caressed his body. The smell, the touch aroused almost instantaneous desire. . . .

And then he heard a laugh.

The water disappeared, the walls surrounded him again, the fragrance was blown away by a cold wind. Gasping, he caught his breath.

"I am sorry," said the sorceress, amused, "but I had to

make certain you were telling the truth. A man your age with no beard, features and skin any woman might envy. I have heard it said that men gained magic at the price of their manhood, but I see that is not so."

Breathing heavily, his body burning with shame and embarrassment, disgust twisting his stomach, Mathew could not reply nor even look at the woman.

"Male children born to you will acquire this gift?"

"They may or may not," answered Mathew, wondering at this unexpected question. Then Auda ibn Jad's description of the Tower of Women came to his mind. He lifted his head and stared at her.

"Yes." She answered his thought. "You will prove quite valuable to us. Male magi!" The sorceress drew in a deep breath of pleasure. "Warriors trained to kill with arcane weapons! We could well become invincible. It is a pity"—she regarded him coolly—"that there aren't more of you. Perhaps Astafas could be persuaded to lend us others?"

"I—I'm certain . . . he would be honored, as would I, t-to serve you," stammered Mathew, not knowing what else to say. The suggestion appalled him, he felt again the touch of the woman's hands on his body, and he hastily averted his face, hoping to hide his repugnance.

It obviously didn't work. "Perhaps a bit more manly than you," the sorceress said wryly. "And now tell me, how did one as young and obviously inexperienced as yourself manage to summon and control an imp of Sul?"

Mathew stared at her helplessly. He was a wet rag in this woman's hands. She had wrung him and wrenched him. He had no dignity, no humanity left. She had reduced him to the level of a beast.

"I don't know!" He hung his head. "I don't know!"

"I thought as much," the sorceress said gently. A hand patted him, an arm stole around his shoulder. It was now a mother's touch—soothing and comforting. She led him back to his chair and he sank down, unnerved and sobbing—a child in her arms.

"Forgive me, my son," said the soft voice, and Mathew raised his head and saw the sorceress clearly for the first time. He saw the beauty, the cruelty, the evil, and that strange compassion he had seen on the face of Auda ibn Jad and the other worshipers of Zhakrin. "Poor boy," she murmured and his own mother could not have grieved for him more. "I had to do this to you. I had to make certain." She stroked his face with her hand. "You are new to the paths of the shadow and you find the walking difficult. So do all who come to us from the light, but in time you will grow accustomed to and even revel in the darkness." The sorceress cupped his face in her hands, staring deeply into his eyes.

"And you are fortunate!" she whispered passionately, a thrill in her voice transmitting itself to Mathew's flesh. "Fortunate above all men for Astafas has obviously *chosen* you to do his bidding! He is granting you power you would otherwise not have! And that means he is aware of us and watching us and supporting our struggle!"

Mathew began to shake uncontrollably as the import of her words and their truth tore open his soul.

"The transition will be painful," said the sorceress, holding him close, pitying his fear, "but so is every birth." She drew his head to her breast, smoothing his hair. "Long I mourned that I could bring only daughters of magic into this world. Long I dreamed of giving birth to a son born to the talent. And now you have come—the Bearer, chosen to guard, to carry our most precious treasure! It is a sign! I take you for my own, from this moment." Her lips pressed against his flesh, stabbing like a knife at his heart. He cringed and cried out with the pain.

"It hurts," she said softly, brushing away a tear that had fallen from her eye onto Mathew's cheek. "I know it hurts, my little one, but the agony will soon end, and then you will find peace. And now I must leave you. The man, Khardan, waits for my ministration so that he may be fit to receive the honor that is going to be bestowed upon him. Here is clothing. Food will be brought to you. Is there anything else you desire— What is your name?"

"Mathew!" The word seemed squeezed out of his chest by his bursting heart.

"Mathew. Nothing else you want? Then make yourself ready. The Vestry convenes at ten this evening, four hours from now. Ah, poor boy." Her tongue clicked against the roof of her mouth. "Fainted dead away. His mind can accept this, but not his heart. It fights me, it fights the darkness. I will win, though. I will win!

"Astafas has given me a son!"

# Chapter 8

In Castle Zhakrin was a great hall made entirely of black marble—perfectly circular in shape. Black columns surrounded a large center floorspace in which the signet of the severed serpent, done in gold, had been inlaid in the marble. There was only one piece of furniture in the room at this time, and that was a small table on which stood an object covered with black velvet. The chamber was rarely opened and then only for ceremonial purposes, for the hall was known as the Vestry and it was here that the followers of Zhakrin met once monthly or, as on this occasion, whenever there was something of special significance to be brought before the people.

Having stored up winter's chill in its stone walls, the cold in the hall froze the heart. The black marble, gleaming in the light of innumerable torches that had been placed in sconces fashioned from the bones of human hands, might have been ice for the freezing breath it gave off. Mathew huddled thankfully within the warm, thick velvet of his new black robes, his hands folded in the sleeves.

At ten o'clock an iron bell rang through the Castle. The people of Zhakrin, with solemn mien, began to arrive in the hall. Swiftly and without confusion each took his or her place in the large circle that was forming around the severed serpent. There were fewer women than men. The women were dressed in black robes similar to those of the sorceress, and many were pregnant. Each woman stood beside a Black

Paladin, and Mathew realized that these must be their wives. He sensed within almost all the women a powerful gift for magic, and no longer did he have to wonder how these people managed to survive under such harsh and hostile conditions.

Sometimes, standing respectfully a few steps outside the circle of adults, was a young person of about sixteen years, this being the age required to first begin attending Vestry. From the comments made by those on entering and from the proud and fond looks given these young people, Mathew guessed that they were children of the Paladins. Again he marveled at the strange dichotomy of these people—the love and warmth extended to family members and friends; the heartless cruelty extended to the rest of the world.

The Black Sorceress appeared suddenly next to him, materializing out of the chill air. Remembering what had occurred between them in the room, Mathew lowered his head, a burning flush spreading over his skin. He knew he had fainted, he knew someone had dressed him and warmed him like a child, and he suspected who that person had been. The Black Sorceress gave no sign, either by word or look, that she was aware of his confusion. Standing beside him, she watched calmly and proudly as her people took their places in the circle. It was almost complete, with the exception of several gaps, and these were apparently left deliberately vacant.

"In time, you will be able to take your place with us in the Holy Circle," said the sorceress. "But for now you may not. Wait here and do not stir until you are summoned forth."

"How is Khardan?" Mathew asked softly.

In answer, the Black Sorceress turned her head slightly. Mathew followed her gaze and saw Kiber and another *goum* leading Khardan into the room. The Calif was pale and obviously confused and amazed by what he saw. But he walked firmly and steadily and there was no trace of pain on his face.

"And Zohra?" Mathew continued, swallowing, wondering at his daring.

"Zohra?" The sorceress was only half attending to his words; her eyes were on the gathering assembly.

"The woman who was with us?" Mathew pursued.

The sorceress glanced at him and shook her head, her eyes darkening. "Do not hold onto any interest in her, my son. There are many other women here as beautiful as that wild desert flower. That one is not for you. She has been chosen by another."

The Black Sorceress's voice was reverent and hushed. Thinking she meant Auda ibn Jad, Mathew was startled to see her look at the Black Paladin with a slight frown and a creased brow. "No, and not for him, either. I hope he does not take that ill." Shaking her head to prevent the young wizard from speaking further, the sorceress gave Mathew a reassuring smile, then left him, walking over to take her place in the circle beside the Lord of the Black Paladins.

A solemn hush fell over the assembly. All bowed their heads and clasped their hands before them. The Lord took a step forward.

"Zhakrin, God of Evil, we gather in your name to do you honor this night. We thank you for the safe return of our brother, Auda ibn Jad, and for the fulfillment, at last, of all that we have worked to achieve these many years."

"We thank you, Zhakrin," came the response from around the circle.

"And now, according to ancient tradition, we do honor to the fallen."

The Lord of Black Paladins turned to his wife, who drew near the black velvet-covered table. Removing the cloth, she lifted in her hand a golden chalice. Its foot was the body of a coiled snake, bearing a cup wrapped in its coils. Placing her hand over the chalice, the Black Sorceress whispered arcane words and sprinkled a powder from inside a golden ring she wore on her finger. Entering the circle, she walked slowly across the black marble floor and handed the chalice to Auda ibn Jad. He accepted it from her reverently, bowing his head. Turning to the empty place beside him in the circle, Auda raised the chalice.

"To our brother, Catalus."

"To Catalus," came the response.

Ibn Jad put the chalice to his lips, sipped at whatever was inside, then solemnly moved across the circle to present the chalice to a woman dressed in black.

She spoke in a language Mathew did not understand, but there was an empty place in the circle beside her, as well. The chalice went from hand to hand. Mathew gathered from those words he could understand that many of those being remembered here had died in the city of Meda. Several of the Black Paladins wept openly. A man put his arm around the shoulders of a woman; they drank out of the chalice together, and Mathew understood that a beloved son had been among those who killed themselves in the Temple rather than permit their souls to be offered up to Quar. The grief of these people moved Mathew deeply. Tears came to his eyes and might have fallen had not the chalice passed again to the Lord of the Black Paladins. He handed it to his wife, who held it reverently.

"Now it is the time to put grief aside and prepare for joy," said the Lord of the Black Paladins. "Our brother, Auda ibn Jad, will now relate to us what he has done on his journeys in the name of Zhakrin."

Auda ibn Jad stepped forward and began to speak. There followed a tale of such atrocities that Mathew's tears were burned out of his eyes and he grit his teeth in order to keep from crying out. Villages burned, the elderly and very young slaughtered without mercy, the fit and strong captured and sold into slavery. Ibn Jad spoke proudly of the murder of the priests and magi of Promenthas who had been so unlucky as to set foot upon the shores of Tara-kan. He described their deaths in detail and went on to relate the sparing of the life of the young sorcerer who—as it turned out—had been sent to them by Astafas.

Cringing, Mathew kept his head lowered, chills shaking his body. He was aware of eyes upon him—eyes of those standing in the circle, the eyes of the Black Sorceress, the eyes of ibn Jad. Mathew was acutely aware, too, of another pair of eyes watching him, and he felt a swift, secret thrill of sweet pain. It was the first time Khardan had ever heard Mathew's story, and he could sense the Calif regarding him with sympathy and dawning understanding.

Auda ibn Jad continued his story, relating how Khardan and his nomads had wrecked the bazaars of Kich, how they had stolen Mathew from ibn Jad, and had then ravaged the Temple of Quar. Ibn Jad did not seem to mind telling tales against himself and related Khardan's bravery and valor in terms that won the Calif murmurs of approval and a grim smile from the Lord of the Black Paladins.

Auda went on to relate how the Amir had taken out his wrath at this effrontery to Quar by attacking the nomads, taking their women and children and young men prisoner, and scattering the tribes. The people of Zhakrin regarded

Khardan with the shared compassion of those who have suffered a similar fate. Mathew saw now that ibn Jad was purposefully establishing Khardan as a hero in the eyes of Zhakrin's followers. The words the Black Sorceress had spoken, the "honor to be bestowed upon him" came to Mathew's mind. It all sounded well, as if Khardan were out of danger. But Mathew's uneasiness grew, particularly as he listened to what had occurred during their journey from the desert of Pagrah north—the cold-blooded butchering of innocent people in the city of Idrith. Now he knew it was their blood—drained from the bodies—contained in those ivory jars, and his soul recoiled in horror as he remembered leaning against the jars on board the ship.

Khardan, too, must be wondering at the Black Paladin's intent. His face dark and suspicious, the Calif watched ibn Jad warily. There was a saying among the nomads that Mathew had heard, and he knew Khardan must be thinking of it now.

"Beware the honeyed tongue. It oft drips poison."

Ibn Jad finished his tale. It was applauded with soft murmurs from the women, deeper-voiced approval from the men. The Lord of the Paladins spoke of his pleasure and the Black Sorceress rewarded Auda with a nod and a smile and another drink from the chalice. Mathew had no idea what the cup contained, but he saw a rising flush come to Auda ibn Jad's pale, stern cheek; the cruel eyes glowed with increasing ferocity. The chalice was then passed from one person in the circle to the next, each taking a drink. It never, apparently, ran dry, and as the cup passed from hand to hand, Mathew saw that each person began to burn with an inner flame.

Ibn Jad returned to his place within the circle, and the Lord stepped forward.

"Now we will speak our recent history, that each may hear it once again so that it echoes forever in the heart. To those who are new to us and hearing this for the first time"— his eyes went to Mathew and Khardan—"this will help you to better understand us.

"Long ago, Zhakrin was a rising power in this world. And as is often the way of Sul, when the Facet of Evil began to glow more brightly in the heavens, the Facet of Good gleamed brilliantly as well. Many and glorious were the encounters between the Black Paladins of Zhakrin and the White Knights of Evren, the Good Goddess." The Lord's voice softened, his aged eyes looked far away. "Just barely do I remember that time. I was no more than a boy, squire to my knight. Brave deeds were done in the name of both the Dark and the Light, each striving for supremacy with honor, as becomes knights.

"And then there came a time when the price of honor was too dear." The Lord sighed. "Immortal beings who had long served us no longer answered our prayers. The power of our God Himself was weakened. The people sickened and died, women grew barren. Some turned, then, to other Gods and Zhakrin grew weaker still. And it was in this hour that the followers of Evren began to persecute us—so it seemed— and, in anger and desperation, we fought back. Like dogs, we hunted each other down, expending our dwindling energies in savage hatred. Our numbers lessened, as did theirs, and we were forced to withdraw from the world, to hide in places dark and secret, and then we spent our days and nights searching each other out." The Lord's face grew grim. "No longer were the contests glorious and brave. We could not afford that. We struck by night, by stealth, as did they. Knives in the back replaced swords face-to-face.

"And then came the time when the fire in our hearts turned to black ash, and we knew our God was defeated. All but the most faithful left us then, for we were weak and had only the power within us with which to fight the battle that is this life. We fled here, to this place. With the strength we had remaining, we built this Castle. We cursed the name of Evren and plotted to destroy her followers if it cost us every last drop of our blood.

"Then a God came to us. It was not our God. It was a strange God we had never before seen. He appeared before us, standing in that very place." The Lord gestured at the head of the snake in the floor. "We asked his name. He said he was known only as the Wandering God"—Mathew glanced at Khardan in astonishment; the Calif's mouth sagged open— "and that he brought urgent news. It was not Evren who caused our Zhakrin's downfall. She herself was gone as well, and all her immortals hid away as did we.

" 'Your fight is not with each other,' " said this Wandering God. 'You have been duped by one called Quar, who tricked you into nearly destroying each other, and while you were fighting, he took the field and claimed the victory. He seeks to become the One, True God; to make all men bow down and worship him.'

"The strange God disappeared, and we discussed this long

among ourselves. We sent our knights to investigate. They found that the Wandering God had spoken the truth. Quar was the rising power in the world. It seemed that there were few who could stop him. Then it was that Auda ibn Jad—at great peril to his life—disguised himself as a priest of Quar and penetrated the very inner circles of the God's Temple in the Emperor's court of Khandar. Here he discovered the essences of Zhakrin and Evren, held prisoner by Quar. Auda ibn Jad summoned my wife to his aid. Together and in secret they succeeded in snatching the souls of the Gods from Quar, who even now, perhaps, is not yet aware that they are gone.

"Last time we met, you heard my wife's story of this daring theft. You heard her relate their final triumph. She and her knights traveled back here, drawing off pursuit, leaving Auda ibn Jad and his brave soldiers to slip unobserved into Ravenchai with the precious treasure they guarded. This night you have heard him relate his adventures in returning home to us. And now you—"

Mathew heard no more. The sound of pounding waves, the roar of rushing wind throbbed in his head. Pressing his hand over his breast, he felt the crystal globe cold and smooth against his skin.

The Bearer.

He knew now what he carried. Two fish—one dark, one light . . .

Mathew stared at the knights aghast, saw them all turn to look at him. The Lord's mouth was moving, he was saying something but his words were obliterated by the throbbing in Mathew's head and he couldn't hear. The Black Sorceress stepped into his line of vision and into his heart and his mind. She was all he could see, could think about. Her words alone he could understand, and when she raised her hand and beckoned, he responded.

"Let the Bearer come forward."

Moving slowly, Mathew stepped toward the Holy Circle. It broke and opened for him, it absorbed him and closed around him.

The Black Sorceress came to stand directly before the young wizard.

"Give me that which you bear," she said softly.

There was no denying her. Mathew's hand moved by her will, not his own. Reaching into the bosom of his black robes, he drew forth the crystal globe and held it in his trembling palm.

The golden fish remained motionless in the center of the globe; the black fish swam about in wide circles, its mouth opening wide, striking in excitement at his crystal walls.

Breathing a reverent sigh, the Black Sorceress lifted the globe gently and carefully. Mathew felt the slight weight leave his hands and a great weight, not noticed until now, leave his heart. The sorceress carried the globe to the table and laid it down beside the chalice. Then she covered both with the black velvet cloth.

"Hear me, my people." Her voice rang triumphantly through the Vestry. "Tomorrow night, our god, Zhakrin, will return to us!"

There was no sound from the God's followers, no cheering. The matter touched the soul too deeply for the voice to echo it. Their victory shone in their eyes.

"He will be weak and thus He has chosen to reside in a human body until He can gain strength and return to His immortal form. This will mean the death of the body in which He chooses to reside for His short stay upon this plane, for He will be forced to suck it dry of its life's juices to feed him—"

Auda ibn Jad sprang forward. "Let Him take my body! "

"Mine! Mine!" shouted the Black Paladins, breaking the circle, vying with each other for the honor.

The Black Sorceress raised her hand for silence.

"Thank you all. The God takes note of your courage. But He has made His choice and"—the sorceress smiled proudly—"it is to be the body of a female. As man is born of woman, so shall our God be brought forth in the body of a woman. Because He will not diminish the number of his followers, He has selected one of our female prisoners—the newest one. She is strong in magic, which the God will find useful. She is intelligent, strong-willed and spirited—"

"No!"

Mathew's mouth formed the word, but it was Khardan who shouted it.

"Take my body, if it's flesh you need to feed your accursed God!" the Calif cried fiercely, struggling to break free of Kiber and the *goum*, straining against them with such strength that Auda ibn Jad left his place within the circle and moved near Khardan, his hand on the hilt of the sword he wore at his waist. Turning, the Paladin looked back at the sorceress with a raised eyebrow.

She nodded, appearing well pleased. "It is as you said, ibn Jad. The nomad is noble and honorable. We know that he is strong and his spirit that of a warrior. You may begin his training tonight." Her eyes fixed upon Khardan. "Your offer becomes you, sir. But to accept such a sacrifice would be a tragic waste, abhorred by our God. You have proven your merit and will, therefore, serve Zhakrin in another way. You will begin your preparation to become one of the Black Paladins."

"I serve Akhran, the Wanderer, and no other!" Khardan retorted.

"As of now you serve Him. That will change," said the Black Sorceress gravely. "Since the circle has been broken, our Vestry is concluded. Auda ibn Jad, you will take the man below. His preparation will begin at once.

"We will reconvene tomorrow night at eleven o'clock," the sorceress continued, speaking to all. "The ceremony begins at midnight—the ending of one day and the beginning of another. So shall our God's return mark the beginning of a new time for the world."

"One question before we depart," said the Lord of the Black Paladins.

The sorceress turned respectfully to face her husband.

"We have here two holy beings—Zhakrin and Evren. What will we do with the Goddess of Good?"

"Because she is a Goddess and we but mortals, we are powerless to offer Her either help or harm. Her fate rests in the hands of Zhakrin."

The Lord nodded, and the people began to file out of the Vestry. The Black Sorceress remained, beckoning several of the women to join her. Their conversation was low and hushed, probably discussing tomorrow night's ceremony. Auda ibn Jad ordered Kiber, with a gesture, to bring Khardan, and together they left the Vestry.

Mathew glanced around. No one was paying any attention to him. He could see ibn Jad and his men traversing a narrow corridor. If I'm going to follow them, I must do so now, before they leave me behind. Silently, after one final look, he stole from the Vestry.

The eyes of the Black Sorceress did not mark his passing, but his footsteps resounded in her heart.

# Chapter 9

When did I begin to lose control? Khardan wondered angrily.

For twenty-five years, I've held life in my hand like a lump of cold iron ready for the forging. Then, suddenly, the iron changed to sand. Life began to slide through my fingers, and the harder I grasped hold of it, the more fell away from me.

It all started with the God's command that I marry Zohra and wait for that accursed Rose of the Prophet to bloom. What have I done to offend the God that he treats me thus? What have my people done? Why has Akhran allowed me to be brought here when my people need me? Instead of helping us to defeat our enemies, why has he chosen to appear to these *kafir* and assist them in their evil plots?

"Hear my prayer, Akhran!" Khardan muttered angrily. "Send my djinn to me! Or appear here with your fiery sword and free me!"

In the passion of his plea, the nomad strained against the leather thongs that bound his wrists together. Kiber growled, and a knife flashed in the light of a torch. Whirling, Khardan turned to face his attacker. Bound as he was, he was prepared to fight for his life, but Auda ibn Jad shook his head. Reaching out, he took the knife from Kiber, grabbed hold of Khardan's arms, and pushed him up against a wall. The knife sliced through the leather thongs.

"That will be all for the night, Kiber," Auda said. "You have leave to go to your quarters."

The *goum* bowed and, after giving Khardan one final, threatening glance, departed. Walking back down the hallway, Kiber seemed not to notice—since he had been given no orders concerning the matter—the black shape moving some distance behind them that vanished precipitously into the deeper darkness of an open doorway at the *goum*'s approach.

Khardan rubbed his wrists and stared suspiciously at ibn Jad. The two were alone in a shadowy hallway that was spiraling downward, taking them deep beneath the ground level of the Castle.

"Fight me!" Khardan said abruptly. "Your sword. My bare hands. It doesn't matter."

Auda ibn Jad appeared amused. "I admire your spirit, nomad, but you lack discipline and common sense. What have either of us to gain by fighting? Perhaps you could defeat me, although I doubt it, for I am well trained in forms of hand-to-hand combat of which you have no conception. Still, by some mischance you might win. Then what? Where would you go? Back to the ghuls?"

Khardan could not help himself; a shudder shook his body. Ibn Jad smiled grimly. "Such was my purpose in allowing them to attack you. I wouldn't have let them kill you, you know. You are far too valuable to us. Blossom's rescue of you was quite unexpected, although highly instructive, as it turned out. Strange are the ways of the God," he murmured reflectively and stared back down the hall in thoughtful silence. Shaking his head, breaking his reverie, ibn Jad continued. "No, I will not fight you. I have released your bonds so that we may walk together as men—with dignity."

"I will not serve your God!" Khardan said harshly.

"Come, let us not spend our time in pointless argument," Auda made a polite, graceful gesture with his slender hand. "Will you walk with me? The way is not far."

"Where are we going?"

"That will be seen."

Khardan stood irresolutely in the hallway, glancing up and down the torchlit corridor. Carved out of granite, it was narrow and grew narrower still up ahead. Torches lit the way, but they were placed upon the wall at intervals of about twenty or thirty feet and so left patches of darkness broken by circles of light. Farther back, at the beginning of the hall, after they'd left the Vestry, they had passed doorways and the arched entrances to other corridors. But soon these were left behind. The walls that had been made of smooth, polished stone gave way to rough-hewn blocks. There were no windows, there was absolutely no way out.

And if there was, there were the ghuls. . . .

Khardan began to walk down the hall, his dark brows lowering, his face grim and stern. Auda ibn Jad accompanied him.

"Tell me, is it true that your God— What is His name?"

"Akhran."

"—Akhran is known as the Wanderer? Could it be your God who came to us with news of Quar's duplicity?"

"Yes," Khardan admitted. "Akhran has warned us of Quar's treachery, and we have seen it for ourselves."

"In the Amir's attack on your people?"

"I did not flee the battle, dressed as a woman!"

"Of course not. That was the doing of Blossom and your wife, Zohra. A remarkable woman that one. I cannot imagine that she would be the kind to drag a man out of battle. Did she give you any explanation for this irrational behavior?"

"Something about a vision," Khardan replied irritably, not wanting to discuss the matter, not wanting to think about Zohra. Despite the fact that she had dishonored him in his bed, despite the fact that she had thwarted his marriage to Meryem and made him ridiculous in the eyes of his fellow tribesmen by forcing him into the position of accepting a man into his harem, she was his wife, deserving his protection, and he was helpless to grant it.

"A vision?"

"Women's magic," muttered Khardan.

"Do not disparage women's magic, nomad," said Auda ibn Jad gravely. "Through its power and the courage of those who wield it—courage as strong or stronger than any man—my people have survived. This vision was important enough to the woman to cause her to act upon it. I wonder what it was. And still more, how it might affect what I do now."

Khardan could hear the Paladin's unspoken words as plainly as the spoken; the thoughtful, brooding expression on Auda's face indicated how seriously he took this matter. Khardan began to regret that he had not questioned Mathew further on this point.

The Black Paladin did not speak for several minutes, while they continued to walk the winding hallway. At length, the light of the torches ended. Beyond them was impenetrable darkness and an evil whose depths were unfathomable.

Khardan stopped. A sudden weakness came over him. Trembling, he leaned against the wall. A draft wafting up those shadowy stairs caused him to shiver uncontrollably. It was as chill and damp as the breath of Death; its touch upon his skin was like the cold touch of a corpse.

Auda ibn Jad took a torch from a sconce on the wall and held it aloft. The light illuminated stone stairs descending in a sharp spiral.

"Courage, nomad," said the Paladin, his hand on Khardan's bare arm.

"What is down there? Where are you taking me?"

"To your destiny," answered Auda ibn Jad.

Khardan was about to hurl himself at the Black Paladin, make a last, desperate, hopeless attempt to battle for his life; but the man's dark eyes met his, caught and held him motionless.

"Is this courage? To fight in despair like a cornered rat? If it is death you face down there, surely it is better to face it with dignity."

"So be it!" said Khardan. Shaking off Auda's hand, the Calif walked ahead of the Paladin down the staircase.

At the foot of the stairs they came to another hallway. By the light of ibn Jad's torch, Khardan could see a series of heavy wooden doors placed at intervals on either side of a narrow corridor. All the doors except one were closed. From that one shone a bright light, and Khardan could hear faint sounds emanating from it.

"This way," said ibn Jad, with a gesture.

Khardan walked slowly toward the doorway, his legs seemingly unwilling to carry him forward, his feet heavy and clumsy. Fear crawled like a snake in his belly, and he knew that if it were not for the black eyes of ibn Jad watching him, the Calif would have broken down and wept like a terrified child.

The sounds grew clearer the nearer he drew to the open door, and the snake in his gut twisted and turned. It was the sound of a man moaning in death's agony. Sweat broke out on Khardan's face, trickling down into his black beard. A tremor shook him, but still he kept going. Coming opposite the doorway, he felt the touch of Auda's hand upon his arm and came to a stop. Blinking against the brightness inside the room, he looked within.

At first he could see nothing but a figure of darkness outlined against blazing firelight. A small, shrunken man with an oversized head and a wizened body glanced at Khardan with shrewd, appraising eyes.

"This is the one, Paladin?" came a voice as wizened as the body.

"Yes, Lifemaster."

The man nodded his huge head. It seemed balanced so precariously upon his scrawny neck, and he moved so carefully and with such deliberation, that Khardan had a fearful, momentary impression the head might topple off. The man was dressed in voluminous black robes that stirred and rippled in waves of hot air wafting from the room. From behind him, running like a dark undercurrent to his words, came the low, moaning sound.

"You arrive in good time, Paladin," said the man in satisfaction.

"The rebirth?"

"Any moment now, Paladin. Any moment."

"It should prove instructive to the nomad. May we watch, Lifemaster?"

"A pleasure, Paladin." The small man bowed and stepped aside from the doorway.

Khardan looked inside, then hastily averted his eyes.

"Squeamish?" said the wizened man, scurrying over to poke at Khardan with a bony finger. "Yet here I see scars of battle—"

"It is one thing to fight a man. It is another to see one tormented to his death!" Khardan said hoarsely, keeping his head turned from the gruesome sight within.

"Watch!" said Auda softly.

"Watch!" said the old man. The bony hand crawled over Khardan's flesh and he cringed in disgust, then started and gasped. Needle-sharp pain raced through his nerve endings. The small man held no weapon, but it was as if a thousand piercing thorns had driven into Khardan's flesh. Choking back his cry, he stared at the black-robed man, who smiled modestly.

"When I came to Zhakrin, I wondered how best I might serve my God. This"—he spread his thin arms, the yellowed skin hung from the bones—"is not the body of a warrior. I could not win souls for Zhakrin with my sword. But I could win them another way—pain. Long years I studied, traveling to dark and secret places throughout Sularin, learning to perfect the art. For art it is. Look, look at this man."

The fingers caressed Khardan's skin. Reluctantly, he turned his gaze back upon the figure in the room.

"He was brought in yesterday, Paladin. Look at his armor!" The wizened man pointed a palsied finger toward a corner of the room.

"A White Knight of Evren!" said Auda in awe.

"Yes!" The small man smiled proudly. "And look at him now. One of her strongest, one of her best. Look at him now!"

The man, his arms chained to the wall, sprawled naked upon the stone floor. He stared at the Lifemaster with wild, dilated eyes. His body was covered with blood—some of it still flowing—from numerous wounds, the skin was ashen gray. The low moaning sound came from his throat; then suddenly his body jerked convulsively. He screamed in agony, his head dashed back against the wall as though he had been struck by a giant hand.

But no one had touched him. No one had gone near him.

The wizened man smiled with quiet pride. "Pain, you see"—he nudged Khardan—"is in two places. Body and mind. The pain you feel"—his fingers twitched and Khardan felt the needles race through his flesh again, this time sharper and seemingly tipped with fire. He could not forbear crying out, and the wizened man grinned in satisfaction—"that was in your body. You are brave, nomad, but within fifteen minutes, with my instruments and my bare hands, I can reduce you to a quivering mass of flesh promising me anything if I will only end your torment. But that is nothing, nothing to the pain you will endure when I enter your mind! I am there now, in his." The wizened man pointed at the White Knight. "Watch!"

The Lifemaster slowly began to clench his tiny fist, the fingers curling inward. And, as he did so, the man chained to the wall began to curl in upon himself, his muscles clenching spasmodically, his entire body curling up like that of a dying spider, scream after scream bursting from his throat.

"Honor?" Turning to the Black Paladin, Khardan sneered, though his face ran with sweat and his body shook. "What honor is there is torturing your enemy to death?"

"Death?" The wizened man appeared shocked. "No! Senseless, wasteful!"

"He is dying!" Khardan said angrily.

"No," said the Lifemaster softly, "he is praying. Listen. . . ."

Reluctantly, Khardan turned his gaze back to the tortured body. Evren's Knight hung from his chains, his strength nearly spent. His screams had ceased, his broken voice whispered words that could not, at first, be heard.

The Lifemaster raised a hand for silence. Hardly breathing, ibn Jad leaned forward. Baffled, Khardan glanced from one to the other. A look of triumph was on each face, yet the Calif could not understand their victory. A dying man praying to his Goddess to accept his soul . . .

And then Khardan heard the man's words clearly.

"Accept me . . . in your service . . . Zhakrin. . . ." The man's voice grew stronger. "Accept me . . . in your service . . . Zhakrin!"

*Preparation to become a Black Paladin.*

Evren's Knight lifted his head, tears streamed from his eyes. He raised his manacled hands. "Zhakrin!" he whispered reverently. "Zhakrin!"

The Lifemaster shuffled across the stone floor. Drawing a key from his robes, he removed the manacles. The knight fell to his knees, embracing the man around the legs. Clucking like a mother over her child, the wizened old man lifted a bowl of water and began to cleanse the tormented flesh.

"Naked, covered with blood, we come into this life," murmured ibn Jad.

Sickened and dizzy, Khardan slumped back against the stone wall. The tortured man's body was muscular; he was obviously strong and powerful. A bloodstained sword rested in the corner, his armor—adorned with a lily—was dented and scratched. He had apparently fought his captors valiantly. He had been the sworn enemy of this God, and now he offered Zhakrin his life.

"So did many of us come to the God," said ibn Jad. "The path of fire cleanses and leads the soul to the truth. And so it will be with you, nomad." He gripped Khardan's arm. "In years to come, you will look back on this as a blessed experience. And with you, it will be a twice wonderful transformation, for you will be reborn almost at the same moment as will our God!"

The Lifemaster had the knight on his feet, his scrawny

arm around the strong body, holding him tenderly. "Take him, Paladin. Take him to his chamber. He will sleep and wake refreshed and renewed in the morning."

Auda ibn Jad accepted charge of Evren's Knight, who was still murmuring the name of Zhakrin in holy ecstasy.

Leading the knight back down the hallway, Auda glanced over his shoulder at Khardan. "Farewell, nomad. When we meet tomorrow, I hope it will be to call you brother."

Khardan surged forward, with no hope of escape, with only some dim view in his mind of smashing his head into the stone wall, of dashing out his brains, of killing himself.

Bony fingers closed over his wrist. Pain mounted up his arm, running from tiny nerve to tiny nerve, seeping through his veins like slow-moving ice water. He stumbled to his knees, resistance gone. The Lifemaster grabbed hold of his other wrist and dragged him across the stone floor into the sweltering heat of the room.

Flame leaped high in Khardan's vision, heat beat upon his body. The manacles snapped shut around his wrists. The old man shuffled across the floor to where an iron cauldron hung over the roaring fire. Reaching inside, his flesh seemingly impervious to the searing heat, he drew forth a thin piece of red-hot, glowing iron and turned back with it to face Khardan.

"Akhran!" Khardan shouted, plunging against the manacles, trying to rip them from the wall. "Akhran! Hear me!"

The old man shuffled closer and closer until his huge head loomed in Khardan's vision. "Only one God hears your screams, nomad. Zhakrin!" The hissing breath was hot upon Khardan's cheek. "Zhakrin!"

# Chapter 10

Mathew crept silently down the stairs behind Auda ibn Jad and Khardan, his way lit only by the faint afterglow of the Black Paladin's torch. Peering cautiously around the corner at the bottom, he saw the long, narrow hallway with its rows of closed wood doors and realized that to go any farther would lead to certain discovery.

He had no choice but to retreat back up the stairs, feeling his way in the darkness, moving cautiously so that he would not be heard. He came to a halt about halfway up the staircase, pressed against the wall, holding his breath to hear. The men's words came to him clearly; a trick of the stone carrying it to his ears almost as plainly as if he stood beside them.

Thus Mathew heard everything, from Evren's tortured Knight's agony to his final, ecstatic prayer to Zhakrin. He heard the scuffling sound of Khardan's futile try for freedom, he heard the Calif cry out in pain, and the sound of a heavy weight being dragged across the floor. But he heard something else, too. Auda ibn Jad was coming back this direction. Moving as swiftly as he dared in the total darkness, Mathew dashed to the top of the stairs. Reaching the level floor but not expecting it, he staggered and fell. The footsteps grew louder. Fortunately, ibn Jad was weighted down by the burden of the weak knight he was supporting and so was forced to move slowly. The Knight's murmuring prayers to Zhakrin kept the Black Paladin from hearing Mathew's scramblings.

Rising hastily to his feet, Mathew looked despairingly down the long hall. A torch burning on the wall about twenty feet away illuminated much of the corridor brightly, leaving only a swatch of shadow between it and the next torch; Mathew could not hope to run the length of the hall without being seen. Near him, just at the edge of the circle of torchlight, a darker shadow offered his only hope. Darting to it, Mathew discovered what he had been praying for—a natural alcove in the rough rock walls. It wasn't very big and seemed to grow smaller as Mathew attempted to squeeze his slender body into the fissure. If he had been standing directly beneath the blazing torch, he could not have imagined himself more visible. Turning his face to the wall in an effort to hide the milk-white skin that would show up in the light, Mathew drew his hands up into the sleeves of his black robes and held his breath.

Ibn Jad and the knight passed within inches of him. Mathew could have reached out and plucked the Paladin's sleeve with his hand. It seemed that they must see him or hear him; his heart thudded loud enough to wake the dead. But the two walked on by, continuing down the hall without once looking in his direction. Exhaling a relieved sigh, Mathew was about to offer a prayer of thanks for the protection when he remembered uncomfortably which God it was who ruled the Darkness.

An agonized scream welled up from below, echoing in the hallway. Khardan . . .

Mathew's legs gave way and he sank down weakly onto the stone floor, the terrible sound reverberating in his heart. Trembling, his hand went to the pouch he wore at his waist, his fingers closed over the obsidian wand.

The darkness hissed. "Say the word, Master, and I will save your friend from his suffering."

"I did not summon you!" Mathew said shakily, aware that he had no control over this creature.

"Not by word," replied the imp, sniggering. "I read the wishes of your heart."

Another cry rent the air. Mathew shrank back against the wall. "By saving him, you don't mean taking us away from here, do you?" he questioned. His chest constricted painfully; it was difficult to breathe.

"No," said the imp, drawing out the word, ending in a throaty growl. "My Demon Prince would not like that at all.

If you leave, then so must I, and my Prince commands that I stay. He is delighted to hear of his brother God's return and more delighted still to know that the Good Goddess is in Zhakrin's power."

"What will he do with her?"

"Stupid mortal, what do you think?" the imp returned, its shriveled body writhing in eager anticipation.

"He can't destroy—" Mathew began, appalled.

"That remains to be seen. Never before has one of the Twenty been so weakened. Her immortals are not here to help her; her mortal followers, as you have seen, are succumbing to Zhakrin. His power grows as Evren's wanes."

Mathew tried to think, to feel some sense of loss at the terrible fate of the Goddess, tried to force himself to contemplate what this upset might do to the balance of power in heaven. But Khardan's screams were in his ears, and suddenly he cared about nothing but what was happening on earth.

"Free him, free Zohra! Take me to your Prince," Mathew begged, sweat beading on his lip.

The imp pursed its shriveled lips. "A poor bargain, trading nothing for something. Besides, Zhakrin has requested the woman's body. Astafas would never offend his brother by stealing her away."

Khardan's screams ceased abruptly, cut off by a choked, strangled city. In the awful silence, a glimmering of understanding lit Mathew's darkness. The perplexing behavior of the Wandering God was no longer perplexing. The young wizard longed to fan the tiny spark of the idea that had come to him, to blow on the coal and watch it burst into flame. But he dared not. The moment the thought came to mind, he saw the imp's tongue lick its lips, the red eyes narrow.

Drawing the wand from his pouch, Mathew held it up before the imp. "I want to talk to Khardan," the young wizard said evenly, keeping tight control on his voice. "Lure his tormentor away."

The imp laughed, sneering derisively.

"What would happen," Mathew continued calmly, though his body trembled beneath the black robes, "if I were to give this wand to the Black Sorceress?"

The imp's red eyes flared. Too late, it hooded them with thin, wrinkled lids. "Nothing," said the creature.

"You lie," Mathew returned. "I begin to understand. The wand serves to summon the immortal nearest our hearts. Meryem used it to call one of Quar's minions. When the wand came into my hands, however, its power acted on an immortal being of the Gods in which I believe, and because its magic is black, it called you."

The imp's long red tongue lolled out of its mouth in derision. Its teeth showed black against the red, its eyes burned.

Mathew averted his gaze; looking directly at the wand he held in his hand. "If I gave this wand to the Black Sorceress, she could use it to summon an immortal being of Zhakrin's."

"Let her try!" The imp's tongue rolled up into its mouth with a slurp. "His immortals have long since disappeared."

"Nonetheless, *you* would be banished."

"As long as you are here, I am here, Dark Master," said the imp, grinning wickedly.

"But powerless to act," Mathew returned.

"As are you!"

"It seems I am powerless either way." Mathew shrugged. "What do I have to lose?"

"Your soul!" hissed the imp with a wriggle of delight that nearly twisted the creature in two.

Mathew saw the Hand reaching out for him; he saw the vast void into which he would be cast, his soul wailing in despair until its small cry was swallowed up by the eternal darkness.

"No," said Mathew softly. "Astafas would not have even that. For when I give the wand to the Black Sorceress, I give myself to her as well."

The imp was caught in mid-writhe. One leg twined about the other, one arm wrapped about its neck. Slowly it unwound itself and crept forward to glare at Mathew.

"Before I would allow that, I would snatch your soul away!"

"To do that, you would have to have me killed, and I would be dead, and you would lose entry to this place."

"It seems we are at an impasse!" the imp snarled.

"Do for me what I ask. Help me to see Khardan—alone."

Its tongue curling and uncurling, the imp considered. It peered into Mathew's mind, but all it saw there was a theological muddle. As far as the imp was concerned, theology was good for only one thing—leading the overzealous scholar into deep and dangerous waters. While occasionally amused to hear mortals argue with firm conviction over something they knew absolutely nothing about, the imp generally found theological discussion somnambulic. The imp thought it odd (even for Mathew) to choose this time to discuss theology with a man being tortured, and the creature probed Mathew's mind deeply. The young wizard appeared to have nothing more treacherous planned, however. Not that anything he attempted would do him any good anyway. The imp decided to humor the mortal and gain a valuable concession at the same time.

"If I obey your commands, then you must swear fealty to Astafas."

"Anything!" Mathew said shortly, eager to reach Khardan. This ominous silence was more terrifying than the screams.

"Just a moment!" The imp held up a splay-fingered hand. "I feel it only right to tell you that your guardian angel is not present, and so you have no one to intervene in your behalf before you make this commitment."

Why this news should have distressed Mathew, who did not believe in guardian angels any more than he believed in other nursery tales, was a mystery. But he felt a sudden heaviness in his heart.

"It is of no matter," he said after a moment. "I pledge my loyalty to the Prince of Darkness."

"Say his name!" hissed the imp.

"I pledge my loyalty to . . . to Astafas." The word burned Mathew's lips like poison. When he licked them, he tasted a bitter flavor.

The imp grinned. It knew Mathew lied. It knew that though the human's mouth spoke the words, they were not repeated by his soul. But the mortal was alone on this plane of human existence, his guardian angel was no longer there to shield him with her white wings. And now Mathew knew he was alone. Despair, hopelessness—these would be the imp's instruments of torture, and when the time came—as it would soon; the imp, too, was starting to form a plan—the young wizard would be all too willing for the torment to end, to lapse into the soothing comfort of dark oblivion.

"Wait here!" the imp said and vanished in an eyeblink.

A voice came out of the torchlight, sounding so near and so real that Mathew started to his feet, looking around in terror.

"Lifemaster! Come swiftly!" Auda ibn Jad sounded angry, upset. "This knight. There is something wrong with him! I think he is dying!"

The hall was empty. The Black Paladin was nowhere in sight. Yet the voice seemingly came from near Mathew's shoulder.

"Lifemaster!" Ibn Jad commanded.

"What is it?" a shrill voice answered from below.

Mathew scrunched back into the alcove, holding his breath.

"Lifemaster!" The Black Paladin was furious, insistent.

Steps rasped upon the stairs. The Lifemaster, wheezing, slowly made his way to the top and stared down the hall.

"Ibn Jad?" he queried in a tremulous voice.

"Lifemaster!" The Black Paladin's shout echoed through the corridor. "Why do you tarry? The knight has gone into a fit!"

His oversized head jutting forward, peering this way and that, the Lifemaster shuffled down the hallway, following the sound of ibn Jad's voice that grew increasingly angrier as it grew increasingly more distant.

# Chapter 11

Strong arms held Zohra close, warm lips tasted hers, hands caressed her. The aching of desire burned within her, and she cried out for love, but there was nothing. The arms melted away, the lips turned cold, the hands withdrew. She was empty inside, longing desperately for that emptiness to be filled. The pain grew worse and worse, and then a dark figure stood above her bed.

"Khardan!" Zohra cried out in gladness and held forth her arms to draw the figure near.

The figure raised a hand and a bright, white light shone in Zohra's eyes, burning away the dream.

"Waken," said a cool, smooth voice.

Zohra sat up, her eyes watering in the sudden brilliance. Holding up her hand to shield them, she endeavored to see the figure that was reflected in the white light.

"What happened to me?" Zohra cried fearfully, the memory of the arms and lips and hands all too real, her body still aching for the touch even as her mind revolted against it.

"Nothing, my dear," said the voice, a woman's voice. "The drug was given you prematurely." The white light became nothing more than the flame of a candle, illuminating the taut, stretched skin of the sorceress. Placing the candlestick on a table beside Zohra's bed, the sorceress sat down next to her. The flame burned steadily and unwaveringly in

286

the depths of the woman's ageless eyes. Reaching out a hand, she smoothed back Zohra's mane of tangled black hair.

"I believe, however, that it has proved most instructive. You see now that you are ours—body, mind, and soul."

"What do you mean?" Zohra faltered, drawing back from the woman's touch. Finding herself naked in the bed, she grasped hold of the silken sheets on which she lay and clasped them around her body.

The Black Sorceress smiled. "Had not another requested you, my dear, you would have now been languishing in the arms of one of the Black Paladins; perhaps within a few months, bearing his child."

"No!" Zohra tossed her head defiantly, but she kept her eyes averted from the stern, cold face.

The Black Sorceress leaned near, her hand touching Zohra's cheek. "Strong arms, soft kisses. And then nothing but cold emptiness. You cried out—"

"Stop!" Zohra thrust the hand from her, glaring at the woman through tears of shame. Clutching the sheets to her breast, she scrambled back as far as possible from the woman—which wasn't far until the carved wooden bedstead blocked her way. "I will eat nothing, drink nothing!" she cried passionately. "I will never submit—"

"The drug was not in your food, child. It was in the clothing you put on. The fabric is soaked in it, and the drug seeps through your skin. It could be in these bed sheets." She waved a hand. "The perfume with which we anoint your body. You would never know, my dear. . . . But"—the sorceress rose languidly to her feet. Turning from Zohra, she walked away from the bed and began to pace the floor slowly—"do not concern yourself. As I said, you have been chosen by another, and though He wants your body, it is not for the purpose of breeding new followers."

Zohra remained silent, disdaining to question. She was barely listening, in fact. She was trying to figure some way to avoid the drug.

The Black Sorceress looked toward a small leaded glass window set into the wall of the cheerless room. "It is only a few hours until the dawn of what will be for us a new day, a day of hope. When the mid hour of night strikes, our God will return to us. Zhakrin will be reborn." She glanced around at Zohra, who—catching the sorceress's gaze and seeing that some response was required—shrugged.

"What is that to me?"

"Everything, my dear," the Black Sorceress said softly, her eyes glittering with an eager, intense light. "He will be reborn in your body!"

Zohra rolled her eyes. Obviously the woman was insane. *I have to get out of here. The drug . . . perhaps it was that musky odor I smelled. There must be an antidote, some way to counter it. Usti might know, if I can persuade the blubbering coward to help me—*

A pang of fear struck Zohra. She glanced around hastily and saw her rings lying on the table beside the bed, gleaming brightly in the candlelight. She sighed in relief.

The Black Sorceress was watching her gravely. "You don't believe me."

"Of course not!" Zohra gave a brief, bitter laugh. "This is a trick to confuse me."

"No trick, my dear, I assure you," said the Black Sorceress. "You are to be honored above all mortals, your weak flesh will hold our God until He attains the strength to abandon it and take His rightful place among the other deities. If you do not believe me, ask your djinn." The sorceress's gaze fixed upon the silver ring. Zohra's face paled, but she pressed her lips tightly together and said nothing. The sorceress nodded. "I will give you a few moments alone to ease the turbulence of your soul. You must be relaxed and peaceful. When I return with the dawn, we will begin preparing you to accept the God."

The Black Sorceress left the room, shutting the door softly behind her. There came no sound of a lock, but Zohra knew hopelessly that if she tried to open it, the door would not yield. Silently, unmoving, clutching the sheets to her bosom, Zohra lifted the ring.

"Usti," she called out in a small, tight voice.

"Is she gone?"

"Yes!" Zohra checked an impatient sigh.

"Coming, Princess." The djinn drifted out from the ring—a thin, wavering wisp of smoke that writhed about on the floor before finally coalescing into a flabby body. Subdued, miserable, and frightened, the fat djinn had the appearance of a lump of goat's cheese melting beneath the desert sun.

"Usti," said Zohra softly, her eyes on the candle flame, "is what she said true? Can they . . . give my body . . . to a God?"

"Yes, Princess," said the djinn sadly, bowing his head. His chins folded in on one another until it seemed likely his mouth and mose would be swallowed up by flesh.

"And . . . there is nothing you can do?" Her spirit broken, her fears beginning to conquer, Zohra asked the question in a wistful, pitiful tone that wrung the djinn's nonexistent heart.

"Oh, Princess," Usti wailed, twisting his fat hands together in anguish. "I have been a most worthless immortal, all my life! I know that! But I swear to you that I would risk the iron box—I swear by *Hazrat* Akhran—that I would help you if I could! But you see!" He gestured wildly at the door. "She knows I am here! And she does nothing to try to stop me. Why? Because she knows I am helpless, powerless to stop her!"

Zohra bowed her head, her black hair tumbling over her shoulders. "No one can help me. I am all alone. Mathew has deserted me. Khardan is undoubtedly either dead or dying. There is no escape, no hope. . . ." Slowly, despondently, she let the sheet slide from nerveless hands. Tears trickled down her cheeks and dripped onto the sheet, spotting the silk.

Usti stared at her in dismay. Flinging himself upon the bed, nearly upsetting it in the process, he cried, "Don't give up, Princess! This isn't like you! Fight! Fight! Look, aren't you furious with me? Throw something! Here"—the djinn grabbed hold of a water carafe. Splashing water recklessly over the bed, he thrust it into Zohra's unresponsive hands— "toss that at me! Hit me on the head!" Usti snatched off his turban, offering his bald pate as a tempting target. "Yell at me, scream at me, curse me! Anything! Don't cry, Princess! Don't cry!" Tears rolling in torrents down his own fat face, Usti dragged the bedclothes up over his head. "Please don't cry!"

"Usti," said Zohra, her eyes shining with an eerie light. "I have an idea. There is one way to prevent them from taking my body."

"There is?" Usti said warily, lowering the sheet and peering over it.

"If my body was dead, they could not use it, could they?"

"Princess!" Usti gasped in sudden terrified understanding, flinging the sheet over his head again. "No! I can't! I am forbidden to take a mortal life without permission from the God!"

"You said you would risk anything for me!" Zohra tugged at the fabric. Slowly, the djinn's face emerged, staring at her woefully. "My soul will plead for you to Holy Akhran. The God has done nothing to help us. Surely He will not be so unjust as to punish you for obeying the final request of your mistress!"

Usti gnawed on the hem of the sheet. Zohra's gaze was steadfast, unwavering. Finally, the djinn stood up. "Princess," he said, his chins quivering, but his voice firm, "somewhere within this fat body I will find the courage to carry out your command."

"Thank you, Usti," Zohra replied gently.

"But only at the last moment, when there is no . . . no hope," the djinn said, the final word lost in a knot of choking tears.

"At the last, when there is no hope," Zohra repeated, her gaze going to the window to watch for the dawn.

# Chapter 12

Mathew waited until he saw the Lifemaster's bulbous head gleam in the flame of the most distant torch lighting the hallway, then the young wizard slipped from his alcove. Keeping to the shadows, he ran to the stairs and, clinging to the wall, fumbled his way down them. Once at the bottom, he could see the light streaming from the room where he knew Khardan must be held. No sound came from it. All was silent, silent as a tomb, he thought, his heart aching in fear.

Outside the door the memory of those agonized screams returned, and this courage failed him.

"Coward!" he cursed himself bitterly as he stood trembling in the doorway, fearful of entering, terrified of what he might find. "*He* is the one who is suffering and you shake in terror, unable to move to help him!"

"Help," he scoffed at himself. "What help can you offer? What hope? None. Words, that's all. What do you fear? That you will find him dead? Shouldn't that be your wish for him, if you truly care about him? Or are you selfish as well as cowardly? And what if he isn't dead? You will exhort him to accept more torment. Better to leave, better to let him go. . . ."

"No! You're wrong!" Mathew argued resolutely, pushing back his doubts. He recognized that voice, it was the same one that had told him to give up when he'd been captured by the slave trader, the voice that had whispered to him of the sweetness of death. "I'm wasting time. The tormentor will be back soon."

Clenching his jaw tightly, Mathew walked into the torture chamber.

"Khardan!" he murmured. Compassion rushed in to fill fear's dark and empty well. Mathew forgot that the tormentor might return any moment. He forgot the imp, forgot his own danger.

Khardan sat on the stone floor, his back against a wall, his arms chained above his head. He had been stripped of his clothes. Burn marks scorched his bare chest, blood oozed from strategically inflicted wounds. The Calif's head lolled forward, he had lost consciousness. Tears stinging his eyes, Mathew pressed his hand to his lips, forcing back a choking cry of anguish.

"Leave him!" the voice urged. "Leave him this one moment of peace. It will be all he has. . . ."

Shaking his head, blinking back the tears, Mathew summoned all his strength and courage—a far more difficult task than summoning demons—and knelt down beside the Calif. A bowl of water stood on a table nearby, just out of reach, probably placed there to enhance the tormenting of the chained man. Lifting it, Mathew dipped his fingers in the cool water and dabbed them upon the Calif's blood-caked lips.

"Khardan," he said. The name came out a sob.

Khardan stirred and moaned, and Mathew's heart was wrung with pity. The hand touching the lips trembled, tears blinded him momentarily and he could not speak. He forced himself to quash the sympathy, the vivid imaginings of what it must be like to endure such torture.

"Khardan," he repeated, more firmly, with a sternness he knew to be a prop holding him up.

Khardan raised his head suddenly, looking about him with a wild terror in his feverish eyes that pierced Mathew to his soul.

"No more!" the nomad muttered. His arms wrenched, trying to drag the chains from the wall. "No more!"

"Khardan!" Mathew stroked the man's hair back with a gentle, soothing hand and held the water bowl to his lips. "Khardan, it's Mathew! Drink. . . ."

Khardan drank thirstily, then retched, moaning in agony, bringing most of the water back up. But his eyes lost their wild look, a glimmer of recognition flickered in the dark depths. He leaned back weakly against the wall.

"Where is . . . *he!*" The horror with which Khardan said the word sent chills through Mathew. He set down the water bowl, his shaking hand was spilling most of it.

"He is gone, for the moment," Mathew said softly. "The creature I . . . control . . . led him away." ﹣

"Get me out of here!" Khardan gasped.

Removing his hand from the man's forehead, Mathew sat back, looking into the black, hopeful eyes. "I can't, Khardan." No words ever fell more reluctantly from Mathew's lips. He saw the eyes flash in contempt and anger, then they closed. Khardan sighed.

"Thank you for this much, at least," he said slowly, painfully nodding toward the water. "You had better leave now. You've risked a great deal in coming to me. . . ."

"Khardan!" Mathew clasped his hands together pleadingly. "I would free you if I could! I would give my life for you if I could!" Khardan opened his eyes, looking at him intently, and Mathew flushed. He hadn't meant his words to come out stained with his heart's blood. Lowering his head, staring down at the bowl of pinkish water sitting on the floor at his knees, Mathew continued speaking in more subdued tones, all the while nervously twisting the black velvet robes between his trembling fingers. "But I can't. It would be pointless. There is nowhere to go, no hope of escape."

"We could at least die like men, fighting until the end," Khardan said warmly. "We would die, each in the service of his God—"

"No!" Mathew said stubbornly, suddenly clenching his fist and driving it into his knee. "That's all you think about—you nomads! Death! When you are winning, life is fine; when you are losing, you decide to give up and die!"

"To die with honor—"

"Honor be damned!" Mathew cried angrily, lifting his head and glaring at Khardan. "Maybe your death isn't what your God wants! Did you ever think about that? Maybe you're of no use to Him dead! Maybe He's brought you here for a reason, a purpose, and it's up to you to live long enough to try to find out why!"

"My God has abandoned me," Khardan said harshly. "He has abandoned all of us, it seems, for now He talks to these unbelievers."

"That's what they want you to think!" Impulsively, Mathew reached out to take the pale, suffering face in his hands. "Believe your God has abandoned you, and you will abandon your God!"

"What do you know of my God, *kafir*?" Khardan jerked his head away from Mathew's touch, averting his eyes.

Clasping him by the shoulders, Mathew moved so that the black eyes had nowhere to look but at him. "Khardan, think about what we heard up there! Think about what these people have endured, have suffered for their faith. Their God was dead, and still they didn't forsake Him! Are you less strong? Will you give in?"

Khardan stared at him thoughtfully, brows furrowed, eyes dark and unreadable. His glance went to Mathew's hands, the thin, delicate fingers, cool from the water, against the Calif's burning skin.

"Your touch is gentle as a woman's," he murmured.

Flushing in shame, Mathew snatched his hands away.

"*More* gentle than some women's—like my wife's," Khardan continued with a ghastly smile. "I don't envy the one who tries to take her body. God or no God, He's going to be in for an interesting time—" Khardan gasped in pain. His body doubled over, nearly wrenching his arms from their sockets.

Mathew looked about frantically for the source, but saw nothing and realized it must be coming from within. Helplessly he watched Khardan writhe, his body jerking convulsively, and then the spasm passed. Breathing heavily, his flesh glistening with sweat, Khardan slowly lifted his head.

Mathew saw himself reflected in the red-rimmed eyes. He might have been the one tormented. His face was ashen, he was shaking in every limb.

Khardan smiled gently. His lips almost instantly twisted in a pain-filled grimace, but the smile remained in the dark, shadowed eyes. "You better go," he spoke almost inaudibly. "I don't think . . . you can take . . . much more of this. . . ."

Praying that the imp was still leading the Lifemaster a merry chase, Mathew caught up Khardan's bloodstained shirt and, dipping it in the water, washed the man's feverish forehead and face with cooling liquid. Khardan's eyes closed, tears crept from beneath the lids. He gave a shuddering sigh.

"Khardan," said Mathew softly, "there is a way out, I think, but it is desperate, almost hopeless."

Khardan nodded weakly, to show he understood. He had

strength for nothing more, and Mathew—seeing his suffering—
nearly gave way. "Be at peace," he longed to say, "go ahead
and die. I was wrong. Give yourself rest." But he didn't.
Gritting his teeth, dipping the cloth in the water again, he
continued, the knowledge of what he was going to ask making
his heart wrench. "We must try, somehow, to gain possession
of the two Gods before Zhakrin can come back into the
world. Once we have them both, we must free Evren, the
Goddess who is Zhakrin's opposite. With Her power—weak
as it is—on our side, I think we might succeed in escaping."

Khardan moved his head, the eyes opening the tiniest
crack to look at Mathew intently. Mathew laid down the
cloth. Gently, he ran his fingers through the crisp, curling
black hair. Unable to meet those eyes, he gazed above them,
at his own hand. "To do this, you must gain admittance to the
ceremony," Mathew said, his voice catching in his throat. "To
gain admittance, you must be a Black Paladin. . . ."

Khardan's jaw muscles twitched, his teeth clenched.

"Do you know what I am saying?" Mathew persisted,
emotion choking him. "I am saying you must hold out until
the point . . . the point of . . ." He couldn't continue.

"Death. . . ." murmured Khardan. "And then . . . convince them I am . . . one. . . ."

Mathew froze. What was that? Fearfully he listened. Footsteps! On the stairs!

Khardan did not move. His face was livid, blood trickled
from the corner of his mouth.

Shivering so he could barely stand, Mathew somehow
managed to regain his feet. His legs seemed to have gone
numb, however, and he thought, for a moment, he must sink
back down to the floor again. Hesitating, he looked at Khardan.

I should forget this! The idea is insane. Far better to give
up now!

Khardan's sunken eyes flickered. "I . . . will . . . not . . .
fail!"

Nor will I! Mathew said to himself in sudden grim determination. Turning, he fled from the chamber, darting farther
down the hallway, out of the light, to hide himself in the
shadow of another cell.

Muttering irritable imprecations down upon Auda ibn Jad
for disturbing his work for nothing and then having the nerve
to try to deny that he had done anything, the Lifemaster
shuffled back into the chamber.

Mathew heard the small man's dragging footsteps cross the room; he heard them stop and could almost picture the tormentor bending over Khardan.

"Ah, had a visitor." The Lifemaster chuckled. "So that's what all that rigmarole and fal-de-ra was about. Whoever it was gave you back a bit of strength, I see. Well, well. No thanks to whoever it was. We'll just have to work a little harder. . . ."

Khardan's scream tore through the darkness and through Mathew's heart. Putting his hand in his pouch, gripping the wand tightly, the young wizard spoke the words of magic and felt impish hands grab hold of him and pluck him into the darkness.

# Chapter 13

"Take me to the Tower of Women," Mathew ordered wearily.

"To see the Black Sorceress? I think not!" the imp returned.

"No, I must talk with—" Staring around him, Mathew swallowed the word with a gulp.

The imp had returned Mathew to the room where the young wizard had been first taken on his arrival. Materializing within it, both Mathew and his "servant" were unpleasantly astonished to see the Black Sorceress standing before the cold ashes left scattered in the fireplace.

"Talk with whom?" inquired the woman. "Your other friend?"

"If you have no further need of me, Dark Master—" whined the imp with an obscene wriggle intended for a bow.

"Do not leave yet, creature of Sul," commanded the sorceress.

"Servant of Astafas!" hissed the imp angrily, its tongue sliding out between its sharp black teeth. "I am not a low demon of Chaos, madam!"

"That could be arranged," said the Black Sorceress, her brows coming as close together as was possible on the tightly stretched skin of her face. She glanced at Mathew. "Make me a gift of this creature."

"I cannot, madam," said Mathew in a low, respectful tone. He had little to fear. The sorceress might try to take the wand from him by force, but the imp would most certainly fight—if not to protect him, then to protect its own shriveled skin.

"You are wise for one so young." The sorceress gazed at him searchingly. Moving close to him, she laid a hand upon his cheek. Her touch was like the bony fingers of a skeleton. Mathew shivered but did not move, caught and held by the mesmerizing stare of the woman's eyes. "Your wisdom comes not from years but from the ability to see into the hearts of those around you. A dangerous gift, for then you begin to care for them. Their pain becomes your pain." She lingered on the word, her fingers softly caressing, and the chill touch began to burn, like ice held in wet hands.

Trembling, Mathew held himself very still, though the pain increased immeasurably.

"You have seen what you should not have seen," the voice breathed all around him. "You have been where you should not have gone. In time, when you were ready, I would have shown you all. Now, because you do not understand, you are confused and disturbed. And you have done nothing for your nomad friend except increase his torment. Why did you go? Did you think you could free him?"

She didn't know! Blessed Promenthas, she didn't know, didn't suspect!

"Yes, that was it!" Mathew gasped.

"A hopeless, foolish thought." The Black Sorceress made a clicking sound with her tongue; the noise flicked on Mathew's exposed nerves. "How did you think to accomplish your escape, and why didn't you go ahead and attempt it?"

"Madam," interposed the imp, rubbing its hands as though they ached, "the nomad was too far gone for us to be able to help him. Madam will forgive us," added the imp, licking its lips, "if we do not tell her our plans for assisting the nomad to escape."

"Why will madam forgive you?" The sorceress smiled cruelly at the imp, keeping her hand on Mathew's cheekbone, the young man not daring to move, though it seemed his teeth were on fire and his brain was expanding in his skull.

"Because, madam, you hope that Astafas will forgive you for harming one of His own." The imp sidled nearer to Mathew. Elongating, stretching its small form like rubber, it closed its splay fingers over the hand of the sorceress. "When Zhakrin returns to the world, He will require the help of Astafas in the fight against Quar." The imp's narrowed red eyes were fiery slits against its blackened, wrinkled skin. "Zhakrin has Astafas's help and freely given, but Zhakrin is not to forget that this young one is ours, not His." Like slithering snakes, the imp's words wound around Mathew, tightening their coils.

Slowly, the sorceress removed her hand, though her fingers lingered long on Mathew's skin. "You are weary." She spoke to Mathew, but her eyes were on the imp. "Sleep now." The pain eased, submerged in a wave of drowsy warmth.

A soft pillow was beneath his head; he was lying in a bed. Darkness enfolded him, banishing pain, banishing fear.

"Thank you," he murmured to the imp.

"Payment will come," whispered the darkness back to him. "Payment will come!"

# Chapter 14

Dawn—The sun's light struggled feebly to penetrate the shroud of gray mist that overhung the Isle of Galos—and the day began to march inexorably toward night, time moving far too slowly for some, far too swiftly for others.

Mathew slept the sleep of exhaustion, waking well past midday. His sleep had been neither restful nor refreshing, however. Filled with terror, his dreams tormented his soul as the Lifemaster tormented Khardan's flesh.

In the halcyon days in his own land, the young man had never given much thought to eternity, to the soul's repose after its sojourn through the world with the body. Like most young people, he assumed he would live forever. But all that had changed. In those terrible days of enforced travel with the slave caravan, when death seemed the only end to his suffering, Mathew thought with longing of his soul ascending to a place where he would find comfort and ease and hear a gentle voice say, "Rest now, my child. You are home."

Now he would never hear that gentle voice. Now he would hear only harsh laughter, crackling like flame. There would be no rest, no sweet homecoming. Only an empty void without and within, his soul gnawing at the nothingness in a hunger that could never be assuaged. For I have dared use the power of Astafas; not only used it—(Promenthas might be able to forgive that, considering the circumstances), but—and Mathew admitted this to himself as he stood in the sunlight trickling feebly through the leaded glass window—I have enjoyed it, exulted in it!

Deep beneath the shock at the imp's appearance had run an undercurrent of pleasure. He had felt the same thrill last night when the imp did his bidding, and lured away the tormentor.

"I should cast away the wand," Mathew said to himself firmly, "destroy it; fall to my knees and pray for Promenthas's forgiveness; and give myself up to whatever fate awaits me. And if it were just me, if I were alone, I would do that. But I can't. Others depend on me."

Flinging himself back onto his bed, Mathew shut his eyes against the light.

"I said I would give my life for Khardan," he said through trembling lips. "Surely I can give my soul!"

And Zohra—exasperating, foolhardy, courageous. Zohra—fighting her weaknesses, never seeing that they were her strengths. Trapped in these walls, without even the poor comfort of being able to exchange a few words as had Mathew and Khardan, Zohra must imagine herself completely alone. Had her courage given way at last? Would she go meekly to her dread fate? Perhaps, like Khardan, she believed that her God had abandoned her.

"I must go to her," Mathew said, sitting up, brushing the tangled red hair out of his face. "I must reassure her, tell her there is hope!"

His hand went to the wand in the pocket of his black robes. As his fingers closed over it, a surge of warmth washed pleasurably over Mathew. Drawing forth the wand, he examined it admiringly. It was a truly fine piece of workmanship. Had Meryem made it, or had she purchased it? He recalled reading of certain dark and secret places in the capital city of Khandar where devices of black magic such as this could be bought if one had the proper—

Mathew caught his breath. His hand began to shake, and he dropped the wand upon the bedclothes. When he'd first discovered the wand on board ship, when he'd first lifted it, his fingertips had tingled painfully, a numbing sensation had spread up his arm. His hand had lost all sense of feeling.

Now its touch gave him pleasure. . . .

"Master," hissed the imp, appearing with a bang, "you summoned me?"

"No!" Mathew cried in a hollow voice, shoving the wand away from him. "No, I—"

A thin curl of smoke drizzled into the center of the room and began to take form. Staring in astonishment, Mathew saw the many chins and round belly of a djinn emerge from the cloud.

"Usti?" he gasped.

He wasn't certain even now, when the djinn appeared as a mountain of flesh before him, that it *was* Usti to whom he was speaking. The djinn had lost at least two chins, his rotund stomach was no longer capable of holding up his *pantalons* that sagged woefully around his middle, revealing a jeweled navel. The djinn's ordinarily fine clothes were torn and dirty and disheveled, his turban had slipped down over one eye.

"Madman!" Usti fell to his knees with a thud. "Thank Akhran I have found you. I—" He stopped, staring at the imp. "I beg your pardon," said the djinn stiffly. "Perhaps I have come at an inopportune time." The immortal's flabby form began to fade.

"No, no!" cried Mathew. "Don't go!"

The imp darted Mathew a narrow-eyed, suspicious glance. "How clever of you, My Dark Master. Do you not find it confusing, serving so many Gods?"

"Whom do you serve, sir?" inquired Usti with a sniff, eyeing the imp's skinny body with disfavor. "And doesn't He feed you?"

"I serve Astafas, Prince of the Night!"

"Never heard of Him," replied Usti.

"As for food," continued the imp, its red eyes flaring, its splay-fingers twitching and curling, "I dine off the flesh of those whose souls my Prince drags shrieking into the Pit!"

"From the looks of you," said Usti, with a pitying glance, "the Prince's larder must be rather bare. I should stick to mutton—"

The imp gave a piercing shriek and made a dive for Usti, who gazed at it in offended dignity. "My dear sir, remember your place!"

Hastily grabbing the wand, Mathew pointed it at the imp. "Be gone!" he ordered harshly, wrenching back a hysterical desire to laugh, at the same time choking on tears. "I have no more need of you."

"How sweet will be the taste of your soft flesh, Dark

Master!" The imp's red eyes devoured Mathew, its hand groped toward him.

"Be gone!" Mathew cried in desperation.

"Ugghhh." Looking at Mathew's slender form, Usti grimaced. "There is no accounting for taste. Mutton," he advised the imp, "sliced thin and grilled with mustard and pepper—"

The imp vanished with a deafening shriek and a blast that shook the room. Mathew rose hurriedly from the bed. Afraid that they had roused the entire Castle, he stared fearfully at the door. He waited expectantly, but no one came. They must all be preparing for the ceremony, he thought, and turned to the djinn, who was still going on about mutton.

"Usti, where did you come from? Are the other djinn with you?" Mathew asked hopefully. "I remember that Khardan had a djinn—a young man with a foxlike face."

"Pukah," said Usti distastefully, mouthing the name as though it were a bad fig. "A lying, worthless—" The djinn's fat face sagged. "But for all that, he might have been useful."

"Where is he?" Mathew nearly shouted.

"Alas, Madman." Usti heaved a quivering-chinned sigh. "He and the djinn of Sheykh Majiid were taken captive during the battle by Kaug, the 'efreet of Quar—may dogs relieve themselves in his shoes."

Hope's flame died, leaving behind cold ash. "So that is why Pukah did not answer Khardan's summons," Mathew murmured. "How did you escape?"

Usti was instantly defensive. "I saw the great horrible hairy hands of the 'efreet sweep Sond's lamp and Pukah's basket up into his arms. I heard his booming laugh, and I knew that I was next! Is it to be wondered that I fled to a place of safety?"

"Meryem's ring," guessed Mathew grimly. "So you thought you'd try life in the palace of the Amir?"

"You have sadly misjudged me, Madman. I would never desert my mistress, no matter how wretchedly she used me, no matter that she made my life a living hell!" Usti regarded Mathew with wounded pride. "I had no doubt that you would stop the rose-colored whore in her vicious plot. When you clouted her upon the head, I took that opportunity to escape her, causing the ring to slip off her finger and commanding it to hide in your pouch."

Mathew had his doubts about this; he considered it far more likely that Usti had been cowering in the ring and that he'd been taken up by sheerest accident. It was pointless to argue; time was pressing.

"Your mistress, Zohra, how is she? Is she all right?"

Usti's fat face crumbled with true, sincere distress. "Ah!"—he clasped his chubby hands—"that is why I have come to you! The Princess I knew and feared is gone! She wept, Madman, wept! Oh what wouldn't I give"—tears crept down the fat cheeks, losing themselves in the crevices of the djinn's remaining chins—"to be back in my dwelling as it goes sailing through the air! To sew up my mistress's ripped cushions! To . . . to feel an iron pot she has thrown at me wang against my skull!"

The djinn flung wide his arms. "My mistress has commanded me to kill her!" he sobbed.

"What?" Mathew cried, alarmed. "Usti, you can't!"

"I am sworn to obey," said the djinn solemnly, with a hiccup. "And, indeed, I would do that rather than see her suffer." Usti's voice grew gentle. "But that is why I came to you, the first chance I had. My mistress says that you have deserted her, but I did not believe that, so I came to see for myself." Usti glanced dubiously at where the imp had been standing. "And I find a creature of Sul who calls you Dark Master. Perhaps, after all, the Princess is right." Usti's eyes narrowed suspiciously. "You have betrayed us, gone over to the side of darkness!"

"No, no! I haven't!" Mathew lowered his voice. "Trust me, Usti! Tell Zohra to trust me!—And don't harm her. I have a plan—"

A knocking came at the door. Mathew cringed. "Who is it?" he managed to call out, in a voice that he hoped sounded as though he'd just awakened.

"I have food and drink," came the answer, "to break your fast."

"Just . . . just a moment!" Mathew couldn't delay long. Moving slowly toward the door, he spoke hastily to the djinn, who was already beginning to disappear. "Tell Zohra to have faith in her God! He is with her!"

Usti appeared dubious. "I will give her the message," he said morosely, "if I have the chance. Already the witch-woman has taken her and begins some evil process of purification—"

There came the grating of a key in the lock; the door began to swing open.

"Don't carry out Zohra's command!" Mathew begged to the vanishing smoke. "Not unless all is lost!"

He spoke to empty air. Sighing, he barely glanced at the slave who entered with a laden food tray. He did notice, however, a Black Paladin standing guard outside his door, and he knew there would be no more opportunities to walk freely through the Castle.

The slave placed the tray upon a table and left without a word; Mathew heard the door lock click. Feeling little appetite, but knowing he should eat to keep up his strength, he sat down to his gloom-ridden breakfast.

Up above him, in the shadows of the ceiling, the imp glared at the young wizard. "He has a plan, does he? You're thinking much too hard, human. I see your thoughts. I believe my Prince will find this most interesting. . . ."

# Chapter 15

Auda ibn Jad opened his casement to the night air, feeling i
blow cool against skin flushed and feverish with excitemen
and anticipation. He reveled in the sensation; then, turning
back to his room, he bathed—shivering in the chill air—and
arrayed himself in the black armor, donning at the last th
black velvet robes. Examining himself critically in the mirror
he searched for the slightest flaw, knowing that the eyes o
his Lord would be hard to please this night. He smoothed the
black beard that ran across his strong jaw, brushed the wel
black hair so that it glistened and tied it behind his head with
a black ribbon. The mustache that grew over his upper li
traced two fine lines down either side of his mouth, flowing a
last like a thin black river to the bearded chin. His pale fac
was stained with an unnatural infusion of blood beneath th
skin, the black eyes glittered in the light.

I must calm myself. This excitement is unholy and ir
reverent. Kneeling down upon the cold stone floor, Aud
clasped his hands in prayer and brought a restful repose t
his soul by losing himself in holy meditation. The Castl
around him was abnormally still and quiet. All were in thei
rooms alone, preparing themselves with prayer and fasting
They would remain there until the hour for the Gatherin
came. Eleven times the iron bell would toll, calling all fort
to the Vestry.

It lacked an hour till that time yet. Ibn Jad rose to hi
feet, his prayers concluded. His mind was clear, his racin

pulse once more beating slowly, steadily. He had a matter of importance to attend to before the Gathering. Walking from his room, his booted feet making as little noise as possible upon the stone so as not to disturb the others in their holy solitude, ibn Jad went forth. He left the upper recesses of the Castle, making his way down to the chambers below the surface of the earth.

He had seen the Lifemaster this morning. Exhausted from having had no sleep throughout the day and night, the man was on his way to his room to eat a morsel (the strictures of the fast being required only of the knights) and then nap a few hours. An assistant, one to whom he was teaching his heinous skills, had taken over with the subject.

"The nomad is a strong man, ibn Jad," said the Lifemaster, his oversized head bobbing upon its spindly neck. "You chose well. It will be nightfall before we break him."

"The only man alive who ever bested me," said Auda ibn Jad, remembering Khardan raiding the city long months ago. "I want the bonding, Lifemaster."

The Lifemaster nodded, as if this did not surprise him. "I thought as much. I heard about Catalus," he added softly. "My condolences."

"Thank you," said ibn Jad gravely. "He died well and for the cause, laying the blood curse upon the priest who seeks to rule us all. But now I am brotherless."

"There are many who would be honored to bond with you, Paladin," said the Lifemaster emotionally.

"I know. But this man's fate and mine are bound together. So the Black Sorceress told me, and so I knew in my heart from the moment we looked upon each other in the city of Kich."

The Lifemaster said nothing more. If the Black Sorceress had set her word upon it, there was nothing more to say.

"The critical time will come this evening. His pain and anguish will have drawn him near death. We must be careful not to allow him to slip over." The Lifemaster spoke with the modest air of one who has mastered a delicate art. "Arrive at ten strokes of the bell. The bonding will be stronger if it is your hand that leads him away from death."

The final strokes of the iron bell were just fading away when Auda ibn Jad entered the Lifemaster's dread chamber.

Khardan was very far gone. Ibn Jad, who had murdered countless of his fellow beings and felt without a qualm their

blood splash upon his hands, could not look at the nomad's
tortured body without feeling his stomach wrench. Memories
of his own conversion to Zhakrin, of his own suffering and torment in this very chamber, seared through the blackness of
deliberate, blessed forgetfulness. Auda had seen others endure
the same fate without thinking back to that time. Why? Why now?

Face pale, a bitter taste in his mouth, the Black Paladin
sank weakly back against a wall, unable to wrench his gaze
from the dying man who lay limply on the floor. Khardan was
no longer chained. He no longer had the energy left to
escape or fight his tormentor.

The Lifemaster, busy with his work, spared ibn Jad a
glance. "Ah," he said softly, "the bonding starts already."

"What . . . what do you mean?" ibn Jad asked hoarsely.

"The God has given you back the memory He once bless-
edly took away. Your souls share pain, as your bodies will
soon share blood."

Falling to his knees, ibn Jad bowed his head, thanking
Zhakrin, but he flinched and came near crying out when the
Lifemaster grasped hold of his arm.

"Come forward!" the tormentor said urgently. "It is time!"

Auda moved near Khardan. The nomad's face was ashen,
his eyes sunken in his head. Sweat gleamed on his skin.
Mingling with blood, it trickled in rivulets over his body.

"Call to him!" ordered the Lifemaster.

"Khardan," said ibn Jad, in a voice that trembled despite
himself.

The nomad's eyelids shivered, he drew a quivering breath.

"Again!" the Lifemaster's voice was insistent, fearful.

"Khardan!" called Auda more loudly and stronger, as though
shouting to one about to walk blindly off a cliff. "Khardan!" Ibn
Jad grasped hold of a limp hand that was already devoid of the
warmth of life. "We are losing him!" he whispered angrily.

"No, no!" said the Lifemaster, the huge head whipping
about so rapidly it seemed it must fly off the thin, brittle
neck. "Make him call upon the name of Zhakrin!"

"Khardan," cried ibn Jad, "pray to God—"

"There, he hears you!" said the Lifemaster in what ibn
Jad noted was a tone of relief. The Black Paladin glanced
coldly at the man, his displeasure obvious, and the Lifemaster
quailed before Auda's anger.

But ibn Jad had no time to spare upon the tormentor.

Khardan's eyelids flickered open. Rimmed with crimson, the pupils dilated, the nomad's eyes stared at Auda without a glimmer of recognition.

"God?" he said inaudibly, the barest hint of breath displacing the bloody froth upon his lips. "Yes, I . . . remember. Mathew . . ." His words died in what ibn Jad feared was his final breath. The Black Paladin clutched the man's hand.

"Call upon the God to spare you, Khardan! Offer him your soul in exchange for your life, for an end to this torment!"

"My soul . . ." Khardan's eyes closed. His lips moved, then he fell silent. Slumping forward, his head rested on his chest.

"What did he say?" ibn Jad demanded of the tormentor.

"He said . . . 'Zhakrin, I give you my life.' "

"Are you certain?" Ibn Jad frowned. He had heard the words "give you my life," but the name of the God to whom the man prayed had been indistinct.

"Of course!" the Lifemaster said hastily. "And look! The lines of pain upon his face ease! He draws a deep breath! He sleeps!"

"Truly, life returns to him," said ibn Jad, feeling the hand he held grow warm, seeing color flow into the bloodless cheeks. "Khardan!" he called gently.

The nomad stirred and lifted his head. Opening his eyes, he looked around him in astonishment. His gaze went to the Lifemaster, then to ibn Jad. Khardan's eyes narrowed in obvious puzzlement. "I . . . I am still here," he murmured.

An odd reaction, thought ibn Jad. Still, this was an unusual man. I've never seen one draw so near death and then have the strength to turn back.

"Zhakrin be praised!" said ibn Jad, watching the nomad's reaction closely.

"Zhakrin . . ." Khardan breathed. Then he smiled, as though seeming to recall something. "Yes, Zhakrin be praised."

Scrambling to his feet, the Lifemaster hastened over to a table and returned bearing a sharp knife, whose blade was already stained with dried blood. Seeing it, Khardan's eyes flared, his lips tightened grimly.

"Have no fear, my . . . brother," said Auda softly.

Khardan glanced at him questioningly.

"Brother," repeated ibn Jad. "You are a Black Knight, now. One who serves Zhakrin in life and in death, and you are therefore my brother. But I would go further. I have requested that you and I be bonded, that our blood mingle."

"What does this mean?" asked Khardan thickly, propping himself up, his face twisting in pain as he moved.

"Life for life, we are pledged to each other. Honor bound to come to the other's defense when we can, to avenge the other's death when we cannot. Your enemies become my enemies, my enemies yours." Taking the knife from the Lifemaster, the knight made a slash in his own wrist, causing the red blood to well forth. Grasping Khardan's arm, he cut the skin and then pressed his flesh against the nomad's. " 'From my heart to yours, from your heart to mine. Our blood flows into each other's bodies. We are closer than brothers born.' There, now you repeat the oath."

Khardan stared searchingly at ibn Jad for long moments; the Calif's lips parted, but he said nothing. His gaze went to the arms, joined together—ibn Jad's arm strong and white-skinned, the veins and sinews clearly visible against the firm muscles; Khardan's arm, pale, weak from the enforced inaction of the past few months, stained with blood and filth and sweat.

"To refuse this honor would be a grievous insult to the God who has given you your life," said the Lifemaster, seeing the nomad hesitate.

"Yes," muttered Khardan in seemingly increasing confusion, "I suppose it would." Slowly, haltingly, he repeated the oath.

Auda ibn Jad smiled in satisfaction. Putting his arm around Khardan's naked back, he lifted the nomad to his feet. "Come, I will take you to your room where you may rest. The Black Sorceress will give you something to ease the torment of your wounds and help you sleep—"

"No," said Khardan, stifling a cry of anguish. Sweat beaded his upper lip. "I must . . . be at the ceremony."

Auda ibn Jad looked his approval but slowly shook his head. "I understand your desire to share in this moment of our victory, but you are too weak, my brother—"

"No!" insisted Khardan, teeth clenched. "I will be there!"

"Far be it from me to thwart such noble courage," said ibn Jad. "I have a salve that will help ease the pain somewhat and a glass of wine will burn away the rest."

Khardan had no breath to reply, but he nodded his head. The Lifemaster draped a black cloth over the nomad's naked body. Leaning upon Auda ibn Jad, the Calif—weak as a babe—let himself be assisted from the chamber.

# Chapter 16

Mathew had remained locked in his room throughout the day. He had spent the incredibly long hours of waiting pacing the floor, his fears divided among Khardan, Zohra, and himself. He knew what he must do, knew what he *had* to do tonight, and he mentally prepared himself, going over and over it again in his mind. It was no longer a question of courage. He knew himself well enough now to understand that his bravery sprang from desperation. Matters were desperate enough. This was their only chance to escape, and if it meant surrendering his soul to Astafas, then that is what he was prepared to do.

"And even that is a cowardly act," he said to himself, slumping exhausted in a chair, having walked miles in his little room. "It is all very well to say that you are sacrificing yourself for Khardan and Zohra, both of whom saved your life, both of whom were dragged into this because of you! But admit it. Once again, you are acting to save your own skin, because you can't face the thought of death!

"That was a very fine lecture you gave Khardan. All about having the courage to live and fight. Fortunately he couldn't see the words were stained yellow with a coward's bile as they fled your mouth. He and Zohra both are prepared to die rather than betray their God! You're prepared to sell your soul for another few moments of keeping life in a craven's body that isn't worth the air it breathes!"

Night had darkened his window. The tones of the iron bell had rung out at such long intervals during the day that Mathew often wondered if the timekeeping device had broken down. Now the peals dinned in his ears so often he was half convinced that they had let the clock run loose, chiming the quarter hours on whatever whim took it.

To distract thoughts that were threatening to run as wild as time, Mathew rose to his feet and threw open the window. A freshening wind from the sea blew away the foul-smelling, yellowish tinged fog that had clung like a noxious blanket to the Castle all day. Looking outside, Mathew could see a cliff of black jagged rocks—below that, the seashore, whose white sand gleamed eerily in the starlight. Dark waves broke upon the shoreline. A black patch against the water, the ship of the ghuls swung at anchor, its crew no doubt dreaming of sweet, human flesh.

Movement near the window casement caught Mathew's attention. He looked out to find a horrid figure looking in. Springing backward, Mathew slammed shut the window. Grabbing hold of the velvet curtains, he drew them closed with such force he nearly ripped them from their hangings. He left the window hastily, hurrying back to his bed, and sank down upon it.

A *nesnas*! Half human and half . . . nothing!

Mathew shuddered, closing his eyes to blot out the memory and succeeding only in bringing it more clearly to his mind. Take a human male and chop him in two, lengthwise, with an axe, and that is what I saw from my window! Half a head, half a nose and mouth, one ear; half a trunk, one arm, one leg . . . hopping, horribly . . .

And that is what we must face when we leave the Castle! *You are the Bearer. Nothing can harm the Bearer!*

The words came back to him comfortingly. He repeated them over and over in a soothing litany. But what about those with me? They will be safe, he assured himself. Nothing out there will harm them, for I will be the master, the master of all that is dark and evil. . . .

What am I saying? Cowering, shivering, Mathew slid from the bed and fell to his knees. "Holy Father," he whispered, folding his hands and pressing them to his lips, "I am sorry to have failed you. I had supposed that you kept me alive, when so many more worthy than myself died, for some purpose. If so, surely I have upset that purpose through my foolish actions. It's just that . . . that I seem so alone! Perhaps what the imp said about a guardian angel is true after all. If that is so, and she has forsaken me, then I know why. Forgive me, Father. My soul will go to its dark reward. I ask only one last thing. Take the two lives in my care and deal mercifully with them. Despite the fact that they worship another God and are barbaric and savage in their ways, they are both truly good and caring people. See them safely back to their homeland . . . their homeland. . . ." Tears crept down Mathew's cheeks, falling among his fingers. "The homeland they long to see once more, to parents who grieve for them.

"What a wretch I am!" Mathew cried suddenly, flinging himself away from the bed. "I cannot even pray for others without finding myself sucked into the mire of self-pity." Glancing up at heaven, he smiled bitterly. "I cannot even pray . . is that it? They say that those who worship the Prince of Darkness cannot say Your Holy Name but that it burns their tongues and blisters their lips. I—"

There came a knock on his door. Fearfully, Mathew heard the clock begin to chime. One . . . five . . . eight . . . his heart counted the strokes . . . ten . . . eleven. . . .

A key rattled in the door lock.

"You are wanted, Blossom."

Swallowing, Mathew tried to answer, but the words would not come. His hand moved to grasp hold of the black wand. It was an unconscious act; he did not know he was touching it until he felt its sharp sides bite into his flesh, its reassuring warmth wash over him like the dark waters of the ocean waves, crashing on the beach below.

The door swung open. Auda ibn Jad stood framed in the doorway, silhouetted against a backdrop of blazing torches. The flickering light burned bright orange on his black armor, glittered off the eyes in the head of the severed snake that adorned his breastplate. Beside ibn Jad stood another knight, dressed in the same armor.

The torchlight gleamed on curly black hair, lit a face that had been in Mathew's thoughts all day—a face that was pale and wan, drawn with pain yet alight with a fire of fierce eagerness, a face that looked at Mathew with no recognition at all in the black eyes.

"You are wanted," said Auda ibn Jad coolly. "The hour of our triumph draws near."

Bowing his head in acquiescence, Mathew walked out the doorway. Ibn Jad entered the room and began to search it. What he might be hunting for, Mathew hadn't any idea— perhaps the imp. Drawing near Khardan, the young wizard took the opportunity to look once more into the face of the Calif.

One eyelid flickered. Deep, deep within the blackness of the eyes was the glimmer of a smile.

"Thank you, Promenthas," Mathew breathed, then bit off his prayer, thinking he felt a burning sensation in his throat.

# Chapter 17

Once again the circle of Black Paladins formed in the Vestry around the signet of the severed snake. This time, however, all the followers of Zhakrin were present in the room. Black-robed women, many with the swollen bellies that held future followers of the God, sat in chairs in one corner of the huge hall. Kiber and his *goums* and the other men-at-arms in service to the Black Paladins stood ranged around the hall, their weapons in hand. The naked blades of sword and dagger, the sharp points of spears, gleamed brightly in the light of thousands of black wax candles set in wrought-iron flambeaux that had been lowered from the high ceiling.

Behind the soldiers, huddled on the floor, their faces pale with fear, the slaves of the followers of Zhakrin waited in hopeless despair for the return of the God that would seal their fate forever.

Flanked by Khardan and Auda ibn Jad, Mathew entered the Vestry. He walked closely between the two knights; more than once Khardan's body brushed against his, and Mathew could feel it tense and taut for action. But he could also hear the breath catch in Khardan's throat when he moved, the stifled groan or gasp of pain that he could not quite suppress. The Calif's face was pale; despite the intense chill of the great hall, sweat gleamed upon his upper lip. Auda ibn Jad glanced at him in concern and once whispered something to him

urgently, but Khardan only shook his head, gruffly answering
that he would stay.

It occurred to Mathew, as he entered the huge, candlelit
chamber, that Khardan was suffering this because of him,
because of what he'd said. He has faith in me, thought
Mathew, and the knowledge terrified him. I can't let him
down, not after what he's endured because of me. I can't!

Gripping the wand more tightly, he entered the circle of
Black Paladins, who moved aside respectfully to make room
for them.

Within the center of the circle of men and women had
been placed an altar of such hideous aspect that Mathew
stared at it, appalled. It was the head of a snake that had
been cut off at the neck. Carved of ebony, standing four feet
high, the snake's mouth gaped open. Glistening fangs made
of ivory parted to reveal a forked tongue encrusted with
rubies. The tongue, shooting upward between the fangs,
formed a platform that was empty now, but Mathew guessed
what object soon would rest there. Around the altar stood the
tall ivory jars that Mathew had seen on the boat. Their lids
had been removed.

Beside the altar stood the Black Sorceress. Her gaze fixed
on Mathew when he stepped into the circle. Aged, ageless,
the eyes probed the young wizard's soul and apparently liked
what they saw there, for the lips of the stretched face smiled.

She sees the darkness within me, realized Mathew with a
calmness that he found startling. He knew she saw it because
he could feel it, a vast emptiness that felt neither fear nor
hope. And over it, covering the hollowness like a shell,
spread exultation, a sensation of power coming into his hands.
He reveled in it, rejoicing, longing to wield it as a man longs
to wield the blade of a new sword.

Glancing at Khardan, he wondered irritably if the man
would be of use to him now, injured as he was. Mathew
fretted impatiently for the ceremony to get under way. He
wanted to see that smile on the woman's drum-skin face
vanish. He wanted to see it replaced with awe!

The Black Sorceress laid her hands upon the emerald eyes
of the snake's-head altar, and a low sound thrummed through
the Vestry, a sound that was like a wail or moan. At the sound,
all excited talk that had flowed among the circle of Paladins
and whispered through the women waiting in the corner of
the Vestry ceased. The men-at-arms came to stiff attention,

their boots scraping against the stone floor. The circle parted to admit four slaves carrying a heavy obsidian bier. Staggering beneath the weight, the slaves bore it slowly and carefully into the center of the circle that closed around them. Reverently, the slaves brought their burden before the Black Sorceress.

Upon the obsidian slab lay Zohra, clothed in a gown made entirely of black crystal. The beads' sparkling edges caught the candlelight and gave off a rainbow-colored aura whose heart was darkness. Her long black hair had been brushed and oiled and fell from a center part in her head around her shoulders, touching her fingertips. She lay on her back, her hands stretched out straight at her sides. Her eyes were wide open, her lips slightly parted; she stared at the candles above her, but there was no sign of life on her face. From the pallor of her complexion, she might have been a corpse, but for the even rise and fall of her chest that could be detected by the faint shimmering of the crystal beaded gown.

Mathew felt Khardan flinch and knew this pain the man experienced did not come from his wounds. He cares for her more than he admits, thought Mathew. Just as well, it will give him added incentive to serve me.

The Lord of the Paladins stepped forth and made a speech. Mathew shifted from foot to foot, thinking they were taking an inordinate amount of time to conduct this ceremony. He had just heard the clock chime three-quarters of the hour gone, when he suddenly stared intently at one of the slaves carrying the bier.

At that moment the slave Mathew was watching set his end of the bier down suddenly, groaning from the strain and wiping his face. The bier tilted, jostling Zohra and causing the Black Sorceress to glare at the slave with such ire that everyone in the Vestry knew the wretched fellow was doomed.

Usti! recognized Mathew, staring in blank astonishment. How he had managed the transformation, Mathew didn't know. He was certain the djinn hadn't been among those who first carried the bier into the Vestry. But there was no mistaking the three chins, the fat face rising from bulging shoulders.

The other bearers started to set down their ends, but the Black Sorceress said sharply, "No! not here in front of me! Beneath the altar."

With a long-suffering groan, Usti lifted his end of the bier

again, helping to shift it around to place it where indicated.
Mathew saw the jeweled handle of a dagger flare from the
djinn's sash wound around his broad middle. Usti's fat face
was grim. His chins shaking with intent and purpose and
resolve, Usti took his place at his mistress's head.

A hushed silence descended upon the Vestry; breath short-
ened, hearts beat fast, blood tinged the faces of those who
had worked and waited and dedicated their very lives to the
attaining of this moment of glory. The iron chimes began
their toll. . . .

One.

The Black Sorceress drew forth from her robes the crystal
globe containing the swimming fish.

Two.

Reverently, she laid the globe upon the forked tongue of
the snake.

Three.

Turning to one of the ivory jars, the Black Sorceress
dipped in her hand and drew it forth, stained with human
blood.

Four.

The Black Paladins began to call upon their God by name.
"Zhakrin . . . Zhakrin . . . Zhakrin . . ." whispered through
the Vestry like an evil wind.

Five.

The Black Sorceress bent over Zohra and drew an S-shape
on her forehead in the blood of the murdered innocents of
the city of Idrith.

Six.

The chant rose in volume, increased in speed. "Zhakrin,
Zhakrin, Zhakrin."

Seven.

Mathew's hand slowly began to draw forth the black wand.

Eight.

The Black Sorceress lifted the crystal globe and placed it
upon Zohra's breast.

Nine.

The chant became frenzied, triumphant. "Zhakrin! Zhakrin!
Zharkin!"

Ten.

The Black Sorceress dipped her hand again in the blood
in the ivory jar and smeared it over the crystal globe.

Eleven.

Removing one of the razor-sharp, ivory fangs from the mouth of the altar, the Black Sorceress held it poised above the globe, above Zohra's breast. . . .

Twelve.

"In the name of Astafas, I summon you! Bring the fish to me!" cried Mathew.

He raised the wand, the imp appeared. A shattering explosion blew out the lights of the candles and plunged the room into darkness.

# Chapter 18

The chanting dwindled into confusion, swallowed up by shouts of outrage and anger.

"Torches!" cried some of the Paladins, starting to leave.

"Do not break the Circle!" the Black Sorceress's voice shrieked above the cries, and Mathew heard movement around him cease.

But the men-at-arms standing outside the Circle were free to act. Hastening into the hallways around the Vestry, their booted feet skidding and sliding on the slick floors in their haste, the soldiers grabbed torches from the walls and were back into the Vestry before Mathew's eyes had yet grown accustomed to the darkness.

Blinking in the blazing light that caused his eyes to ache, Mathew saw the Black Sorceress staring at him, her face livid, her eyes burning more fiercely than the flames reflected in their dark depths. She did not say a word or make a move but only gazed upon him, testing his strength. Between her and Mathew stood the imp, its splay-fingered hands outstretched, its red eyes flaring threateningly around the circle, its tongue lolling in excitement from its drooling mouth.

Nobody moved or spoke. All eyes were on him. Mathew smiled, secure in his power. "Bring me the fish," he ordered the imp again, his voice cracking with impatience. "Why do you delay? Must I speak the name of Our Master again? He won't be pleased, I can assure you."

Slowly, the imp turned and faced Mathew, its red eyes flickering, its shriveled skin glistening with slime in the torchlight. "You speak the name of My Master glibly enough," said the imp, pointing at Mathew with a crooked finger, its feet sliding noiselessly over the floor as it drew near him. "But Astafas is not convinced that you are His servant. He demands proof, human."

"What more proof does he want?" Mathew cried angrily, keeping the wand pointed at the imp. "Isn't it enough that I am capturing these two Gods, bringing them to Him to do with as He pleases?"

"Are you?" inquired the imp, grinning. "Or are you using that as an excuse to aid you in your escape from the Castle, knowing that if you have the magical globe in your possession, no one can harm you? Will you truly offer the fish to Astafas?"

"I will! What can I do to prove it?"

The imp's pointing finger began to move. "Sacrifice, in the name of Astafas, this man." The finger stopped. It was aimed at Khardan's heart.

Mathew sucked in his breath. The wand in his hand began to writhe and change and suddenly he held an onyx dagger with a handle of petrified wood. The breastplate melted from Khardan's body, leaving his chest bare, the wounds of his torment clearly visible on his skin. The Calif regarded Mathew complacently, obviously thinking this was part of the plan. He made no attempt to escape, and Mathew knew he would not.

He has faith in me!

Not until Mathew plunged the dagger into his heart, would Khardan realize he'd been tricked, duped.

"There is nothing else I can do!" Mathew whispered, raising the dagger, enveloping himself in the darkness that had suddenly become a living, breathing entity.

And thus he did not see, behind him, torchlight flare off the drawn blade of the sword of Auda ibn Jad.

# Book Eight

# THE BOOK OF AKHRAN

# Chapter 1

Death led Asrial from the *arwat* through the crowded streets of the dead city of Serinda. Glancing back, the angel could see Pukah sitting disconsolately near the window, his face against the glass, staring into nothing. For the first time since Asrial had come to know him, the djinn looked defeated, and she felt an aching in her chest in what Pukah would have termed her heart. Repeating to herself that immortal beings did not possess such sensitive and wayward organs did little to ease the angel's pain.

"I've been around humans too long," Asrial rebuked herself. "When I go back, I will spend seven years in chapel and do penance until these uncomfortable, very wrong, and improper feelings are expunged from my being!"

But the strong, shielding walls of the cathedral of Promenthas were very far away. A mist began to rise up around the angel, obliterating the sight of the *arwat* from her view. The sounds of the city of Serinda faded in the distance. Asrial could see nothing except the gray fog that swirled around her and the figure of Death near.

"Where are we?" asked Asrial, confused and disoriented in the thick mist.

"One might say this is my dwelling place," responded Death.

"Dwelling!" Asrial peered through the mist, attempting to see past the wispy rags of fog that wrapped and whorled and meandered around them. "I see no dwelling!"

"You see no walls, no floor, no ceiling, you mean," Death corrected. "Such structure makes—for you—a dwelling. Yet how should I—who know the impermanence of all things—put my faith in the frail and fragile elements? Were I to live in a mountain, I would eventually see it crumble around me. Speaking of that which is frail and fragile, I will show you the human in whom you take such an interest."

The mists swirled and then parted, swept from before the angel's eyes by a blast of cold wind. She stood in the Vestry. Mathew—dagger in hand—faced Khardan. Behind Mathew stood Auda ibn Jad, his sword slowly and noiselessly sliding from its scabbard. And standing near them all, its red eyes gleaming in glee—

"A servant of Astafas!" cried Asrial. "And I am not there to protect Mathew! Oh, I should never have left him, never!"

"Why did you come?"

"I was told I had to, or else my protégé would lose his soul," Asrial faltered, her eyes on the imp.

"And who told you this?"

"A . . . fish," Asrial said, flushing in embarrassment. "How could I be so foolish!"

"The fish was the Goddess Evren, child." Death seemed amused. "Trying to regain Her immortals, so that She can return to power, if She manages to return to life."

"I don't understand."

"The two fish you see in the globe on the altar are, in reality, the God Zhakrin and His opposite, the Goddess Evren. They are in the hands of Zhakrin's followers. The Black Sorceress, the woman standing beside the altar, was just about to bring Zhakrin back into the world by placing His essence into the body of a human when your Mathew decided to interfere.

"The young man came into possession of a wand of evil magical power. He succumbed to the temptation to use it and so—without you to guard him—he is easy prey for Astafas. Your Mathew is attempting to take possession of the fish."

"To save Evren!" Asrial breathed.

Death shrugged. "Mathew is a human, child. The war in Heaven is not his concern. Under the growing influence of evil, the only person he intends to free is himself. Once he has possession of the globe, the magic surrounding it will protect him from harm. If he takes it, he would dare not free the Gods. And it would not make much difference if he did.

Without their immortals, Zhakrin and Evren will soon dwindle, and this time they will vanish completely. Quar's power is ten times what it was when he first caught them. Their followers will be obliterated from the earth."

The vision changed. Asrial saw the future. A mighty armada sailed the Kurdin Sea. Hordes of men, bearing the standard of the golden ram's head, landed upon the beach of the Isle of Galos. The followers of Zhakrin fought desperately to save their Castle, but it was all in vain. They were overwhelmed. The bodies of the Black Paladins lay hacked and mangled upon the beach. Their line had not broken; each died where he stood—side by side with his brother. In the Castle, the Black Sorceress and the women fought with their magic, but that, too, could not prevail against the might of Quar. The Imam called down their ruin. The 'efreet, Kaug, surged up from the volcano, bringing with him deadly ash and poisonous fume. He shook the ground; the Castle walls cracked and crumbled. The armies of Quar fled to their boats and sailed hastily back to the mainland. The volcano blew asunder; molten rock flowed into the boiling sea. Steam and cloud wound their winding sheets about the Isle of Galos, and it vanished forever beneath the dark waters.

"They are a cruel and evil people," said Asrial, reliving in her mind the murder of the priests and magi upon the shores of Bas. "They deserve such a fate. They are not fit to live."

"So Quar teaches—about the followers of Promenthas," said Death coolly.

"He is wrong!" Asrial cried. "My people are not like those!"

"No, and they are not like Quar's followers. And therefore they must either become like Quar's followers or they must die, for 'they are not fit to live.' "

"You must stop him!"

"Why should I care? What does it matter to me if there is one God or twenty? And it is not your concern, either, is it, child? Your concern is for that one mortal whose life and soul stand poised upon the blade of a dagger. I fear there is little you can do to save his life"—Death caused the vision of Mathew to return and gazed upon it, an expression of insatiable hunger on her pallid face—"but you might yet be able to save his soul."

"I must go to him—"

"By all means," said Death nonchalantly. "But I should

remind you that in order to reach the city gate, you will have to traverse the streets of Serinda."

The angel stared at Death with stricken face.

"But I can't! If I should die—"

"—you would live again, but without any memory of your protégé."

"What do you want of me?" Asrial demanded through trembling lips. "You brought me here, you showed me this for a purpose."

"Can't you guess? I want Pukah."

"But you have him!" the angel answered despairingly. "You said yourself that there is no way for him to escape!"

"Nothing in Sul is certain," replied Death sagely, "as I— above all others—have reason to know. You love him, don't you?"

"Immortal beings cannot love." Asrial lowered her eyes.

"*Should* not. It reduces their efficiency, as you yourself can plainly attest. You have committed a double sin, child. You have fallen in love with a mortal and an immortal. Now you must choose between them. Give me Pukah, and I will set you free to go to the rescue of your mortal's soul, if not his body."

"But it will be too late!" Asrial gazed, terrified, at the vision before her.

"Time has no meaning here. One day passes in this realm for every millisecond in the mortal realm. Bring me the tourmaline amulet this night, leave the djinn defenseless, and I will see to it that you arrive in time to fight for Mathew's soul."

"But you said Pukah had until morning!"

The woman showed her teeth in a grin. "Death is without pity, without mercy, without prejudice . . . without honor. The only oaths I am bound to keep are those I swear in Sul's name."

Asrial looked again at Mathew. She could see the darkness already folding its black wings around him. The sword of Auda ibn Jad was sliding forth slowly, ever so slowly, from its scabbard and she saw Mathew—his back turned to the Black Paladin—raise his dagger against a man who had trusted him, a man he loved.

Asrial bowed her head, her white wings drooped, and she found herself standing in the street, in front of the *arwat* in the city of Serinda.

# Chapter 2

"My enchanting one!" Pukah shouted, spying Asrial from the window. Springing to his feet, he raced outside the *arwat* and accosted the angel in the street. "You came back!"

"Of course," said Asrial sadly. "Where did you think I could go?"

"I don't know!" Pukah said, grinning. "All sorts of wild ideas went through my head when I saw you disappear with Death. Like maybe she might send you back to be with that madman of yours—"

"No!" cried Asrial wildly. Pukah looked at her, startled, and she flushed, biting her lip. "I mean, no, how silly of you to imagine such a thing." Reaching out her hand, she clasped hold of Pukah's and gripped it tightly. Her fingers were a bit too cold for those of an ardent lover, and her grasp was more resolute than tender, but so thrilled was Pukah at this expression of caring, that he immediately overlooked these minor inconsistencies.

"Asrial," he said earnestly, gazing into the blue eyes that were raised to his, "with you here, I'm not afraid of anything that might happen to me tomorrow."

The angel lowered her eyes, hurriedly averting her face, but not before Pukah saw a tear glisten on her cheek.

"Forgive me! I'm a wretch, a beast! I didn't mean to talk about tomorrow. Besides, nothing's going to happen to me. There, I'm talking about it again! I'm sorry. I won't say another word." He drew her near, putting a protective arm

329

around her and glowering at those in the street who were lustfully eyeing the lovely angel. "I think we should go someplace where we can be alone."

"Yes," said Asrial shyly. "You're right." Her eyes looked to the upper windows of the *arwat,* from where sounds of sweet laughter drifted out into the street. "Perhaps—"

"By Sul!" Pukah caught her meaning and stared at her, amazed. "Are you serious?"

Pressing her lips together firmly, Asrial moved nearer Pukah and rested her head against his chest.

The djinn flung his arms around the angel, hugging her close, never minding that it was similar to embracing the hard and unresisting trunk of a date palm. Her lips were stiff and did not kiss back.

"She does not want to seem too eager," said Pukah to himself. "Quite proper. I wonder if the wings are detachable."

Keeping his arm around Asrial's waist, the djinn led her back to the *arwat.* "A room," he said to the *rabat-bashi.*

"For the night only, I suppose." The proprietor grinned wickedly.

Pukah felt Asrial tremble in his arms and glared at the man. "For a week! Paid in advance." He tossed a handful of gold into the immortal's hands.

"Here's the key. Up the stairs, second door to your left. Don't wear yourself out tonight. You'll need to be fresh for the morrow!"

"I'll be fresh enough for *you* on the morrow you can be sure of that!" muttered Pukah, hurrying the near-collapsing angel up the stairs. "Don't pay any attention to that boor, my dearest."

"I'm . . . not," said Asrial faintly. Leaning against the wall, while Pukah fumbled with the key, the angel looked at him with such a sorrowful gaze that Pukah couldn't bear it.

"Asrial," he said gently, hearing the lock click, but not yet opening the door, "wouldn't you rather go sit somewhere and talk? Maybe the fountain by the Temple?"

"No, Pukah!" Asrial cried fiercely, flinging her arms around his neck. "I want to be with you tonight! Please!" She burst into tears, her grip tightened until she nearly strangled him.

"There, there," he said soothingly, feeling the heart beating wildly in the soft breast pressed against his bare chest. "You and I will be together, not only this night, but all nights in eternity!" Opening the door, he led the angel inside.

The rays of the setting sun beamed brightly through an open window. Asrial drew away from his arms as soon as they were in the room. Pukah locked the door, tossing the key on a nearby table, then hurried over to shut out the red, glaring light, slamming closed the wooden shutters and plunging the room into cool darkness.

When he turned around, his eyes growing accustomed to the dimness, he saw Asrial lying upon the bed that was the room's prominent feature. The wings—about which he had been so worried—spread out beneath her, forming a white, feathery blanket. Her long hair seemed to shine with its own light, bathing the angel in silver radiance. Her face was deathly pale, her eyes shimmering with unshed tears. Yet she held out her arms to him, and Pukah was very quick to respond.

Unwinding his turban, he shook free his black hair and crawled into bed beside her. Asrial did not look at him, but kept her eyes lowered in a maidenly confusion that made Pukah's blood throb in his temple. Slowly, her arms cold and shaking, the angel drew his head to her bosom and began to mechanically stroke the djinn's curly hair.

Pukah nestled into the softness of the wings and, placing his lips upon the white throat, was just about to lose himself in sweetness when he noticed that Asrial was singing.

"My dove," he said, clearing his throat and trying to lift his head, only to find that the angel held him close, "your song is beautiful, if a bit eerie, but so mournful. Plus"—he yawned—"it's making me sleepy."

The angel's hand motions were lulling and soothing. Pukah closed his eyes. The enchanting song bubbled into his mind like the rippling waters of a cool stream, quenching desire. He let the waters take him up and bear him away, floating on the top of the music until he sank beneath its waves and drowned.

Asrial's voice died. The djinn slept soundly, his head on her breast, his breathing regular and even. Rolling his body over gently, she sat up beside him. She had no fear of waking him. She knew he would sleep soundly for a long, long time.

A very long time. Sighing, Asrial gazed at the slumbering Pukah until she could not see him for the tears in her eyes. The slim, youthful body, the foxish face that thought itself so clever. Her hands stole around his chest and drew him close. She buried her face in his chest and felt his heart beat.

"No immortal can have a heart!" she wept. "No immortal can love! No immortal can die! Forgive me, Pukah. This is the only way! The only way!"

Taking hold of the amulet in her shaking hands, Asrial slowly removed it from around the djinn's neck.

# Chapter 3

A djinn awoke in a dimly lit, cavernous chamber. Sitting up and looking around him, he could barely make out tall marble columns reflecting the orange light of glowing flame off their polished surface. The handsome djinn had no idea where he was and no recollection of how he got here. He had no recollection of anything, in fact, and felt his head to see if there was a lump on it.

"Where am I?" he asked rhetorically, more to hear the sound of his voice in the shadowy darkness than because he expected an answer.

An answer was returned, however.

"You are in the Temple of Death in the city of Serinda."

Startled, the djinn glanced quickly around and saw the figure of a woman clad in white standing over him. She was beautiful, her marble-smooth face reflecting the flame in the same manner as the towering columns. Despite her beauty, the djinn shivered when she approached. It may have been some trick of the indistinct light, but the djinn could have sworn there was something strange about the woman's eyes.

"How did I get here?" the djinn asked, still feeling his head for swellings or bruises.

"You don't remember."

"No, I don't remember . . . much of anything."

"I see. Well, your name is Sond. Does that sound familiar?"

Yes, the djinn thought, that seemed right. He nodded gingerly, expecting his head to hurt. It didn't.

"You are an assassin—a skilled one. Your price is high. Few can afford you. But one did. A king. He paid you quite handsomely to kill a young man."

"A king shouldn't have to hire an assassin," said Sond, rising slowly to his feet and staring at the woman suspiciously. What was there about her eyes?

"He does when the killing must be kept secret from everyone in court, even the queen. He does when the person to be assassinated is his own son!"

"His son?"

"The king discovered the boy plotting to overthrow him. The king dares not confront his son openly, or the boy's mother would side with him, and she has her own army, powerful enough to split the kingdom. The king hired you to assassinate the young man; then he will spread the news that it was done by a neighboring kingdom, an enemy.

"You tracked your quarry to this city, Serinda. He stays in an *arwat* not far from here. But beware, Sond, for the young man is aware of you. Last night, you were attacked by his men who beat you and left you for dead. Some citizens found you and brought you to the Temple of Death, but you recovered, with my help."

"Thank you," said Sond warily. He moved nearer the woman, trying to see her more clearly, but she stepped back into a shadow.

"Your thanks are not required. Does any of this bring back memories?"

"Yes, it does," Sond admitted, though it seemed to him more like a story he'd once heard a *meddah* relate than something that had happened to him. "How do you know—"

"You spoke of it in your delirium. Do not worry, it is not unusual for memories to flee a person's mind, especially when they have taken such a brutal beating."

Now that she spoke of it, Sond did feel pain in his body. He could almost see the faces of his attackers, the sticks they carried raining blows down upon his body while the young man whom they served stood looking on, smiling.

Anger stirred in his heart. "I must complete my mission, for the honor of my profession," he said, feeling for the dagger in the sash at his waist, his hand closing reassuringly over the hilt. "Where did you say he was staying?"

"In the *arwat* the next street over to the north. It has no name, but you can tell it by the lovely girls who dance on the

balconies in the moonlight. When you enter, ask the proprietor to show you the room of a young man who calls himself
Pukah."

"His guards?"

"He believes you to be dead, imagines himself safe. You
will find him alone, unprotected." In her hand the woman
held an amulet, swinging it by its chain.

Sond paid scant attention to the jewel. Eager to get on
with his work, his memories growing clearer and more vivid
by the moment, he looked about for an exit.

"There." The woman pointed, and Sond saw moonlight
and heard faint sounds of a city at night.

He hurried forward, then stopped, turning. "I am in your
debt," he said. "What is your name?"

"One you know in your heart. One you will hear again
and again," said the woman, and her lips spread over her
teeth in a grin.

Sond had no trouble finding the *arwat*. A huge crowd was
gathered outside to watch the girls dancing on the balcony.
This Serinda was a lusty, brawling city, apparently. If Sond
was at all worried about how the murder of a Prince might be
viewed here, his fears were quickly eased. Life was cheap in
Serinda, to judge by what he glimpsed in dark alleyways as
he made his way through the streets. With only a glance at
the dancing girls, one of whom seemed vaguely familiar,
Sond entered the inn.

He found the proprietor—a short, fat man, who glanced
at him and nodded in recognition, though Sond couldn't
recall ever having seen him before.

"I am looking for a man called Pukah," said Sond in a low
undertone. The woman had said the Prince's guards would
not be about, but it never hurt to be cautious.

The *rabat-bashi* burst into wheezing, gasping laughter,
and Sond glared at him angrily. "Shut up! What is so funny?"

"A small joke just occurred to me," said the proprietor,
wiping his streaming eyes. "Never mind. You wouldn't understand. A pity, too. Don't glower so and keep your knife
where it is, or you'll regret it, friend." Steel flashed in the
proprietor's hand. He could move fast, it seemed, for one so
round. "Your man is upstairs, second door to the left. You'll
need a key." Knife in one hand, he fumbled at a ring at his
waist with the other. "Sure you don't want to wait until sunrise?"

"Why should I?" Sond asked impatiently, snatching the key from the man's hand.

"No reason." The *rabat-bashi* shrugged. "You know your business, I guess. He was with a woman—a beauty, too. But she left some time ago. I'll wager you'll find him sleeping like a babe after his . . . um . . . exertions."

Scowling, Sond didn't wait to hear anymore but ran up the stairs, taking them two at a time. Pausing outside the door, he laid his ear to the keyhole, but it was futile to attempt to hear anything above the wailing of the music and the howls of the crowd outside. Ah, well, the noise would muffle any sound—such as a scream.

Quickly, Sond inserted the key, heard the lock click, and silently pushed open the door. The curtains were closed; he could only see a dark shape lying on white sheets. Padding softly across the floor, the djinn opened the curtains a crack, allowing moonlight to spill through and shine upon the figure in the bed. He wouldn't want to kill the wrong man by mistake.

But this was his man, he was sure of it. Young, with a thin, pointed-chinned face and an expression on his countenance indicating that—even in sleep—he thought very well of himself. Though Sond couldn't say he recognized the face, that smug, self-satisfied look evoked a response—a highly unpleasant one.

Drawing his dagger, Sond crept over to the bed where Pukah lay, apparently in deep slumber. To his consternation, however, the young man's eyes suddenly opened wide.

The dagger's blade gleamed in the moonlight. There was no mistaking the murderous intent on Sond's face. He gripped the dagger in his sweating palm and prepared to fight.

But the young man lay in bed, staring at him with an odd expression—one of sorrow.

"Pukah?" questioned Sond grimly.

"Yes," replied the young man, and there was a tremor in the voice as of one who holds very tightly to courage.

"You know why I am here."

"Yes." The voice was faint.

"Then you know that I bear you no malice. I am but the hand at the end of another's arm. Your vengeful spirit will not seek me, but the man who paid me?"

Pukah nodded. It was obvious he could not reply. Rolling over on his stomach, he hid his face in the pillow, gripped it with both hands. His body was covered with sweat, he quivered, his lips trembled.

Sond stood over him, looking down at him, contemptuous of his victim's fear. Lifting the dagger, the djinn drove it to the hilt between Pukah's shoulder blades.

# Chapter 4

The entire population of the city of Serinda gathered to celebrate Pukah's funeral. The *arwat*'s proprietor (a new one; the former had been dispatched during the night in a quarrel over the price of a room) discovered the djinn's body in the morning when she made a tour of the rooms, throwing out any guests too drunk to stagger forth on their own.

Death came to view the body as it was being carried forth, accompanied by a mockery of solemn state and ceremony. The dancing girls preceded it. Dressed in sheer, filmy black silk, they wept copiously and disappeared rapidly; there being those in the crowd who offered to comfort them in their affliction. The *arwat*'s musicians played funeral music to a festive beat that started an impromptu street dance as the bearers carried the djinn's corpse on their shoulders to the Temple of Death. Several fights broke out along the route— those who had placed bets on the time of death were arguing among themselves vehemently, since no one was quite certain when he'd died.

Death walked behind the body, smiling upon her subjects, who instantly cleared a path for her, scrambling to get out of the way of her coming. The hollow eyes scanned the mob, searching for one who should have been in attendance but was not. Death did not look for the assassin. She had taken Sond last night. Several immortals, convinced that they were the "Prince's" bodyguards, cornered the djinn in an alley and effectively avenged the death of their imagined monarch. Sond lay once again in the Temple where he would be restored to life as a slaver, perhaps, or a thief, or a Prince himself.

"Where is the angel?" Death questioned those who gathered to watch. "The woman who was with the djinn yesterday?"

Since few to whom she spoke remembered yesterday or knew anything about the dead man other than that it was rumored he had sought to destroy their city, no one could answer Death's question. Asrial had come to Death last night, bearing the amulet, and had given it into her hand without a word. Death promised that the angel should leave at sunset the following day, when the bargain was concluded. Asrial had seemed ill at ease, inattentive, and had vanished precipitously without responding to Death's offer.

"Truly she loves that liar," said Death to herself, and it occurred to her as she walked among the crowd that Asrial might have attempted to prevent the djinn's assassination and could very well have fallen victim to Sond's knife herself. Death shrugged, deciding it didn't really matter.

Pukah was laid upon a bier of cow dung. The singing, dancing immortals strewed garbage over him. Soaking the bier in wine, they made preparations to burn it with the setting of the sun.

Death watched the proceedings until, bored, she left to follow the Amir's troops into battle against another city in Bas. This city was proving obstinate—refusing to give up without a fight, refusing to acknowledge Quar their God. Death was certain to reap a fine harvest from this bloody field. The Imam had ordered every *kafir*—man, woman, and child—put to the sword.

She had all day until she must return to Serinda and see her bargain with Pukah completed.

Death had time to kill.

# Chapter 5

"Dark as Quar's heart," muttered Pukah to himself, opening his eyes and staring around him confusedly. "And the air is thick! Has there been a sandstorm?" Dust flew into his mouth, and the djinn sneezed. Sitting up to see where he was, he received a smart rap on the head.

"Ooof!" Dizzily, Pukah lay back down and, moving more cautiously, slowly extended his hands and felt around him. Above his head, apparently, was a slab of wood. And he was lying on wood—dirty, dust-covered wood by the feel and the smell.

Just when the djinn had decided that he was lying in a wooden box—for Sul only knew what reason—Pukah groped about farther and felt his hand brush into soft material on either side of him. "A wooden box with curtains," he commented. "This gets stranger and stranger." One hand slid completely underneath the material. Figuring that where his hand could go, he could follow, the djinn scooted across the floor, raising a huge cloud of dust, and nearly sneezing himself unconscious.

"By Sul!" said Pukah in astonishment, "I've been lying under a bed!"

Sunlight streaming through a dirty window revealed to the djinn the place where he'd apparently spent the night. It was the same bed on top of which he'd been lying in a state of bliss with . . .

"Asrial!" Pukah cried, looking around him frantically.

He was alone and his head felt as though it were stuffed with Majiid's stockings. Pukah had the vague memory of singing in his ears, then nothing. Slowly he sank down on the bed. Batting himself on the forehead several times, hoping to displace the stockings and allow room for his wits, the djinn tried to figure out what had happened. He remembered Asrial returning to the *arwat* after his bargain with Death. . . .

Bargain with Death!

Pukah's hand went to his chest. The amulet was gone!

"Death's taken it!" Gulping, he leaped up from the bed and staggered across the room to peer out the window. The sun was low, the shadows in the street were long.

"It's morning!" Pukah groaned. "Time for the entire city to try to kill me. And I feel as if camels have been chewing on my brain!"

"Asrial?" he called out miserably.

No answer.

She probably couldn't bear to watch, Pukah thought gloomily. I don't blame her. I'm not going to watch either.

"I wonder," the djinn said wistfully after a moment, "if I was good last night." He heaved a sigh. "My first time . . . probably my last . . . And I don't remember any of it!"

Flinging himself upon the bed, he pulled the pillow over his aching head and moaned a bit for the hardness of the world. Then he paused, looking up. "It must have been wild," his alter ego said upon reflection, "if you ended up under the bed!"

"I've got to find her!" Pukah said decisively, scrambling to his feet. "Women are such funny creatures. My master the Calif told me that one must reassure them in the morning that one still loves them. And I do love her!" Pukah said softly, clasping the pillow to his chest. "I love her with all my heart and soul. I would gladly die for her—"

The djinn stopped short. "You undoubtedly will die for her," his other self told him solemnly, "if you go out that door. Listen, I have an idea. Perhaps if you stayed hidden inside this room all day, no one would find you. You could always slip back underneath the bed."

"What would the Calif say—his djinn hiding beneath a bed!" Pukah snorted at himself in derision. "Besides, my angel is probably roaming the city now, thinking in her virgin heart that I have had my way with her and now will abandon her. Or, worse still"—the thought made him catch his breath—"she might be in danger! She has no amulet, after all! I must go find her!"

Checking to make certain his knife was tucked into his sash, the djinn hurled open the door and ran down the stairs, feeling as though he could take on the entire city of Serinda. He paused outside the beaded curtains.

"Ho! Come out, you droppings of goats, you immortal refuse of swine! Come! It is I—the gallant Pukah—and I challenge one and all to do battle with me this day!"

There was no response. Grimly Pukah charged through the curtains into the main room.

"Come, you horses' hindquarters!"

The room was empty.

Frustrated, Pukah fought his way through the swinging beads and leapt out the door, into the street.

"It is I, the challenger of Death, the formidable Pukah. . . ."

The djinn's voice died. The street was empty. Not only that, but it seemed to be growing darker instead of lighter.

What with all the confusion, the shouting and yelling and flinging himself about, Pukah felt his head begin to throb. He gazed about in the gathering gloom, wondering fearfully if his vision was beginning to go. A fountain stood nearby. Bending his head at the marble feet of a marble maiden, he allowed her to pour cooling water from her marble pitcher upon his fevered brow. He felt somewhat better, though his vision did not clear up, and he was just sitting down on the fountain's rim when he heard a great shout rise up some distance away from him.

"So that's where everybody is!" he said triumphantly. "Some sort of celebration. Probably"—he realized glumly—"working themselves into a blood frenzy."

He jumped to his feet, the sudden movement making his head spin. Dizzily he fell back into the fountain, clinging to the marble maiden's cold body for support. "Maybe they're tormenting Asrial! Maybe Death took her from me in the night!"

Fury burning in his imaginary veins, Pukah shoved the maiden away from him, knocking her off her pedestal and sending the statue crashing to the pavement. He ran through the empty streets of Serinda, using the shouts as his guide, hearing them grow louder and more tumultuous as the darkness deepened around him. No longer trying to figure ou what was going on, knowing only that Asrial might be suffering, and determined to save her no matter what cost to himself, Pukah rounded a corner and ran headlong into the Temple plaza.

He was stopped by a crush of immortals blocking his path. Their backs to him, they were staring at something in the center of the plaza and cheering madly. Standing on tiptoe, trying to see over veils and turbans, laurel wreaths and steel helms, golden crowns and tarbooshes and every other form of head-covering known to the civilized world, Pukah could make out a wisp of dark, foul-smelling smoke beginning to curl into the air. He saw Death, standing next to something in the center of the Plaza, a look of triumph upon her cold, pale face.

But what was it she was gazing at with those hollow, empty eyes? Pukah couldn't see, and finally, exasperated, he increased his height until he towered head and shoulders above everyone in the crowd.

The djinn sucked in his breath, a sound like storm wind whistling through taut tent rigging.

Death was looking triumphantly at him!

But it wasn't the him standing at the edge of the cheering mob. It was a him lying prone upon a bier of cow dung, flames flickering at its base from torches thrown by the crowd.

"*Hazrat* Akhran!" Pukah gasped. "There really are two of me! I've been leading a double life and I never knew it! Suppose"—a dreadful thought struck the djinn—"suppose he's the one Asrial fell in love with!" Pukah shook his fist at the body on the bier. "You've been so understanding, so sympathetic! And all the time it was you making love to her!"

Jealousy raging in his soul, Pukah began to shove his way through the mob. "Get out of my way! Step aside there. What are you staring at? You'd think you'd seen a ghost. Move over! I have to get through!" So intent was he upon confronting himself with betraying himself, the djinn did not notice that—at the sight of him—the immortals fell back, staring at him in shock.

Striding angrily down the path cleared for him by the shaken immortals, Pukah came to the bier. Death gaped at him, her mouth open, her jaw working in unspeaking rage. Pukah never noticed. His eyes were on himself lying, covered with garbage, upon the smoldering dung heap.

"You were with her last night!" Pukah cried, pointing an

accusing finger at himself. "Admit it! Don't lie there, looking so innocent. I know you, you—"

"Kill him!" Death shrieked, her hands clenching to fists. "Kill him!"

Howling in fear and fury, the mob surged toward Pukah, their screams and curses bringing him to his senses at last.

"I'm not dead!" he said. "But then who—"

The mob attacked him. The fight was hopeless; he was one against thousands. Falling back across the bier and the body on it—the body whose identity he now knew, the body who had given her life for his—Pukah raised his arm instinctively to ward off the blow. Averting his eyes from Death, his gaze rested on the face he loved, a face he could see beneath the mask it wore.

"Holy Akhran, grant my prayer. Let us be together!" Pukah whispered. Looking at Asrial, he did not see the sun vanish beneath the horizon.

Death saw. The dark eyes stared into descending darkness, and she gnashed her teeth in her wrath.

"No!" she cried, raising her hands to Heaven. "No, Sul! I have been cheated! You can't take this away from me!"

Night came to Serinda; the sun's afterglow lit the sky, and by its dim light the immortals watched their city begin to crumble and fall into dust.

Staring at the body on the bier, Pukah saw it change form. Blue eyes looked into his. "You've won, Pukah," the angel said softly, her silver hair shining in the twilight. "The Lost Immortals are freed!"

"Because of you!" Pukah caught Asrial's hand and pressed it to his lips. "My beloved, my life, my soul . . ." The hand began to fade in his. "What—" He grasped at it frantically, but he might as well have been clutching at smoke. "What is happening? Asrial, don't leave me!"

"I must, Pukah," came a faint voice. The angel was disappearing before his eyes. "I am sorry, but it has to be this way. Mathew needs me!"

"Stop, I'll go with you—" Pukah cried, but at that moment he heard a harsh voice booming in his ears.

"Pukah! Your master calls you! Have you been purposefully avoiding me? If so, you will find your basket being used to roast squid upon your return!"

"Kaug!" Pukah licked his lips, peering into the Heavens. He felt himself slipping away, as though he were being sucked into a huge vortex. "No, Kaug! Please!" The djinn fought frantically, but he couldn't help himself.

A last glance at the city of Serinda, the dying city of Death, revealed all the immortals looking around themselves in vast confusion. A seraphim dropped a wine goblet, staring at it in horror, and hastily wiped his lips in disgust. A virginal goddess of Vevin glanced down at her own scantily clad form and blushed in shame. Several immortals of Zhakrin, who had been leading the murderous assault upon Pukah, suddenly lifted their heads, hearing a voice long stilled. They vanished instantly. A deity of Evren dropped a sword she had been waving and lifted her voice in a glad cry. She, too, disappeared.

Sond staggered out of the Temple, looking dazed.

"Kaug?" he muttered, shaking his head muzzily. "Don't yell! I'm coming."

Pukah tumbled through the ethers, whirling round and round.

Death stood in the midst of the ruins of an ancient city lying silent and forgotten, sand blowing through its empty streets.

# Chapter 6

Khardan understood little of what was transpiring around him. It was magic—magic more powerful and terrifying than he could have ever believed was possible to exist in this world. At first he had assumed that this was all part of Mathew's plan to help them escape—until he saw by the deperate, half-crazed look in the youth's eyes that Mathew truly meant to kill him. Khardan could do nothing to defend himself. Pain-numbed and shocked, he stared at Mathew in a stupor.

And then his eye caught movement.

Swiftly, silently, Auda ibn Jad drew his curved sword. Light flashing on the arcing blade, the Black Paladin swung it in a slashing, upward thrust aimed at Mathew's back. True to his oath, Auda was going to save his brother's life.

Khardan's sluggish heartbeat quickened; action's heat surged through him, driving off the chill of helpless fear of the unknown. This he knew. This he understood. Steel against steel. Sinew and bone, muscle and brain against another man's bone and brain and brawn. Counting life's span by each panting breath, each thud of the heart, knowing any second it might end in a blood-red explosion of pain.

Far better than dying by magic.

Mathew did not see his danger. Eyes squinched shut, the youth lunged at Khardan with a despairing, clumsy thrust. Stepping lightly to his left, avoiding the dagger's jab, Khardan clasped his right hand around Mathew's wrist and yanked the boy past him and out of danger, sending him sprawling on his stomach to the stone floor. In the same movement, the nomad's left hand knocked aside Auda's sword thrust. Khardan intended to follow through with a knee to the groin, incapacitating his enemy, but ibn Jad quickly recovered and blocked the jab. Falling back before the nomad's rush, Auda kept his sword easily clear of Khardan's frantic grasp. His blade flaring in the torchlight, ibn Jad faced Khardan, who drew his own sword and fell on his guard.

"Tell me," said ibn Jad, his hooded eyes glittering, "the name of the God you serve?"

"Akhran," answered Khardan proudly, keenly watching the other's every move.

The Black Paladins gathered round, watching, not drawing their weapons. It was Auda's privilege to dispatch his foe himself. They would not intervene.

"That is impossible!" ibn Jad hissed. "You spoke the name 'Zhakrin'!"

"Zhakrin, Akhran"—Khardan shrugged wearily, his wounds aching—"they sound alike, especially to ears listening for what they want to hear."

"How did you manage to survive?"

"All my life I have made demands of my God," said Khardan in a low, earnest voice, never taking his eyes from the eyes of ibn Jad. "When He did not answer in the way I wanted, I was angry and cursed His name. But in that terrible chamber, my pain and torment grew more than I could bear. My body and my spirit were broken and I saw—as you meant me to see—a God. But it was not your God. It was Akhran. Looking at Him, I understood. I had been fighting His will instead of serving Him. That is what had led me to disaster. Stripped naked, weak and helpless as when I first came into this world, I knelt before Him and begged for His forgiveness. Then I offered Him my life. He took it"— Khardan paused, drawing a deep breath—"and gave it back."

Auda lunged. Khardan parried. The swords slid blade to blade to the hilts, the two men locked in a struggle that each knew would prove fatal to the one who faltered. They strained against each other, foot braced against foot, body shoving against body, arms locked.

Ibn Jad smiled. Khardan's breath was coming in painful, catching jerks. Sweat broke out on the Calif's forehead, his body began to tremble. Khardan sank to one knee, bowed down by ibn Jad's strength. He held his sword steady until, striking like a snake, Auda dropped his weapon, and seizing the wrist of the nomad's sword arm, he gave a sharp, skilled twist. Khardan's sword fell from a hand that had suddenly ceased to function.

Retrieving his weapon, the Paladin prepared for the kill.

Khardan made a last, feeble effort to fight. His hand reached out for his sword that lay on the stone floor at Auda's feet. The Black Paladin caught hold of Khardan's arm. Blood flowed from a reopened wound on the nomad's wrist—a cut that had been made with the Black Paladin's own knife. Blood from that wound was on ibn Jad's fingers—the blood of his bonded brother. . . .

Mathew hit the floor hard, the fall slamming the air from his lungs and sending the dagger-wand flying from his grasp. He tried to draw a breath, but his breathing pattern had been disrupted, and for several horrifying moments he could not inhale. Panic-stricken, he gulped and gasped until air flowed into his lungs at last. His breathing resumed its normal rhythm. Panic subsided and fear rushed in to take its place.

Mathew heard shouts behind him. The remembered flash of ibn Jad's sword, glimpsed from the corner of his eye, filled Mathew with terror. The wand had changed back from dagger to its usual form. It lay only inches from his hand.

"Grab it! Use it! Kill!" The imp's shrill command dinned in Mathew's ears.

Scrambling forward, Mathew stretched out his hand to seize the wand when he felt something like feathers tickling the back of his neck. Startled, thinking someone had crept up on him from behind, he lifted his head and looked frantically around. No one was there. He started to turn his attention back to the wand when he saw the Black Sorceress. Ignoring the confusion and turmoil going on about her, she had lifted the ivory fang of the altar snake and was preparing to drive its pointed edge into the crystal globe that rested upon Zohra's chest.

"Stop her! Use the wand!" hissed the imp.

The young wizard lunged forward, his fingers closed over the handle of petrified wood.

"Command me!" begged the imp, panting, its hot breath burning Mathew's skin. "I will slay her! I will slay them all at your word, Dark Master. You will rule, in the name of Astafas!"

Rule! Mathew lifted the wand. Its evil power shot through his body with the tingling blast of a lightning bolt.

The imp's red eyes left Mathew and gazed at something that had seemingly appeared above the young wizard. "In the name of Astafas, I claim him as mine!" the creature crowed triumphantly. "You are too late!"

"In the name of Promenthas," came a whisper soft as the touch of a feather upon Mathew's skin, "I will not let you take him."

War raged in Mathew's soul. Turmoil and doubt assailed him. The hand holding the wand shook. The hands of the Black Sorceress, holding the ivory knife, descended.

Fear for Zohra swept over Mathew like a cleansing, purifying fire, burning away terror, panic, ambition. He had to save Zohra. The magic was in his hand that could do so, but Mathew knew—and finally admitted to himself—that he was too young, too inexperienced to call upon it. Acting out of desperation, he did the first thing that came to mind. He lifted the obsidian wand and threw it, as hard as he could, at the Black Sorceress.

He missed his aim. The wand crashed instead into the crystal globe, knocking it from Zohra's chest, sending it rolling and bouncing over the marble floor. With a piercing scream, the Black Sorceress left Zohra to chase after the precious globe.

"Our only way out!"

Scrambling to his feet, Mathew joined in the pursuit of the crystal fish bowl. Though he was faster, the aged sorceress was closer. She must win the prize.

"It's over!" Mathew whispered to himself. Their brief, futile, hopeless battle was coming to its only possible end.

And then, suddenly, the globe vanished, swallowed up by what seemed to Mathew's dazed eyes a mound of flesh.

Flopping on his fat belly, Usti had flung himself bodily upon the bounding crystal globe.

"Thank Promenthas!" Mathew cried, lunging forward. "Usti! Give me the globe! Quickly!"

"Give it to me, meddlesome immortal," shrieked the sorceress. "I might yet spare you the fate of an eternity locked away in iron!"

Ignoring threats and cajoles alike, the djinn lay prone

upon the floor where he had landed, his arms stretched out above his head in an attitude that might have been mistaken for prayer until it became obvious to the two tense, eager observers that Usti seemed to be endeavoring to dig up the marble and crawl beneath it.

The sorceress gave an impatient snarl, and—at this dreadful sound—Usti lifted his head. His chins shook, the fat face was the color of tallow, congealing into lumps of fear. The djinn's eyes darted from one to another.

"Madam, Madman"—Usti raised himself up slowly off the floor—"I fear that I cannot accommodate either of you, no matter what"—the djinn gulped—"you threaten to do to me!"

"Give me the fish, Usti!" Mathew demanded in a cracked, terror-laden voice.

"—to me, or I'll rip out your eyes!" hissed the sorceress, clawlike hands twisting, taloned nails ready to sink into immortal flesh.

"I cannot!" Usti cried, wringing his hands. Sitting back on his fat knees, he gazed despairingly down at the front of his rotund belly. Water soaked the front of the djinn's silk blouse; the torchlight winked off shards of blood-smeared crystal poking out of his stomach. On the floor before him, two fish flopped feebly in a puddle.

"I broke it!" said Usti miserably.

# Chapter 7

" 'From my heart to yours, from your heart to mine . . . closer than brothers born.' "

Khardan heard the whispered words, felt ibn Jad's grip on him relax. Pulling Khardan to his feet, Auda tossed the Calif his sword and then put his back to the nomad's. The Black Paladins, who were waiting for ibn Jad to finish his opponent, stared at their comrade in wordless astonishment.

"What are you doing?" Khardan demanded, his voice thick, his breathing ragged.

"Keeping my oath," said ibn Jad grimly. "Have you strength to fight?"

"You're going against your own?" Khardan shook his head in confusion.

"You and I are bonded by blood. I swore before my God!"

"But it was a trick! I tricked you—"

"Don't join your arguments with those of my own heart, nomad!" Auda ibn Jad snarled over his shoulder. "I am already more than half inclined to sink my blade in your back! Do you have the strength to fight?"

"No!" gasped Khardan. Every breath was burning agony. The sword had grown unaccountably heavy. "But I have the strength to die trying."

Auda ibn Jad smiled grimly, keeping his eyes on the Paladins. At last beginning to understand that they had been betrayed, they were drawing their weapons.

"Nomad—you have stolen from me, cheated me, tricked

351

me, and now it seems likely you are going to get me killed by
my own people." Ibn Jad shook his head. "By Zhakrin, I
grow to like you!"

Swords slid from scabbards, blades gleamed red in the
torchlight. Their faces grim, confused no longer, the Black
Paladins closed the circle of steel.

Broken! Mathew stared bleakly at the water dribbling
down Usti's belly, the shards of crystal on the stone floor, the
fishing lying—gasping and twitching—in a puddle. But the
globe couldn't break! Not by mortal hands! But, perhaps, an
immortal belly? . . .

"You could have had much, but you wanted it all!" whispered the Black Sorceress in Mathew's ear. Hands gripped
his arm, and he flinched at the touch, knowing in sick despair
that there was worse—far worse—to come. "What would
Astafas have given you for them that I couldn't give you?"

Her hands crawled over his chest, up his neck.

Mathew couldn't move. Perhaps the sorceress had laid a
spell on him, perhaps it was her awful presence alone that
stung him, paralyzing him. He stared at her, seeing her
emerge from her unnatural youthful shell like some dreadful
insect crawling out of its husk. The flesh receded from the
fingers; they were pincers with bloodstained talons scraping
his chin, tearing his lips.

"First the eyes!" Her breath was hot and foul against his
skin, her gaze mesmerizing, and Mathew felt his blood con-
geal, his senses go numb. The pincers clawed over his cheeks,
piercing the flesh. "Then I will turn you over to the torturer
and watch while he removes other parts of you. But not the
tongue." A thumb caressed his mouth. "I will save that for
last. I want to hear you beg for death—"

Mathew shut his eyes, a scream welling up inside him.
The pincers were on his eyeballs, they began to dig in . . .

Suddenly there was a soggy thud, a muffled groan.
The pincers twitched and relaxed. The hands slide horribly
down his face, his body, but they were limp and harmless.
Opening his eyes, Mathew saw the Black Sorceress lying
unconscious at his feet, a bruised and bloody mark upon her
forehead.

"Mat-hew," said a groggy voice at his side, "you must
learn . . . to defend yourself. I cannot always . . . be rescuing
you. . . ."

The voice faded. Mathew turned, but Usti was there to catch his mistress as she slumped over sideways, the blood-rimmed ivory lid of one of the tall jars slipping from her fingers. Lifting Zohra in his flabby arms, his face reddening with the exertion, Usti turned to Mathew.

"What now, Madman?"

"You're asking me?" Shaking in reaction to his horrifying experience, the young wizard stared at the djinn. "Take us out of here!"

Usti drew himself up with dignity.

"I can take myself out of here. Poof, I'm gone! But humans are entirely another matter. You do not easily 'poof.' Only my vast courage and undying loyalty to my mistress keeps me here—"

"And the fact that they've taken the ring and you have nowhere to hide!" Mathew muttered viciously beneath his breath, noting that all the jewels had been removed from Zohra's fingers. Frustrated, frightened, he ceased to listen to the djinn's self-aggrandizements. The Black Sorceress was dead—at least Mathew hoped to Promenthas she was dead—but their danger had not lessened. If anything, it was now greater. He could picture to himself the fury of these people when they discovered their witch-queen murdered.

Where was Khardan? Was he still alive? Sounds of fighting coming from the opposite end of the Vestry, near the door, seemed to indicate that he was. How to reach him? How to win their way out of this dread Castle against so many opponents?

"I can take you out of here, Dark Master!" came a whining hiss at his elbow. "Speak the name of Astafas—"

"Be gone!" said Mathew shortly. "Return empty-handed to your Demon Prince—"

"Not empty-handed!" flashed the imp. With a gurgling cry, he snatched the golden fish up in his shriveled fingers, then vanished with a bang.

Mathew stared at the black fish, resting near the hand of the sorceress. The fish's spasmodic twitchings were growing more feeble, its heaving gills showed blood-red against its black scales. Mathew scooped up the fish in his hands. Cupping his fingers, cradling the slimy amphibian in his palms, the young wizard turned slowly around to face the followers of Zhakrin.

"Listen to me—" His voice cracked. Angrily, he cleared his throat and began again. "Listen to me! I have defeated your Black Sorceress, and now I hold in my hands your God!"

His call thundered through the Vestry, echoing off the ceiling, rising above the clash and clamor of the combatants. All faces, one by one, turned toward his, all sound died in the vast chamber.

Mathew could not see Khardan, there were too many people standing between them. But Mathew knew from the sound of battle where the Calif must be. The young wizard began to hedge slowly in that direction.

"Follow me!" he shot out of the side of his mouth.

Regarding Mathew with a look of amazed respect, the djinn hurriedly fell into step behind him, bearing the unconscious Zohra in his arms.

Coming up upon a line of Black Paladins that had formed in front of him, Mathew felt his heart pounding so that it came near to suffocating him.

Mathew tilted his hands slightly so that they could all see the black fish.

"Let me pass," he said, drawing a shivering breath, "or I swear I will destroy your God!"

# Chapter 8

On the eastern shores of the Kurdin Sea was a small fishing village. It was located far enough from the Isle of Galos that the people dwelling there could see only the perpetual cloud that hung above the volcano.

Swirling over the village like the tide that ruled their lives, night had reached its flood stage and was beginning to ebb when a boat took to the water. A man was setting out fishing.

Not such a strange occupation for a resident of this tiny village, whose houses appeared at first glance to be nothing more than pieces of debris washed up on the shore during the last storm. Or at least it wouldn't have been strange to see the boat setting sail with all the others of the village, the fishermen casting out their baited hooks by the first rays of the sun. This fisherman was out in a boat by himself, in the dead of night, the oars muffled with old rags, the oarlocks greased with tallow so that no sound betrayed him.

No long length of rope was coiled at his feet, no hooks were baited with juicy squid. The solitary fisherman's only fishing equipment was a net and lantern of his own clever devising, for he could be clever if he chose—this fisherman—especially when it came to the crafty, the sly, and the deceitful.

Made of brass, the lantern was completely closed on all four sides and open only at the bottom, a narrow crossbar stretching from side to side. On the center of this crossbar rested the stub of a candle, and the light that this lantern shed streamed out from the bottom; no glimmer of flame could be seen shining from the sides. An odd sort of lantern, one might think, and certainly not practical for walking at night.

But highly practical for unlawfully catching fish.

Crouched at the boat's stern, the man, whose name was Meelusk, held the lantern up over the water, watching in high glee as the fish—attracted to the light—came swimming all goggle-eyed and gasping-mouthed to get a better look. Meelusk waited until he had a fair number, then gathered in his net with his wiry arms.

Dumping his catch in a basket made of twisted wire, Meelusk took time to cackle silently at the slumbering village of dolts who had no more brains than the fish they caught. They worked throughout the day, from dawn to dusk, those codheads, and oftimes came back with little to show for their labors. Meelusk worked only a few hours each night and never came in empty-handed.

Oh, he made a fine pretence of taking his boat out every day, but never fished with the rest, claiming to have a secret spot all his own. So he did. Every night he sailed to a secluded alcove and lowered his wire basket, full of fish, into the water. Every day he returned to this alcove—well hidden from the eyes of his neighbors—and slumbered peacefully through the heat of the afternoon. Waking with the setting of the sun, Meelusk hauled in his catch and sailed back to the village, to greet his neighbors with gibes and taunts.

"What, no luck this day, Nilock? And you with a family of ten to support! Try selling children in the market, instead of fish!"

"The God of the Sea favors the righteous, Cradic! Quit ogling your neighbor's wife, and perhaps your luck will change!"

With a cackling laugh, always cut short by a wheeze, for Meelusk complained of a weakness in his lungs (a weakness his neighbors devoutly hoped would carry him swiftly to his just reward), the skinny, bent, little man would caper away to his wretched hut, which stood far apart from the rest of the village. Meelusk lived by himself; not even a dog would have anything to do with him. Eating his miserly dinner, Meelusk stopped occasionally to wrap his arms around his scrawny body, hug himself, and think with delight how his neighbors must envy him.

Envy was not the word.

All knew about the poaching. All knew about the cunning lantern. All knew about his "secret fishing spot." And there was more. Meelusk did not steal only fish. They told stories of how the greedy old man dropped pebbles in the cups of blind beggars and filched the coins; how he grabbed the wares sold by poor cripples and ran off, taunting them to catch him. He was not a follower of Benario. Such thieves risked their lives to steal the rubies from a Sultan's hand while the man slept. This little man stole shirts drying on the line, snitched bread from the ovens of poor widows, snatched bones from the mouths of toothless dogs. Followers of Benario spit upon Meelusk. He was a craven coward who believed in no God whatsoever.

This night, shortly after midnight, Meelusk flashed his lantern light into the water and cursed. There was something amiss with the fish, it seemed. Few came near the light. Those that had been taken in his net were wretched little creatures, hardly worth the effort, too small to eat. Other fishermen would have thrown them back, making suitable apologies and asking them politely to return when they were bigger. Meelusk left the little things in the bottom of the boat, taking a mean, nasty satisfaction in hearing them flopping helplessly about. It was the only satisfaction he was liable to get this night, the old man thought sourly, tossing out his dripping net without much hope of bringing in anything.

He shone the lantern in the water, peering down, and gave a wheeze of delight. Something shiny and bright glittered right below him! Eagerly he took a pull at the net and grunted in amazement. The net would barely budge! A spasm of excitement shook Meelusk's bony frame. Truly this was big! Perhaps a dolphin—those kind an gentle daughters of Hurn that the fools on shore always treated with such respect, petting them when they rubbed up against the boats or actually leaping overboard and frolicking in the sea with them! Meelusk grinned a gap-toothed grin and, throwing all his weight into the task, heaved again on the net. He could imagine what they'd say when he dragged this big fish to market; they'd berate him, of course, for killing an animal known to be good luck to mariners. But he knew that in reality they would be eaten alive with envy.

By Sul, it was heavy!

Veins bulging on his bony arms, his feet braced against the gunnel, Meelusk pulled and grunted and panted and sweated and hauled and pulled. Slowly the net rose dripping from the water. His arms trembling from the strain, fearing at the last moment his muscles would give out and he would drop it back into the dark depths, Meelusk threw everything he had and then some into dragging the net over the side of the boat.

He made it, heaving it over the hull with such tremendous effort that he heaved himself along with it and sprawled flat on top of his catch. Pausing to catch his wheezing breath, Meelusk was so done in by his exertions that he resembled the unfortunate fish he'd landed, able only to gape and gasp. Finally, however, the stars quit bursting in his head; he was able to stand and stagger to a seat. Lifting the cunning lantern, he eagerly looked to see what he had caught.

Undoing the net with trembling fingers, Meelusk lifted up his first object and spit out a filthy, nasty little word. "A basket," he muttered. "Nothing but a water-soaked old basket—belonged to a snake charmer by the looks of it. Still, I can probably get a few coppers for it—

"Ah, ha! What's this? A lamp!" Dropping the basket, Meelusk grabbed the lamp and stared at it with greedy, rapacious eyes. "A fine brass *chirak*! This will fetch a fair price in the market—not once but several times over!" Meelusk was adept at selling something to an unsuspecting merchant, then snitching it and reselling it again.

Tipping the lamp upside down, Meelusk shook it to drain out the water. More than water came out of the lamp, however. A cloud of smoke issued from the spout, assuming the form of an incredibly large and muscular human male. Arms clasped before his bare chest, the gigantic man regarded the little, dried-up Meelusk with humble respect.

"What are you doing in my lamp? Be gone! Get out!" screeched the old man in high dudgeon, clutching the lamp to his bosom. "I found it! It's mine!"

"*Salaam aleikum, Effendi*," said the man, bowing. "I am Sond, the djinn of this lamp and you have saved me! Your wish is my command, O master."

Meelusk cast the djinn a disparaging gaze—noting the silken *pantalons*, golden arm rings, earrings, jeweled turban. "What do I want with a pretty boy like you?" the little man snorted in disgust. "Get you gone!" he was about to add, when suddenly the basket at his feet stirred, the lid flew off, and another cloud of smoke materialized into the form of a man—somewhat thinner and not as handsome as the first.

"And who might you be?" growled Meelusk warily, keeping a firm grip on the lamp.

"I am Pukah, djinn of this basket, *Effendi*, and you have saved me! Your wish is my command, O mast—" Pukah stopped speaking abruptly, his gaze becoming abstracted, his foxish ears pricking.

"I know, I know," mimicked Meelusk irritably, "I'm your master. Well you can just hop back into the sea, Fancy Pants, because—"

"Sond," interrupted Pukah, "our master talks too much. Hear how his breath rattles in his lungs? It would be far more healthful for him to speak less."

"My thought exactly, friend Pukah," said Sond, and before Meelusk knew what was happening, the firm, strong hand of the djinn clamped the little man's mouth tightly shut.

Pukah was listening intently, his head cocked toward the plume of smoke that was a dark splotch against the moonlit horizon. Enraged, Meelusk whined and whimpered until the young, foxish djinn gazed at him severely.

"Friend Sond, I fear our master will do himself an injury if he persists in making those annoying sounds. For his own benefit, I suggest you render him unconscious!"

Seeing the djinn clench an enormous fist, Meelusk immediately ceased his pitiful screeching. Nodding in satisfaction, Sond turned to Pukah. "What do you hear?"

"Khardan, my master—former master"—Pukah amended, with an obsequious bow to the muffled Meelusk—"is in dire peril. Over there, from whence issues that cloud of steam." The djinn's face paled, his eyes widened. "And Asrial! Asrial is there, too! They are fighting for their lives!"

Sond removed his hand from Meelusk's mouth. "What place is that, *Effendi*?"

"The Isle of Galos!" Meelusk whined. "A dreadful island, so I've heard, populated by demons who eat human flesh and evil witches who drink the blood of babes and terrible men with great, shining swords who lop off heads—"

"It seems to me, *Effendi*," said Pukah solemnly, "that you have had, your entire life, a burning desire to visit this wondrous isle."

Somewhat slow-witted when it came to things other than cheating and stealing and lying, Meelusk smugly shook his head. "No, you are wrong, Puke-up, or whatever your name is. I am content with my home." He gave the djinn a cunning glance. "And I command you to take me there, this instant!" Another thought occurred to him. "After we've caught all the fish in the sea first, of course."

"Fish! Alas, all you think of is work, I fear, *Effendi.* You are such a conscientious man." Sond gave Meelusk a charming smile. "You must take some time off to pursue pleasure! As your djinn, *Effendi,* it is our duty to fulfill the wish of your heart. Rejoice, *Effendi!* This night, we sail for the Isle of Galos!"

Meelusk's gap-toothed mouth dropped open. He nearly swallowed his tongue and was, for a moment, so occupied in attempting to cough it back up that he could only splutter and slobber.

"I fear the master is going into a fit," said Pukah sadly.

"We must keep him from choking on his spit," added Sond solicitously. Snatching up a slimy rag used to slop the deck, the djinn stuffed it neatly into Meelusk's gabbling mouth.

"Throw these little fellows overboard!" Pukah ordered, and began to hoist the boat's tattered and torn sail.

Gathering up the fish, accepting graciously their cries of thanks, Sond tossed them back into the ocean and sent the net and cunning lantern down after them.

"We need some wind, my friend"—Pukah stated, looking critically at the sail that hung limp in the still night air—"or we will arrive at the battle two days after its conclusion."

"Anything to oblige, friend Pukah. You take the tiller."

Flying out over the calm water, Sond began to swell in size until he was twenty feet tall—a sight that caused Meelusk's eyes to bulge from his head. The djinn sucked in a deep breath that seemed to displace the clouds in the sky and let it out in a tremendous blast of wind that billowed the sail and sent the fishing boat skipping and dancing over the water.

"Well done, friend Sond!" cried Pukah. "Look! The Isle of Galos! You can see it!"

The Isle of Galos loomed large on the horizon. Ripping the gag from his mouth, Meelusk began to beat his breast and wail. "You're going to get me killed! They will eat my flesh! Chop off my head!"

*"Effendi,"* said Pukah with a sigh, "I sympathize with your vast excitement and your eagerness to fight *nesnas* and ghuls—"

"*Nesnas!* Ghuls!" Meelusk shrieked.

"—and I am aware that you are thankful to us—your djinn—for providing you with the opportunity to draw your sword against Black Knights, who are devoted to torturing those they capture—"

"Torture!" Meelusk screeched.

"—but if you go on flinging yourself about in this manner, Master, you will upset the boat." One hand on the tiller, Pukah reached out his other and picked up Meelusk by the scruff of his neck. "For your own good, Master, in order that you be rested and ready to do battle when we go ashore—"

"Battle!" wailed poor Meelusk.

"—I am going to offer you the loan of my dwelling," continued Pukah with a magnanimous bow.

Meelusk's mouth thought what was left of Meelusk's brain was going to order it to say something and worked away at forming the words, but no sound came out.

Pukah nodded solemnly. "Sond, our master is speechless with gratitude. I fear, Master, that you will find the basket cramped, and there is a redolent odor of Kaug, for which I apologize, but we were just now released from imprisonment, and I have not yet had time to clean." So saying, Pukah stuffed Meelusk—headfirst, feet flailing—into the basket, firmly slamming shut the lid upon the man's protests and screams.

A peaceful silence descended over the dark water.

Sitting back calmly at the tiller, Pukah steered a direct course for Galos. Sond flew along behind the boat, adding a puff every now and then to keep it skimming over the waves.

"By the way," said Pukah, comfortably extending his legs and giving the basket, from which muffled howls were starting to emerge, a remonstrating nudge with his foot, "did you discover the reason why that Goddess—what was her name—slipped into Kaug's dwelling and rescued us from that great hulking oaf?"

"The Goddess Evren."

"Evren! I thought she was dead."

"She seemed very much alive to me, especially when she ordered her immortals to pick up our dwellings and hurl them into the sea."

"Why would she do that? What are we to her?"

Sond shrugged. "She said she owed Akhran a favor."

"Ah," remarked Pukah with a sigh of admiration, "*Hazrat* Akhran always did have a way with the ladies!"

# Chapter 9

"Stand aside! Let the wizard pass!" ordered the Lord of the Black Paladins.

The line of armored men slowly parted, their eyes burning with hate, clouded with fear.

Keeping the fish in his cupped hands, deathly afraid he would drop the wiggly, slimy thing, Mathew walked through their ranks, feeling their gazes pierce him like sharp steel. Trotting along behind him, carrying Zohra in his arms and panting from the strain, came the djinn.

"Madman," gasped Usti in a low undertone that echoed resoundingly through the silent Vestry. "Where are we going?"

Mathew's breath caught in his throat. Where *were* they going? He hadn't any idea! His one thought was to get out of this nightmare chamber, but then what? Go out into the night, to face the one-armed, half-headed *nesnas*?

"To the sea!" came the cool pronouncement. "The God must be taken to the sea!"

Mathew looked down the row of men that lined his path like black, armor-plated columns. Standing at the end was Auda ibn Jad, sword stained crimson, more than one of his fellow knights lying wounded at his feet. Beside him, face ashen with pain and exhaustion, blood smeared over his bare chest and arms, was Khardan.

To Mathew's wild-eyed gaze, it seemed ibn Jad must have been fighting in defense of the nomad. And it was assuredly his voice that had ordered the wizard to take the fish to the sea. The sea! There were boats! . . .

"Ghuls!" cried Usti, his round, frightened eyes looking like holes punched in bread dough.

"One worry at a time," Mathew snapped.

He glanced warily at the Black Paladins. They were muttering darkly; he saw his death in their grim faces, saw it in the white knuckles that clenched over the hilts of swords or around the hafts of spears, saw it in the bristling mustaches, the lowering brows.

He continued walking forward.

The fish in his hands gave a spasmodic jerk, flipping out of his grasp, taking Mathew's heart with it. Frantically he clutched at it, caught it by the tail, and closed his hands over it with a relieved sigh. The mutterings among the Paladins grew louder. He heard footsteps coming up behind him, steel sliding from a scabbard.

"Master!" whimpered Usti.

"I'll kill it!" Mathew shouted, sweat trickling down his face. "I swear!"

And then ibn Jad was at his side, guarding his back, a dagger in one hand, his drawn sword in another.

"Let them go," came the order. The face of the Lord was a terrifying sight—contorted with fury, pale with fear. Mathew darted a glance at the Black Sorceress lying on the floor at her husband's feet. Her women were gathered around her, endeavoring to bring her back to consciousness. But it appeared that it would be a long time—if ever—before she spoke to her people again. "We can do nothing more," the Lord added grimly. "My wife is the only one who could tell us if Zhakrin is truly in peril and she cannot speak."

Catching sight of Auda ibn Jad's face over his shoulder, Mathew saw a ghostly smile flicker across the thin, cruel lips. What the man might be thinking, Mathew couldn't fathom. From the expression on Auda's face, he wasn't at all certain he wanted to know.

Mathew kept walking.

Footsteps followed him across the stone floor; the wizard could feel the thud of boots jar his body. Behind the Paladins came their men-at-arms, and behind them the black-robed women.

The fish lay in his hands, its unblinking eye staring upward, the heaving of its gills growing weaker.

"If that fish dies, so do you!" hissed ibn Jad.

Mathew knew that all too well. Focusing his attention on the fish to the near total exclusion of all else, he willed the creature to live. Each breath it drew, he drew. He was only dimly aware of Khardan joining them, of the nomad taking Zohra from the arms of the djinn, of Usti's protest. "My Prince, you can barely walk yourself!" Of Khardan's stern reply. "She is my wife." Of Usti's muttering, "I shall soon have to carry both of you!" But the words drifted past the young wizard, less real than the sudden sensation of cool, night air blowing upon his face.

They were outside the Castle, moving in a torchlit procession down the pathway, and still the fish clung to life. His gaze fixed upon it, Mathew slipped and slid precariously in the loose gravel of the path until ibn Jad's strong arm caught hold of him and braced him.

They were crossing the narrow bridge with its grinning, gruesome heads, when the fish stopped breathing. Mathew glanced in fear and consternation at ibn Jad, who shook his head grimly and hurried the wizard along, now half carrying the young man. The others followed, and the Black Paladins followed them.

Salt spray cooled Mathew's feverish skin. He could hear the waves rolling to shore. Leaving the bridge, setting foot on the ground once more, he looked down the cliff of shining wet black rock and saw the vast ocean before him, the moon's white light forming a glistening path on the top of the black water.

At the smell of the sea, the touch of spray upon its scales, the fish jerked and gasped, and Mathew began to breath himself. The crossing of the bridge had slowed the Black Paladins. Cautiously he began to descend the slick, steep steps.

"Hurry!" urged ibn Jad in Mathew's ear. "The damned thing's about finished! When we reach the sand, head for the boats!" he added in a piercing whisper.

Looking ahead, Mathew saw a line of boats drawn up in the sand near the water's edge. But he also saw the ship, swinging at its anchor, its sailors crowded on the deck, watching the unusual activity on shore with hungry eyes.

"What about the ghuls?" returned Mathew frantically, fighting to keep calm, avoiding the longing to break into a panic-stricken run. Behind him, he could hear Khardan's labored breathing, Usti's frightened whimpers.

"Once we're on the boat, I'll take care of Sul's demons! Whatever you do, keep hold of that fis—"

Mathew had just set foot upon the shore when, "Stop them!" The shrill cry of a woman rang like a hideous bell from the topmost turret of Castle Zhakrin.

"Too late! Run!" cried Auda, giving Mathew a rough push.

Mathew stumbled. The fish flew from his hands and plopped into the murky water.

"Stop them!" came the enraged sorceress's command, and it was echoed by the furious shouts of the knights.

Mathew reached down into the crashing waves and began to grapple frantically for the fish.

"Never mind!" Grasping him by the back of his wet robes, Auda jerked him upright. "You can't fool them any longer. It's all over! Run!"

Looking behind him, Mathew saw swords flash. The Paladin had turned to face alone the onslaught of charging knights, when there came a blinding flash of light. The djinn, Sond, exploded in their midst like thunder.

# Chapter 10

Springing up from the sand, full ten feet tall, wielding a scimitar it would have taken four mortal men to lift, Sond stood between the captives and their attackers. Fanatic fighters though they were, the Black Paladins could not but be awed by this fantastic apparition appearing before them. Coming to a halt, they glanced askance at each other and at their Lord. Above them, the Black Sorceress called down death from the Castle spires, but she was far from the towering, grim-faced djinn and his scimitar that gleamed wickedly in the bright moonlight.

"Master, Master!" cried a voice excitedly. "Over here! Over here!"

Khardan raised his eyes—even that took a supreme effort it seemed—to see a rotting, leaking, tattered-sailed fishing boat nudging the shoreline, rocking back and forth with the waves. On board was Pukah, waving his turban like a flag, and a small, wizened man crouched at the tiller, who shook in such paroxysm of fear that the chattering of his teeth could be heard above the clash of steel.

Khardan forced his weary, aching legs to drag him forward another step. Fire burned in the muscles of shoulders and arms from carrying the unconscious Zohra, his wounds pained him, his strength was gone. Pride alone kept him from collapsing before his enemies.

Seeing his master begin to give way, Pukah leapt from the boat and ran toward the Calif, taking Zohra from him just as

Khardan's eyes rolled back in his head and he pitched forward onto the sand. Mathew stopped in his own headlong flight and knelt to help him.

"Run for it, Blossom!" Auda ibn Jad commanded harshly.

"I can't leave Khardan!"

"Go on!" Auda hauled Mathew roughly to his feet. "I swore to protect him with my life! I will do so!"

"I will fight alongside you!" Mathew insisted doggedly.

Ibn Jad glowered at him, then gave a grudging nod. Several of the Paladins started forward, only to be confronted by the djinn. Undaunted, the knights were prepared to fight even the immortal when the voice of the Black Sorceress rang out again from the tower.

"You are commanded to"—it seemed she choked on the words—"let them go!"

"Let them go?" Turning to face her, the Lord of the Paladins stared up at his wife in astonishment. "Who commands such a thing?" he shouted.

"Zhakrin commands!" came a deep voice that seemed to well up from the ground.

At the sound, several of the Paladins sank to their knees. Others remained standing, however, including their Lord. Sword in hand, he glared balefully at Mathew.

The volcano rumbled. The earth shook. Many more Paladins fell to their knees, looking at their Lord in fear.

Reluctantly, the knight lowered his sword.

"It seems our God owes Akhran a service," the Lord of the Black Paladins growled. "Leave quickly, before He changes His mind!"

Together, Mathew and Auda ibn Jad lifted Khardan to his feet and dragged him across the sand to the waiting boat.

"What did you mean when you told me—'you can't fool them any longer'?" Mathew asked the Black Knight.

"Surely you knew, didn't you, Blossom"—Auda's black eyes, glittered in the moonlight—"that you did not hold a God in your hands?"

Mathew stared at him, aghast. "You mean—"

"You held in your hands nothing but a dying fish!" A ghostly smile touched Auda's thin lips. "The Black Sorceress was not the only one who would be aware of the presence of the God within the fish. I was there during the ceremony when we freed the God from the Temple in Khandar. I was myself the Bearer for a long time after that. The God left when the djinn—or should I say *Hazrat* Akhran—broke the crystal."

"But you— Why didn't—" Mathew's lips went numb. He felt the blood drain from his face, his strength seep from his body when he recalled how he had walked down that black-armored aisle of death.

"Betray you?" Ibn Jad released Khardan into the strong arms of Pukah. "Ask the nomad when he awakens."

Gently lifting up the Calif, the young djinn carried him through the water to the waiting boat and deposited Khardan next to his wife in the bottom. Pukah hurried back to pluck at Mathew's sleeve.

"Come, Mad—" The young djinn's gaze went to a point above and behind Mathew, his expression softened; indeed, it became almost enraptured. Looking around, startled, Mathew could have sworn that he caught a flash of white and silver. But there was no one near him. "Come, Mat-hew," amended Pukah gravely and respectfully, holding out his hand to assist the young wizard through the sea water. "Hurry! We could throw this wretch of a fisherman to the ghuls if they decided to chase after us, but I doubt his scrawny body would content them for very long."

Turning, Mathew waded into the rippling waves, then realized that Auda ibn Jad was not with him.

"Aren't you coming?"

The Black Paladins had risen to their feet and were swarming down toward the boat. Pukah was tugging at Mathew's sleeve. Sond splashed into the water beside him, appearing prepared to lift up the young wizard and carry him aboard bodily.

Auda ibn Jad shook his head.

"But . . ." Mathew hesitated. This was an evil man, one who murdered the innocent, the helpless. Yet he had saved their lives. "They will take their wrath out on you."

Ibn Jad shrugged, and—ignoring Mathew—the Black Paladins descended on their fellow knight. Auda surrendered without a struggle. The Paladins divested him of sword and dagger. Wrenching his arms painfully behind him, they forced him to his knees before their Lord.

"Traitor!" The Lord of the Paladins stared coldly at ibn Jad. "From now on, every second will bring your tortured body one step closer to death—yet never close enough!"

Raising a mail-gauntleted hand, he struck the Black Paladin across the face.

Ibn Jad fell back in his captors' arms. Then, shaking his head to clear it, he raised his eyes to meet Mathew's.

"As was our friend's, my life is in the hands of my God." He smiled, blood trickling from his mouth. "Do not fear, Blossom. We will meet again!"

The Paladins carried him off the beach, their Lord remaining behind. His eyes, blazing in the moon's pale rays, were so filled with enmity that their gaze alone might kill. Mathew no longer needed Pukah's exhortations and pleadings (all given in the most respectful tones) to hasten through the silver-laced, black sea water. Catching the young wizard up in his strong grip, Sond tossed him headfirst over the hull.

"The ghuls! They're watching! They smell blood! Oh, make haste, make haste!" Crouched on a seat, Usti wrung his hands.

But Sond, shaking his head, was examining the boat with a frown. At the bottom lay Khardan and his wife. Pukah had taken advantage of their unconscious state to rest Zohra's head upon her husband's shoulder and drape Khardan's arm around her protectively.

"Truly, a marriage made in Heaven," sighed the djinn.

Heaven! I've had enough of Heaven, thought Mathew wearily. Hunching down on his knees in the boat's stern, oblivious to the inch or so of sea water that sloshed around him, he laid his cheek on a wet basket and closed his eyes.

"Well, what are you waiting for?" screeched the little old man from the tiller. "Get this thing moving."

"Master, shut up," said Pukah politely.

"The boat's too low in the water. There's too much weight," stated Sond. "Usti, get out!"

"Don't leave me! You can't!" wailed the djinn. "Princess, please don't let them—"

"Stop blubbering!" snapped Pukah. "We're not going to leave you. And don't wake your mistress. We want a peaceful trip after what we've been through, to say nothing of what faces us when we reach shore. Crossing the Sun's Anvil on foot. If we survive that, we must then raise an army to defeat the Amir—"

None of it mattered to Mathew. It was all too far away.

"We need a new sail," grunted Sond. "Usti, you'll do fine!"

"A sail!" The djinn drew an indignant breath. "I will not—"

"Was that a ghul I heard, smacking his lips? . . ." inquired Pukah.

"I'll do it!" cried Usti.

The boat heaved and floundered. Startled, jolted to wakefulness, Mathew opened his eyes and beheld an astounding sight.

Curling his feet under the boom, groaning and protesting over the hardness of his life, Usti grabbed hold of the mast with both hands. His massive body stretched and expanded until all that remained recognizable were his woeful eyes, his turban, and numerous chins.

Sucking in a deep breath, Sond let it out in a whoosh. Usti filled with air.

"Swells up like a goat's bladder!" commented Pukah in awe.

The fishing boat began to move over the water. Taking the tiller, Pukah steered the vessel into a path seemingly laid down for them by the moon.

Mathew closed his eyes again. The wind sang in the rigging. Pukah began to relate some improbable escapade about himself and Mathew's guardian angel in a City of Death. Usti whimpered and complained. Sond blew and puffed. Mathew paid no attention to any of it.

It seemed to him that he felt a gentle hand touch his cheek. A blanket of feathery softness wrapped him in warmth, and he drifted into a relaxed sleep.

A last image drifted into his mind, that of an imp appearing before Astafas, Prince of Darkness, bearing in its splay-fingered hand . . .

A dead fish.

# Glossary

*agal:* the cord used to bind the headcloth in place
*aksakal:* white beard, village elder
*Amir:* king
*Andak:* Stop! Halt!
*ariq:* canal
*arwat:* an inn
*aseur:* after sunset

*baigha:* a wild game played on horseback in which the *"ball"* is the carcass of a sheep
*bairaq:* a tribal flag or banner
*Bali:* Yes!
*bassourab:* the hooped camel-tent in which women travel
*batir:* thief, particularly horse or cattle thief (One scholar suggests that this could be a corruption of the Turkish word "bahadur" which means "hero.")
*berkouks:* pellets of sweetened rice
*Bilhana:* Wishing you joy!
*Bilshifa:* Wishing you health!
*burnouse:* A cloaklike garment with a hood attached

*Calif:* prince
*caftan:* a long gown with sleeves, usually made of silk
*chador:* women's robes
*chirak:* lamp
*couscous:* a lamb stuffed with almonds and raisins and roasted whole

*delhan:* a monster who eats the flesh of shipwrecked sailors
*dhough:* ship
*divan:* the council-chamber of a head of state

*djinn:* beings who dwell in the middle world between humans and the Gods

*djinniyeh:* female djinn

*djemel:* baggage camel

*dohar:* midafternoon

*dutar:* two-stringed guitar

*Effendi:* title of quality

*efreet:* a powerful spirit

*Emshi besselema:* a farewell salutation

*eucha:* suppertime

*eulam:* post meridien

*fantasia:* an exhibition of horsemanship and weapons skills

*fatta:* a dish of eggs and carrots

*fedjeur:* before sunrise

*feisha:* an amulet or charm

*ghaddar:* a monster who lures men and tortures them to death

*ghul:* a monster that feeds on human flesh. Ghuls may take any human form, but they can always be distinguished by their tracks, which are the cloven hooves of an ass

*girba:* a waterskin; four usually carried on each camel of a caravan

*goum:* a light horseman

*haik:* the combined headcloth and face mask worn in the desert

*harem:* "the forbidden," the wives and concubines of a man or the dwelling places allotted to them

*hauz:* artificial pond

*Hazrat:* holy

*henna:* a thorn-shrub and the reddish stain made from it

*houri:* a beautiful and seductive woman

*Imam:* priest

*jihad:* holy war

*kafir:* unbeliever

*Kasbah:* a fortress or castle

*khurjin:* saddlebags

*kohl:* a preparation of soot used by women to darken their eyes

*madrasah:* a holy place of learning
*Makhol:* Right! (exclamation)
*mamaluks:* originally white slaves; slaves that are trained warriors
*mehara:* a highly bred racing camel
*mehari:* a plural of mehara
*mehariste:* a rider of a mehara
*marabout:* a priest
*mogreb:* nightfall

*nesnas:* a legendary, fearsome monster that takes the form of a man divided in half vertically, with half a face, one arm, one leg, and so on

*palanquin:* a curtained litter on poles, carried by hand
*paranja:* a woman's loose dress
*pasha:* title of rank

*quaita:* a reed instrument
*qarakurt:* "black worm," a large species of deadly spider
*qumiz:* fermented mare's milk

*rabat-bashi:* innkeeper

*saksul:* a tree that grows in the desert
*salaam:* an obeisance, a low bow with the hand on the forehead
*salaam aleikum!:* Greeting to you
*saluka:* a swift hunting dog
*seraglio:* the quarters of the women of the harem
*Sheykh:* the chief of a tribe or clan
*shishtick:* strips of meat grilled on a skewer
*shir:* lion
*sidi:* lord, sir
*sirocco:* the south wind, a windstorm from the south
*souk:* marketplace, bazaar
*spahi:* native cavalryman
*Sultan:* king
*Sultana:* wife of a Sultan, queen

*tamarisk:* a graceful evergreen shrub or small tree with feathery branches and minute scalelike leaves
*tambour:* similar to a tambourine
*tel:* a hill
*tuman:* money

*wadi:* river or stream
*wazir:* an adviser to royalty

*yurt:* semipermanent tent

## About the Authors

Born in Independence, Missouri, Margaret Weis graduated from the University of Missouri and worked as a book editor before teaming up with Tracy Hickman to develop the *Dragonlance* novels. Margaret lives in a renovated barn in Wisconsin with her two teenage children, David and Elizabeth Baldwin, and her three cats. She enjoys reading (especially Charles Dickens), opera, and rollerskating.

Born in Salt Lake City, Utah, Tracy Hickman resides in Wisconsin in a 100-year-old Victorian house with his wife and three children. When he isn't reading or writing, he is eating or sleeping. On Sundays he conducts the hymns at the local Mormon church.

**The Darksword Trilogy** marked Margaret and Tracy's first appearance as Bantam Spectra authors. They followed up with *Darksword Adventures,* a companion volume and game book set in the same world. They've just finished writing **The Rose of the Prophet Trilogy**—*The Will of the Wanderer, The Paladin of the Night,* and *The Prophet of Akhran*—which will be published in 1989. Margaret and Tracy are about to begin working on the first of volume of their new series.

# The Darksword Trilogy
## by
# Margaret Weis and Tracy Hickman

Here are the adventures of the angry young Joram, born into a world where his lack of magic powers means an instant death sentence. When he meets the catalyst Saryon, they become allies and together forge a sword capable of absorbing magic: the Darksword. Joined by the young mage Mosiah and the trickster Simkin, Joram embarks on a perilous journey, rising to power he never dreamed of, and finding himself faced with the greatest challenge of his people's history.

☐ **Forging the Darksword** (26894-5 • $4.50/
$5.50 in Canada)

☐ **Doom of the Darksword** (27164-4 • $4.50/
$5.50 in Canada)

☐ **Triumph of the Darksword** (27406-6 • $4.50/
$5.50 in Canada)

☐ **Darksword Adventures** (27600-X • $4.50/$5.50 in Canada) An exciting, groundbreaking gaming manual— the first ever in paperback—which requires no peripheral equipment. It's also an indispensable companion to *The Darksword Trilogy*, full of fascinating background information and lots of surprises.

Buy **Forging the Darksword, Doom of the Darksword, Triumph of the Darksword** and **Darksword Adventures** now on sale wherever Bantam Spectra Books are sold, or use this page for ordering:

------------------------------------